The Oath We Swore

Brenda Glazer

The Oath We Swore

Brenda Glazer

Colonsay Press
Calgary, Alberta

This is a work of fiction. Descriptions of historical events, people, and places are used within the context of this fiction. Names situated in the present time are fictional and any resemblance to actual people is purely coincidental.

ISBN 978-1-7782916-0-9 (softcover), 978-1-7782916-2-3 (EPUB), 978-1-7782916-1-6 (kpf)

The quoted excerpt from "*Ja nus hons pris*" is from John Gillingham, *Richard I*. Yale University Press, 1999, p. 243. Translated into English by Kate Norgate.

Photo credits:

Cover photo of a ruined section of present-day Acre's (Akko's) wall, the sketch of Jerusalem, and the etching of the Glastonbury ruins are from istock-photo.com.

Templar illustration from alamy.com.

"A medieval chess game" from Codex Manesse, 14th century CE, Zurich, Switzerland. Accessed from World History Encyclopedia: Medieval Chess Game. Ancient.eu. Public domain. Accessed March 3, 2021.

"The Coronation of Richard I" from Wikimedia Commons, File: Lvisrde korunovace 1189.jpg. Accessed March 4, 2021.

Richard I's crest during the Third Crusade from "Richard I. (Richard the Lionheart)," Militaer-Wissen.de. 5-Graf-von-Poitou-dieses-Wappen-führte-Richard-auf-dem-Dritten-Kreuzzug.png. Accessed November 1, 2020.

"King Richard and King Philip accepting the keys to Acre" from Gallica Digital Library, under the digital ID btv1b84472995/f484, Public Domain, https://commons.wikimedia.org/w/index.php?curid=3845930

"A Medieval Infirmary." Public Domain. Ms. Gaddi 24, f. 247. Laurentiana Library, Florence. Accessed October 23, 2021.

Photo of the Templar Tunnel from Wikimedia Commons. File: Accre [sic] Israel (9567499367).jpg. Accessed July 17, 2021.

Photos of Richard I's effigy and of Fontevraud Abbey are by the author.

By the same author:

Who Looks Inside, © 2016, 2nd Revised Edition © 2019
Nor Me Without You, © 2020

Digital versions are available from Amazon Kindle, Kobo, and Apple Books. Hard copies are available from Amazon.

To my dad, whose guidance I really could have used during this project. And to Joe, whom I neglect.

N'est pas mervoillee se j'ai le cuer dolant,
Quant mes sires met ma terre en torment.
S'il le membrast de nostre soirement
Quo nos feïsmes andui communement,
Je sais de voir que ja trop longuement
Ne seroie ça pris.

#

No marvel is it that my heart is sore
While my lord tramples down my land, I trow;
Were he but mindful of the oath we swore
Each to the other, surely do I know
That thus in duress I should long ago
Have ceased to languish here.

—Richard I, "Ja nus hons pris", Stanza 4
Written in captivity

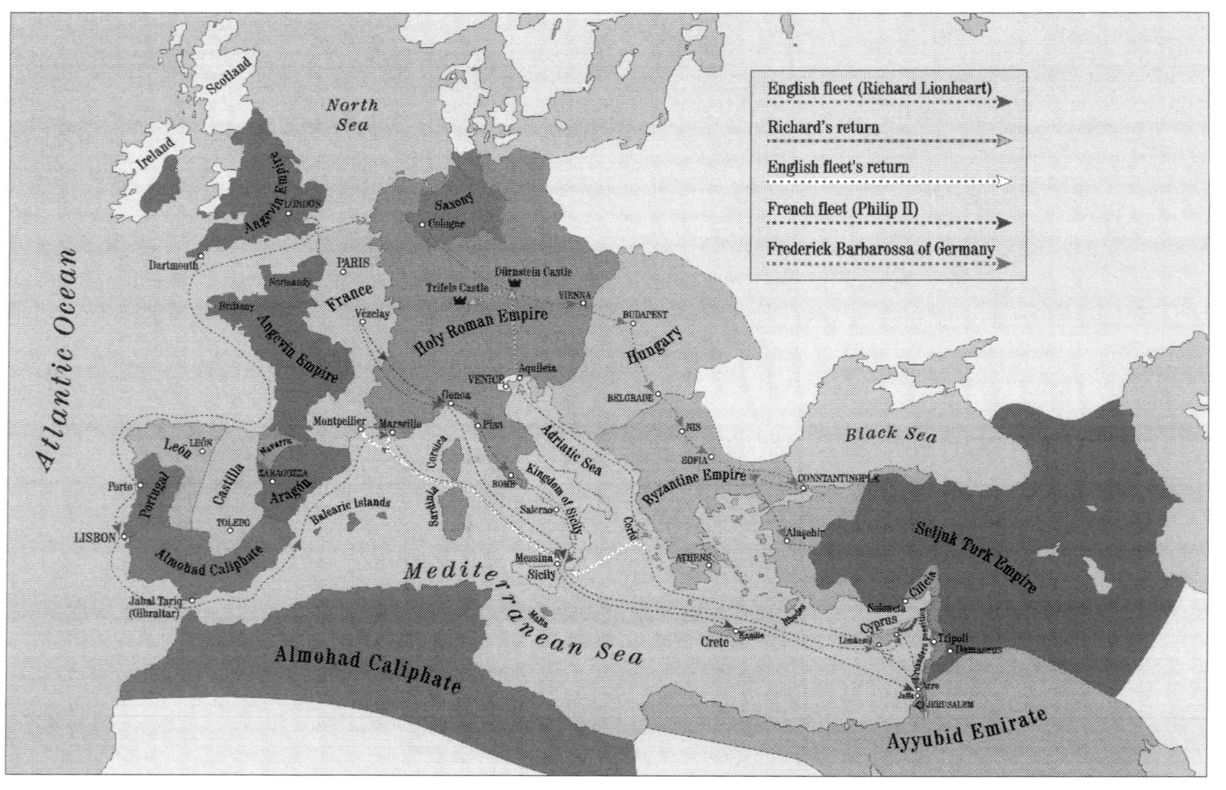

The Third Crusade

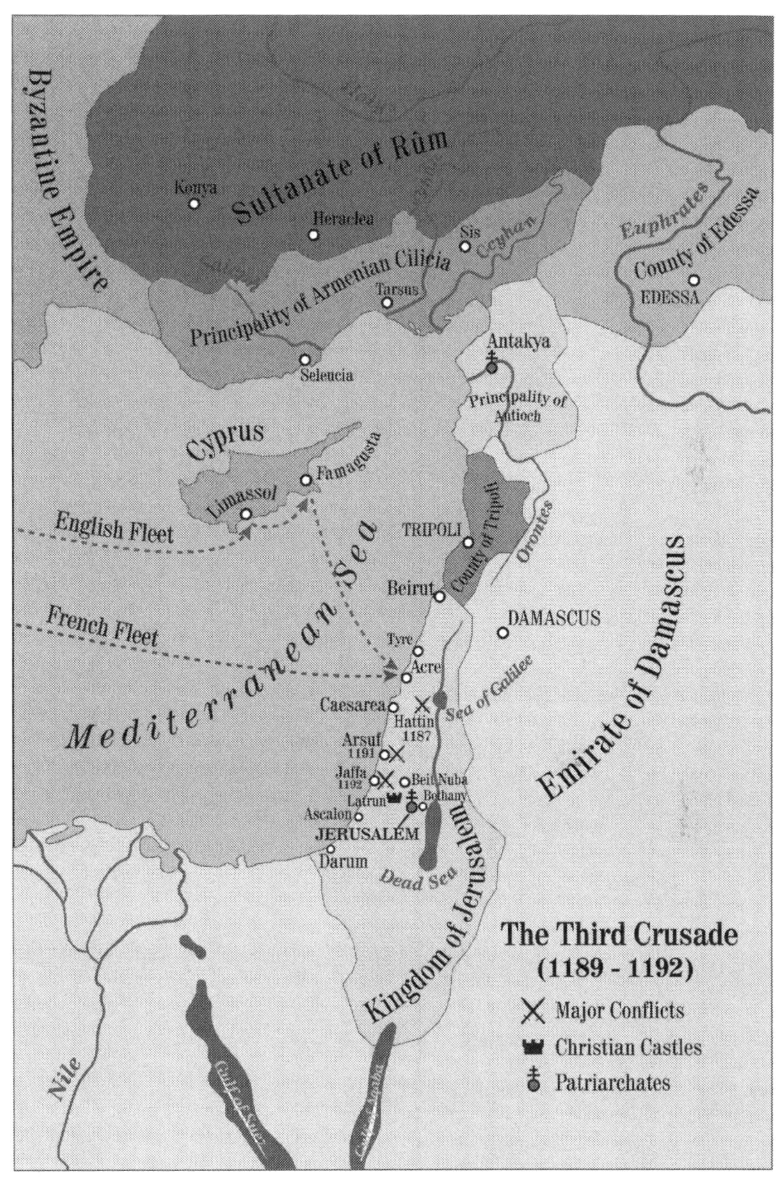

The Holy Land

An Informal Glossary

Aics: Modern-day Aix-en-Provence.

Angevin: The name of the dynasty that began with Henry II, in 1154, and ended with the death of Richard III in 1485. Both a noun and an adjective, it's a derivative of Anjou, the region where Henry's father was from. The dynasty was renamed "Plantagenet" in the fifteenth century.

Avicenna (from Ibn Sina): An eleventh-century Persian polymath whose text, the *Canon Medicinae*, remained one of the standard medical texts until the seventeenth century.

Baldric: A belt worn over one's shoulder and across the chest, which carries a sword on one side.

Bliaut: A type of dress characterized by sleeves that widen considerably at the elbows, sometimes reaching floor length.

Buisine: A long, medieval version of a trumpet, used ceremonially. Buisines are shown in the illustration accompanying the chapter heading of "1187."

Clarion: A shrill, narrow war trumpet.

Cloister garth: An open courtyard, most often a garden, surrounded by the cloister arcade in a monastery or abbey. A photograph of the Fontevraud Abbey cloister garth introduces the year 1200 chapter in this work.

Cog: A broadly-built medieval ship with a rounded prow and stern.

Compline: Final prayer service of the day, at about 7:00 p.m., or bedtime.

Dalcop: Dumbass. Literally, "dull head." In the context of this novel, directed at Evan, the word would not have been meant as a true insult.

Destrier: A warhorse. These stallions were bred for size, strength, and fearlessness under battle conditions.

Dinner: The major meal of the day, taken anywhere from about 10 a.m. to noon. For that reason, breakfast, if there was any, was perhaps just some gruel or bread.

Donjon: The inner tower, or residence, of a castle. "Keep" came into use in the later Middle Ages. This is not to be confused with "dungeon," which is, nevertheless, a derivative of the word.

Dromon: A large, medieval, three-masted, galley ship.

Fin'amor: This later became known as *amour courtois* or "courtly love."

Fluxus: Diarrhea. This could be a sign of dysentery.

Frank (adj. Frankish): Strictly speaking, descendants of German invaders of Gaul who had become thoroughly integrated. However, Mediterranean peoples typically lumped the English in with them.

Galen: A revered second-century Greek physician, surgeon, and philosopher in the Roman Empire. It was Galen who formulated the humoral theory.

Gambeson: A quilted, padded defensive jacket.

Great chamber: A medieval living room and gathering place for the lord's family in the donjon.

Hauberk: A sleeved coat of mail reaching to the knees (see illustration below).

Holy Roman Emperor: A title from Charlemagne's time, in the twelfth century simply the ruler of most of modern Germany and Austria.

Hose: worn by both men and women in Europe from the twelfth until the late eighteenth century. At the time of this novel, they were made from loosely-woven linen or wool, cut on the bias for a snugger fit. They came up past the knee and were secured with a garter. The most common colour seems to have been white.

Jabal Tariq: Gibraltar

Jeux de tables: Backgammon

Joseph of Arimathea: According to the gospels, the man responsible for Jesus's body after the Crucifixion.

Knights Hospitaller: Originally a religious order founded in Jerusalem to care for sick and wounded pilgrims. With time, they evolved to play a military role in the crusades.

Livre (fem.): Unit of medieval French currency equaling a pound of silver. Twenty *sols* (or *sous*) equaled a *livre.*

Mangonel: A military device for throwing stones and other missiles. A type of trebuchet—see entry further on

Matins: Prayer service at about 2:00 a.m.

Medicus (pl. medici): A lesser physician in the hierarchy of medieval medical personnel. He could do simple procedures but lacked higher preparatory education.

Mixolydian mode: A medieval church scale that begins and ends at G.

Nones: Prayer service at about 3:00 p.m.

Oncos: Cancer

Outremer: Literally, "beyond the sea." The crusader states in the Holy Land.

Pasch: Norman French word for Easter.

Patten: A wooden sandal, strapped onto shoes or boots, to protect from water or other damage.

Phthisis: Tuberculosis.

Prime: Prayer service at about 6:00 a.m.

Quadrivium: Upper level of education, comprising arithmetic, geometry, astronomy, and music.

Saracen: Used by the crusaders to describe Infidels/Muslims/the enemy, regardless of nationality.

Sard: A vulgar early English word for our "fuck." The earliest known use of the latter is the fourteenth century.

Sext: Prayer service at about noon.

Shipman: Sailor

Shipmaster: The medieval equivalent of "captain."

Supper: The evening meal, taken anytime from about 4 to 6 p.m.. Lighter than the mid-day meal, it often comprised mainly a substantial soup—hence the French *souper*, from which the English word is derived—or perhaps leftovers from the day's dinner.

Solar : Bedroom belonging to the lord and/or lady of a castle.

Studium generale (pl. studia generalia): Although the word "university" had been coined in Bologna in the eleventh century, the word was not yet in common use.

Surcoat: A sleeveless knee-length garment worn over mail. In the crusades, the colour and sewn-on crosses indicated the wearer's country of origin (white cross for English, red for French, black for German, red Maltese cross for Templars). On other occasions, the owner's crest could be sewn on. (see illustration below)

Trebuchet: A long-armed catapult.

Trencher: In informal meals, a large, round flatbread used to soak up the sauces from the meals, and also eaten. Note that spoons and knives were the only table cutlery in use in the twelfth century.

Trivium: The lower division of the seven liberal arts, comprising grammar, logic, and rhetoric.

Trouvère: Northern French dialect for a troubadour or poet. Their works were often of epic length, much longer than those of minstrels.

Vespers: Prayer service at about 6:00 p.m.

Villein: Contemporary Norman French word for a tenant farmer who would, in later centuries, be called a serf. They were tied to the land, owed the lord service, and could only be freed by him.

A twelfth-century Templar wearing a surcoat over a mail hauberk.

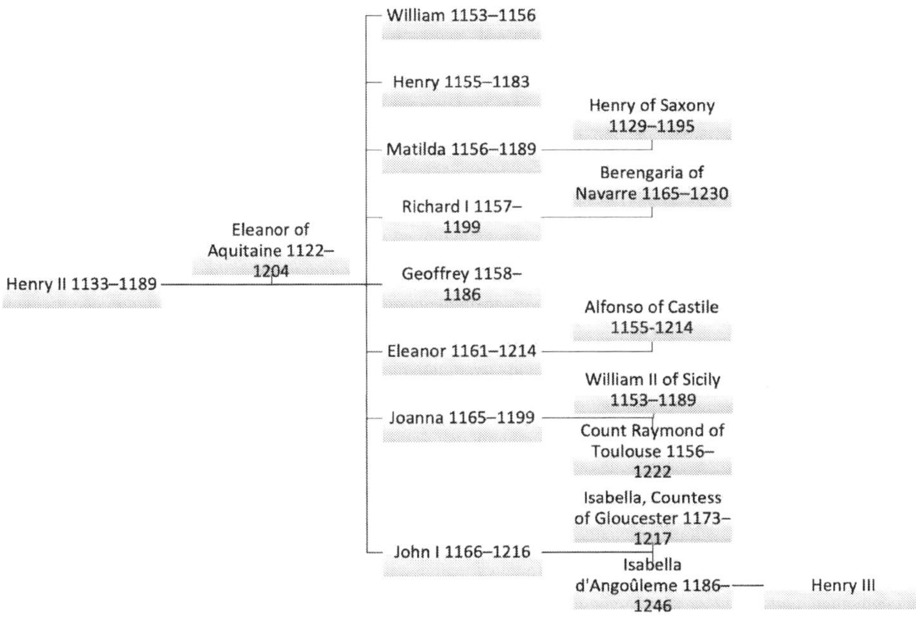

Official Family Tree of the Angevin Dynasty from Henry II to Henry III, as is relevant to this work

1187

A medieval chess game

I warn you against shedding blood, indulging in it and making a habit of it, for blood never sleeps.
—Attributed to Saladin

-I-
Steven's Crisp

Fifteen-year-old Evan de Montmorency is having another Steven dream. Once again, he is seeing through the eyes of a boy about his own age. This time, he's sitting on a tall bench, in a small, white-walled room with cupboards, a counter, and various implements on the wall beside him. Evan has no idea what they are for; does Steven? His bench is covered with some thin, white substance that crackles when he moves. Inside the counter is a square, steel basin, on the far edge of which is a shiny, tall, curved pipe of some sort. The room is very brightly lit, considering there are no windows. He looks up and sees that the light source is two long tubes in the ceiling, covered by translucent sheets of some unknown material. How is this possible*?*

Two women are with him. One of them, he knows by now, is Steven's mother; the other is younger and wearing a white coat. She must be someone in authority because Steven's mother is deferential to her. The woman in the white coat is sewing stitches into Steven's left hand, between his thumb and index finger. Although she is piercing Steven's skin, he feels no pain.

"So, tell me again how this happened, Steven?" she asks with a smile, though her cautious, watchful eyes belie her friendly manner. Why, Evan wonders.

"Mom made me help her peel apples for a crisp."

"Guilty as charged, doctor!" his mother replies, laughing. "Only because he said he wanted one!"

"Doctor" laughs in turn. "You do know there's such a thing as a vegetable peeler, don't you? A couple of bucks at Dollarama." Steven's answer must have been acceptable to her because her eyes are no longer wary.

His mother says, a little defensively, "Well, for peeling apples, I like a knife, myself."

The doctor ties off the last stitch and begins binding Steven's hand with a pristine white dressing. "Okay, just about done here. Ms. Rickert, keep this dressing on for two days. Steven, don't get it wet, and try not to move your thumb. Good thing it's your left hand. After that, keep it clean. Soap and water twice a day. Again, try not to move your thumb more than necessary. Come back in a week, and we'll see about removing those stitches. Tylenol for the pain if you need it, but come back if you start to see redness around the edges, okay?"

"Okay, doctor," says Steven.

"What do you say, Steven?" says his mother in a slightly nagging, though still pleasant voice.

"Thanks, doc!"

The women laugh.

Evan woke up on his twelfth-century pallet outside Lord Rupert de Villiers's bed chamber. It was a rainy June morning at Amesbury Castle in Wiltshire, where he was being billeted. This was his fourth Steven dream. However, telling his parents, Lord Robert and Lady Branwen de Montmorency, about the dream would have to wait for a while: they were two days' ride away, in Shaftesbury Castle in northeast Dorsetshire.

Mama would be able to explain the mysterious things he saw in this dream. However, although she always seemed to know exactly what he was talking about, she was evasive about their context. And she never would say how she understood both that foreign tongue and the myriad little details Evan noticed in that strange place.

"Wait," she'd always say. "We'll explain it all to you when you're old enough."

Whenever he related these dreams, the door in the great chamber was closed behind them, and they'd swear him to silence. At one time, Evan loved the secret. He felt special, pampered; it was something he had that his brother and sister did not. But lately, he'd been thinking with increasing impatience, When will I be old enough?

Because he was fairly sure he'd figured something out.

Evan had had Steven dreams about every three years since he was six. In every one, he was in a place where women were tall and very immodest. Everyone wore blue breeches and had excellent, straight, white teeth. By now, he was old enough to realize that while Shaftesbury Castle was a sophisticated place that welcomed a lot of guests from all over, *nowhere* in his world did people remotely look, talk, and act like the people in his dreams. Therefore, these dreams must also be taking him to another *time.*

Other boys his age would always remember with clarity the day they'd first lain with a girl. For Evan, it was the day of this stunning epiphany. A few months before, his tutor had quoted Marcus Aurelius: "Time is like a river of passing events, and strong is its current." Later that day, it came to him as he tossed a stone into the Amesbury Castle moat and observed the resulting ripples: yes, but there are eddies and whorls in the current! Had Mama had dreams, too? By some miracle, could Mama have been swept into one such eddy? How, when, and how often, then? No wonder she and Papa insisted on secrecy. Although twelfth-century Britons easily lived with the duality of church doctrine and ancient, pagan beliefs in magic and spirits, one never sought to draw the unwelcome gaze of the Church.

Until now, Steven had always been engaged in some outdoor activity: flying a "kite," riding a "bike," kicking a "soccer" ball. In the dream Evan had when he was six, Steven had been joined by a younger brother. However, much as Mama and Papa enjoyed hearing about his dreams, they were especially curious about Steven's *mother.* Did she seem well and happy with her husband? They were always delighted when Evan replied that, yes, that was his impression.

This particular dream was longer, took place indoors, and was much more detailed. There was also a lot more dialogue than in the others, which only contained a sentence or two. What was a "doctor"? Some kind of physician, apparently, but a *woman?* Why did he feel no pain as the doctor pierced his skin? Also, what was with this word "okay"? What was "Tylenol"? "Bucks"? "Dollarama"? And what was a "crisp"? Some kind of sweet, perhaps?

And Steven's mother's name: "Mizrikert," was what he thought he heard. It certainly seemed like a strange-sounding name to him.

He knew Mama could tell him. Patience, he had to be patient.

Most upper-class twelfth-century children would have long since completed their formal education, but none of the Montmorencys were typical for their time. Learning was highly valued in Shaftesbury Castle. His parents even had books: twelve, the last time he looked, carefully locked away in their great chamber cupboard. Otherwise frugal, this was what his parents spent their money on—also, on rugs, which sensuously beautified the floors of every bedroom, unlike the straw matting here at Amesbury Castle.

All the children in Shaftesbury Castle, including Evan's younger sister Marie, had been instructed by Rabbi Jacob d'Orléans, a famous Jewish scholar, and the best there was. Rabbi Jacob had heard about the enlightened culture in the castle and had ridden up to the gate one day, offering his services. No thought was wasted about the man's faith; Branwen had stared people in the eye and told doubters to get used to him. Although the Montmorency children had been infected to varying degrees by the ingrained anti-Semitism of the time, they quickly came to adore him. He never birched them; instead, he would just gaze at them sorrowfully, as if to say, "How could you disappoint me so?" They certainly never wanted to disappoint Rabbi Jacob.

Lord Rupert and Lady Christine de Villiers were friends of long standing with the Montmorencys. Respecting their desire that Evan's instruction continue until his return home at about eighteen, the Villiers had engaged the Aurelius-loving John of Winchester at some expense. Master John was knowledgeable but strict and humourless. Once he understood how precocious Evan was, he was all about serious, hard work. He had taken Evan past the trivium and into the quadrivium, the highest level one could reach in a liberal arts education at the time. He'd told the Villiers that, frankly, he was running out of things to teach him, and the boy never seemed to forget a thing.

Two days after Evan's Steven dream, Master John was demonstrating the Mixolydian mode in church music when they heard a commotion in the bailey.

"What's going on?" Winchester called down from the great chamber, where they were working.

"It's Cuthbert! He's cut his hand! There's blood all over the place!" yelled back one of the stable hands.

The dream.

"Master John, may we go see?"

"Why? Does it give you some pleasure to see a person in pain?" Winchester retorted sarcastically.

"Oh, no, Master John, it's not like that! It's just that—maybe we can help."

"We? *You?!*"

Thinking quickly, "My mother is Welsh, as you know. The Welsh know some things about physic and she taught me. Please, I think I can help."

Winchester looked doubtful. "Well, all right. But if you can't do any good, at least get out of their way."

His knife having slipped while cutting twine, Cuthbert had indeed produced an impressive gash on the palm of his hand. Someone had poured wine over it, and they were trying to stanch the flow of blood with cloth. Wine was a good disinfectant, but they were in the stables—hardly the brightly lit, immaculate room Steven had been treated in.

Winchester asked, "Do you mind if we approach? Young Evan here thinks he knows what to do."

The others stood back, dubious. Everyone knew Evan was very bright, but he was, after all, only a boy of fifteen. He sat on a stool to examine the wound. It was an inch long and about a quarter of an inch deep.

"Right," he said. "I need the cleanest water you have, soap, linen thread, a needle, and very clean cloth."

"Now?" said Albert, the head groom. "Don't we have to wait for pus or something?"

"No," replied Evan with certainty. "We must close the wound now."

By the time the dinner bell rang, Cuthbert's hand was stitched and dressed. Evan had put in four stitches. He had no idea if this was adequate—he hadn't counted Steven's. It had hurt Cuthbert, and Evan wished he knew why Steven had felt no pain. Did people not feel pain in that time? Amazed at himself even as he spoke, he repeated the doctor's instructions, omitting the "okays."

He asked, "Is there anything for pain here?" A crowd had

now gathered, including Lord Rupert and Lady Christine.

"Yes," she said, "he can have a little of my poppy liquid. Just a little."

The assembly parted quietly before him as he and Master John stood to leave. Lord Rupert was staring at him speculatively. No one was saying anything, but Evan was sure that the minute he was out of earshot, he'd be the talk of the castle. He prayed the "Welsh knowledge" explanation would suffice.

Giddy from what he had just done, he said, "Master John, forgive me, but do you mind if we suspend my lessons for today? I'm afraid I won't be able to concentrate on the Mixolydian mode."

"Yes, Evan," Master John quietly replied. "I don't mind in the least. We will resume tomorrow."

Evan had been at Amesbury Castle for eight years now. While the style of living here was certainly richer than it was at home, he continued to miss his people: his parents; their loyal servants; older brother Edward and his wife Jeanne; younger sister Marie, thankfully soon to be coming here with Jean de Villiers, to whom she would be wed. They'd been betrothed since she was four, and she worshipped him. The residents of Amesbury castle were in full preparation mode for this wedding.

Beyond that, Evan missed the harmony of everyone pulling for the same cause. He missed the sparkling conversations around the dinner and supper table, the undeniable devotion his parents had to each other and their children. The best part of living in Amesbury Castle, in Evan's view, was when he got to go home at Pasch and Christmas.

Evan was a second son. Edward, ten years older, was being groomed to take over his father's barony. As a second son, Evan had no rights of inheritance. He would have to make his own way in life, but this gave him a freedom that Edward made no secret of envying. Robert and Branwen had always made it clear to Evan that his life was his to do with as he wished, with the sole promise that he never do anything to bring shame on the house of Montmorency.

The previous night's dream was taking him in new, thrilling directions. This was more than jolly stories of kites and soccer balls. It was instructional. And, more, he had found out something about himself: He was good at repairing wounds. He was not at all squeamish. Just the opposite: he'd felt confident, knowing that he was treating this man properly. This was something he could do, he just knew it, and the thought that these dreams were coming to be relevant to his own life—that they were not just interesting glimpses into another time and place—made him practically delirious with excitement.

-II-
Straw on the Floors

A fortnight later, the entire Montmorency family and their retainers descended on Amesbury Castle for Marie and Jean's wedding. All were excited to be part of this joining of a beautiful young couple, a true love match by the looks of it. In this way, Marie and Jean were fortunate; they'd known each other since childhood, had grown up together in Shaftesbury Castle while Jean billeted there, and had come to care for each other deeply. In fact, there was a perceptible heat between them. Despite stern warnings to her daughter, Branwen was not at all sure that Marie was still a maiden; her eyes had drifted when Branwen had taken her aside to describe her "marital duties." So, Branwen was as thrilled as anyone that the marriage was actually about to take place.

At fourteen, Marie was taking on the appearance of the beautiful woman she would become, a younger version of her mother: raven-black hair, sapphire-blue eyes, milky-white skin. However, unlike the generally serious and purposeful Branwen, Marie was a bouncy, vivacious girl, secure in herself as the pampered youngest child and only daughter.

As Lady Christine showed everyone to their quarters, Branwen discreetly inspected the castle grounds and interiors. Despite the appearance of opulence—marble floors, glass windows that were garlanded with roses for this occasion—the place was not up to her standards. She hadn't expected it to be. Branwen was notably particular: the bailey at home was raked clean; the great hall floor was bare and also swept clean; cats kept the vermin under control; the straw bedding was changed weekly. Water was either spring-sourced or boiled and was safe to drink.

She knew the wedding and banquet would be grand. Over two hundred were coming, and the Villiers were never shy about spending money. Edward and Jeanne's celebrations had been much more modest—many of the guests made their excuses when they learned that Rabbi Jacob and his wife had been invited to the wedding—but people still talked about the inventive and delicious banquet she and Cook had planned and prepared. The recipe for her exquisite lemon *tartelettes* was still requested. And Robert and Branwen henceforth had a very clear idea of who their friends were.

First to be dropped off were Edward and Jeanne, who'd be quartered in separate bedrooms on the second floor, along with their retainers.

"Th-thank you, Lady Villiers," said Jeanne in her quiet voice. "We w-will be most comfortable here."

Though upper-class, arranged twelfth-century marriages were always a gamble, Edward and Jeanne seemed to get along well, and they'd produced two healthy children so far: Pierre and Isabelle. Jeanne was even-tempered and sweet-natured. She never challenged Branwen on any domestic matter in the castle. Her tongue had been burned when she was a child in an unsuccessful attempt to cure her stutter, and her confidence, already low, had worsened through the years. Despite concerted efforts on everyone's part to prop up her self-esteem, she remained shy, and because of that stutter, entirely disinclined to open her mouth at dinner and supper.

This weighed on Edward. Out of her presence, he had occasionally worried to his parents, "Mama and Papa, what will Jeanne do when she's in charge?"

Robert had replied, laughing, "Well, don't plant your mother and me in the ground quite yet!" Both of them felt that, with time and maturing, Jeanne might well learn to assert herself more.

Robert and Branwen's quarters would be cozy. Lady Christine must have learned that they normally shared a bed—to her undoubted relief, no doubt, because, with this influx of guests, accommodations were tight. Their retainers would have to sleep on pallets in the same chamber. A large room on the third floor, the walls were panelled in oak and covered with colourful hunting and unicorn tapestries that Lady Christine had worked herself. It was certainly a beautiful room, obviously the best the Villiers could offer, and after the wedding it would serve as Jean and Marie's solar. However, as

Branwen had expected, on the floors were not the colourful, soft, exotic rugs of Shaftesbury Castle, but straw. Yes, it was fresh and sweet-smelling, but it wasn't *clean*.

"This will be lovely, Lady Christine. Thank you," Branwen said. It would only be for a couple of days, after all.

Branwen cast an approving glance at her younger son, who had bounded up the stairs ahead of them to their quarters. How he was growing and filling out! Since she'd last seen him at Pasch, she was sure he'd grown a couple of inches. She judged him almost as tall as his father. Clearly, he was thriving here.

Only a year older than Marie, Evan, too, had taken on the look of his adult self. Both her sons resembled their father. However, unlike the tall, handsome, black-haired Edward, Evan's hair was a sandy brown, thick and curly, and it never seemed to want to behave. A narrow diastema between his two front teeth imparted a slightly mischievous air to his grin. But Evan's most remarkable feature was his eyes: an arresting grey-green framed by strong brows and long lashes, which intensely focused on people when they talked to him. Evan listened, and remembered. No one knew where those eyes came from.

Unlike Edward and Marie, Evan had never been betrothed to anyone. Branwen had been adamant about that. Let *one* of the children be free to make their own choice, she insisted, and Robert had reluctantly conceded.

Evan was restless this day, his manner one of controlled agitation.

"Mama and Papa," he said, "when you have a moment, would you mind if I spoke to you alone?"

She and Robert glanced at each other. By the light and excitement in his eyes, he must have had another Steven dream.

"Of course," she replied. "How about after supper this evening. In here?" They couldn't wait.

When Evan left his parents' chamber that evening, he knew what "doctor," "Tylenol," "Dollarama," and "crisp" meant. Branwen and Robert knew something more important: they knew that a seer's long-ago prophecy about their son was likely going to prove true.

On July 4, 1187, a week after the wedding and just before Evan's sixteenth birthday, a fierce Sunni Kurd, Al-Nasir Salah al-Din Yusuf ibn Ayyub—quickly corrupted to "Saladin"— decisively routed an opposing army of Knights Templar and Hospitaller in the Holy Land. It would become known as the Battle of Hattin. Low-ranking surviving knights, if not beheaded, were sold into slavery. Three months later, on October 2, Jerusalem fell.

This insult to Christendom could not be tolerated, and both King Henry II and his son Richard vowed to take up arms. Henry even imposed a "Saladin" tax.

Robert and Branwen, in the privacy of their solar, said to each other, "And so now it starts."

1189

Coronation of Richard I, September 3

It is certain because it is impossible.
—Latin saying

-I-
Mould in the Broth

On July 13, 1189, five days after Evan turned eighteen, he and Marie were abruptly summoned home. She was five months' pregnant with her second child. Jean was welcome as well, of course, but Branwen said she wanted all her family together, now. Evan, Marie, and Jean decided they could make better time by leaving their little son Rémy safely at home to be coddled by the grandparents, wet nurses, and attendants. Even so, due to her "condition," Marie would have to go by carriage. They hurriedly packed a few personal items for a night's stay at Sir Chastain's manor and then set off, the horses at a brisk trot.

This is what Branwen knew: King Henry II had died on July 6 at Chinon, in Normandy. Robert had been called to arms in June to defend Henry against his sons' rebellions, the third time in sixteen years. This time, Robert had rounded up a hundred good men. Henry's assembled army had lost the final skirmish at Le Mans, nonetheless. On Henry's death, Robert would have kneeled and sworn obeisance to the legitimate next-in-line, Richard, although he personally had no use for this bellicose and disloyal son. Montmorencys had always been loyal to the rightful heir to the throne. So, Richard I, *vive le roi.*

Branwen had heard all this from one of Robert's men, arriving on a fast horse. With it, he brought more worrisome news: His Lordship had taken an arrow in the thigh. The wound had been treated on site, he assured her, and Lord Robert would be home as soon as he was able.

On July 15, late in the afternoon, Robert and his guards entered the bailey. All the family were there waiting for him. Evan, Marie, and Jean had barely arrived themselves. He was pale and exhausted and had to be helped off his destrier, Merlin II.

At Branwen's direction, Edward and Evan helped him over to a ground-level room on the south side, one that usually housed guests, where she'd had the bed readied and her usual assortment of remedies organized. She then asked everyone to leave the room, so that she could be alone with her husband.

Branwen took off his hose to examine the wound. It had been disinfected with wine, then stitched and dressed, but it was now blood-soaked. The wound was not large, but it wasn't healing and showed signs of infection at the edges. He was also running a fever. She bathed the wound with soap and boiled water. She smeared a poultice of silverweed, crushed garlic, and dead nettle mixed with honey on the wound and re-dressed it with clean, white linen. She gave him a tea of feverfew and poppy liquid for his fever and pain.

She whispered angrily, "Don't you dare die and leave me here alone, Robert de Montmorency! Don't you *dare!*"

Then she lay beside him and remained there, in his arms, all night.

When Robert awoke, it took him a moment to remember that he was really at home, though not in his bed. He turned to see Branwen lying beside him. She was awake, watching him. It was clear by the shadows under her eyes that she had barely slept, if at all. After all these years, the first thing his eyes sought in the morning was her.

He lay back, troubled by recurring, obsessive thoughts he'd had since Chinon.

"What are you thinking about?" she asked.

After a moment, he replied, "All the way home, I kept thinking, Why, *three times,* have I been summoned to help save Henry from his sons? How could a father so fail them? Or had they failed him? We were so outnumbered at Le Mans, we never had a chance. He was dying, anyway, of a stomach ulcer, we were told, brought on by anxiety and stress. In spite of all their betrayals, he loved those boys so much. He forgave them every single time. He just could never understand why they kept rising up against him. And then, to hear that his precious favourite John had also turned on him …"

"How can a son betray his father like that? What a disgrace," Branwen muttered. Prince John was only twenty-three at this time, but he already had a reputation for laziness and double-dealing.

"You know how a wounded animal runs home to its lair?" Robert continued. "That was Henry, dragging us all back to Chinon so he could die in his home. For thirty-five years, he was a great king, but he died, crying that he'd failed in what was most important. It was a terrible way for a man like him to leave this world. I was told that when Richard came to view his father's body, all he did was stand there, emotionless. Then, he just turned away."

He paused. Then he whispered, "Tell me that this will never happen to me."

Branwen stared at him in alarm. It was the pain talking, of course. "My love, look at me. You are not Henry, promising one thing, doing another, playing one side against the other. Christine de Villiers told me that he even lay with Richard's fiancée! What kind of man would *do* that?"

He had actually heard that bit of shocking gossip and had chosen to keep that to himself; his loyalty to his king ran deep. Henry had been a legendary philanderer, but Robert thought this a bit much even for Henry.

"You are a good man whose sons want only to live up to your example. *This will never happen to you.*"

He smiled weakly and held her close. His marshal, Geoffrey Longstreet, had urged him to remain in Normandy until he was well enough to travel. However, the thought of dying anywhere other than his birthplace and ancestral home, in any other person's arms than those of his beloved wife, had filled him with panic. In that respect, he was little different from Henry.

Evan is in a room—it seems to be a classroom—with other pupils his age, young women, too. Their teacher is standing in front of them, pointing to a series of pictures behind him. Steven has a flat device in front of him, on his desk, and he is moving his fingers quickly over flat squares with letters on them. Magically, whatever letters he touches appear on this flat machine. He's summarizing what the teacher is saying: "It's amazing how some of the world's greatest discoveries happened by accident. Newton with the apple hitting his head, leading to the Law of Gravity, for one. Here's another: Alexander Fleming went on holiday, leaving Petri dishes on his lab table with bacteria-filled medium in them. When he got back, you can imagine how annoyed he was that there was mould on most of them. But before he threw them all away, he looked under his microscope and saw the mould had killed the bacteria. It was a common, air-borne mould, Penicillium notatum. *Eventually, this mould was refined to produce penicillin. It isn't much used anymore, but imagine the lives that it and its descendants have saved!"*

He woke up, his mind racing. He knew nothing about this Newton/apple/gravity thing. Nor did he know who Fleming was. But this ordinary mould: How could he reproduce it? He went down to the kitchen and asked Jack for a bowl of broth. He carefully carried it up to the roof of the tower and left it in the sun, with instructions that no one go near it, especially not the cats. Sure enough, a couple of days later, a sort of slimy green mould had formed on the surface. Meanwhile, Father Benedict had twice daily conducted special masses for His Lordship.

Evan carried the bowl down to his father's sick bed. The wound was no better, but it was no worse.

He said, "Mama and Papa, with your permission, I'd like to try something."

Branwen took one look at the disgusting-looking bowl and recoiled.

"Please, Mama, I *saw* it!"

"You mean, in a dream?" they asked together.

"Yes, the night you came home, Papa."

His parents exchanged a glance and then nodded uncertainly to him.

He removed the dressing, as well as the stitches, which he suspected were the source of the infection. After bathing the wound again with soap and water, he smeared some of the slime into the wound. After that, he said, "Leave the wound be for the moment, to let this penetrate. May I put some more on this evening? Then re-stitch it?"

Robert said, "Tell us what you saw."

Evan relayed his dream and what he saw Steven write on that tablet of his. He saw anew the recognition in his mother's eyes. When Evan had finished, they all sat silently for a short while.

Robert said, "You have no idea whether the mould you have

applied to me is this 'penicillin' or not, do you? For all we know, it's a poison, not a cure."

"You're right, Papa, but what choice do we have? Do you not think there is a reason why I had a Steven dream, at this time? Is it not worth the risk?"

Evan returned that evening to reapply the slimy mould. Taking a waxed linen thread and needle, he carefully re-stitched the wound. Robert clenched Branwen's hand as he gasped in pain with that. If only there were a way to relieve the pain of this step! By the third day, the redness around the edges had disappeared and the wound was scabbing nicely. On the fourth day, with the aid of a crutch that one of Marshal Geoffrey Longstreet's sons had fashioned, Robert was helped outside and up to their solar. He was grumpy with inactivity but otherwise much better. All the castle denizens believed that his recovery was a blessed gift from God. But the three who'd been in that room knew that yes, it had indeed been a blessed gift, but not quite in the way everyone thought.

When Evan had been just a toddler, a chiromancer had predicted that he would be a "great healer." Evan's treatment of the stable boy's injury at Amesford Castle two years before was impressive enough. Even without this miraculous slime, they had witnessed for themselves his calm confidence as he treated his father. Clearly, this was what he was meant to do. They also knew it was time to tell him who Steven was and why Branwen, too, understood his dreams.

After dinner on the fourth day, Robert drew Evan aside and said, "Join us up in the great chamber. We need to have a talk."

The great chamber was the family's private gathering place. It was simply furnished but comfortable, the focal point of which was a large fireplace. Windows in three of the walls ensured that lighting was generous. The walls were whitewashed, with blue wainscoting. On the walls were large tapestries that Grandmama Maude had embroidered herself. Tapestries served a dual function: decoration and insulation. Chairs were set around a substantial oak table that sat before the hearth. A glass vase held a spray of roses today; Branwen always liked fresh flowers in the room. Next to the west-facing windows was a long table, with two chairs. This was where Robert and Branwen read. In the far corner stood Branwen's loom. Beside it was a large, locked cupboard where their books were kept. The planked floor was warmed by oriental rugs.

Soie, one of the castle cats, followed them into the room. As far back as Evan could remember, cats had been in the castle to get rid of the vermin. Typically, Branwen would have someone snatch a stray female kitten from off the streets in Shaftesbury, not that anyone would notice or care: stray dogs and cats littered the streets. But, periodically, in bouts of religious paranoia, the local cats would be almost completely exterminated. Black cats had it the worst, and even Branwen always instructed the kidnapper not to take a black cat, for fear of unhinging the castle inhabitants.

When they were sure of not being overheard, they closed the door and took their seats. Soie jumped on Branwen's lap. Stroking her, she began her tale.

"The name of the mother in your dreams is Stacey."

In the autumn of 2012, a twenty-three-year-old student named Stacey Rickert had signed up for a past-life-regression hypnosis experiment that went awry. Because of a simultaneous seizure in both women, their consciousnesses had been exchanged: Stacey to 1170 CE, Branwen to the twenty-first century and a city called Calgary in an as-yet-unknown continent across the ocean.

To Evan's start of surprise, Branwen said, "Believe me, dear, there are two vast continents out there. The Norsemen have already found the northern one, but England won't for more than three hundred years."

"So, the Day of Judgement won't have happened yet?"

Branwen smiled. "No, and doesn't it gladden your heart to know that we are not all going to be judged *any day now?*"

"What is 'past-life regression'? 'Hypnosis'?"

"Have patience, my dear. I'll explain it all another time."

She went on, "Our adventure lasted three months. You might think we spent the whole time in hiding, terrified we'd be found out. We were, at first—Stacey, especially. But, in fact, it was the most marvellous experience for both of us, so much so that we prayed we could spend the remainder of our lives there. Still, we had to be cautious. Our identities were carefully protected by the few who knew who we were: Stacey by your father, me by her sister and the experiment's designers. Then, another seizure caused us to return to our times; I cried privately for weeks after that." Robert squeezed her hand. "I had only your wonderful, understanding papa to help me through it."

Miraculously, no one except Robert seemed to realize either that Branwen's body had been inhabited by a visitor or that the real Branwen had returned. Branwen and Robert believed all of this had been by design, though what the design was they still didn't know for sure.

Stunned by these revelations, Evan asked, "You mean, no one even *suspected?*"

"Well," Branwen replied, "I'm sure Enith did. She knows me like I know myself. She must have guessed, but neither of us has ever brought it up. Some things are better left undiscussed, and she knows that."

Enith was Branwen's Welsh maid, who had tended her from the time Branwen was ten.

Through the years, Evan had heard castle gossip from old timers suggesting that the autumn of 1170 had been a remarkable one to witness, and it began with the fit. Lady Branwen was warmer and more approachable; she instigated the boiling of water and the sweeping of the bailey, among other changes; her relationship with her husband became, and remained, closer. She was never again the brittle woman she'd been before the fit. Lord Robert, who'd previously seized on any excuse to get out of the castle, since that time had to be pried out of it. All the castle residents religiously believed that the fit had been heaven-sent: the castle from then on had a positive energy that had been entirely lacking before. Thinking about this, given what he now knew, Evan understood how no one would want to look too closely into such a gift.

Branwen continued, "It doesn't matter if you don't understand the exact way it came about. I'm not even sure myself though it would surely be called witchcraft or heresy here. What matters is that it happened. I'd had the falling sickness when I was a child, though it stopped in my twelfth year. Since my return to this time in December of 1170, I've never had another fit. Both your papa and I believe that, once my condition had served its mysterious purpose, it was simply no longer needed. Seen in that light, an affliction I'd always thought of with shame and embarrassment could almost be considered a gift."

This jogged a little memory of Evan's, back when Marie was getting married, and Grandmama Generys grandly arrived at Amesbury Castle. Mama and Grandmama were not close; he'd only met her once before, at Edward's wedding.

Having likely forgotten that her grandchildren had been taught Welsh, she hadn't considered that Evan might be listening when she asked, "Are you still quite well, dear? There have been no … incidents?"

Mama had quickly brushed her off. "Of course, Mam. I'm perfectly well. Besides, everyone in the castle has known about it for years."

That had shocked Grandmama. "What? You mean—"

"Yes, and no one cares."

"Well, I must say that *is* a surprise. But I'm glad to hear it, dear. You know how much I worry about you."

"So, that's what Grandmama was talking about when she asked about your 'incidents.' I wondered about it at the time."

Branwen smiled. "Yes, I worried for a while that you and your curiosity would hound me for an explanation. But, to continue, the language you are hearing in your dreams is English."

English? The language of the *villeins?*

"Yes, I know," Branwen said. "It shocked me, too. While our Norman French will disappear, English will change and grow to become a great world language. As the Bible says, 'For everything there is a season.'"

Evan knew it'd take some time to absorb all this. In the meantime, he returned to what concerned him most. "Then what does Steven have to do with me?" This had been bothering Evan since the very first dream.

His father replied, "There are Infidels in the East who believe that after death, one's spirit lives on, to be born again. It's heresy to Christians, but as Rabbi Jacob often said, 'There are many paths to God.' You must understand the continued need for secrecy about this. We cannot have the Church hearing of it."

"So, you think Steven is me, reborn."

"It appears that way, yes. It's the only explanation we can think of."

"Then is Stacey you, Mama, reborn? Is my father in the dream you, Papa?"

Branwen replied, "Stacey and I thought about it a lot at the time—I still have her memories and thoughts while she was here—and I've thought a lot about it since. But my answer to that is 'no.' We felt no spiritual connection with each other. She never felt any sense of having lived this before. I still have no idea why we two were chosen."

Robert said, "But for the father in your dream, it's *possible*. I, too, once had a dream of the future in which I met Stacey. Just one dream, but it didn't reveal if I married her."

Branwen said, "If, by God's will, I am also reborn, it must be at some other time. Either that, or I'm unconnected to you two, which saddens me." She patted Robert's hand and smiled at him.

Evan thought of his Steven dreams. A time and place where people were happy, healthy, and incredibly rich, it seemed to him, though no one seemed to have any attendants. He asked, "Do you still wish you were back there?"

She paused for a moment, considering. "I have a good life here, as you know. I have a husband and family that I prize more than any jewel or possession. But, yes, to this day, I wish I could return, and take you all with me. To me, it feels like my true home."

She paused once again and gazed directly into Evan's eyes. "Evan, my dear, you will surely have already done the arithmetic. You were conceived then. Although, certainly, I bore you and have always been proud to be your mother, in a wonderful sort of way, both of us believe that Stacey is, too. She wanted nothing more than to remain here and birth you. In a way she perhaps never imagined, with Steven, she got her wish."

Evan sat back on his chair, studying these two people—strangers, they seemed to him now. Papa's hair was streaked with grey, his face creased with the burden of his position. Mama's hair, if ever he glimpsed it at all, was completely white. She had once said it had been like that since her fortieth year. However, her face remained lovely, her skin smooth, save small laugh lines around her eyes and mouth.

He tried to imagine his father as young, handsome, and lusty. Papa's eyes twinkled whenever she explained how she knew things from "Welsh" knowledge. It was a classic feature of their marriage. Everyone assumed he was gently mocking her; but no, quite the opposite, Evan now understood. He was fascinated, as eager for knowledge as she was.

Mama was defined by her restless need for learning and her quest to try new things; she was fortunate to be married to a man whose curiosity matched hers. Evan now knew why he'd so often sensed a frustration, even a sadness in her: she was wishing for things that would not be dreamed of for centuries.

Branwen gathered Soie back onto her lap and said, finally, "Surely you agree that things happened between Papa and Stacey that were best left until you were old enough to hear it."

Robert added, "It may be difficult to hear that I was unfaithful to your mother in this way. You're still young, but can you comprehend that it's possible to love two women, equally but differently? Your mother has always accepted this. I loved Stacey and I always will. Stacey is a part of us. It tortured us that we had no way of knowing what had become of her. Until you had your first Steven dream."

He drew a breath. "Son, I believe these dreams of yours are beginning to serve a purpose, don't you agree, love?" Branwen nodded. "This latest one reminds us of what we have both known for a very long time: that you are meant to be a healer. We have never tried to push this on you. We've always believed that your life is yours to do with as you wish, free from interference from us. But I think you have found your calling, have you not?"

Evan had lived at Amesbury Castle for eleven years. When he was fourteen, as was the custom, he'd advanced from page to squire in the Earl of Amesbury's service. Previously surrounded mostly by women who'd refined his social graces, the plan from then on was to toughen him up by putting him in the all-day company of men. He was Lord Villiers's personal servant: dressing him; assuming total care of His Lordship's horses, saddlery, and mail; serving him at meals; performing every task required of him, no matter how trifling. He'd also learned to hunt.

His military training had similarly advanced. The castle's marshal worked with him extensively on sword and crossbow. He developed skill at the quintain, a suspended sandbag dummy that he charged at with a lance. The trick was to get away fast enough so that it didn't smack him on the back as it swung around. Because both hands were occupied holding a shield and the lance, it meant his horse had to be sensitive to guidance by only the legs and feet. Not a problem for Evan: he and horses had always understood each other.

All the instruments of war that he was being trained on at that time were heavier than what he'd eventually carry. This was meant to build his upper-body strength, as well as to make the actual weapons easy to wield by comparison.

Since the previous year, he'd slept on a pallet outside Lord Villiers's solar, ready to defend his lord if ever the occasion required it and to respond to his every need. Not that Rupert de Villiers was a harsh taskmaster. But he was a stickler for form, for the proper way to do things. It had made Evan tidy about his person and his affairs.

All upper-class parents billeted, trained, and educated their boys, and sometimes their girls, at friendly, neighbouring castles. As hard as it had been to send Edward and Evan away, both Robert and Branwen believed that such training was a necessary component in the formation of young men of their class. It taught humility and responsibility. However, no one, including the Villiers, saw battlefield knighthood in Evan's future; it was too alien to his gentle nature. Besides, it would be a waste of a superb education and brain.

What Robert was saying to him now was that his squirehood was over. It was time for him to leave Amesbury Castle and take his proper place in the world.

Evan nodded. "Mama, will you teach me what you learned there? It may be useful sometime."

"Absolutely. Ask me anytime we're alone—though it was some years ago, and I've forgotten a lot. Your father will be glad to hear it again, too."

"And tell me all about Stacey. I'd like to know her better."

"Of course. Both of us enjoy talking about, and remembering, Stacey."

-II-
Neither Witches, Nor Jews, Nor Women

On Sunday, September 3, 1189, the males of the Montmorency and Villiers families were in London for Richard I's coronation at Westminster Abbey. Women were not allowed, as was the tradition, so Branwen, Jeanne, and the children stayed home, leaving castle affairs in Branwen's capable hands. Branwen didn't much mind, apart from her usual resentment of the pervasive misogyny in this society; she could well imagine the outcry if women were barred from a coronation in the twenty-first century.

However, she did worry about her family's safety. London was a fetid, sewage-ridden cow pad of narrow streets, crowded alleyways, and ne'er-do-wells of every description. Shaftesbury was less disgusting only because it was smaller, but at least she knew most everyone by sight. She felt out of her element in cities, fearful of all those strangers, every one of whom was just waiting for a chance to cheat or take advantage of her, she was sure of it.

She and Enith also shared a Welsh uneasiness about the choice of date. Richard had overridden his advisors' and astrologers' warnings that September 3 was a day of ill-omen. Striving hard not to show her apprehension, she had cautioned them, as they mounted their horses, "Be careful there, my loves!" At compline, matins, and prime, she prayed especially fervently for their safety.

The moment they'd learned the date, Branwen dispatched Michael Halliwell the Younger to London to arrange accommodations at Robert's preferred inn, The Blue Fox. It was situated on an unnamed street a few blocks from the abbey, and it was cheap and clean. Even at that, additional money had changed hands to secure the rooms. Coronations were few and far between, and the opportunity for merchants of every sort to line their pockets was too great to resist.

Nevertheless, despite the greasing of the innkeeper's palm, the Montmorencys were crowded into two small rooms, not three, as they'd been promised, their attendants on pallets along the walls. The fact that the innkeeper had done the same thing to the Villiers provided scant comfort to Robert. Evan had to bunk down with Edward, who snored.

Although it had rained the day before, coronation day dawned bright. Strapping on their wooden pattens to protect their boots from the puddles, garbage, and dung on the streets, and trying to ignore the stink from the Thames, they all made their way to the abbey, early. This way, they wouldn't have to stand at the back.

When the sun was at its zenith, the event began. Many of the nine hundred in attendance had not been alive when Henry took the throne thirty-five years earlier. Those who had been alive remembered The Anarchy, the eighteen-year civil war before that, brought on by rebel barons who would not accept Henry's mother as their sovereign. *Henry's* reign had been contested in the early years as well. So, it was surely a blessing that, for once, this ceremony marked an orderly transfer of power.

Buisines blaring, the assembly parted as Richard arrived, flanked by two bishops. He stood out against the crowd, dressed in a rich red, jewelled silk robe with a white tunic underneath. Even Robert, who'd met Richard before, was impressed at the sight. Richard was undoubtedly the tallest man in the building, with the perfect carriage of a man who'd spent his life on horseback. And he was handsome, with his reddish-blond hair, steel-grey eyes—a magnificent, younger version of his father. He was reputed to have a marvellous singing voice and a sure hand at poetry, too.

He certainly *looked* kingly, was the general whispering. Here was a man still in the flower of his youth, experienced in battle and administration of his duchy of Aquitaine, not some whimpering child or drooling fool. The Archbishop of Canterbury awaited him at the altar, where the throne was placed. When Richard reached him, he removed all his clothes except his breeches and chemise, cleverly open at the front to reveal a muscular chest. The archbishop then anointed him with holy oil on the head, hands, and chest. Just at that moment, a stray bat started swooping about, its flapping wings breaking the sacred silence of the ceremony. Robert crossed himself.

Richard was now permitted to re-clothe himself. He picked up the crown waiting on a pillow and handed it to the Archbishop, who placed it on his head. The new king sat on his throne, and the mass proceeded.

All those attending agreed that the only thing this impressive man lacked was a wife beside him. Instead, that chair was occupied by his mother, the redoubtable Eleanor of Aquitaine, now Dowager Queen of England. Richard had been betrothed for twenty years to Alys, a sister of King Philip of France. Why the delay, people wondered. She was now in her twenty-ninth year, surely a little long in the tooth to be a bride for the first time. Could she even start churning out heirs, at this advanced age?

It was an open secret that Henry, as her guardian, had got to Alys first. There were even rumours, difficult to contain, of a bastard son. The gossip mill wondered if Richard knew of this; if he did, he would certainly not marry goods tainted by his *father*, no less. But what would that do to the delicate alliance Richard had brokered with her brother, King Philip, his partner-in-arms on this crusade? In any case, why was the most eligible bachelor in Christendom still not married at thirty-two?

After the ceremony, guests crossed the street to the great hall of Westminster Palace, where a splendid feast and troupes of entertainers awaited them. The Montmorencys and Villiers were seated at one of the middle tables, some distance below the salt—not up with the top ranks of barons, bishops, Richard's staff, and other dignitaries, but not at the back of the hall, either. Robert expected no more. Their baronies, after all, were far from the halls of power and of middling size.

Suddenly, a commotion at the back of the hall interrupted their dinner. A few knights angrily charged outside, and immediately thereafter, the Montmorencys heard cries of pain and panic. What was going on?

"Stay here," Robert ordered the boys as he ran out to see what was happening. To his horror, an enraged mob, joined by those same knights, were assailing the bloody and broken bodies of three richly-dressed Jews. He recognized the ring on the hand of one of them. He looked, then looked again. It was Jacob d'Orléans.

"*Get away from them!*" Robert shouted, drawing his sword

and waving it in the air. "Haven't you defiled this day enough? Come one step closer and I will gladly run you through! That means you, too, filthy curs!" turning to the knights behind him. *"Shame on you!"*

The assembled crowd outside backed off, but they were now feral in their rage. When they saw that there was no more they could do to the dead Jews, anyway, they took off, looking for fresh blood. The knights withdrew back into the hall.

Robert knelt at Jacob's body. He looked for his pulse and then realized that there was nothing to be done. He crossed himself and whispered, "Walk with God now, Jacob."

Edward, Evan, and Jean burst out the door and sank to their knees, first in shock, then in confusion, and finally rage. Why? Why would anyone do this to such a blameless, elegant man as Jacob? And what was he doing here, anyway, at the steps of Westminster Hall?

Other Jews soon came out of the shadows to quietly pick up and spirit away their dead friends.

The family stood uncertainly on the steps, hardly believing, still, the sight of their lifeless teacher being carried away like a sack of carrots. The thought of going back into that hall, to *eat*, no less, made them want to hurl.

"What do we do now, Papa?" asked Edward. "We can't just walk back in there like we came out to take a piss."

Robert took a deep breath and shook his head. "We must, for all our sakes. Our absence would be noted, if not by Richard, by one of his minions, or even by one of the swine at the back of the hall who helped perpetrate this. Now is not the time to draw unwelcome attention to ourselves. We will each have to do whatever is necessary to get through the rest of this afternoon. Let's all take a moment to compose ourselves and say a prayer for Jacob, then we'll go back in."

They drew together in a group hug and a prayer.

Numb with shock, wooden smiles plastered on their faces, they picked at their meals and chatted politely. King Richard took his leave an eternity later. Robert caught his sons' eyes and discreetly nodded. They calmly walked out, having said their goodbyes to the surrounding guests, who were still unaware of what had happened.

Word of this did, of course, eventually reach the remaining guests. When they did leave, they were obliged to pick their way around the drying blood on the steps and wondered why they were so incommoded on this, of all days.

Only later, back at The Blue Fox, with the help of their wide-eyed retainers, did the group manage to piece together the story. Jews and witches had been expressly warned not to try attending the coronation. The Jewish community leaders therefore knew not to crash the coronation. But the banquet afterwards? Surely, they might be allowed to offer gifts to the new king? Would that not ensure Richard's good will in turn?

The grounds around the abbey and palace were crowded with onlookers, however, and a rumour started of a plot against the life of the King. That was all it took to turn otherwise decent people into a vicious mob. Hatred of Jews was never far from the surface, if it was hidden at all.

Their retainers had stepped outside The Blue Fox for fresh air during the course of the afternoon, only to run smack into the mob on its enraged way to the Jewish quarter after slaughtering the three Jews at Westminster. They'd only just got back safely in the door; otherwise, they'd have been trampled. The smoke from the burning quarter turned the setting sun and sky a carnelian red.

Rupert de Villiers, too, was aghast that such a splendid event had been despoiled. He had taken his son in his arms as Jean wept, "Why? Why?" Although Rupert harboured the usual anti-Semitic tendencies, he knew how much the children under Jacob's tutelage had loved him. He certainly envied the superior level of instruction his son had attained under him. He wondered what people would remember of this day as a result: the lavish coronation or the massacre afterward?

The two families set out for their homes the following day, heartbroken and deeply fearful for what might be in store in the months ahead. Edward's and Evan's sheltered, privileged lives would never be the same. They had seen evil up close and it thrived in people who looked like them.

Later, it came out that thirty Jews had been massacred that day. It didn't matter that when Richard got wind of what happened, he had the main instigators captured and hanged. He needed the

Jews. Especially, he needed their access to money for his crusade. But this taste of blood launched a storm of bloody pogroms across the country that went on for months.

In the months following the coronation, as far south as London and Dorsetshire, strange, glowing curtain-like swaths of light in the night sky were witnessed—mostly green, but sometimes a blood red. The deeply superstitious people of the time read this as an ill omen of the new king's reign. Branwen had seen these lights once during her time in the twenty-first century, where they were understood as a natural phenomenon that inspired awe, not fear. But she said nothing, merely drawing Robert and Evan aside to tell them that these lights were nothing more than one of nature's gifts.

-III-
"I would sell London if I could find a buyer."

A few months later, the Montmorencys were seated at dinner, the third Sunday of Advent. Fortunately, this close to Christmas they had no guests to turn away. This was a relief because the occasion demanded secrecy.

Along with the adult family, several others were in attendance at the great hall: Steward Michael Halliwell the Younger, who had taken over his father's position when he died; Father Benedict, as usual; Marshal Geoffrey Longstreet, a spry sixty-five; Sheriff Roger Boisvert of Shaftesbury; Hugh Scrivens, Robert's bailiff; and, finally, their honoured guest, the Reverend Mother Marie Martel, Abbess of Shaftesbury Abbey, a close neighbour, and perhaps the wealthiest and most important woman for leagues in any direction.

They were assembled to compare notes on what was being expected as a "contribution" to Richard's grandiose crusade plans. Behind the doors of this hall, they were calling it what it was: extortion. Henry had left the state treasury in healthy shape. The Saladin tax had raised a considerable sum, but it wasn't enough for Richard. He needed to raise vast sums because he intended to reach the Holy Land by sea, rightly figuring that it was quicker, easier, and safer than making the trip overland. But it was not *cheaper*. For that, he needed ships, plenty of them, big enough to quarter and feed horses.

Richard knew another country-wide tax would be unpopular, this early in his reign. But when the Bishop of Ely died intestate, allowing Richard to seize his assets, a sly little man named William Longchamp offered to purchase the bishopric for three thousand marks, which went straight into royal coffers. A mark was not an actual coin; it merely held the *value* of one hundred sixty pence. Impressed by the man's initiative, Richard immediately hired him as tax man-cum-chancellor. Now, what else? Together, they cooked up an original scheme.

Ambitious men in England had always been able to buy their way into positions of power and influence. Why not turn this to their advantage? Overnight, everything was up for sale: offices, sheriffdoms, lord- and earl-ships, castles, towns, lands, the lot. If the Reverend Mother wanted to remain abbess of Shaftesbury Abbey, that would be two thousand marks. If Robert wanted to remain earl of Shaftesbury, that'd be another two thousand. How about sheriff of Shaftesbury? Seven hundred—and if Roger Boisvert didn't have it, there would be someone who did, who would gladly pay for the privilege of a gilded position, with lots of opportunity for graft and corruption. Rumour had it that Richard had proclaimed, "I would sell London if I could find a buyer."

The Abbess sighed, her normally cheerful face lined with fatigue. "I can pay it. I will have to sell off some of the gold and silver plate and a piece of land. Who knows who will end up buying it, and even he will have to pay to keep it."

Scrivens said, "Indeed, there's nothing our king won't do to squeeze a few last pence out of us. My nephew signed up for the crusade and then changed his mind. He was fined ten marks."

Everyone gasped at that.

Of course, no one was going to send wagonloads of pence to be carted off to Winchester, where the Treasury was still located. They would be melted down under heavy guard into silver bars at the village smithy. Getting them to Winchester safely would be its own security nightmare. Gangs of brigands were an ever-growing travel hazard, particularly now, with countless sums being transported daily.

As for Robert, although he would muster a show of tired, worried stoicism in solidarity with the others, he had the money. For almost twenty years, he had known this was coming, and he knew more was in store. Everyone knew Robert was thrifty. Only Branwen, Edward, and Michael Halliwell knew just how thrifty.

While Branwen was in the twenty-first century, she'd made a study of the past, coming home with a good grasp of British history for the next few hundred years. She had wondered at first whether telling Robert what she'd learned would be harmful or destroy some timeline. But she had finally decided there was no good reason to keep this from him. She and Stacey had irrevocably changed whatever timeline was in progress the moment they switched; Stacey herself had freely volunteered information about life and culture in the twenty-first century. So, Branwen had told him that Richard and then John would become king and that the tax burden during their reigns would be crushing. She had told him about the Magna Carta, and that Edward would be one of the signatories. From 1170 onwards, Robert therefore instructed Halliwell to quietly squirrel away five percent of net income into what he called a famine fund and prayed it would be enough. And it was, this time, though a significant dent had been put in it. Edward had known of the fund for many years, but not the real reason for its creation.

Knowing the future was a mixed blessing, they'd found. While they now both knew the grand scheme of things, the devil was in the details. Beyond that one, tantalizing bit of information about Edward and the Magna Carta, history was silent about the Montmorencys' role in it. Robert had advance knowledge of the three rebellions of Henry's sons, each time heeding his king's call to arms, each time shaking his head at the inevitability of the future, the past, whatever it was. Just thinking about it twisted his brain. When he last set out for France he knew the battle would be lost, but what he did not know was his own fate. He and Branwen were as relieved as anyone that he'd survived all three campaigns.

Roger Boisvert complained, "Milord, I don't have seven hundred marks. Selling all of our dishes, our house, my wife's fancy dresses and our cow, and emptying my coffer, I think I could bring in perhaps a hundred and fifty. I could press my son-in-law for about fifty more."

Boisvert had been Sheriff of Shaftesbury for twenty-five years. He and Robert weren't exactly friends—it was strictly a professional relationship—but in a "profession" rife with corruption, he was honest and respected. Robert, quite literally, could not afford to lose him. He turned to Michael. "Steward Halliwell, can we make up the difference?"

He sucked his breath in. "Yes, but it will allow us no cushion for emergencies."

The Reverend Mother said, "I could contribute about a hundred."

Boisvert's eyes filled with tears. "Milord, Reverend Mother, my gratitude ..."

Robert waved his hand impatiently and said, "We all know that we must help Sheriff Boisvert. What cow turd would we be stuck with in his place? What we will *not* do is take it from the *villeins* as long as I sit in this chair, is that clear?" He could almost hear a couple of those present, including Boisvert and Scrivens, thinking, "Oh fie. Well, it was a thought ..."

"I will say one thing about Richard. He is taking from people who he's pretty sure can afford it. Let's keep it that way."

When they were alone, Branwen said to Robert, "There's something else, Robert. My marriage portion." When they were married, part of Branwen's dowry had been a brick of pure Welsh gold. It had remained in the safest coffer the castle had: behind a false front in their solar wall. He was fairly sure that only Branwen, Edward, Michael Halliwell and Reginald Poole, his long-time manservant, knew of its existence. All would die before they'd confess its location to anyone.

Robert smiled fondly at his wife. "Yes, my love, I thought of that. From what you told me, there may come a day when we will need it. But we're not at that point yet. We have the money." He kissed her hand.

"Should we tell Evan about the fund?" she asked.

Robert sat, considering. "He may start wondering about how much future knowledge we have, what we might have done to prepare for it. But, for now, I think not unless he asks. Castle finances need not concern him. Let this be Edward's knowledge only."

Branwen nodded in agreement.

Later that day, as the aroma of the evening's comforting venison stew wafted throughout the castle grounds, Evan joined his parents in the great chamber. They were reading, an activity they enjoyed whenever they had an hour or so of free time. He looked around and, seeing they were alone, said, "Mama and Papa, I need to talk to you about something."

Branwen looked up from her reading. This day just wouldn't quit. What now?

When he'd settled himself onto his chair, he announced, "I want to go on the King's crusade as an apprentice *medicus*." A *medicus* could treat wounds and do simple procedures but lacked the prestige of a *studium*-educated physician.

Branwen gasped and Robert jerked back in surprise. Where had *this* come from? When they'd all agreed that Evan was to study to become a physician, they assumed he would spend an amiable few years at Oxford, followed by perhaps another year or so in Montpellier, or even Bologna, for the sake of life enrichment. Preferably the former, though, because it was closer. Salerno also had a renowned medical school that he could probably get into. But trailing after a horde of armed, violent men? Sleeping rough, prey to the elements and disease? Beset by Infidels or brigands? His body chewed at by the wolves that quietly lurked in the forests, in the wake of battle? It was well known that a third of all crusaders never made it home alive. A lot never even made it to the Holy Land. Not that many, surprisingly, died in combat: most succumbed to disease, heat stroke, death by accident or misadventure, sometimes even starvation.

Branwen said flatly, "I will not permit it."

He pleaded, "Mama, please! It's not a combat position—"

"Oh yes it is," Robert cut in. "You'll be trailing at the back of the pack, with the rest of the camp followers, easy pickings. Your wits and sword skills will need to be sharp. You may kill more often than you cure."

Evan hadn't thought of that. The fact was, he hadn't really thought it through at all; he'd assumed his parents would be delighted by this show of initiative. He'd also assumed medical personnel were protected in some way. Well, at least he knew his away around a sword.

Thinking on the fly, he advanced his best argument: "Is not rescuing Outremer from Infidels the noblest of all causes?"

But his parents were too clever for that. "Especially noble is the plunder you bring home with you," Robert scoffed.

This wasn't going well. He took a breath and marshalled another line of reasoning. "But consider: Where do you think I can learn the most? Serve the Lord in the best way? Bring the most honour to this house? By treating every kind of condition in every circumstance, or some old boot's gout—"

Robert snapped, "That's enough! Your Grandmama Maude had gout. Never underestimate what pain relief of any kind does for a person."

Evan wondered if it was possible for him to be more of a jackass. "I'm sorry, I didn't know." He had one last thought. "But, consider this. We will be stopping at ports renowned as centres of learning. I can learn Infidel and Jewish physic while the fleet is docked. Do you not think that, absorbing all this knowledge, I will return as a better healer?"

He could see that he'd aimed true with Mama. What she prized, second only to her family, was knowledge. At that moment, he spied just a flash of envy in her eyes, and he knew he'd won. He exhaled quietly in relief; his final word would have been that he was going whether they approved or not. He saw the wheels turning in his father's mind.

They were all silent for a few moments, the crackling fire the only noise in the room.

Then Robert began, "Your mother and I must think on this. After all, having told you your entire life that your life is yours to do with as you please, we can hardly scuttle your dreams now. But, we will need to mitigate your risk. You'll need mail and a sword; don't argue with me on this. You will immediately recommence wooden sword practice with Oliver Longstreet." Oliver was Geoffrey Longstreet's older son, being groomed to take his father's place as castle marshal.

He went on, thinking aloud, "The horse you have will suffice. A destrier would direct a kidnapper's attention straight to you."

Evan had been hoping for a destrier, like Edward had. Elijah was a good, reliable horse, but, as his father said, nothing special.

"But wouldn't that be better than being shot at like everyone else?"

"The idea is to blend in. You'll be mounted and wearing mail. This'll distinguish you from the infantry. But you'll need to look like you're not really worth ransoming. Let other knights show off with their fancy horses and colours."

He paused. "Further, you will need money for emergencies.

Believe me, wherever an army goes, prices soar. I'll visit the Templars in London to see about getting you a letter of credit you can redeem in any city where they operate. We can send you off with a small amount of spending money in the meantime. It'll be up to you to make all the inquiries about getting hired on, find out what you will need in the way of supplies, and purchase them."

Evan got up to embrace them. "I won't disappoint you, I promise."

Her eyes teary, Branwen ran her hands through her son's untidy hair, his intense green eyes so earnest, and so innocent, still.

Lord, You have played a strong part in this boy's formation. I beg You, don't abandon him now.

1190

Richard I's crest from the Third Crusade

[It is] like teaching a fish to swim.
—Latin saying

-I-
"People will be studying us!"

In late January of 1190, Evan was in London, seeing to the business of getting himself signed on with the crusade. He had signed up at the Chancery at Westminster as an apprentice medicus and had been told to report to Dartmouth harbour within a fortnight of being notified that the fleet would set sail, likely within a couple of months. They would not wait for him.

True to his word, his father had managed to get Evan assigned to Lord William de Fors's command, exactly how Evan had wished: in the medical corps as an apprentice medicus. Fors, Lord Robert de Sablé, and Lord Richard de Canville were the three commanders of the fleet. Fors's reputation was unimpeachable, a man of great military experience and honour. Like other commanders of his rank and experience, he would trust the senior shipmasters to get them to their destinations on time. Robert was convinced that Evan would be in good hands under his command.

At the same time, Evan had learned that many of his father's assumptions about this crusade were wrong. This one was going to be different, a sentiment he'd heard from almost everyone. For example, contrary to what his father had assumed, since he wasn't a knight, he wouldn't need a horse because he'd be making the trip by sea with all the infantrymen and medical personnel. If the need arose on land, it would be up to him to obtain—in other words, steal—one.

Evan had been told a list of things to carry with him beyond the usual personal items, specifically a knife, sword, woollen blanket, helmet, and shield. He was told never to count on being fed once they hit land; if he was, it would likely be deducted from his salary. Armies on the move foraged, typically cutting a swath through the territories where they marched like a swarm of locusts. At sea, of course, he'd get the usual daily rations.

Furthermore, he'd signed his name, agreeing to a contract outlining a) his term of service: until King Richard released him; b) rate of pay as an apprentice medicus: six pence a day, paid at the end of each month; c) amnesty for previous crimes, non-applicable to Evan; d) forgiveness of any debt, also non-applicable; and e) division of spoils: strictly according to rank. The clerk had shown surprise at the facility with which Evan read the contract. Most recruits were illiterate or close to it and certainly incapable of more than an "X."

He and his escorts, Henry and Alwin, were staying with William Wolstone, now practising as a physician after graduating the year before from Oxford. Robert had paid for his studies there. Oxford did not have an organized program of studies—the *studium* itself was still very new, though a renowned Italian physician, Marco da Bologna, had found his way there and had started conducting classes in physic. Everyone knew the Italians were master teachers, so Branwen had insisted William go to Oxford.

William was Joanne Wolstone's son. He was commonly believed to be Robert's unacknowledged bastard, though everyone tactfully refrained from mentioning it. A bright boy, he had wanted to be a physician from the time he was little. When he was seven, with Joanne's eager consent, Branwen had brought him to Shaftesbury Castle as a day student, where he'd enjoyed the same splendid instruction as Jean, Evan, and Marie had.

Now twenty-four, William was treating patients in his neighbourhood of Southwark, across the bridge from the richer, more established north side. The streets in this somewhat disreputable part of town were narrow; the cramped and cheap housing had mostly been thrown together in a hurry by immigrants to the city. The closer one got to the Thames, the more the stench of excrement, tanneries, tallow chandleries, fishmongers, and butchers made the eyes water. True Londoners only noticed it if they left town and returned. Stray or feral pigs, dogs, and cats wandered the streets, often biting pedestrians and threatening those on horseback.

William's treatment room was in one such house on Saint Olave street. Beside the front door hung a sign with a single snake entwined around a rod. Lining the shelves were pottery jars filled with dried herbs and potions, and variously-sized mortars and pestles. An examining table took up much of the outer room. In the drawers were his implements. Despite his modest circumstances, the place was spotless and the wooden floor swept daily. His living quarters were through a door, behind the treatment room. It was monkishly furnished: a bed, a table, a chair. A battle-scarred grey tom, named Cat, came and went as he wished.

Although William had a brazier for warmth and cooking, he mostly took his meals elsewhere. He often had to accept food or livestock as payment for his services and now had three chickens and a goat out back, forming a cramped, chaotic menagerie with Evan's and his escorts' horses. Also at the back was the "necessary," just a wooden box with an opening in the top over a deep hole. A community well was at the end of the street.

He was still young and thus was still working on gaining the trust of the denizens, but he loved being his own man. And Evan noticed that business was steady—not crowded, but enough that William couldn't stray far during the day. For three nights, Evan, Henry, and Alwin had slept on William's floor. Over the course of those few days, he watched, rapt, as William efficiently treated his patients.

Evan wanted to be just like William.

William's smile was broad as he enthusiastically discussed advances in physic—things he and his young cohorts were learning through trial and error that seemed so at odds with the age-old Hippocratic/Galen-centred, humoral-based curriculum that was still the standard. Sadly, that was largely still the case in Northern Europe: thousand-year-old beliefs mixed with herb-based treatment and prayer. An uneasy truce lay between the healing community and the priests who held to the belief that cures lay in God's hands for people whose sins must have caused their maladies in the first place. Most men who called themselves physicians had learned by doing, by apprenticing themselves to other physicians who'd learned in exactly the same way. There were no female physicians, only midwives and wise women who were often viewed with suspicion by the Church and male practitioners.

People were generally mistrustful of physicians, rightly believing that they killed more often than they cured. They would only consult one if home and wise women's remedies had been exhausted, and only if they could afford it. Nonetheless, the concept of a physician as a studium-trained, licensed profession, honourable in itself, was slowly making its way north as medical schools started to crop up in centres like Paris.

William said, "It's exhilarating! We're devising our own physic! Someday, people will be studying *us!*"

Evan fervently wanted to be part of that new breed.

William even quietly divulged that, under cover of darkness, he and a few colleagues had dissected dug-up, hanged prisoners. It was illegal, money was passed under the table, and they had to do it quickly because the corpses decomposed. But they had to see for themselves the structure of a human body. The bodies were subsequently stitched up and quietly reburied.

He was sweeping his treatment room as he said this. He looked up from his broom. Holding Evan's gaze, he said, "I'm only telling you this because you have similar ambitions to mine. At some point, you too will be driven by curiosity to see the miracle that is the human body. Pigs and monkeys just aren't good enough. You understand, of course, that this is between us. If this gets back to me, I'll deny it, and I'll know it was you, *dalcop.*"

Evan nodded. He was good at keeping secrets.

-II-
The Whoreson of a Widowed Weaver

The evening before Evan was to return home, William opened up about what it was like growing up as the bastard son of a baron. Of that, he was sure, though with his auburn hair and brown eyes, he strongly favoured his beautiful mother. She had always assured him that Lord Robert was his father, even if he would never acknowledge him.

Although William's instruction had taken place in the Anglo-Norman-speaking Shaftesbury Castle and he spoke that language well, he remained most comfortable in English, so on William's home turf, Evan used that language. Europe was a place of numerous regional dialects, although Latin remained the lingua franca of educated people. However, Europeans who got around had to be at least bilingual, or even multi-lingual. Robert and Branwen's children were all fluent in five languages: Anglo-Norman French, English, Welsh, Latin, and Parisian French, which Jacob believed was important for his charges to learn. As well, they could all read Greek.

The ales from the local tavern had loosened William's tongue. Cradling his mug, he said, "My mother and I have always been grateful to Lord Robert and Lady Branwen. Me, the bastard son of a widowed weaver, who everyone knew was the Lord's *puterelle,* among other men's. The Montmorencys treated me like another son and never made me feel that I was less than you are. Where would I be without your parents' help and faith in me?"

Nevertheless, as William looked up from his ale, Evan saw, not gratitude, but eyes as bitter as the ale they were drinking.

"But do you know what it's like to always feel beholden? I owe them a debt that can never be repaid, only because I was born on the wrong side of the castle walls. You take your birthright for granted, but you have no idea how much I envy you. There are certain circles where I will never be welcome. To some people, I'll always be the whoreson of a widowed weaver. Who will never be invited to a coronation."

That last sentence stung. William had fit in so well at the castle; he'd excelled in his studies, got along with Edward and Jean. But reflecting on this now, Evan understood how constant *gratitude* could grate at one's soul, how it could warp into bitterness and resentment.

The silence lingered. William said, "I keep thinking that, had I been at the coronation, I might have been able to help Rabbi Jacob."

Evan was still trying to take in what William had told him. He sipped his sour ale and tried to compose his thoughts. "This ale is terrible, isn't it?"

William laughed and nodded. No doubt about it, Shaftesbury Castle brewed the best ale.

Evan beat down that still-raw memory of Jacob on the steps and replied, "No, you couldn't have helped him. His skull had been shattered on the steps. He was already dead when we got to him. The only mercy was that it would have been quick."

William was silent, though Evan could see he was weighing something in his mind. He seemed to decide, then said, "I was in the crowd of onlookers that day. You've seen flocks of starlings, haven't you? How they swoop and soar as one? Well, a mob's an evil version of that. It has its own life, I learned, quite apart from the individual humans that make it up.

"As quick as a cat, the mood changed from celebration to fury, and I had no idea why—only that I felt anger, too. When they rushed to the steps, I had to go along. It was like I, William, no longer existed. Then I saw … And even then, knowing that it was Jacob lying there on the steps, the madness in me thought, Serves him right! Can you *imagine?* I still can't."

He massaged his forehead with his fists, as if trying to wipe the memory, then brushed a tear away. "I saw Lord Robert shout them back. That seemed to snap me to my senses and I felt horror and shame for what I'd been thinking. But then the mob turned to rush to the Jewish Quarter. I was nearly trampled, pushing my way out of that."

Both of them sat silently, remembering their beloved teacher, knowing that it was a guilt William would always carry.

"Our father is a good man," he said, finally.

All the castle children mixed freely, regardless of station, and William had always treated Evan like a pest of a little brother. He was six years older and had been closer to Edward and Jean. So, Evan felt honoured that William had shared this story and was certain he'd told it to no one else.

Eventually, Evan replied, "Yes, he is. Wolstone, I'm sorry, about all of it. I can't relieve your guilt about Rabbi Jacob. But, about the debt? I'm sure they never thought about it like that. You know Mama. She believes everyone who wants it should have schooling. I think they saw it as a way of giving back. They're so proud of you. They're hoping you'll someday return, so they can engage your services."

"You'll get wool from an ass before that'll happen, I hate to say. Here, I have a decent chance of getting by on my own merits, not having my parentage thrown in my face. Besides, London is *the* place to be if you want to get ahead."

William paused, and then spoke again. "My mother was a good mother, you know that, don't you?" Evan had never given it much thought. He only really knew of her by reputation—whispered, overheard conversations among the guards. He realized that the moment she became known as Lord Robert's *pute* on the side, she would never have been able to remarry.

"She fed and clothed me before herself. How was she supposed to support us on just what she made from weaving? My earliest memories are of her chasing me out of the house as Lord Robert pulled up to our gate. Then in the fall of 1170, his visits suddenly stopped for good. Mama never understood what happened, although she did hear that Lord and Lady Montmorency's relations had become more … cordial. They certainly seemed close enough to me."

There it was again. The fall of 1170. Three months that changed everyone's lives—and brought his own into existence. He sensed that William was probing him, hoping for some explanation. Evan let the silence lengthen.

"Don't misunderstand me. Lord Robert has always done what he could for her, and we are grateful. But I asked him to stop when I started this practice. I give Mama half of what I make. She doesn't need men's coin any longer."

Ah, that's why William's lodgings are so modest, Evan thought.

"Why don't you come with me on this crusade? Your parentage would be no barrier there."

"Don't think I haven't thought about it! The chance to learn from the best, to see the world along the way—"

"But you have obligations elsewhere, yes, I see. Your mother and mine will be very proud of you, knowing this. Consider your debt paid in full. If there ever was one. You've accomplished what you set out to do. That's enough for them."

"When you come home, you're going to teach me what you learned. Promise me, Montmorency."

Evan looked across at his childhood friend, eyes glittering with intelligence, avid for learning. "I promise."

"So, what did you think of London?" he asked Henry and Alwin as they headed out of town. Evan expected they'd wax enthusiastic about the pleasures of the big city.

"Can't wait to get back," said Alwin. "We've been ready to go home for days!" They had only been there for four.

Evan chuckled. "I couldn't agree more."

-III-
The Moon Without a Rocket

On his return, still excited from watching William at work, he sought his parents out in the great chamber later the following afternoon, when he figured they'd be just about done their reading for the day. Everyone in the castle knew they liked this quiet time to themselves, and they were generally not disturbed.

Evan said, "Mama, tell me what you know about healing in the twenty-first century."

Branwen had been prepared for this question, but, still, she had to consider what she knew for certain. The last thing she'd ever want would be to give misinformation that could harm a person here. The fact was, she hadn't paid much attention to the healing arts there, being much more interested in history and politics. She also knew that humanity had worked hard through the centuries to attain the knowledge it had; technology such as X-ray machines, ultrasound, and microscopes would not be thought of, much less developed, for centuries. Many of the treatments and cures in that century depended on the knowledgeable use of those machines. Giving Evan this knowledge would be like daring to think one could walk on the moon without knowing how to build a rocket.

Once they were all settled around the fire, she began, "Well, the Lord still finds ways for people to die. Stacey's mother died young of the wasting disease, as you remember, Robert." He nodded. "But, thanks to more abundant food and clean water and so many amazing treatments, people do live longer. Their greatest achievement is that few women die in childbirth, and their babies have a good chance of surviving to adulthood. Unfortunately, those treatments are unavailable to us now. You can only work with what we have. For the most efficient medicinal herbs, you really need to talk to Sister Marguerite at the abbey. She is a powerful healer in her own right."

"So, what *can* you tell me, then?"

"I do know that no one lets blood anymore; neither does anyone subscribe to the humoral doctrine of healing."

Evan gaped. "But this has been truth for a thousand years!" William practised both regularly.

"Well, we all know that just because something is accepted practice, it doesn't make it correct," she reminded him. Now that he thought about it, Mama never let physicians bleed anyone in the castle.

"But if I don't let blood or consult the humoral charts, what can I do?"

"All right, first of all, let's talk about what your father and I think is most important for your future. Steven was treated in a small hospital, which they call a clinic. I know that because I was in one, too."

"What happened?"

"I was foolish. I ate something that made Stacey's body sick. But that's not important. Clinics are independent of churches and treat everyone, regardless of race or faith or, where I lived, ability to pay. Because medicine has made so many advancements, people go to such places with the *expectation* that they will be helped. They are profoundly disappointed if there's nothing physicians can do. Faith and prayer are still important for many people, but it is combined with certainty that human skills and knowledge play a huge role."

She leaned forward, her eyes excited. "What I'm trying to say is that you can build a version of such a place here, like what William is doing but bigger: a place dedicated to healing."

Robert added, "You will likely have to work under the aegis of an abbey or monastery to get it built, but we're sure you'll be up to that challenge."

Branwen nodded and went on, "For treatments, I think I can most confidently tell you about some *preventative* measures I learned, though let me stress that I didn't spend my time studying their physic! Just a few important things. The shipman's disease will be known as scurvy and is entirely preventable with lots of fresh fruit and vegetables. Remember that on your travels. Buy them before you buy meat. The deformation in bones we see among the poor: you won't get it with sufficient milk and cheese and exposure to sunlight. Swamp fever is actually caused by a mosquito, so cover yourself during mosquito season."

This was manna from heaven. "What else?"

Branwen smiled at her son's eagerness. "Well, a big one is cleanliness. Keep yourself and your surroundings clean; there's a reason why we sweep the bailey, why we have rugs in the bedrooms. This will be very important when you treat the injured. Wash your hands with soap and water before and after you touch your patients. Wash the injured area before you treat it. Rain water should be safe; so should spring-sourced water. Otherwise, when in doubt, boil water before drinking it. There are tiny creatures in there, too small for you to see, but they can be harmful to us. In that century, people also heat milk gently for some time because it is thought to kill those tiny, harmful creatures."

"If they're that small, how do they know they're there?"

"They have a machine which allows one to see them very clearly. Furthermore, they've learned that many diseases are spread through the air, among them *phthisis* and pox. Cover your face if you have the least suspicion a patient may have them. Again, wash your hands and keep them away from your face."

At that moment, Jeanne knocked and came in when Robert told her to enter. "I'm s-sorry, am I interrupting?" she asked in her gentle voice. "S-supper is ready."

"Oh no, of course not, dear, thank you," Branwen replied. "Evan was just telling us about what William's doing now." Nodding at Evan, "We'll talk about this again."

Following Branwen's advice, Evan paid a visit to Sister Marguerite a few days later. She was a stout woman of about sixty, with a pink face that radiated good cheer. When Evan mentioned the reason for his visit, she was thrilled. "Come, sit down! And how is Lady Branwen these days? It's been some time since I've seen her."

For twenty years, Branwen had been a frequent visitor at the abbey, dropping by to chat with the Reverend Mother and to borrow books from the large library on the premises.

"Busy, as always!" Evan replied. "She spends a lot of time with her grandchildren, tutoring them. Also, the castle is like an inn, there are so many guests."

He looked around approvingly at her apothecary. This was located on the abbey grounds, not in the cloisters, so local folk could access treatment. It was clean and orderly, all her herbs arranged neatly on the shelves. Drying bunches of rosemary, lavender, and oregano scented the room. It was an inviting, comforting place where he imagined himself sitting cozily by her brazier and confiding his anxieties to her. When he mentioned that he'd been to visit and study under William Wolstone in London, she smiled.

"Oh yes, William," she said. "Very bright and keen to learn. I taught him everything I knew, and it wasn't enough."

Evan remarked, "Clearly, from you, he learned the importance of cleanliness and good order."

Sister Marguerite smiled again at the compliment. "Yes, that is of primary importance. I can't have my herb mixtures contaminated with other herbs or dust."

Forty-some years of foraging, consulting with wise women and midwives, and trial and error—often on herself—made her an impressive storehouse of knowledge. From Sister Marguerite, he learned about salves for aching muscles and lacerated or burned skin. He learned which herbs worked for digestive upset, which for aches and pains, which for anxiety and sleep disorders. She showed him how to reset a dislocated shoulder by placing the hand of the affected arm on the shoulder and massaging the surrounding muscles; it was a method she'd devised herself. All this, Evan soaked up like a child learns his native tongue.

She showed him how to restore life to a drowned or unconscious person by using a combination of forceful pushes with the heels of the hands on a person's chest and breathing into their mouths. She said, "In fact, your mother taught it to me. Did you know she saved Swithin Atwater's life?" Swithin was the Shaftesbury blacksmith.

"*Lady Branwen* taught it to you?" She'd never mentioned it, as far as he knew.

"Yes, years ago. Let's see … 1170, I think. Not long after her fit," she added, her eyes probing. "It doesn't always work, but when it does, everyone says it's a miracle."

"Thank you for telling me, Sister Marguerite. I must ask her about that."

And thank *you*, Stacey, he thought, smiling inwardly.

-IV-
The Name of Your Horse

Five months later, the Montmorency family members were together at supper for the last time. God only knew when they'd have such an occasion again. Henry and Alwin were going to escort Evan the following day as far as Dartmouth, a good four days' ride southwest of Shaftesbury. After months of planning, fundraising, and arms and personnel acquisition, Richard's grand quest was finally about to get underway, three months late. The intention was to set sail on the Feast of Saint John the Baptist—June 24—after all the requisite rituals had been fulfilled, not the least of which was special prayers to God and Saint Nicholas for this momentous undertaking.

Richard was not with the fleet. He was in Aquitaine, rounding up his knights, persuading more people to reach into their pockets, finally meeting up with King Philip in Vézelay to coordinate plans. This was to be the largest, best financed, and best organized crusade so far, truly an international cooperative venture. Although the two armies would take different land and sea routes—Richard overland to Marseille, where he'd meet up with his fleet; Philip to Genoa for the same—the ultimate plan was for the vast fleet to convene at Messina, Sicily by September at the latest, before setting out eastward to Outremer. Duke Leopold of Austria would accompany Philip. A fourth army, led by Frederick Barbarossa, Holy Roman Emperor, was making the entire journey overland, while other, smaller forces were travelling from the Baltic states and Italy.

That afternoon, Robert had given Evan a folded slip of parchment inside a waterproofed leather pouch attached to a long cord of leather that he hung around Evan's neck. It was the letter of credit from the Templars he'd promised him months before. It read, in Latin, *To the bearer, upon proper identification, the amount of money requested, to a maximum of 30 marks.* It was a sizeable sum, and given the recent financial sacrifices Robert had had to make, Evan was touched.

"If you're careful, it'll last you for two years, at least, and may even pay for some of your advanced schooling," he said, squeezing his hands into Evan's shoulders. "Never remove it. Show it to no one. Should you need money, take it to the closest Templar commandery. The agreed-upon code word is 'Stacey.' No one will understand its meaning, and I'm quite sure no one will guess it," he added with a conspiratorial smile.

"If they ask what it means, have prepared some simple story—like the name of your horse when you were a child—and stick to it. The Commander assured me that it is written with a special, waterproof ink from the East. Still, I don't suggest bathing with it on."

That night, as everyone was preparing for bed, Evan found his father in his sitting room. Reginald Poole had just finished attending to His Lordship's evening toilette and was repairing to his own room.

This sitting room and closet was on the new fifth floor, which also comprised Branwen's matching sitting room on the opposite side and an ample, white-washed solar in the middle. The fifth floor had been built three years ago. It was relatively unorthodox in its design, as titled spouses typically maintained separate bedrooms. Since Stacey's time here, Robert had slept in Branwen's bed and both loved this spacious arrangement.

Robert's sitting room was large enough to accommodate walled-off quarters for Poole, who, out of long habit, always wanted to be proximate to his master. For twenty years, Enith had shared a room with Winnifred on the south side of the castle. Accommodations for the servants had always been a problem; although the donjon had several spare bedrooms, it was considered unseemly for servants to occupy them. Hence, they were squeezed in elsewhere on the grounds, mostly in the corner towers. The former solars on the fourth floor were now guest bedrooms frequently occupied by the castle's many visitors.

The Montmorencys were not alone in renovating their living quarters. Castles had originally been built solely with defence in mind. The donjons were drafty, cold, and cramped. But, as the danger of Saxon rebellion and assault passed through the years, the inhabitants increasingly saw these buildings as homes that should provide some comfortable amenities. The outstanding feature of this new solar was a large fireplace.

Evan took a chair. "Papa," he said when they were alone, "Tell me, why did you never acknowledge William as your son?"

Robert stared at him, puzzled. Why was he asking this now? It must be from the time Evan had spent with William in London. He had always known what a wound it was in William's heart that he was an unacknowledged bastard. He wondered if it was about the coronation and William's absence from that event. While he understood the slight William would have felt, some things in life just didn't go one's way. This was one of them. Well, Evan was a grown man now, about to leave them, perhaps forever, and he deserved the truth.

"I never acknowledged him as my son because he isn't."

This was the last thing Evan expected to hear. "But how can you say that? Both William and his mother maintain that he is. Everyone thinks so."

Robert looked his son in the eye. "Son, a lie repeated many, many times has a way of becoming truth, but it is still a lie. From day one, she insisted that William was mine, but how could I know for sure? I started investigating it when you were about four because, of course, if anything happened to Edward, the succession would be at stake.

"The short answer is that I could not have fathered that child. Around that time, I was either on the way to Amesford, or visiting Rupert de Villiers at Amesford, or on the way back. Nor did I visit her on my return because I was ill from something I'd eaten en route."

He watched as Evan struggled to absorb this information.

"I've told her this, many times, but she refuses to believe it. After all, which makes a better story? That his father is a baron, or some unknown, forgotten man? I apprised your mother of this. It made no difference in how she felt about William. She has a great need to see the deserving rewarded, and who better than him? And I happen to agree with her on that matter. Someday, she says it will be possible to succeed solely on one's merits. But not now. William needed help and we gave it to him."

"Could not this midwife have felt pressured to say what you wanted to hear? Could you not be misremembering your activities then?"

Robert glared at him. "Absolutely not. The midwife clearly remembered the date, Palm Sunday, because her father died the same day. I was nowhere near Shaftesbury for a good month on either side of probable conception. William was a healthy, full-term baby of normal weight. Halliwell kept accurate records of my whereabouts in his accounts."

"But surely you'd have known that this would breed resentment? The fact that you brought him to the castle would fuel their hopes that you'd someday acknowledge him? And lead pretty well everyone to assume that he was your son?"

The word "resentment" cut Robert to the bone. If there was one thing he always sought, it was harmony in his corner of the universe. He had always assumed that William was happy at the castle. Should this be cause for concern? Well, the higher he rose—of that, Robert was certain—the less his parentage would matter.

"He would have felt this resentment whether we'd brought him here or not. At least, William got the instruction he deserved, and he's done us all proud. William is clever and ambitious. I know he'll use this false 'connection' to advance his career, and that's to the better. But he is *not* my son, and let that be the end of it."

Evan considered the tangle of emotions enveloping this foursome. He knew Mama must have accepted the arrangement at the time; all high-born wives did, to his knowledge. But how had she felt about the liaison, really? Had she been jealous? Had she laid down the law when she returned from the future?

Then, for the first time, he tried to put himself in Joanne's shoes. The fury and desperation she would have felt, leading to "forgetting" the other man, William's actual father. Yet, she would have still needed Papa's support, so she continued to open her door to him. Until he suddenly stopped coming. The ray of hope when her son was brought to the castle, which dimmed to nothing as the years went by.

"And you've allowed this fiction to stand uncorrected, knowing that it casts you in an unflattering light?"

"Well, I am the Earl of Shaftesbury, and I'll remain so, no matter what people think of me. Other lords have been accused of far worse, believe me. Bastard sons are as common as seashells—you know that. And it does leave the Wolstones their dignity."

"Did you love her, at all?"

Robert took a moment to reply. "She satisfied … needs I had at the time. She was, and still is, a beautiful woman, very desirable. But no. Your mother was always my first love."

His parents had been married for thirty years now. The first ten of them had been strained for no reason he'd ever learned, despite his father's stated love for her. Evan had occasionally wondered about that ten-year gap between Edward and him, years during which his father was almost always away from the castle. But Mama's return from the future somehow effected a harmonious entente. He couldn't think of any way to tactfully ask Papa why he'd had "needs." Perhaps there were secrets that were never meant to be divulged.

"Papa, that mountain tapestry of Joanne's? There are no mountains like that in Britain, are there?" It was Mama's favourite tapestry and had hung opposite their bed for as long as he could remember.

"No. But it highly resembles a landscape your mother saw when she was in the twenty-first century."

"So, did Mama commission the tapestry or has Joanne—"

"It was already completed when Stacey was here. Joanne claimed she'd seen it in a 'dream.' We've never pursued the matter. One of life's small mysteries, is it not?"

Evan nodded. "Thank you, Papa. I'm glad you explained all this. I won't speak of it ever again." He got up to embrace his father, wondering if he would ever truly know his parents.

Robert smiled, regarding his second son, in whom he was well pleased. "And now, I must go. Your mother is expecting me."

Through the following morning, the castle hummed with the busyness and excitement of an imminent, important event.

"Do you have soap? Here, take these dried rosehips!" Branwen fussed, as mothers do. The family and castle staff gathered in the bailey to offer their *adieux* and one last hug and wishes for great good fortune. Over his mail, he was wearing a dark blue surcoat with a white cross that Branwen had made for him. The white cross signified the English contingent in this crusade. She pressed something tiny and gold into his hand. It was an exquisitely-worked frog. A frog, symbolizing harmony, was always on the Montmorency crest. A talisman. He would need one.

"Keep it with you, for good fortune," she said. "Remember: seek harmony in all you do."

Evan gratefully tucked it in his pouch along with the letter of credit and the handful of change his father had given him.

When Edward embraced him, he whispered, "I still want to be you. Do us proud."

As Evan and his guards waited for the portcullis to raise and the drawbridge to lower, he looked back one last time to see the crumpled, sorrowful faces of the castle staff and the stoic, impassive faces of his family, Papa's arm firmly around Mama.

-V-
Naranjas, Alberengenas and *Espinache*

Seven days in, Evan, along with the approximately eighty others on board the cog ship *Saint-Luc,* was dry heaving into barrels that were filling with vomit. Their hammocks pitched as the ship rolled, fighting its way through the fearsome storm. The terrified passengers, if they weren't begging for the Lord's mercy, were groping and competing for access to the closest barrel. In the dark. It was too dangerous to light a candle. Just the stench from the barrels, slopping vomit onto the floors with every heave and roll, was enough to make them sick.

They'd had remarkably fair weather until now, and Evan had been priding himself on his pretty good sea legs. Granted, the accommodations were crowded and primitive, but they only slept down below. During the day, he'd enjoyed the warm sun on his face, the bracing salt air and spray, the schools of dolphins joyfully leaping in tandem, and the increasing mildness of the climate. He'd breathed deeply, exhilarated to be on his own. For the first time ever in his travels, he had no guards watching over him. He was free. Not only that, surveying the convoy of ships surrounding his, he felt part of something great. Perhaps that greatness would rub off on him, a little. Perhaps he could make a name for himself!

The combined fleet was massive. It consisted of over a hundred ships, and scores more would join them in Marseille when Richard and his knights met up with them. Canville's and Sablé's sub-fleets had departed first from Dartmouth, staggered two days apart, to put less strain on the ports where they would be docking. The three separate fleets hugged the coastline along the Bay of Biscay, stopping every day or two to load up on ale, wine, fruits, and vegetables—a welcome supplement to salted beef, pork, fish, hard tack, and, on good days, cheese. The passengers oared over to the towns they stopped at, where they were free to sleep on the beaches and purchase what they desired at exorbitant prices. Some, to Evan's disgust but no surprise, simply took what they fancied. Vacating the ships overnight allowed the shipmen to swab things down and dump the refuse.

Although a physician was aboard every other ship in the fleet, everyone on the *Saint-Luc* other than two priests was medical personnel: medici, surgeons, barbers, bloodletters, apothecaries. Evan was the youngest, as far as he could see, and, given his inexperience, very much the lowest in the pecking order. It was assumed by everyone that he was a mere dilettante, a rich man's son playing around. The senior man aboard was Sir Roger de Crécy, a career military physician and veteran of many campaigns. Given his rank, he had his own quarters. Everyone else was below, two to a hammock.

Evan's hammock mate was Gurci Morgant, a Cornishman whose grasp of English, never mind French, was halting. For the time being, Evan spoke Welsh to him, a language related to Cornish; but both agreed that he would need to learn French, which Evan was teaching him. Evan was thankful that Gurci at least talked to him, unlike everyone else.

Like Evan, he had signed on as a medicus, having learned on the job from his father. He was the youngest of five boys, all of whom were in the family business. Gurci was short and stocky, with black hair and blue eyes. For Gurci, with no chance of inheriting his father's practice, this was the best way to improve his qualifications and see the world in the process. His smile was almost as broad as he was. Though Evan had to endure Gurci's rather pungent feet beside him in the hammock, he felt he'd made a friend. Gurci was absolutely unimpressed by Evan's fancy kit and privileged, Norman-French accent. He'd already begun to tease him about his "girly" hands, soft as a woman's breasts. Evan examined his hands with fresh eyes; well, yes, they were uncalloused, but they seemed manly enough to him.

Evan could only take Gurci's word for it that women's breasts were soft, for despite vivid nocturnal fantasies, Evan had no expertise in that area. He looked forward to rectifying that lack of experience, soon. However, the whores who beckoned him on shore interested him little. The type of woman who kept him awake at night was a well-bred woman, soft of hands, gentle of manner, and quick of wit.

She was also somehow experienced in the art of love. Evan had no idea how to turn such a fantasy into reality.

He asked Gurci if there was a wife waiting back home for him. Mainly, Evan wanted to know if Gurci was as inexperienced as he was.

Gurci replied, laughing, "Plenty of time for that! First of all, I have to have something to offer. I'm hoping the plunder I bring home will be enough to set me up in a practice somewhere. In the meantime, no harm in sampling here and there, right?"

"Right, of course."

They hit the storm as they were rounding the northwest corner of the Iberian Peninsula. For two days, the ship heaved and rolled. Evan lost all track of time.

Please, release me from this vomiting, worse than *death!* His sides ached as he once again dry heaved.

But on the third day, they woke to calm seas and were finally allowed up on deck. They'd lost sight of land and been blown off course by a hundred miles, he heard one of the shipmen say. Nothing for it but to plot a course southeast, back towards the coast. Miraculously, it appeared that no ships in their group had been lost. No word on the other fleets, however.

They docked for two days at Porto, on the west coast of Portugal, to resupply and regroup. Here they learned that the other two fleets had come and gone, having missed the storm entirely, and were off for the planned rendezvous in Lisbon.

Although Porto had been recaptured by the Christians almost two centuries ago, there were still remnants of the former Muslim city, with its elegant mosque, cobblestone streets, cosmopolitan air, and veiled women that hurried by him or slid out of sight if he happened to come near. On the intricately painted tiles, he saw peculiar Arabic squiggles that had a kind of unfamiliar beauty. Five times a day, someone called from the mosque tower in a voice that could be heard to England, surely; all Muslims then stopped what they were doing to face eastward and kneel to pray. Evan thought of himself as a devout Christian (he never skipped matins and prime if he could help it), but not like *that.* The city rose steeply from the port, and many of the streets were so narrow that only one or two people could pass through. Later, he realized that this was intentional and clever: it would be virtually impossible for an invading army to shove its way through.

While other passengers bought fresh meat, per Branwen's instructions, Evan bought produce: lemons, as well as their larger, slightly sweeter, green cousins, called *naranjas*. He pressed fruit on Gurci too, telling him that he'd "heard" that it was good for disease prevention.

His eyes and nose feasted on the exotic fruits, vegetables and spices in the markets. Abundant, ordinary, and cheap—produce that Mama had only occasionally, delightedly, been able to purchase from itinerant traders: dates; olives; a beautiful, purple elongated vegetable called *alberengena*; and bunches of dark, leafy greens (*espinache*) that the traders urged on him as being "Very good for you! Good for energy!"

A sizable church was being built on the north side of the Douro River. The city could now be comfortably called a Christian city. Yet, as he and Gurci explored the walled city, he had the distinct, unpleasant feeling that he was a barbarian, despite his learning and upbringing. London was considered by the English to be a sophisticated city, but it was a pigsty compared to this modest town. The inhabitants certainly treated him like a barbarian, when he wasn't being beseeched to purchase their goods. Evan found it both fascinating and enviable that the two religions seemed to be coexisting in a sort of hard-won harmony.

Everyone learned of the Battle of Tours, the great victory Charles Martel had won against the Saracens in AD 732, effectively halting the Muslim conquest of Europe. It was considered the signal event in European history, a momentous triumph of David over Goliath. Looking around this elegant town, so much cleaner and more prosperous-looking than filthy London, a thought occurred to him: Would it have done us so much harm to learn a little Arabic? Quickly, he repressed that thought.

Two days later, they arrived in Lisbon to find that the other fleets had been busy while they awaited them. Envoys sent ashore reported back that their fleet was denied permission to anchor and disembark. Word was that gangs of crusaders—likely bored with inactivity—had been taking out their frustration on the local Muslims and Jews. It was alleged that shops had been ransacked, their owners roughed up, some women ravished. They'd even stripped the grapes from their vines! King Sancho had closed the gates to the city and thrown the egregiously guilty in prison. He was understandably reluctant to allow this to happen again. Lord Fors vowed that anyone guilty of such abhorrent practices would be dealt with severely, likely keelhauled.

Fors was granted an audience with King Sancho and asked him, "What can we do to demonstrate our good intentions?"

"Well," the King replied, "If you really want to be of use, Muslim insurgents are besieging Santarem, just up the river." The Christians had only recently retaken the region, and pockets of Muslim resistance remained. Would the commander care to lend assistance?

So, the following day, Evan found himself and the *Saint-Luc* on the tail end of a flotilla of ships heading up the Tagus to retake Santarem. The fired-up, fresh, and well-armed crossbowmen and soldiers in Fors's fleet made short work of that insurrection. The *Saint-Luc*'s services were not even needed, to everyone's disappointment.

God's whiskers, Evan thought, if this is what a crusade is like, I'll be home by Christmastide.

-VI-
"Just how ignorant of physic are you?"

The delay caused by the storm and the longer-than-scheduled stay in Lisbon made the combined fleet about two weeks late setting forth again. Canville's ships, once again, took the lead. This time, the intended destination was the final one: Marseille, where Richard's entire, gigantic fleet was intended to rendezvous. There was no way of knowing just where Richard was at that point. If he was on schedule, would he wait around for them? It was well known that he was not a patient man.

Rounding the corner of the Iberian Peninsula, they passed through a narrow strait. *Africa!* The continent was tantalizingly within sight, although it remained just and only that: in sight. They docked for a night at a port called Jabal Tariq, out of which sprang a mountain surrounded by flat land.

Evan was so fascinated by the architecture and the geography of the lands he was seeing that he was seized with an urge to draw them. He'd never considered himself artistic in any way, so this was a rather surprising impulse for him. He particularly wanted to capture Jabal Tariq. He managed to purchase a small, bound book at the bazaar, one with empty paper pages, along with a supply of quills and some ink powder. He had never seen paper, having only ever worked with parchment, which was expensive though undoubtedly more durable. Parchment was too valuable to merely sketch on, however, so this cheaper, commonplace alternative was a revelation for him.

His first drawing of that rock was all wrong, off in scale and detail, as was his second, mainly because some of the ink from page one leaked through in spots. Paper was cheap, all right, but it was much too thin for his liking. He angrily ripped another page out of the book. On his fifth attempt, he finally managed to capture the proportions. He was pleased with himself: something to show the folk at home when he finally returned.

Gurci liked what he was doing and asked, "Can you draw me?"

Drawing a person's face was another challenge entirely. Again, Evan wasted a whole page of paper until he had something that resembled his friend. Gurci was impressed.

"You caught my fine, aristocratic chin very well. A fine-looking fellow, indeed," he joked.

Until they left Hispania, every port they stopped at was still in Muslim hands. They were cordially greeted by people who really had no other choice, but the fleet never stayed longer than a day.

Three weeks after leaving Lisbon, August 22, the entire fleet rendezvoused at Marseille to find that they'd missed Richard. No one was surprised. He'd arrived on schedule two weeks before; discovering his fleet wasn't there, he took off again with his own, smaller fleet to join up with Philip in Genoa. From there, he would see the sights of the Italian coast and pass some time. He'd left word in Marseille that everyone was to depart for Messina, Sicily, the final rendezvous point, where he would certainly connect with them.

The fleet stayed a week to refit and then set out again. During this time, Evan stretched his legs around the port, sketching what he saw. Marseille had a different feel to it: although the Greco-Roman temples were in ruins, the wall, fora, and baths remained intact. The city had the distinct air of an aging courtesan, having seen it all after repeated conquests for over a thousand years.

Three days after their arrival, he was sitting on the harbour wall, sketching the vast fleet docked before him. Completely preoccupied with getting the proportions of the ships correct, he did not immediately hear when Sir Roger de Crécy, the senior medical officer on board the *Saint-Luc,* hailed him.

"You there!" he called. Crécy was a tall, thin man of about forty, saturnine in appearance, with a long, thin nose much in the habit of looking down on other people. He was accompanied by a grey-blond man of about the same age, who Evan assumed must be his manservant. He would later learn that his name was Louis Chapelle. Evan never heard him utter a word beyond, "Yes, Milord."

Evan scrambled up to bow to Sir Roger.

"You're Montmorency, aren't you?"

"Yes, Milord."

"Show me what you're doing." Evan showed him his sketch of the harbour, which was not going well. Crécy studied it, nodding. "Your problem is that you're trying to fit too much into a small space. It lacks a central focus."

"That is my feeling, too, Milord. I was just about to tear it up and start anew."

"I've seen you sketching on board. May I see the pictures of the passengers you've done?" Evan flipped back to the sketch of Gurci, as well as of John Harewood, the shipmaster. He skipped by the one he'd done of Crécy, though not quite quickly enough.

"Stop there. Back a few pages."

Now you've done it, Evan thought. Into the brig for you, imbecile. He nervously opened the book to the portrait of Crécy, who studied it thoughtfully. "It's not a bad likeness, though I don't believe my nose is that long."

Evan could not possibly tell him it had been intended as humorous. But neither could he know, at this point in his sketching career, that it was a thrilling novelty for people to look at representations of themselves, exaggerated or not. If people ever saw images of people at all, they would be of saints and other religious figures, certainly not their unworthy selves.

"I'm sorry, Milord. If you would care to sit for me when you have a free moment, I could try for a more accurate likeness."

"Perhaps, another time. So, tell me, just how ignorant of physic are you?"

"Very ignorant. I am here to learn."

"Have you ever amputated a limb? Set a broken leg? Brought down a fever?"

"Never, Milord."

"Well, you have much to learn, and you will have to learn it fast. Listen and observe. Do not question what you are ordered to do. Do not pretend that you know better than qualified, experienced physicians. We have no time for that sort of nonsense."

"That is what I intend, Milord."

Crécy considered him again. "You strike me as an intelligent boy, well-spoken and well-mannered. I know your family by reputation. Despite your father's eccentric resolve to remain obscure, he is very well regarded in court circles."

Evan nodded. "The Earl of Shaftesbury has always believed he can be of more use seeing to his own barony than lingering around court."

"Agreed. However, to the point. I am a physician of no small repute myself, as you are no doubt aware." He paused, enough time for Evan to nod respectfully.

"When this venture is over, I would like to set down what I have learned, to contribute to the store of general knowledge. There will be maladies and conditions in Outremer unknown in Europe. I'm thinking of an illustrated manual of surgical procedures and diseases. For that, I'll need someone handy with a quill. Do you think you are up to that? Illustrating a properly dressed wound? A clean amputation? A case of pox?"

"I would be honoured to be of assistance. However, I'll need more paper and ink than I have in my possession."

"For the final version, I'm not thinking cheap paper, my boy. Parchment is the way to go. I'll see to it that you have sufficient supplies when the time comes. But, for now, paper will do."

"My humblest thanks to you, Milord," Evan said, bowing.

"We will speak again." And with that, Crécy and Chapelle swept on past him and continued their promenade, the length of the sea wall.

-VII-
"The first is the worst."

Three weeks after that, September 21, the fleet pulled into Messina harbour. Messina was a prosperous port city in the far northeast corner of Sicily, practically swimming distance from the Italian peninsula. Sicily itself was a sizable kingdom that included the lower half of the Italian boot. Philip's fleet had docked a week earlier, with little fanfare; a day later, Richard and his ships arrived.

Evan could only imagine what the inhabitants thought when they saw them all lined up across the expanse of horizon: one hundred fifty-six ships, twenty-four dromons, and thirty-nine galleys. Over thirty-six thousand men, Evan heard. Adding Frederick Barbarossa and his land-based army would put it at close to fifty thousand by the time they reached the Holy Land. The fleet was laden with not only men, horses, and their feed, but also arms, victuals, siege equipment, and treasure.

The thrill of this sight was shortly muted by some shocking news: Barbarossa had drowned, crossing a river in Asia Minor. What about all his now-leaderless troops? No one knew. It was hoped they'd find their way to Outremer with another leader.

Grandly stepping ashore, Richard doubtless expected a warm welcome from both the populace and his younger sister, Joanna, recently widowed Dowager Queen of Sicily. She was all of twenty-five, having been married at twelve to King William II. However, much to Richard's chagrin, not only was the populace surly and unwelcoming, Joanna was not to be seen. Tancred of Lecce, an illegitimate cousin of her late husband, had usurped the throne, putting Joanna into house arrest and seizing her dowry. The dowry itself was substantial and imprisoning his sister was downright rude, but what really upset Richard was Tancred's disregard of a bequest to the English crown in

William's will of a hundred ships, as well as vast quantities of grain and wine. This was meant to help finance the crusade, Richard was sure, and it belonged to him! He immediately sped up the coast to Palermo to set things right. He managed to secure Joanna's release to a monastery, but, to his rage, the dowry, ships, grain, and wine were not forthcoming.

All this, Evan heard third-, fourth-, and fifth-hand. He was still on the *Saint-Luc*. Only Richard's fleet had gone ashore (because of the horses, he was informed). Even so, the sudden influx of a horde of Frankish fanatics destabilized the already fragile peace between Christians, Muslims, and Jews. The demands for food and supplies were inflating the price of everything to a ridiculous degree. While the fleet might have imagined itself as hosts of crusaders off to do good, to the Messinesi, they were just another invading army, one of many through the centuries. Riots broke out, which Richard ruthlessly put down, and while he was at it, he sacked and took control of Messina. The rest of the island fell quickly thereafter.

King Philip was reputedly annoyed about not being consulted, which aggravated his pique about Richard's continued delays in marrying Alys. Word was that Richard had even picked out another bride—some unknown from Navarre called Berengaria, and that she was en route with the Dowager Queen Eleanor!

To the bored armies, all this provided delectable gossip, although Richard's timing puzzled everyone: why hadn't he married this Berengaria person soon after he'd been crowned, while he was still in England? Navarre wasn't that far by sea, and at least his people could have met their queen. Instead, she was slogging across Europe with his aged mother. The best reason anyone could venture was to put off offending Philip as long as possible.

Conquering Sicily cost Richard two dozen knights, and a score more were injured. The *Saint-Luc*'s passengers were finally allowed to come ashore to tend to the wounded. Evan was instructed to watch as the wounds were bathed in wine and left open for a few days to allow the "laudable pus" to form. In this traditional Greek approach to healing, the thicker and creamier the pus, the greater the body's fight to heal the wound—or so went the belief.

Evan said nothing. He decided that, as soon as he could, he would quietly treat wounds his own way.

All smugness vanished, though, when he was ordered to hold an agonized knight down as the remaining part of his near-detached calf was amputated, cauterized with a hot iron to stop the bleeding, and dressed. Evan could tolerate the sight and smell of blood and gore—he had, after all, witnessed animal slaughter since he was a boy. It was the man's anguished screams that sickened him. Was there no way to relieve his fear and pain?

He brought up the hard tack and salted pork he'd had for dinner, to the derisive laughter of the other surgeons.

Gasping and wiping away the sour spittle in his mouth, Evan resolved that he would never embarrass himself like this again. More, he would somehow find a way to ease the pain of amputations, or, better still, render the patient unconscious during the procedure. Fear made the heart beat faster, he figured, making the loss of blood that much more serious.

He learned something about the art of triage that day. "Leave that one, come over here," one surgeon abruptly ordered him, at which point a priest came over to give last rites. Brutal as it seemed, he understood that some men were too far gone, and it was a waste of time and resources to even try. The ability to tell the difference was one he could only acquire by experience.

"The first is the worst," Gurci reassured him afterwards. Evan had been envious of Gurci's cool self-assurance as he assisted in the sawing off of a hand.

"How do you manage to look so calm?"

"Ah, that's the trick. I shit myself the first time I did it. My da told me, 'Never let them see your fear. Focus entirely on your task, and always remember that you are helping this person live.'"

Obviously, it would take Richard a while to sort out this mess, pacify Philip, and see to the money. Evan was not surprised when the news came that the fleet would winter in Sicily, for the sailing season typically ended mid-October, anyway. Passengers would be allowed to disembark but were instructed to spread themselves out across the island and find their own billets. No one was pleased to hear this and, facing possible mutiny, Richard had to dig into his hoard of treasure and compensate his army for room and board.

Well, Evan thought, so much for being home by Christmastide.

We'll all be old men by the time we see the Holy Land. However, far from being disgruntled at this delay, he was elated. A block away from the port of Messina, he'd spied a large, solidly-constructed building with a bilingual inscription in Arabic squiggles alongside a magic word: *Hospital*. It was Infidel, true, but everyone knew they were far ahead of their Christian brethren in this field. Now, if he could just quietly disappear, stay out of sight of Crécy's withering gaze, for a while.

"Where do you think you'll go?" Gurci wanted to know, as Evan packed up his belongings. Gurci was like everyone else, figuring he'd just knock on doors with a friendly, hopeful smile until he found people willing to take whatever he had to billet him, hoping that he wouldn't get a snarl and a knife in his belly for the trouble. Though a wooden fort was being built for temporary accommodation just outside the town, that would likely hold only the elite of the crusader population. Some of the men were remaining aboard ship, but Gurci had never been much of a sailor and was glad to be back on terra firma. If it came to it, he'd build shelter for himself up in the hills. He'd lived through worse, including a fire that had made his whole village homeless over a wet winter.

"I'm going to plant myself at the door of the hospital, and I'm not moving till they let me in. Why don't you come with me?"

"What, Infidel physic? Have you forgotten they're our enemies? Everyone knows they boil Christian babies!"

Evan was shocked. "Well, *I* don't know that! Who told you that, some poppy-addled witch? As far as I'm concerned, the only enemy in physic is ignorance. It's our *duty* to learn. Look, Morgant, I'm doing it, and if anyone asks where I am, especially Crécy, you haven't seen me, right?"

Gurci considered this. Evan was his friend, and what else was he going to do for months? He would hardly be missed.

"Well, they can hardly ask me if I've seen you if they haven't seen me either. I'm in."

-VIII-
One Good Medicus

That afternoon, they knocked at the door of the hospital. They were greeted by a robed and turbaned man who looked to be in his mid-thirties, even with the salt and pepper beard. He eyed Evan and Gurci suspiciously before adjusting his face to one of professional concern.

"Good afternoon, *mes sires*," he said, in accented French. "How may we be of service?"

Evan was relieved. His knowledge of Arabic was nil. Then he remembered. Of course, as the language of government here, French would be the lingua franca, whether the citizens liked it or not.

He bowed to the gentleman and began, "I am Evan de Montmorency and this is my friend, Gurci Morgant. We are *medici* on this crusade, off the medical ship *Saint-Luc*. We are anxious to learn whatever you can teach us about your physic in the time we have here. We will do whatever you ask of us, even if it is washing the chamber pots. We ask for nothing except whatever food you can spare. And a place to lie at night."

The man stood back in surprise. "Well, this is interesting. Come in. Most of your people take the view that there is nothing to learn from us. How much do you know?"

Evan and Gurci glanced at each other. "For myself, my knowledge is very limited. I am on this crusade to serve and to learn. However, my friend here comes from a family of medici. His knowledge of physic is much greater than that of the French we are speaking, I assure you."

The man smiled. "My name is Abdullah ibn Nasir, and I am the chief physician at this facility." He held out his hand for a handshake, and they obliged, though it was not their custom.

"Normally, I would turn down your request, as ours is not a teaching hospital, but there has been an outbreak of fever in Messina, and our staff are stretched thin. You understand, we can't afford to pay you." Evan and Gurci nodded.

"Our faith instructs that we must accept everyone, regardless of race, creed, sex, or ability to pay. We rely totally on contributions from our patients, whatever they can spare. Come with me. And please remove your shoes."

They exchanged glances and shrugged. Indeed, beside them lay two tidy rows of sandals on the tile floor. "Unlike in your culture," Nasir said, barely concealing his disdain, "the soles of shoes are considered unclean and must not be allowed to contaminate the indoors. We can provide you with sandals that are only worn indoors."

Evan agreed. Mama always insisted that people remove their outside footwear in rooms with rugs.

Inside was an open area with benches along the sides.

"Put your bags in this cupboard," said Nasir, gesturing to a large cabinet to their left. "Let me first show you our garden. We're very proud of it."

They followed Nasir through a door where a large, tranquil garden lay before them, much like cloister garths he'd heard of at home. In the centre was a rectangular pool of water with stone benches arranged alongside. The pool was surrounded by beds of herbs, as well as roses. Two patients were being helped around the columned perimeter. To the left, along the west wall, lay the kitchens. Birds chirped in the lone chestnut tree at one end of the pool. Butterflies and bees flitted among the flowering rosemary and thyme, which gave forth resiny, earthy aromas. An almost religious sense of calm and peace floated through Evan, much like going into chapel at prime.

"This space pleases you? Fundamental to healing, we believe, is adequate rest, peace and quiet, a healthy and moderate diet, light, air, and gentle exercise. This garden is meant to be a restful place that, at the same time, gently stimulates the senses of smell, sight, and hearing."

Evan couldn't disagree. He could sit in this garden all day, sketching, if he had the chance.

Pointing to the sheltered arcade on their right, Nasir said, "You may sleep against that wall, with the understanding that at *salat al-fajr,* first prayer call of the day, you pack up your belongings and put them back in the cupboard. We cannot have our patients distracted by the sight of you and your mess. It is unlikely that the elements will trouble you there. Now, if you'll come with me, I'll show you the rest of the facility."

They went back inside. Through a door past the entry Evan noticed an examining area with two tables, as well as shelves laden with pottery jars, rolls of linen, mortars and pestles, and steel implements. Beyond that was a large ward with, perhaps, ten beds on either side, occupied by men bandaged to varying degrees. It was a plain, white-washed room. Although the south wall turned a blind face to the street, four tall windows on the opposite wall gave onto the garden, allowing a mild breeze and importing a pleasurable, herbaceous scent.

"This is our surgical ward. It is at capacity just now because of the recent … hostilities with your people," he said, his voice reproachful.

Past the rows of patients, through another door, lay a smaller ward. Here, there was no visible sign of injury and a few patients were sitting up. "This is our ward for digestive complaints."

Gesturing them through another door, Nasir said, "Through here are eye maladies. We believe that all other wards should be separate from the surgical ward to prevent the spread of infection. Across the street is a ward for those struggling with their mental health."

Each ward was staffed by at least one attending physician, all male.

Messina was not one of the famous centres of medical training, yet here was a hospital of impressive sophistication. Evan was sure it had no equal at home, even the great cathedral hospices. Could he build such a place? William would swoon in delight to see this.

Nasir went on, as if what he was saying was the most natural thing in the world, "The women's ward is across the street, beside the mental health building. Of course, women must be kept separate, and they are attended to by women, for modesty's sake. You are never to set foot in there, is that clear?"

Women? Treated in a hospital?

He continued, "We believe in the recuperation of our patients' bodies, minds, and spirits, but not to the extent that the safety of our female patients is put at risk." He added without irony, "You know how men are, with our uncontrollable urges."

Evan and Gurci nodded solemnly.

"You have female physicians, then?" Evan asked.

"Of course, though not as many as for men. For childbirth and other strictly female issues, they are attended to by midwives and healers at home, mostly.

"Ours is a small hospital. In our great teaching hospitals, there'd be a mosque, also a small chapel for Christians if space allows and numbers warrant."

Nasir glanced again at the two young men. "You seem impressed." They nodded, smiling. "That pleases me. This facility is my life's work. All right, let us now go back to my office for tea."

They trailed after him back through all the doors until they came again to the entryway. Ahead of them was another door. He clapped at an attendant, calling, "Tea, for three," and, once inside the office, bade them sit on the cushions on the floor around a low table. Nasir sat cross-legged, and the younger men awkwardly followed suit, unaccustomed to, essentially, sitting on the floor. A tray was promptly brought with an intricately embossed, spouted brass container and three tall, white glazed cups, of a material unknown to Evan. On the tray was also a bowl of dates.

He poured out the tea and gestured them to drink. Evan had had tea before, though only in the great chamber with the family because it was rare and expensive. But this tea had an elusive, unfamiliar taste. He saw Gurci purse his lips as he swallowed. However, his friend smiled in pleasure at the taste of a date.

Nasir turned to Evan. "You have not seen this type of cup, Evan, if I may call you that?"

"No, Sir." Evan looked more carefully at the cup and then up again at Nasir. "And what should we call *you?*"

"You may call me Sayid. These cups are from the East. We call this material *ceyramik.* It is delicate, surprisingly strong, though breakable, so please be careful."

Turning to Gurci and speaking slowly, "You. Do you have a tongue, or do you just smile idiotically while your friend does all the talking?"

"Oh, yes, Sayid!" Gurci replied, smiling not too idiotically, Evan thought. "I much use my tongue. But in my home, we wait an elder to say we speak. Forgive me, my French is still poor. But my friend here teaches me."

"Admirable custom," said Nasir, with a nod. "What exactly is your native tongue? I understand several."

"Cornish, Sayid. It is like Breton tongue. But only speaks in Cornwall."

"Where is Cornwall?"

"West England."

"I see. So, I have one English who is capable but can't speak, another who can speak but isn't capable. Between you, I have one good medicus."

Evan jumped in. "Both of us learn quickly. You'll see."

Nasir turned again to Gurci. "Have you never eaten a date before?"

"Never. I see in markets. Look like turds, no? But taste like solid honey," said Gurci, helping himself to another date.

Nasir smiled. "Dates are one of Allah's treasures. There are nomadic desert tribes in Africa who can survive for days on only dates. Remember this when you're in the Holy Land. Food may not always be in abundant supply, and dates are very portable. But never take them from the trees because every date palm you see belongs to someone. The dates you will find in Palestine are superior to these, but we enjoy them just the same."

He sipped his tea. "This is anise tea. It is admittedly an acquired taste, but we value it for its digestive properties. We do not drink wine or ale, and neither will you on these premises, am I clear?"

They nodded once again.

"So. These are the rules. You will watch and learn. You will be assigned to a physician who will be your guide and mentor. You will not question his orders. You will eat with the staff by the kitchens. Neither dogs nor any form of pork are allowed on these premises. You will stay away from the women's ward. You will work from sunrise to sunset except on Sundays, which you will have free. You will, of course, be expected to work on our holy day, Friday. Understood so far?"

They said in unison, "Yes, Sayid."

"Always remember that you are to conduct yourselves in a manner that speaks to the dignity of your calling. I particularly mean your conduct on your day off. A certain part of town, down by the port—I'm sure you have found it—you are not to frequent. Doing so would bring shame to this hospital, and I cannot allow that. Do you follow me?"

"Yes, Sayid."

He removed a leather-bound book from the shelf behind him. "Especially, in your free time, you will be expected to read this." It was a massive volume, entitled *Canon Medicinae*, by Avicenna.

"The great Avicenna is our guide in all matters here. We are grateful to have a Latin translation of this great work, which was given to us by a Christian patient. It's our only copy so we treat it very gently. I trust you know how to read?"

They sipped their tea.

Evan replied, "I do. I will gladly translate for my friend."

"One more thing. Your superiors don't know you're here, do they?"

"No, they don't."

"I thought not," said Nasir briskly. "Well then, shall we find you suitable robes and put you to work? Your sword, Medicus Montmorency, will be of no use here."

-IX-
Catgut and Linen

When Evan mentioned "washing the chamber pots," he hadn't expected Sayid to take that literally. However, every morning, before breakfast, the chamber pots at each bedside had to be emptied into a barrel and washed, but not before they had taken note of the contents. They were informed—and Gurci confirmed this—that much information could be conveyed by the state and smell of a patient's urine and bowel movements, particularly if that patient was in the stomach ailment ward. Records of both had to be noted down in a log beside each patient's bed.

Evan quickly learned to recognize what these deposits looked and smelled like in a healthy patient. He could soon detect the signs of a bladder infection by the strong smell; the sweet aroma of a diabetic's urine; dehydration by the dark yellow colour. Avicenna listed the twenty possible colours of urine and particularly noted that sediment was likely attributable to kidney stones. At any sign of *fluxus*, that patient was immediately isolated.

After they finished each morning's collection, they carted the barrel off to the port, where they rowed it out to sea among their ships and emptied it, to the jeering hoots of those still on board. They were always at risk of being recognized. However, they quickly realized that robed and turbaned as they were, with heads down, their people looked right past them, without so much as a second glance. In fact, in view of the malodorous contents of the wagon, they were given a wide berth. They drove right by Crécy and Chapelle one morning, who doubtless took them for yet another pair of wretched Infidels, a waste of skin. They returned from the port each day with the satisfaction of having gotten away with something.

They became attuned to the rhythm of the primarily Muslim community in the hospital. Five times a day—early dawn, just after midday, late afternoon, after sunset, and sometime between sunset and midnight—they heard the relentless call to prayer. Not always, but most often, adherents ritually washed themselves prior to kneeling, in a fashion called *wudhu.* In fact, the overriding ethos Evan sensed in this place was one of cleanliness, both physical and spiritual. Mama would approve, he thought. During these prayer sessions, Evan and Gurci would repair to the garden, where Evan would read some of the *Canon* to him, or they would talk about what they'd seen and learned that day, or just breathe in the soothing atmosphere of the garden. They were glad for the rest; their feet were not yet used to standing and walking about for hours at a time.

Meals were taken communally—at dinner and supper, mostly a stew of some sort, reminiscent of those Mama sometimes had Cook prepare, with exotic seasonings and dried fruit. They noticed, gratefully, that on their "fast" days—Wednesday, Friday, and Saturday—they were fed fish. On those days, they were occasionally offered dishes based on various preparations of chickpeas, surprisingly reminiscent of meals he'd had at home. Evan wondered now if Mama had had these dishes in the future.

They went to sleep each night, first, to the sound of the muffled noise of carousing from the bars at the port and, finally, only the rush of the ocean and the song of crickets. Throughout the day, a dove soothingly *koo KOO kook*-ed. Nasir had taken pity on them, sleeping on the stone floor, and had provided them both with low pallets that they propped up against the wall when they arose each morning. Not that they had even minded sleeping on the floor; after weeks below decks on a hammock in a dark room that reeked of body odour, it was a refreshing change.

In the afternoon, they did rounds in the wards. To Evan's mild surprise, his mentor was Physician Joseph ben Solomon, who wore a similar conical hat to one Rabbi Jacob used to wear. He was a big man, robust in physique and personality. When they were first introduced, Evan asked him if he practised Jewish physic here.

Joseph was startled. "There is no Muslim physic or Jewish physic—or even Christian physic—in this place. There is only the art and science of physic. All of us are dedicated to the best possible care of our patients, no matter what the origin. But yes, generally, I follow Avicenna's guidance in this hospital."

"But are you not warring peoples?"

Again, surprise. "No, why would you think that? All we Jews want is to be left alone to practise our religion and raise our children according to Jewish law. We live amicably alongside our Muslim brothers. It is you Christians who hate and persecute us. Do you have any *idea* what my people suffer every time you and your kind take it in your heads to 'rescue' the Holy Land? Pardon me if I don't fall on my knees and shout 'Hallelujah!'"

From his small experience, Evan had some idea of this suffering, though clearly not the extent of it. He thought he should defend his side a little. "I was tutored by a Jewish scholar."

"Oh? What was his name?"

"Rabbi Jacob d'Orléans. He was a great man."

"Yes, I know of him. He was a famous Talmudic scholar. Until he was murdered a year ago, by your people," he said bitterly.

"Yes. I was at the coronation when it happened. By the time I got to him, he was already dead. I'm so sorry."

"And I am sorry for the loss of someone of whom you were very fond, it appears. Well, if you were taught by Jacob, you may not be completely hopeless. Tell me, what do you apply to an open wound?"

"Traditionally, wine mixed with honey and herbs." Joseph seemed not to pick up on the slight emphasis on the word "traditionally."

"What is the best way to lance a boil?"

"Boil the needle first."

"Very good. What kind of thread do you use to suture wounds?"

"Boiled, then waxed linen thread. Silk, if we can find it, though I have not seen it used."

"We use catgut. No need to wax it."

"*Catgut?*"

And so began a tentative, unacknowledged friendship. Two like minds: men of science, greedy for knowledge, whatever the source, although one was well on this path and the other just beginning.

1191

King Richard and King Philip
accepting the keys to Acre

Love is a kind of warfare.
—Ovid, *Ars Amatoria*

-I-
Opium, Mandragora, Hemlock Juice

By the end of January of 1191, while Gurci was performing surgeries and treatments under a more experienced physician's eye, Evan was now being allowed to assist. Gurci had been right: the first was the worst. Gradually, Evan began to see each patient's body and the parts within it as a problem that he must solve.

Thankfully, they'd been off chamber pot duty since December. Joseph had long since stopped treating Evan like a cretin. He knew to clean superficial wounds with distilled alcohol. He was familiar with tongue depressors, concave scissors, forceps, and ear syringes. He had extracted teeth, set dislocated shoulders, reset broken bones in arms, legs, and a jaw, and had helped perform a tonsillectomy and tracheotomy, in addition to myriad other complaints that brought sufferers into the hospital. He had inserted a hollow syringe into a patient's eye to remove a cataract. He now knew how to use a hacksaw and was no longer sick at the thought of it. He learned that, in Islamic physic, surgeons were respected partners of physicians—not thought of as glorified butchers as they were in Northern Europe.

He had learned the secret to relieving the pain of surgery: a carefully-calibrated, dissolved solution of opium, mandragora, and hemlock juice. It was easy, and they took turns refilling the stock daily. They simply soaked sponges in this solution and let them dry, after which they were tucked away in tightly-closed jars. At the time of surgery, they had only to re-soak the sponge and hold it over the patient's face.

Chiefly, they learned that no medicine was given to a patient unless it had been proven through experience or observation. They both knew that all too often herbs at home were prescribed as medicine simply because they resembled the afflicted part of the body—for example, lungwort for inflammations of the lungs because it vaguely resembled lungs. Islamic physicians roundly rejected such nonsense; instead, the pharmacopoeia of tried-and-true herbs was immense.

From Joseph, Evan learned something of the treatment of arrow wounds from unfortunate citizens who'd annoyed Richard's men. Contrary to what he'd thought, Joseph did not just yank the arrow out. He explained that doing that would most likely pull the shaft from the arrowhead, leaving it lodged in the body where it would only cause further damage. Arrow wounds were therefore tricky: one had to be careful not to worsen the trauma when removing the weapon. All kinds of delicate things like arteries and veins were often close by. So, they waited for a few hours with the arrow secured in place until the blood had well clotted, then enlarged the wound so they could probe around with their fingers and gently pull it out. Sometimes, in the case of arm and leg wounds, it was easier to simply push it out the other side. The patient was, of course, sedated. The wound was then doused with wine and stitched after the laudable pus was detected. Even so, about half the time the patient died anyway—almost all the time if the wound was in the abdominal cavity.

Joseph took him aside one day and said, "I want to pass on a piece of advice that all of us here have heard. Even if your patient is at death's doorstep, tell him that he will pull through. To the concerned relatives, tell them the situation is dire. On the one hand, it'll encourage the patient to make an effort; on the other, the relatives will spread word of what a marvellous physician you are if he lives. Never make the mistake of doing the opposite." It was the first time, but not the last, that Evan would be made aware of the strong connection between body and mind.

He learned that, advanced as Islamic physic was, they could not distance themselves from the thousand-year-old belief in such practices as bloodletting and humoral balance. However, physicians did recognize the limits of what they could do. Every physician here referred to the wasting disease as *oncos*. Sometimes, if the tumour was visible, they would surgically remove it. Even so, in most cases, all they could do was relieve the pain.

Evan had never been so happy. Learning something new every day, being of actual use, gaining the respect of the other physicians, he sometimes privately wished as he went to bed each night that he'd be forgotten by the fleet and could just stay on here.

He and Gurci had even been invited to supper at Joseph's home before Christmas. There, they met his wife and four children. Joseph was at pains to point out that what they were celebrating that evening was Hanukkah, which had nothing to do with the Christian celebration a few weeks later.

Joseph's children eagerly explained the miraculous story behind the lighting of the candles. Joseph said, sardonically, "It celebrates *our* recapture of Jerusalem from our Syrian oppressors. It *is* our city, by the way. Everyone seems to forget that, but we never will."

Mostly, Evan and Gurci held their tongues, relishing Madame Joseph's cheese pastries and observing the lively interaction of the family around the table. Their children were encouraged to voice their opinions, and they were impressed at how the resulting discussion evolved into an opportunity to teach them something of the nature of the world.

As they walked back to the hospital that night, Gurci commented, "My da would have cuffed me across the back of the head if I ever ventured an opinion. 'Who asked *you*, you insolent pup?' he'd shout. When my older brothers got big enough, they shouted back. He'd hit them, they'd hit him back, but that was only when they were pretty sure they could take him on. Mam would never dare interfere. Meal times weren't pleasant, let's just say."

Evan had to admit he didn't know anything about violent, chaotic mealtimes. Neither of his parents had ever struck him. Mama had, only once, been furious with him. This was when he was about five, and he never forgot it, nor the lesson he learned that day. At dinner, Freddy was serving water when the jug slipped and he spilled a bit of water on Evan's lap. Evan had said, snottily, "Careless churl!" He didn't really know what the word meant, but he'd overheard the servants use it dismissively about their own.

His parents sucked in their breaths. Then she lit into him. "Apologize right now and go to your room! We'll see to *you* about this later!"

Evan, shocked, had apologized and fled in tears. He lay there, dreading the moment when she might come in with a birch stick or something. Marie had come up and excitedly announced, "Are *you* in trouble, Evan! They're still angry!"

Later, Branwen had simply sat on their bed and given him a hug, reassuring him that she still loved him. She'd said, "All the blessings you two enjoy, people obeying your every command, will only last as long as they believe that you deserve it. Remember this: We need them more than they need us. Always, always treat them with kindness and respect."

This evening, filled with intelligent exchange of ideas, brought back memories of meals at Shaftesbury Castle, where people constantly "happened" to be in the neighbourhood around mealtime. Their price of admission was news, gossip, and stimulating conversation, and they rarely disappointed.

For Evan, the only thing different about Joseph's family and his own was that Mama and Papa insisted on quiet voices, no interrupting their elders at the table.

It couldn't last. Although Evan stuck close to home, Gurci moved about freely on his Sundays off. Eventually, he must have been spotted and tailed. Or, perhaps it was a patient who noted the two English medici at work in the hospital. Whatever it was, Abdullah ibn Nasir opened the front door one day in early February to find Sir Roger de Crécy demanding to see Evan de Montmorency. He had it on good authority that he was not only practising physic in these quarters, but was said to be *living* here, as well. He was politely but firmly told that Medicus Montmorency was occupied but would be with him shortly. Crécy was not accustomed to being told to wait and was in a filthy mood when Evan eventually came out.

"So *here* I find you! In *this* place! Among heathens!" he bellowed. "I should have you whipped and sent home!"

Evan gritted his teeth. Although Crécy would never do that to a medicus whose skills he could well use at some point, never mind to the son of a baron, he knew this sojourn had come to an end.

He composed his face in an attitude of sorrow and contrition.

"Milord, my friend and I needed a place to stay, and I needed to learn. This hospital was kind enough to take us in. I'm so sorry to make you angry. I hadn't intended to hide from anyone." Although he had.

"Well, fortunately, I found you before you became completely corrupted. Pack up your bags. You're coming with me."

"What about Morgant, Milord?"

"He can stay here, for all I care. It's you and your drawing skills I need."

"As you wish, Milord. May I say goodbye to my friends in here?"

Crécy was not without a heart. The word "friends" seemed oddly to pacify him a little. "Yes, but be quick about it. I don't like to be kept waiting." He strode out the door.

Evan embraced Gurci, Joseph, Nasir, and as many others as he saw. To Gurci, he said he'd be seeing him soon. To the others, he thanked them for the honour of knowing and learning from them. Perhaps someday he would return.

"*Yahmik Allah*," said Nasir, clasping his hand. "You will always have a place here."

"Follow me," said Crécy, when Evan came out the door. "I'm quartered at the Mategriffon up the hill." This was the wooden fort that Richard's builders had hurriedly thrown together for rough accommodation. "I've heard that the King wants to dismantle it before he leaves, so that he can reconstruct it at Acre! Damn fool idea, if you ask me." Messina was a hilly city, and they were both puffing before long. "Tell me you have at least kept up your drawing."

"When I've had time, yes, Milord. I've been practising on the patients. I believe I'm getting the knack of the human body."

"Very good. You must show me when you're settled. It's not much of a fort, but it's a roof over our heads. A damn sight better than on a floor, outside, like a common beggar, is my information," he panted. "What would your father say."

Evan decided to say nothing. He suspected that his father would say it was a valuable life experience.

-II-
The Undeclared War

All that winter, Richard continued his negotiations. By the beginning of March, he had secured Joanna's dowry from Tancred and got the will bequest reread in his favour. Trickier was his alliance with Philip. Berengaria was by now making her way through the length of Italy with her sixty-nine-year-old future mother-in-law. Word of their slow progress had reached Richard, and, from there, almost everyone else: *They've reached Rome! They're in Naples!*

Renouncing Alys after a twenty-one-year betrothal took all the diplomatic skill Richard had, plus ten thousand marks to buy himself out of the deal. It helped that he could besmirch Alys's reputation by throwing the "fact" of her bastard son by Henry in Philip's face. Still, the once solid alliance with Philip was now irrevocably broken. While Richard may have felt he'd emerged from the debacle relatively unscathed, Philip would never forgive this insult to his sister. Henceforth, it was hard to tell with whom he was more at war: the Saracens or Richard. The only real difference was that his war with the Saracens was declared.

Berengaria and Eleanor arrived in Messina, finally, on March 30. Evan was among those in the crowd at the port when they disembarked. He'd seen Eleanor, of course, at the coronation and continued to be impressed that a woman of her age was as vigorous and formidable as most women half that age. Of regal and dignified bearing, she reminded him of Mama.

He strained to get a look at the next queen of England. Perhaps it was exhaustion after months of being on the road, perhaps it was the crowds bearing in on her, perhaps it was the absence of her future husband, who was nowhere to be seen, but at first sight, she was unimpressive.

Small in stature and build, dark, she looked terrified. Word was that she and Richard had met when they were younger. It was easy to see that she would have been smitten with him, but what would have attracted Richard to her, so much that he'd risk Philip's wrath? The answer came to Evan: probably, nothing. She was a good catch. As a bridge between Hispania and the Angevin possessions on the Continent, Navarre was a useful ally to have.

The two ladies were shown into a carriage and quickly spirited away, followed by their entourages and train of baggage. For reasons of propriety, they were evidently not to be in the same building as Richard.

Evan spotted Gurci in the crowd. The two friends embraced each other warmly, then repaired to a local tavern for a quick ale and catch-up.

Gurci bragged, "Sayid Abdullah's now allowing me to perform surgeries unassisted! Why, I excised a hemorrhoid just the other day!"

"Oh really," Evan drawled. "You must tell me how sometime."

"And, speaking of which, do you know there's an elixir of water mixed with mashed, dried plums that's great for getting you shitting again!"

While Evan chuckled at that, he couldn't claim as much. He was now under Crécy's close watch. He was sharing a tent with nine other men, but at least it was inside, he told Gurci. He spent most of his days trailing around after Crécy, pretending to be rapt, watching as Crécy's physicians worked on their patients, doing very little of interest, while he sketched their procedures under Crécy's careful eye.

"Watch as I cauterize this wound, boy!" he would command. Out of Crécy's sight, he would surreptitiously offer the patient a sweetened tea made from green willow bark, having collected the twigs from a tree close to the port.

As for Richard and Berengaria, a quick wedding would have ordinarily ensued, but it was, unfortunately, Lent: sex and feasting were forbidden during this time. Understanding this, Eleanor rested up for four days and, then, pleading business to attend to in England, left to make the long journey home, entrusting Berengaria to her daughter Joanna's care.

-III-
The Emperor of Cyprus

Eventually, the day came—April 10, to be exact—when all were ready to depart. All the ships left with their holds packed to the rafters: their first landfall would be a rendezvous point in Crete, over two hundred fifty nautical miles away, at least a week away over open water. Mategriffon had indeed been disassembled and was stowed in sections across various ships. Philip's fleet had left some time before and, reportedly, was already in the Holy Land, besieging Acre. Again, for reasons of propriety, Berengaria and Joanna were installed on a different ship, the *Reine-de-Sicile* [Queen-of-Sicily]. Richard himself sailed at the front of the fleet in his great vessel, *Trenc-la-Mer* [Slice-the-Sea], lighting an enormous lantern above the stern deck at night so that the others would see the way. Painted red, the ship was unmistakable.

Evan was back in the hold of the *Saint-Luc,* Gurci's feet once again in his face. Both now knew that before long blood would be shed with a purpose. They would likely be in harm's way, if not from Saracen arrows, then from the myriad other ways an unforgiving climate could kill them. The Third Crusade was finally underway.

The third day out, Good Friday, the fleet hit a storm. Once again, Evan was sick into the barrel, praying that his life would not be taken in such a futile and purposeless way. Three days later, the passengers were allowed on deck, where they saw that the two-hundred-plus fleet was now twenty-five. Where were they? Where were all the others? There was no sign of Richard's lantern. According to star charts, they had blown past Crete. They were, in fact, closer to Cyprus. Since all the ships were meant to reconvene there, anyway, there seemed no other choice but to sail onward. Perhaps everyone else was already there, waiting for them.

More calamity ensued as they approached the south Cyprus shore. The waves were still fierce from the remnants of the storm, and *Saint-Luc's* shipmen were unfamiliar with the coastline. They ran aground, the hold quickly filling with water, and thinly disguised panic seized the men. It was every man for himself as they grabbed what they could and jumped off the foundering ship and into the water. Evan wisely abandoned his mail, but he had never learned to swim. Why would he have needed to? He had never been in waves, never felt their horrific power. Twice, he did a complete forward somersault. Taking in water, sucked under and tossed up again, he again begged, *No! Not like this!*

And then, a guardian angel in the form of a short, squat Cornishman grabbed his vest and shouted, "Let me pull you! Don't try to help!" Stumbling and gasping, spitting out sand, briny water, and seaweed, he and Gurci collapsed onto the beach. They were alive. Many others weren't, including one well-dressed, middle-aged man whom they recognized: Richard's vice-chancellor and seal-bearer.

When they looked up, they saw they were not alone on the beach. Lined up the length of the beach were men whose smiles were not those of welcome or concern, but of greed. Arrows were pointed straight at their hearts. It was useless to try to fight them off. They could barely stand, never mind breathe. Besides, they were not soldiers. They were medical personnel.

A richly dressed, swarthy man stepped up to them. "Who's in charge here?"

Crécy and John Harewood, the *Saint-Luc*'s shipmaster, answered in chorus, "I am." They glanced at each other before nodding in tacit agreement. Crécy had the greater authority.

"I am Sir Roger de Crécy, master physician aboard the medical ship *Saint-Luc*. We mean you no harm. We are merely one small part of a great fleet. We are on crusade." He looked at them expectantly, perhaps hoping that they would be awed, or, at least, impressed by this.

"Yes," the man replied drily, "We've been expecting you. Your French fellow men-at-arms have already been here. They were not well-behaved. Where is your king?"

They all looked back out to sea at the ships still out there, now at anchor, and counted. There was no sign of the *Trenc-la-Mer.*

However, one ship was recognizable by the dual flags: a diagonal, red-and-white checkerboard stripe on a field of blue, and a second one of crossed gold chains on red. It was the *Reine-de-Sicile.* Did these men know what those flags signified?

Those two women were hostage bait, and no one was inclined to point out the importance of that ship.

Crécy merely replied, "He's not with us. Those twenty-two ships are only a tiny portion of the fleet. Either the rest have blown ahead of us, or they are behind. In any case, they will not stop looking for us. They will surely arrive *soon.* Can you tell us where we are?"

"You are at Limassol, Cyprus." Gesturing to the city walls, he went on grandly, "I am Emperor Isaac Komnenos. You will come with us."

Gurci and Evan glanced at each other. "*Emperor?*" Of this island? Was he joking?

Evan turned to retrieve his bag, which he saw washing ashore behind him.

"Where are you going?" demanded one of the men.

"Just to get my bag, sir," replied Evan.

"Absolutely not. And while you're here, for our security we will take your sword. It will be returned to you on your departure."

Everything Evan had was in that bag, including his precious sketchbook, which would be ruined anyway by now. Well, not quite everything. He could still feel the small pouch, hanging from his neck.

Crécy blustered, "In the name of King Richard, I strongly object to this treatment!"

"Your objection is noted. However, until your King arrives, consider yourselves prisoners of war."

-IV-
"Up the street, on your left"

Three weeks later, the survivors of the three wrecked ships were still crammed into underground cells in Limassol Castle. Crécy had huffed and puffed and got a cell with just Harewood and Chapelle as his cellmates. Nonetheless, they were all filthy, stinking, and constantly hungry. No one had seen daylight since they'd landed and *fluxus* was rampant. Evan and Gurci had been spared so far only because they both knew from their time at the hospital to never touch their hands to their mouths. They "drank" their meals as best they could. Evan felt sticky, cold, itchy, and very sorry for himself. Also, he was sure he now had lice.

One morning, Evan overheard Harewood ask Costas, one of the guards, if his ship was salvageable.

Costas laughed. "Hah! It's been taken apart and used to help fortify the beach against your king."

The men passed the time by talking about their families, women they'd carnally known, places they'd seen. Sometimes they sang bawdy shanties. They slept intermittently, persistently uncomfortable. Only the regular chiming of church bells summoning people to prayer services seven times a day helped them to track the time. Sneering at the Emperor's fantasy of making money off them as hostages, they kept themselves going with the certainty that Komnenos would wish he'd never been born the moment Richard's massive fleet docked. It could only be a few more days, at most. After all, it was his fiancée and sister that were among the missing.

The guards were surprisingly chatty. It turned out that Komnenos the Despot was indiscriminate in his plundering—a man of voracious appetites, reputed to have raped wives, defiled virgins, and reduced formerly-prosperous merchants to rags. It had not taken him long to decipher who was aboard the princesses' ship, and he'd tried unsuccessfully since then to lure them ashore. But Harewood was fairly sure they'd be well victualed—all they had to do was wait for Richard to find them.

The prisoners whispered among themselves that Richard would find unexpected, ready assistance from their guards.

Evan was philosophical about the likely loss of his sword, mail, and small other belongings. However, his lost sketchbook weighed heavily on him. True, many of the most recent drawings were prosaic, rubbishy likenesses of Crécy's procedures, surgical and otherwise. It was the loss of the faces, the landscapes—those drawings, even Crécy's, represented hours and hours of struggle, frustration, and, finally, illumination.

Mama had told him that, in the twenty-first century, exact likenesses of people could be captured and put on paper and other surfaces. This was miraculous enough, but if, by misfortune, one lost this likeness, one could always retrieve it from some "cloud" and order another one exactly like it, provided it had been saved somewhere on a machine such as Steven's or on a special, small "stick." She only knew that this "cloud" had something to do with a vast machine somewhere that stored it all. But why call it something as ephemeral as a cloud if it was a big, earthbound machine?

Mama's eyes always shone when she talked about the twenty-first century. To this question, she could only reply, smiling, "Evan, dear, there is much about that century that I will never understand. And neither do they. Truly, it is a world of wonders."

But what about him, in the here and now? He couldn't save his drawings to any "cloud." He either had them or he didn't. Father Philip, the former castle chaplain, used to rant about the sin of becoming too attached to earthly possessions. His replacement, Father Benedict, was not nearly as austere and strict as Philip had been, but even he could occasionally summon a thread of righteousness and guilt, invoking the Bible's "easier for a camel to go through the eye of a needle than a rich man to get into heaven." Perhaps this was God's punishment for his pride in his work? Well, his current situation certainly seemed to confirm that view, but he wasn't ready to give up yet on his new-found passion.

As soon as they were released, he figured he had two options: scour the markets for another paper book or prevail upon Crécy to purchase him another. While the latter had the advantage of being free, it would shackle him to Crécy for the remainder of his service. He would never be permitted to draw what he fancied, certainly not reproduce the sights and faces he'd seen.

Or maybe, just maybe, he could have both. The pocket change he'd had was lost to either the sea or Komnenos's men. He would have to dip slightly into the letter of credit. When his cellmates were asleep the first night of their confinement, he'd surreptitiously checked his pouch. To his great relief, the letter of credit was there, blurry but still legible, as was his little talisman. This close to the Holy Land, there must be a Templar commandery here.

The following day, Costas rushed up to their cage, unlocking it. "Your king is here! He got past our defenders with no trouble!" He described how Richard's crossbowmen let loose a storm of arrows on the city's defenders as they rowed ashore, catching them unawares. Apparently, they'd expected a more traditional charge of men and swords.

"Where is Komnenos?" asked Harewood.

"Oh, he's gone. He's fled the city. Your king is pursuing him right now. And *you're* getting out of *here!*"

Just like that, a hundred and eighty prisoners were free men.

Evan asked Costas if there was a Templar commandery nearby.

"Oh, yes. Out the door, turn left. It's just up the street. You'll recognize it by the black cross on the white flag."

Good. Now, to get away without Crécy seeing him.

Evan whispered to Gurci that he'd find him later. They all staggered up the stairs and out the door. Then everyone stopped, blinded by the sun. Using their temporary blindness and the general confusion of the day as cover, he squinted and groped his way up the street. He quickly spotted the distinctive flag. The commandery was like every other building here, in a town like every other he would visit in the Holy Land: low, stone, and flat-roofed, all the better to keep the heat out, with stairs to the roof on the outside.

Opening the door, he found a large room abuzz with activity. All the men were wearing the Templar uniform of a white surcoat with a red cross sewn on the front. Things were advancing quickly on the political front and no one was sure who would fill the power vacuum now that Komnenos appeared to be finished.

He tapped one such man on the shoulder and said, "Excuse me, sir, but can I make a small withdrawal on a letter of credit here?"

The man eyed the ratty-looking, stinking wretch before him. Wrinkling his nose, "You have proof?"

"Indeed, I do, sir."

"Then follow me."

He was led into a small room with a cupboard, desk and two chairs. "Show me this proof." Evan fished into his pouch and produced the letter of credit.

"One moment, please." The Templar opened the cupboard and brought out a thick tome. "Name?"

"Evan de Montmorency. The account was opened by my father, the Earl of Shaftesbury, in London."

He flipped through the pages, which appeared to be in order of origin, each page dedicated to one account. "Yes, here it is. What is your date of birth?"

"Saint Theobald's Day, 1171. Or July 8, however it was recorded."

"And what is the code word that accompanies this account?"

"Stacey."

The Templar assessed this wretched-looking young man again. "I take it that you have spent the last few weeks as a guest of Emperor Komnenos."

"Yes, I was just released. I need to purchase a few items, and all the coin I had was gone as soon as I jumped into the water."

"How much money do you require?"

"Perhaps five shillings?" A shilling was worth twenty pence.

The Templar laughed. "Well, I think we can spare that!" He looked again at the account. "Stacey. That's an unusual word. What does it mean?"

"It was the name of my horse when I was young. It's short for 'Anastasia.'"

"Ah yes, a Greek word. It means 'resurrected.' Still an odd name for a horse." The Templar reached into a drawer, from where he retrieved a locked metal box. Opening it from the key at his waist, he poured out the coins onto a weighted scale. "Someday," he muttered, "perhaps some bright fellow will devise a less cumbersome form of currency."

"Yes, larger denominations would make it easier, for sure," Evan replied as he clutched at the coins and put them in his pocket. In addition to a sketchbook, he would certainly need a small purse to put them all in. Maybe some new clothes, too.

"We might as well issue you a clean, new one," the Templar said as he looked at the smudged lettering. From a drawer, he took out a new square of parchment, on which he wrote, in Latin, *Replacement of letter of credit first issued in London.* He wrote down the sum of money transferred in his log, and, on the back of the letter of credit wrote, *Exchanged 5s, May 10, 1191 at Limassol, Cyprus.* Then he stamped the Templar seal beside it. He returned the letter to Evan.

"We take pride in the accuracy of our records. You will likely find that at whatever Templar house you next go to, your account will be up-to-date. Try not to get this one wet."

Evan shook his head in amazement at such efficiency and thanked him, smiling.

The Templar coughed in distaste as another waft of Evan's stench came his way. "Ahem … young man, you may be free, but you still look and smell like a beggar. Here, take this bag. It belonged to one of our number who died recently. He has no more use for it. You can keep your pence in it." It was a sturdy leather bag that fastened around the shoulders and had pockets inside, as well as a blanket. "There is a *hammam*—a bath—farther up the street on your left. You will recognize it by a door with a blue tile with white wavy lines on it. It belongs to us and those approved by us. I suggest you take immediate advantage of it. Knock at the door and tell him Commander Guy de Cluny sent you. With so much going on here today, it's unlikely that you will encounter anyone else. The Muslims are our avowed enemies, but let me tell you, this will change your life. It will cost you five of your pence, but you won't regret it. You are about to be 'resurrected.'"

Evan thanked him, wished him a good day, bowed, and turned to leave. Just then, Cluny added, "Oh, and may I advise you not to ruin such an experience by talking."

Two hours later, Evan had indeed been resurrected, in his opinion. Mama had told him of her near ecstasy when she'd stood under her first hot shower, the day of her arrival in the twenty-first century, about as scared and lost as she'd ever been. Mama, this may come close, Evan thought as he walked out the door that afternoon.

When he'd been admitted inside and handed over the pence, he'd been given a blue-and-white-striped linen towel, a pair of wooden sandals, and a modesty-saving white loincloth. He was instructed to go into the room adjoining, where he was to remove his clothes. The attendant told him that they would be washed and almost dry when he came out. He tucked his pouch in the loincloth. Then, he opened the door to a steamy, tiled room with a large, raised marble slab in the centre. An attendant, clad in a similar white loincloth, instructed him to lie face down on the slab. There, he was scrubbed with an abrasive cloth to within an inch of his life.

At first, in near agony, he was tempted to beg the man to stop, but, gradually, his body became inured to the scraping as weeks of collected grime, sweat, and salt from the sea were rubbed off. Then, oil of rosemary was massaged into every muscle in his body. Evan worried as the masseur approached his private parts but relaxed once he realized that no part of that area was going to be touched or exposed. Groaning in pleasure, the spell was only broken when the masseur started rubbing the soles of his feet. He had always been ticklish there. He was then shaven and his hair and nails trimmed.

Shortly afterward, he was told to get up at his leisure and go into the room adjacent, where he was to stand under the fall of water and to bathe. In that room was, indeed, a shower of warm water, with soap, where he rinsed off the excess oil and washed his hair. Also in the room was a tiled pool of steamy warm water. How is this possible, he wondered, as he gingerly stepped into the water. There was no sign of the wood fires necessary at home to laboriously heat pails of water. How was the temperature of the bath being maintained? He drifted off and was only awakened by the sound of church bells, summoning the faithful to some service, he cared not which.

Eventually, he hauled himself out of the bath, refastened his loincloth, and passed through the third door. This was a coolish room with benches. What was he to do here? Then, he realized, nothing. It was merely a place to rest, cool down, and prepare one's body for going outdoors again. Sometime later, he got up and exited via the door opposite, finding himself once again in the first changing room. There he found his clothes, laundered and folded, warm from the heat of the sun, though still a bit damp. But they'd be dry soon enough. The white cross looked like new again.

Coming back into the main reception room, he smiled at the attendant and thanked him for the experience. He asked, "Might you know where I could find a small book filled with blank paper here, as well as writing supplies?"

"Oh yes, you will find a stand right up the street, on your left." Of course. Everything here was "up the street, on your left."

A short while later, feeling proud indeed of his purchases, Evan headed back down the street.

"Montmorency! There you are! I've been looking all over for you! Where have you been that you look like a poncy eunuch?" It was Crécy. Louis Chapelle, as usual, was two paces behind him.

"Milord, I needed money from the Templar commandery just down the way. They referred me to the bath house back yonder. It was magical! Look, they even cleaned my clothes!"

Crécy sniffed. "Not only that, you *smell* like a eunuch! Shaven clean as a baby's bottom, no less!"

Evan wasn't sure what a eunuch was. He resolved to ask Gurci when he next saw him.

"We've been assigned quarters, aboard ship," said Crécy. "King Richard does not intend this to be a long stay, so we will not be billeted in town." He'd heard that since the prisoners no longer had their ships to report to, they were being spread out among the fleet.

"Which ship, Milord?"

"The *Reine-de-Sicile*. We are fortunate. The ship will likely be well protected. It's not quite the *Trenc-la-Mer*, but I had to pull a few strings to get us on it."

"Ah." This sounded promising. Surely quarters aboard this ship would be a step up from the *Saint-Luc*.

"Get your head out of the gutter. You will never sully the royal women with your presence. When they are on deck, everyone else is below."

"Of course, Milord. I hadn't considered it!" Really, he hadn't. "And do you know where my friend Morgant has been assigned?"

"I have no idea. It's no concern of mine."

Evan stopped. "Milord, he saved my life."

Crécy stopped to consider this forthright, unusual young man. For one so young, he was remarkably self-possessed and blessed by Fortune. Yet there remained an innocence about him that evoked certain protective feelings in his hardened soul, a little like adopting a stray puppy. Evan reminded him of his favourite son, who had died of the pox when he was twelve.

"Very well. I will ask about. One more person shouldn't make much difference. Now tell me about this den of iniquity that you call a bath house."

"So, first of all, you tell them Sir Guy de Cluny sent you …"

-V-
Some Local Worthy's Wife

On Saint Pancras Day, May 12, 1191, Limassol was humming. Everyone knew that Komnenos was finished, his forces routed. "What now?" was the burning question.

Komnenos had holed up in the hills, where he assumed he'd be safe, but he was unprepared for the roar of charging forces, with the English king fearlessly at their head. Even the horses were a shock, as he'd wrongly believed they would be unfit for riding after a month at sea. Completely surrounded, his own men fleeing in wild panic, he had been forced to sue for peace, begging not to be put in irons. So, Richard did not put him in iron chains. He put him in *silver* chains and handed him over for imprisonment to the Knights Hospitaller. And while he was at it, he helped himself to Komnenos's treasure, grain, and much fitter horses. And then he put the Templars temporarily in charge of the island.

Richard's conquest of Cyprus was an unexpected but brilliant tactical move, as the location was a vital staging and resupply area. It was so close to the Holy Land that some locals claimed the cedar groves in the Lebanese mountains could be seen on a fair day from atop the hills.

This day, Richard was finally to be married to Berengaria in Saint George's chapel in Limassol. It was a hastily arranged wedding, but there was really no other place to get it done. Here was definitely better than in Acre, right under Philip's outraged nose.

The local denizens were thrilled. A royal wedding, here, of all places! Unfortunately, the chapel was rather small, so only a few select guests were invited. However, the feast would last three days, and pretty well everyone was invited to that. Evan and Gurci, once again crammed together on the *Reine-de-Sicile,* rowed in to partake of the abundance of freshly prepared food. Later that day, as the music and dancing subsided, Evan sat on the sea wall and sketched what he remembered of the royal pair: her eyes, worshipful, on him; his, absently looking out to sea, his mind already elsewhere.

Opportunities for solitude were rare, especially with a party going on. A figure alone in this century tended to draw attention, but Evan was like his mother: for him, solitude was restorative. Since this expedition started, he'd rarely enjoyed it.

As he worked, chewing his lip in concentration, trying to get the proportions right, a well-dressed woman in a mauve silk dress approached him, trailed by two attendants. He stood to bow to her. She was a few inches shorter than he was—in other words, tall for a woman—slim, with a pale complexion and large, grey eyes in a striking, angular face. Judging by the colour of her eyebrows, Evan figured her hair would be reddish-blonde. She was most comely.

She nodded in acknowledgement to him but then said, "Please, don't stop on my account. Pray, continue." She stood by him, making him nervous and a little irritated with this infringement on his precious alone time.

"I'm making you nervous."

"Oh no, Milady, I'm just not accustomed to people watching me work."

"You're drawing the newlyweds, I see."

"I am attempting to, yes. It's difficult drawing their faces at an angle."

She watched him work for another few moments. "Not intended for posterity, I imagine?"

"Heh, heh, no, not these miserable scribblings, Milady. They're only for my memories, to show my people at home, and for practice."

"Have you been drawing for a long time?"

"No, I started on the voyage from England. I wanted some way to show my family what I'd seen, people I've met."

"But this looks like a new book."

"Yes, the other was lost when we were shipwrecked here."

"You were one of the prisoners, then?"

"Yes. It was an *interesting* few weeks, let's say."

"I'm sorry to hear about that, and also for the loss of your book." She stood there for a moment or two longer. "Indeed interesting. And unconventional. But it is accurate. I will leave you to your solitude. Good day to you, sir." And she and her companions carried on down the wall walk.

Hmm, I wonder who she is, Evan thought. Probably some local worthy's wife. He returned to his drawing.

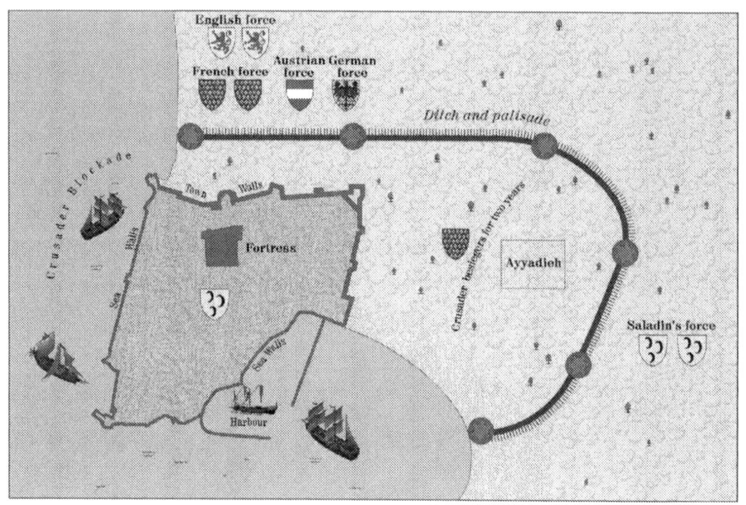

The Siege of Acre: July, 1191

-VI-
Melons and Grapes from Syria

Sailing down the coast of the Holy Land at last, early in June, Evan witnessed battle action, but that was all he could do: witness, as the *Reine-de-Sicile* was kept safely away from the action. On June 7, the reassembled fleet intercepted a gigantic Muslim dromon approaching Acre, the largest ship anyone had ever seen. It was doubtless intended to reinforce and resupply Saladin's army that was besieging the French forces under Philip and Leopold, which were, in their turn, besieging Muslim-controlled Acre. A siege in one form or another had been going on for almost two years, and both sides were nearing the end of their tether, never mind the hapless garrison and residents of Acre.

There was no way that Richard could let this ship pass. Indeed, capture and confiscation of the ship's cargo was the whole point. Richard's galleys drew close enough to the ship to hail arrows on the men aboard, but even though the dromon was badly outnumbered, men kept appearing from below as those on deck fell under the onslaught of the arrows. Bodies were simply piled and shoved out of the way. Just how many men *were* on that ship? Fifteen hundred, was the consensus, though that surely was an exaggeration, Evan thought. Even as the English fleet suffered its own losses under Greek fire, the massive dromon eventually ran out of men.

It was at that point that the English fleet witnessed an act of immense courage: the shipmaster ordered the ship to be set ablaze, scuttling it, rather than allowing it to be captured. All those surrounding the dying ship stood silently on their decks, the odour of burning wood and flesh filling their nostrils and stinging their eyes, pitying the lost, screaming souls on that immense ship, albeit Infidel souls. No one had ever seen death on this massive a scale.

"Should we not be of assistance to the injured on the other ships?" Evan asked Crécy.

"No, we aren't needed now," he replied. "Each of those ships has physicians aboard."

"Shouldn't we at least try to save some of the Infidels in the water?"

Crécy regarded him as if he was questioning Evan's basic intelligence. "And do what with them, exactly?"

Gurci joined them then. "Why deprive them of the martyrdom they seek?"

Steven is stretched out on one end of a long black leather divan that could seat three, easily. On the other end is a pretty young woman—long, dark brown hair, loose around her shoulders. Dark brown eyes. She looks exotic, somewhat like the women in Portugal and Hispania that Evan has seen. The corners of her mouth naturally turn up, giving her a good-humoured, pert, though sensuous countenance. She's wearing a loose grey top over the usual blue breeches, just like Steven. Soothing, quiet music plays in the background. On her left hand is a thin gold band with a small diamond on it. Their legs are loosely entwined and they seem comfortable and happy together. Steven is reading a thick book with small print, she a thin, cheap-looking one entitled The Pale Horse, *accompanied by a name: Agatha Christie. It looks like she's almost finished reading it. Evan somehow knows that the girl's name is Gaby.*

"Is that book any good?" Steven asks. "Would I like it?"

"Well," she says, "it's a Christie, but at least it's one I haven't read. Half the time, I get halfway through before I think, 'Wait a minute, I've read this one!'"

"How come you keep reading her, then?"

"I don't know … It's kind of reassuring, reading her books: a vanished world where everyone knew their place, order was always maintained, and nothing ever disturbed afternoon tea."

She pauses, and then continues. "And yet, she upends all that coziness because the murderer is almost never some shady outsider, but a perfectly respectable person right at home."

Steven laughs. "Do you think that vanished world ever existed, really?"

"I don't know. Maybe not. But it's fun imagining that it did."

"What's it about?"

"It's complicated, but it has to do with slow poisoning with thallium. Poison's her favourite way to knock people off, I notice. Odourless, tasteless, except people's hair falls out and funny things happen to their fingernails. They die of it eventually."

"What's thallium?"

Gaby laughs. "Damned if I know, Steve! You're the science nerd! For all I know, she just made it up!" Leaning forward, she massages one of his socked feet and says, smiling mischievously, "Feel like a bit of a break?"

"C'mere," he replies.

Evan awoke, delighted to catch up with Steven again. So, "Steve" now. Fortunate man! He was in love. Evan could still feel the warm sense of ease and comfort Steve felt being around this Gaby. Evan was in love, too, just from "meeting" her briefly. She was perfect. But the way they were sitting was so indecorous!

And "Gaby": What kind of name was that? And what was a "nerd"?

He thought a moment about that Agatha Christie who could write books about murder. A *woman?* Writing a book about such a topic? Imagine that. His thoughts then turned to Gaby's "vanished world." What did she mean by that? Of course, everyone knew their place. How else could it be? Villeins thinking they were lords? Lords thinking they were kings? Was that what Mama was talking about when she'd scolded him that time about being polite to the servants? He would have to ponder that another time, but, for now, more important, what was this "thallium"? Evan had never heard of it either. Did it matter? Maybe the essence of the dream was that their conversation was about a *poison.*

He went happily back to sleep with the thought of that beautiful girl in his arms.

Richard did not leap ashore at their arrival at Acre. He spent two days appreciating the situation, despite Philip's pleas that he "do something." It was not looking good. Only two dozen of his ships were anchored outside Acre; the rest of the entire fleet was becalmed and stuck farther up the coast. Disappointingly, only five thousand of Frederick Barbarossa's men had doggedly made it there on their own. The situation on land was chaotic, and everyone was exhausted. Emissaries were sent to Philip, Saladin, and other allied armies. Saladin sent back crushed ice and Syrian melons and grapes, as if to say, "Welcome to the party."

On day two, Crécy poked Evan and Gurci on the shoulders and said, "We're all needed ashore."

During the siege, German and Baltic physicians had organized a field hospital just outside the north wall. It had been reasonably well protected by the ditch and spiked wall erected by the crusaders as protection from Saladin's forces. Crécy was charged with enlarging it and resupplying it with staff and supplies. He separated patients in need of urgent care from those in recovery; the former were given round-the-clock care. Evan and Gurci, being merely medici, were among those assigned the night shift.

On day three, Richard brought up his trebuchets to pummel Acre's outer walls, already in bad shape.

The siege now looked like this: Richard's crusaders had joined those of Philip, Leopold, Frederick, and the other forces, besieging Acre from the north. Their ships formed a complete blockade of the city to the west and south, cutting off all means of resupply and reinforcement. Other crusader forces that had been trying to recapture Acre for almost two years were camped just east of the city walls, behind the ditch and palisade they'd constructed. Saladin's camp was to the east of them, and his forces were taking pot shots at all the crusaders now—but, to their pleasant surprise, he was refraining from all-out attack.

The otherwise healthy and fit English took mostly arrow wounds, although an early, surprising casualty was Lord Richard de Canville, victim of a well-aimed arrow to the neck. All the other crusader besiegers were in appalling shape: thin, dirty, suffering from exhaustion, starvation, gum disease, and scurvy. There were even shocked whispers of cannibalism during the worst of the siege. The countryside surrounding Acre had once been rich with orchards, but those had long since been destroyed.

Word was sent back to the becalmed fleet up the coast: Pilfer, buy, do whatever is necessary to feed these men. Go back to Cyprus if you have to.

And then, on day five, disturbing news reached those under

the medical tent. Richard himself was ill and so was King Philip. Weak, feverish, little appetite. What could be the cause? A couple of days later, Richard's hair reportedly started to fall out. The diagnosis, according to his physicians: *léonardie*. He was being bled, to excise the evil humors. Richard was down but not out, however. From his litter, he gamely fired arrows at the city's defenders.

"*Léonardie,*" my eye, thought Evan. Hair falling out. If his suspicions were correct, "funny things" would soon happen to his fingernails. He had no idea whether thallium was available or even known in this part of the world, but similar-acting poisons likely were. How to convey this message to his king?

He decided to approach Crécy.

"Milord, I believe I know the cause of the King's illness."

"And what would that be? Some scrap of dubious Infidel 'knowledge' that you have retained?"

"Yes, Milord. I believe he is being poisoned. It's easy to do. Melons and grapes from Syria! Or, failing that, all it would take would be for someone to slip it into his wine. It is odourless and tasteless. That's why no one else is sick."

Crécy was dubious but not entirely dismissive. He himself had never heard of this *léonardie,* and it was much too soon for it to be any of the more common afflictions. Richard had only *just* arrived! Surely not the shipman's disease, which in his experience was caused by poor diet; even if his men ate roughly, Richard got the best available. If it was some unknown contagion, why was no one else within the ranks afflicted, including himself? Why only Richard and Philip? Crécy himself would have put his money on swamp fever, a common plague in the Holy Land. It was hideously hot and humid, certainly swamp fever season, but it still didn't explain why only the two dominant figures in the crusader camp had come down with it.

The young man pressed him. "Milord, just ask his physicians one thing: Is anything happening with his nails? If so, he is indeed being poisoned. Instruct his cooks that only one person be entrusted with his food and that it be carefully guarded. He should not consume anything that this one person can't vouch for personally."

"What is the name of this 'poison'?"

"Thallium, Milord."

"Never heard of it."

"Neither had I, until recently. I pray you, before it's too late, just ask his physicians. It will do no one any harm to have his regimen strictly monitored."

Crécy nodded. "I'm on good terms with his chief physician, Ralph Besace. I'll have a word with him at dinner today."

Three days later, Crécy and Evan were summoned to King Richard's tent.

Crécy couldn't elaborate why, but he assumed "their" suggestion had been heard.

Evan worried as they approached. "What do I say? What do I do?"

"How should I know! I've been in the same room with him, but hardly in his *presence*," Crécy replied. "My guess is the usual. Don't speak until spoken to. Keep to the point. Bow out when it's obvious he's finished with us."

Evan had only seen Richard from a distance at the coronation and the wedding, when he was looking his best. While still the dominant presence in every room, up close the man before him was much changed. His wavy, red-blond hair was thinning on top. He was pale and sweaty from the oppressive heat. He had lost two of his fingernails. But his eyes were alive with purpose, and the restless energy that Richard always exuded was still evident. His father had been just the same, according to Papa. The King was sitting up, maps arrayed on his table. Several advisors hovered about. To the side were a simple cot, cupboard, and bedside table, where his crown sat.

Crécy and Evan bowed deeply.

Richard didn't waste time with pleasantries. Eying Evan shrewdly, "Are you Montmorency, the young medicus who put forth the theory of poison?"

Evan shot a quick glance of startled gratitude at his mentor.

"Yes, Your Grace. During our stay in Messina, I spent some time at a Muslim hospital, learning my craft." Well, a lie repeated many, many times has a way of becoming truth. And one good turn deserved another. "Sir Roger was kind enough to relay my thoughts."

"By last night, I was feeling much better. I believe we all owe you our thanks."

"It was our honour."

"Your father fought against me at Le Mans. He unhorsed me. No one had ever done that before. He could have killed me then, but he tipped his sword and rode on. He kneeled obeisance to me as soon as the King passed away."

Evan was surprised that Papa had never mentioned this episode, but he never was one to brag. "Yes, Montmorencys have always, and will always, swear fealty to the rightful monarch."

"He was injured and in pain. I had to help him up."

"Thank you, Your Grace. I didn't know that."

"Did he recover?"

"Yes, he did, Your Grace. Completely, thank you for asking."

"I take it that you're Lord Montmorency's younger son."

"Yes, I am, Your Grace."

Richard studied him thoughtfully and nodded, having fixed him in the established order. "I've always believed in the adage 'Know thy enemy.' Infidel physic may have its uses. Don't go far. I may be calling on your assistance again."

He looked back down at his maps.

Crécy and Evan glanced at each other, nodded, and took that as their cue that they were dismissed. They bowed and withdrew.

But before they were completely clear of the tent, Richard called after them. "Where are your mail and sword, Montmorency? You should at least be wearing your mail, wandering about here. We're in a battle situation."

"Lost at sea when we were shipwrecked at Cyprus, Your Grace."

"Hmm, we will have to see what we can do to remedy that."

"A thousand thank-yous, Your Grace." Although Evan, to be honest, was glad to be rid of both. The heat was a live thing that wrapped him in a suffocating embrace. He knew how much the mail-clad men were suffering with all that protective clothing—fifty pounds of added weight when fully kitted out. Even the infantrymen suffered under their padded gambesons.

Soon after his arrival at Acre, Evan had ditched his shoes, hose, and garter in favour of simple sandals he'd purchased at a local stand. Doing so had quickly cleared up a bothersome heat rash near his nether regions. Initially mocked for "going Infidel," he'd noticed some of the other physicians were doing the same—but not Crécy, who found such exposure shocking. The annoying hose had been hurriedly put back on at the King's summons.

"Thank you, Milord," said Evan as they walked back to the makeshift hospital. "Most men would have taken the credit for themselves."

Crécy smiled. "I believe that if we look out for each other, we are both in a position to see our stars rise. By the way, I mentioned your theory to King Philip's physician. 'Bah,' he said. 'Impossible!' We'll just see, won't we."

Since they'd disembarked, all the medical personnel were sleeping on cots under the same tents as their patients. The following day, when Evan returned to his in the morning, he found a folded-up hauberk of mail, as well as a fine, gleaming sword. Both were "gently used," from some unknown and now deceased crusader. He took it for the gesture it was.

Gurci snickered as he saw the metal. "So, you're now a fancy man again, are you? Don't forget us little folk as you claw your way to the top. I'm available if you need a companion some evening."

Henceforth, Evan and Gurci were on day shift.

-VII-
"You'll be hearing from me."

Richard intensified the assault on Acre, bringing up God's Own Catapult and Bad Neighbour, his two fearsome mangonels. Daily pummelling continually weakened the walls, with more than just rocks as projectiles: severed heads, excrement, refuse, rotten carcasses—anything to make life as unbearable as possible for the wretched defenders. Finally, on July 12, Acre surrendered. It was agreed that the prisoners' lives would be spared in exchange for two hundred thousand dinars and the return of a portion of the True Cross, said to be in Infidel hands.

The three-storey Acre fortress had survived the siege relatively undamaged. Until four years ago, it had headquartered the Knights Templar and resembled a typical European castle. Since then, under Muslim occupation, the usual bailey had been replaced by a garden quadrangle in the centre, with a reflecting pool and tinkling fountain.

In this peaceful setting, during what should have been a triumphant, joyful moment of victory for the crusaders, childish bickering did its leaders in.

Whose flag should fly over the city? And in what order? Richard was incensed that Leopold of Austria hung his flag at the same height as his and Philip's flags—he, who had really only tagged along, done none of the hard work of planning or fund-raising. Besides, he was only a duke! Richard angrily ordered the flag torn down.

This enraged Leopold, as well as his good friend Philip.

Leopold shouted, "How *dare* you rip down my flag! Who appointed *you* as leader! You're nothing but a loud-mouthed bully who's found himself king of a *rain-soaked backwater!*"

Richard's Angevin temper got the best of him, and he slapped Leopold. Everyone gasped. A lethal silence ensued, during which the two men glared at each other.

"APOLOGIZE!" Leopold roared. "On your KNEES!"

"I will NOT!"

Hearing this reply, Leopold took a moment to consider his options. He could never seek satisfaction in a duel. He would lose. Richard had about nine inches and fifty pounds on him. But he knew how to get to Richard, where it would hurt.

In a low, icy voice he said, "I dislike this place, I dislike losing men, and I especially dislike *you.* I'm leaving on the morrow, and I'm taking my men with me."

"You 'dislike' this place? You expected the Elysian Fields, perhaps? So, leave! Be my guest! You'll hardly be missed." And Richard stomped off.

This was hardly a private shouting match. It took place in full view of bishops, knights, dukes, and other leaders in the crusader cause. Word of this exchange travelled like wildfire. By supper that evening, even the lowliest washerwoman knew of it. It was all people were talking about.

As Evan cut into his fish, he commented, "If what we're hearing is correct, Richard has just made himself a mortal enemy. Leopold will never forgive this insult."

"Bah," replied Gurci, picking a bone out of his teeth. "Richard will come out of it smelling like a rose. Men like him always do. He'll just marry off some sister of his to one of Leopold's half-witted brothers. All it takes, right?"

Evan wasn't so sure. He had a bad feeling that they hadn't heard the last of Leopold.

Leopold, his men, and his ships left the following day. So did Philip, to everyone's shock, with most of his army, leaving Hugh of Burgundy, a vassal of Philip's, in charge of the French contingent. The official reason was "continuing ill health." Everyone knew, however, that Philip's departure wasn't as simple as that.

Philip was in a perennial snit. He was incredibly frustrated at his illness, which didn't seem to be abating, and he knew he was being shamed and humiliated by his departure. He was miffed that Richard hadn't offered him half of Cyprus. He was miffed that just because Richard was taller, louder, wealthier, and had more men, he seemed to be taking over the whole operation when it had been agreed this expedition would be an equal partnership. What right did Richard have to take control of everything? While Richard had been chasing around the Mediterranean and getting himself married, with all the pleasures that entailed, Philip and Leopold had been beating off Saladin in this godforsaken, stinking-hot hellhole since April and had lost many men. And he was still plenty miffed about Richard's spurning of Alys. Bringing that Navarrienne nobody here, of all places, was the last straw.

However, on the bright side, now that Richard was safely here, as opposed to *there,* disputed lands back home could be seized in his absence, and Philip was free to craft his own story about what *really* happened in the Holy Land.

Philip would become a devious, implacable enemy.

As for Richard, he'd now lost two important allies and a third was dead.

As soon as it was deemed safe, Richard ordered quarters prepared for him in the fortress. Berengaria and Joanna were to be installed there as well, safely out of the way while Richard and his army marched to Jerusalem. He ordered Mategriffon to be reassembled outside Acre's walls, to house a permanent garrison there.

Meanwhile, he impatiently awaited the ransom money for the prisoners, as well as the piece of the True Cross. Saladin claimed it was taking time to raise the money—which, granted, was an enormous sum—but it surely seemed like dithering to Richard.

Evan, from afar, witnessed the two ladies and their procession of servants and baggage as they were helped off the ship. They must surely be hoping that this stay would be for longer than a couple of days. Little Berengaria, he recognized. But the other woman … She very much had the look of—Lord in Heaven, she *was!* The Dowager Queen Joanna of Sicily! She had popped up in his dreams a few times since that evening in Limassol—probably because she was the only woman he'd talked to for months, he figured, but he'd always wakened a little aroused. He squirmed at the memory of his disrespect that evening.

The most severely injured, along with selected medical personnel, were also moved inside Acre to what was left of the hospital.

Richard immediately set men to work on its repair and enlargement. While the injured took over the wards, Evan, Gurci, and all the others settled under a tent adjacent to the hospital.

Evan was delighted to spot not only rosehips in the garden but also a few precious ginger plants. Worth their weight in gold, the roots could be sparingly doled out in the form of a restorative tea. However, he and Gurci found the cupboards in the hospital apothecary almost bare of the herbs they'd come to trust and rely on. They would need to immediately begin harvesting and drying what was still alive in the garden.

They approached Crécy with a list of herbs they believed necessary to treat their patients. Would Sir Roger trust them to seek out these supplies, or would he prefer to handle it himself?

Crécy glanced at the list. Procuring supplies was a skill he was proud of; that, and organizing men was why he was the army's chief physician. It would be an interesting, distracting challenge. Moreover, his increasingly symbiotic relationship with these young men amused him.

"Leave this to me, boys. You see to your patients."

Exotica such as myrrh, camphor, hemp, and mandragora seemed to magically appear on the shelves a short while later. It was no magic: Crécy's well-kept secret was to have Chapelle quietly approach the local midwives, who in turn referred him to eager retailers. Predictably, as the crusade wore on, local entrepreneurs, hearing that there was a lucrative market for their native herbs and spices, knocked directly at the hospital's door. Initially bemused by this influx of Infidel mysteries that only Montmorency and Morgant seemed to know anything about, the crusade apothecaries gradually noticed other medical personnel were requesting them, as well.

In these early days, the medical corps were so busy treating the injured from the siege that no one noticed Evan and Gurci quietly stitching and dressing wounds right after they'd been cleaned, knocking their patients out when necessary with a wet sponge. What *was* noticed was that these patients were up and about when others were still lying there looking at their laudable pus and, often, getting gangrene. Taking notice, the other physicians started doing the same, even Crécy.

After supper one evening, Evan decided that this quiet, pre-sunset time afforded a good chance to get some sketching in. Everyone else seemed to be readying themselves to retire or maybe go gambling or whoring. He walked down to what was left of the city walls, thinking that a ruined tower, with Richard's fleet in the background, would make a pleasing picture. He hoped to make a better job of it than the last time he tried to sketch a multitude of ships.

He had just settled himself down to his task, pleased at the aesthetics of the site he'd chosen, enjoying the cooling ocean breeze on his face, when a female voice said, "Well, hello again!"

He knew the voice. This time, he scrambled up to bow deeply to her. "Your Highness, good evening, I'm sorry, I failed to recognize you the last time we met … Is it not dangerous for you to be walking here?"

She replied, smiling, "I'm glad you didn't. I wish it happened more often. As for my safety, don't worry, my guards are discreet, but they're ever-present. And who are you, now that we're practically old friends?"

"I'm Evan de Montmorency, no one important. Just a humble medicus-in-training and beginning artist."

Joanna frowned, then cocked her head in curiosity as she remembered. "Oh, but you *are* someone important, I think! You're the medicus who saved my brother's life. We are all grateful to you. May I see what you're drawing?"

Evan showed her what he'd done so far: a sketch of the tumbled-down wall on the left of the page, with a few ships in the background.

She studied it. "It will be small, detailed work, won't it … the bricks in the wall, the small sails and masts beyond. I like how you're creating a feeling of depth by making the ships smaller in the distance. It looks so true! I didn't know one could do that."

"Thank you, neither did I. I'm still figuring it out. The last time I tried it, in Marseille, I made a mess of it. This time, I'll do fewer ships, even if it won't look strictly accurate."

"May I see your other one, of my brother and his wife?"

"Certainly, Your Highness." He flipped back to the now-completed image.

"Yes. I think you captured the gaiety of the guests very well, as contrasted with the thoughtfulness of the King and Queen." She studied him again, with interest. "You've had an adventure or two in this crusade so far, haven't you? I would like to hear sometime about your experiences as a prisoner."

Evan liked the sound of that very much. So close to any woman, never mind one as pretty as this one, was pleasurable after so many weeks in rough male company. She was a reminder of how life used to be before he saw mangled and moaning bodies lined up in front of him, every morning. Some dead ones, too.

To his disappointment, she turned as if to leave him, but then paused. She gently laid her hand on his arm, startling him. Impure thoughts tumbled through his head, and he strove mightily to suppress them. He must pray for forgiveness at matins tonight.

"Would you care to draw me?" she asked with surprising hesitancy. Her attendants giggled. She glared at them, though she removed her hand.

His eyes widened in surprise. "Why yes, Your Highness. It would be an honour. I must warn you, however. I've never drawn a portrait of a woman."

"Oh, I doubt it'll be much of a problem for you. Now that I know where to find you, you'll be hearing from me."

-VIII-
"Try for more of my body"

The following day, a knight approached Evan as he was setting a broken leg. "The Dowager Queen of Sicily requires your presence in her chambers, at your earliest convenience for the reasons previously discussed."

Well, that was fast. What would she call "earliest convenience"?

"Would after supper today be suitable?"

"I'll come and fetch you then." The knight bowed and strode off.

Sure enough, the knight was waiting for him as he went to wash his hands after supper.

"Where are *you* heading in such a hurry?" Gurci asked.

"I'll tell you later. I have to go." He jogged back to his cot to collect his materials.

Evan and the knight walked silently up the hill until they came to the fortress gate. Trying to appear calm, as if being admitted to the chambers of a dowager queen was something he did every day, he worried, What if she doesn't like it? What if I make a mess of it? Does she have the Angevin temper? Will she scream at me as my ass gets the sharp end of her shoe? He didn't think he would get over the humiliation.

The guards recognized the knight and quickly raised the portcullis for them.

He took a moment to appreciate the garden before he was led through dimly lit, vaulted stone hallways. He resolved that, if ever he was fortunate enough to have property and a bit of money to spare, he would recreate such gardens for himself. They climbed a set of stairs at the end of a hallway. Another hallway on their left ended with a door.

The knight knocked. They were commanded to enter.

Inside, they found Joanna and her attendants in a large sitting room. The windows were small, but they did overlook the garden. The room had been softened with deep pink, diaphanous curtains swaying in the late-afternoon breeze. Gold thread—such luxury!—had been decoratively woven into them. Two European-style chairs were arranged against the windows. Low, silk-upholstered divans sat against the walls, with a large Oriental rug warming the floor. In the middle of the room was a low, square wooden table, on top of which was a silver bowl full of luscious-looking cherries and peaches. The wall in front of him featured a large door, which he presumed led to her solar. Though Joanna had doubtlessly done what she could to make her quarters pleasant and welcoming, this room and all the others had been built by men, for men, with scant thought of comfort.

She was dressed as she would have been at supper, with a jewelled gold band around her head, ruby-encrusted necklace and gold bands around her wrists. She was wearing a rich blue, silk *bliaut.*

"Welcome, Medicus Montmorency. Thank you for coming on such short notice. That'll be all, Lord Pummeroy. Agnes, Nicolette, you may leave us now, as well."

Agnes and Nicolette exchanged an amused glance, bowed, and withdrew.

Lord Pummeroy? Serving as a queen's errand boy? No wonder Papa never wanted to be around court.

As they closed the door behind them, Evan found himself in a mild panic. Alone, with a woman, a beautiful one, not a relative? In a closed room?

Joanna settled herself on one of the chairs by the windows. "Don't worry, Medicus, I won't turn into Medusa or anything. I won't keep you long tonight, just until the daylight fails."

As Evan nodded, tongue-tied and fumbling in his bag for his supplies, she asked, "Is this setting suitable for the light? Against the window?" She was clearly trying to put them on an easier footing.

"Yes, that will be excellent, Your Highness." Gesturing to the other chair, "If I may?" She nodded in turn. He picked it up and placed it about six feet in front of her.

As Evan studied her, preparing himself mentally to sketch a regal woman, he was surprised and shocked to see her remove her crown and unfasten her veil and wimple. Then all jewellery, except what must have been her wedding ring. Her thick, red-blonde hair, so like that of her brother and their father, was braided around her head.

She then proceeded to unclasp the braid to let it drape along the front left side of her body, where it ended at her slim waist. While she did, she casually asked, "Do you not find Infidel furniture rather too low, Medicus? We had these chairs brought from the ship."

Evan was again rendered speechless. Before him, stripped of royal trappings, sat a graceful woman, younger-looking now and somehow vulnerable. To his surprise, he observed just a trace of nervousness.

"I'm sorry. I was trying to put you at ease, but I see I have done the opposite. I merely thought that your task might be a little easier without all the other distractions of jewellery and so on."

In fact, this would make his work incredibly hard. The "jewellery and so on" was what he'd been counting on to keep this engagement professional.

"However you feel most comfortable, Your Highness. Perhaps, for now, just replace your crown."

She put the circlet back on. "Please, between us, 'Milady' will be fine. I get so tired of the other all day."

"As you wish, Your—Milady, I mean." He strove to collect his wits. "Let's get started, then, while we still have good light. How would you like me to draw you? Just your face? Or …?"

"Well, for tonight, perhaps just my face would be easiest?"

"I agree, Milady. All right, how you're sitting is fine, but perhaps if you could turn your face at a slight angle to the right, and hold that pose? Try not to talk while I'm working?"

"Do you want me to smile? Or look like my pet rabbit just died?"

The tension between them broke, and Evan laughed. He wanted to capture that vulnerable look she'd had just now. "I think, Milady, I'd like you to think of how you felt when you learned you were to accompany the Princess Berengaria on this crusade."

"You mean, *What?* You want me to go *where?* With *her?*"

Evan laughed again at the sight of her, her mouth agape with mock outrage. "No, not like that. Perhaps as you were about to board the ship."

She nodded. "Oh, I see. Perhaps a bit scared, wondering what my brother's grand schemes were getting us all into? I understand, though I'm surprised it's the expression you are seeking."

She sat silently for a moment, conjuring the memory, and gradually her face settled into that vulnerable countenance again. Perfect. Then she said, quietly, "Actually, our new queen is a sweet woman who has become a good friend. I don't know what I would have done without her company on this expedition. I've never had a good friend, until her." And then her eyes took on a look of wistfulness. Even more perfect. Her hair was spun gold in the setting sun.

"Hold that expression, please, if you can."

Sometime later, as the church bell rang for compline, having lost the last of their light, she stood to draw the curtains, and he packed up his supplies. She had proven to be an excellent subject, remaining motionless and silent, although holding that expression had been difficult. He'd noticed that she would catch her mood drifting, stop, and rearrange her face.

"May I see?"

"Certainly, Milady."

She drew near to him. She carried a light, flowery scent. Lily of the valley, Evan thought. She studied what he'd done.

"It's not quite finished," he explained. "I think I need to do a bit more shading around your cheekbones, perhaps with a bit of charcoal because your face is very … interesting. It has angles. Contrasts, might be the word."

Not to mention beautiful, expressive eyes, framed by long lashes and sensuous lips—Stop it, Evan, right now! Stop it, you dalcop!

"If I may say," he chattered on, "you don't resemble the King, except for your hair and eyes."

"No, I take after my mother. I like what you've done. It's not an expression I allow myself when I'm around other people. Why did you think that this would be the best representation of me? I'm curious."

"Well, I see something of my mother in you."

She laughed. "Your *mother*? Thank you very much!"

He scrambled to explain. "No, not old like she is now! But,

like you, she is a noble lady. She is very clever, and in her youth, she was famously beautiful. She still is. Her life has always been privileged but tightly bound by duty. She is certainly content in her life with my father, but sometimes I catch a look on her face of wishing she were not the Countess of Shaftesbury, but someone else. Someone freer."

That was all he was going to say about that. "I wondered if you, too, had felt that on occasion, and I wanted to capture it."

She searched his eyes for a moment. "I would like to meet your mother someday." And then she took his face in her hands. She lowered it to gently, tentatively, and lay her lips on his. Without his bidding, his body responded. He took her in his arms and returned the kiss, not gently, but urgently. A hot surging desire flooded him, like the nighttime—and occasional daytime—dreams he had but this was the real thing and oh Lord …

She was the first to pull away.

He stammered, horrified and ashamed, "I-I'm sorry! That was unforgivable. I'll leave now."

He ripped out the page. "Here—it's yours to keep. I think it is a fair likeness as is." He turned to gather his supplies and hurriedly throw them in his bag, willing his erection down.

"Please don't apologize. I too forgot myself for a moment. I'm unused to a man staring at me so frankly, for so long. It won't happen again." She sat back down on her chair and smiled at him. "But I would like you to return tomorrow at the same time. To try for more of my body, if that's agreeable to you."

Gesturing towards the bowl of fruit on her table, she said, "Please, take as much as you wish. I know fruit is in short supply down there."

He bowed. "As you wish, Milady." He shoved a handful of cherries in his bag. "Thank you."

He bowed and walked backwards and out the door. The last he saw of her, she had turned away from him, having pulled back a curtain to gaze out the window.

-IX-
"Call me Joanna."

Evan barely slept that night, replaying those last few moments together. God's whiskers, she could have had him flayed alive for what he'd done! But instead, he'd felt her desire, too. "*To try for more of my body*"? What was *that* supposed to mean? Surely not what he was feverishly imagining. Just a sketch, waist up, was all she meant. Perfectly innocent and acceptable. Of course, he was nothing to her, just someone to amuse herself with. He, the second son of a provincial baron. Not exactly the quality she was accustomed to. Love of Heaven, she was the Dowager Queen of Sicily, even if she was, what, only twenty-six by now? What was he thinking. And then the memory of those last moments took hold of him, and he circled back on it all again, and again.

"So where *were* you last night?" Gurci asked after prime the following morning. "Poirier got a good game of knucklebones going." Poirier was one of the French physicians. Although Richard had banned games of chance below the level of knight, that had been largely ignored. The men had to do something in their spare time. "Looks to me like you were sketching again," looking at Evan's blackened nails.

That was the thing about sketching, Evan had to admit. It was tough to get the ink out. "I had a sort of commission. I was asked to sketch a likeness of a lady in town."

"A 'lady in town'? What lady? Is there any lady left in this shithole of a place? Except, are you talking about—"

"Quiet! It's nothing. Just a sketch. But I'm to return again this evening, to finish. Don't tell anyone, please. You could get me into a lot of trouble."

"I won't. But just remember, this is a small place. Word will get out eventually."

"I know. I'm hoping we all leave before it has a chance to."

As he was finishing supper that evening, he glanced to his left and saw Lord Pummeroy at the edge of the garden, waiting for him. Evan nodded at Gurci, who took in the knight at a glance and then went back to his supper.

This time, Evan had his bag already packed and ready to go. After washing his hands, he joined Pummeroy.

"So, who do you think you are, that I must waste my time escorting you?" Pummeroy asked him, as they walked up to the fortress. Acre was a major centre of commerce and trade in the eastern Mediterranean. The city was rapidly recovering from the siege; most of the damaged buildings were well on the way to repair, and there was a general atmosphere of hustle, relief, and optimism that life might soon return to normal.

"I'm no one special. Only the second son of the Earl of Shaftesbury, here to serve God and the King and apprentice to become a physician."

"The Dowager Queen is a good woman. I will happily run you through if I even hear a peep of a bad word about you from her. It is not seemly that you are alone with her."

"I will conduct myself appropriately." But he knew he couldn't promise this, and he prayed that Pummeroy wouldn't ask him to swear. He didn't.

They knocked at the door and were bidden to enter. Pummeroy bowed and took his leave. So did Agnes and Nicolette.

Right. How long could the lid be kept on this impropriety?

"Good evening, Medicus—or may I call you Evan? Thank you for coming again."

"Good evening, Milady. Yes, you may, and it's my pleasure."

Tonight, she was prepared for him, in a deep red silk gown—on any other woman, plain and in need of accessories—but on her, enough. Her braided hair was already down, and she was wearing her gold circlet band on her head. His chair was ready for him.

"The red becomes you," said Evan. "Unfortunately, I have no dye. I can always put it in later. So, the same seated position, the same countenance as last night's? Or would you prefer something different?"

It occurred to him that he was babbling again.

"Perhaps, tonight, I may be permitted a slight smile? That expression is easier to hold."

"As you wish," he replied. All was going well so far. Strictly a client and a hireling.

He assembled his materials, and then sat back, studying her. The silence was electric. Lord, keep her away from me.

He cleared his throat and took out a stylus. This would trace a thin mark on his paper that would be unnoticeable when covered with ink. This was one sketch he did not want to make a shambles of. He felt his control waver as he struggled to trace the slight curves of her breasts, the tapering of her torso to her narrow waist, her graceful hands, folded on her lap. He returned to her face. The gentle repose of her initial countenance had now been subtly replaced by something else: her eyes were alive, with anticipation. They stared at each other.

They rose and came together, eagerly grasping the other's body, lips greedy. She ran her hands through his disorderly hair, his hands fumbled with her braid.

"What are you doing to me?" he mumbled into her hair.

"Nothing that we haven't wanted since first we met," she whispered.

"We have no time."

"We have until the compline bells ring. It is enough time."

They lay arm in arm afterwards, on her bed in her inner chamber. As beautiful as she was clothed, she was even more so naked. Pale, flawless, baby-soft skin. He ran his hand down her slim thigh.

She stretched languorously. How long had it been since she'd felt this good? Perhaps once or twice with William.

"This was your first time, wasn't it?" she asked gently.

"Yes, it was. Was it obvious?"

"Only that I could see you'd never undressed a woman before."

He smiled, relieved that she'd refrained from mentioning his tentativeness as his hands explored her body. "I was afraid I wouldn't know what to do, that I'd disappoint you." She hadn't disappointed *him*, that much had been obvious. Her hands had been knowledgeable. Her hair tumbling over her shoulders, her grey eyes sparkling with pleasure, Evan thought he'd never seen anything so beautiful.

"You didn't disappoint me," she replied, smiling. She straddled him, surveying his body approvingly. She reached for a cherry and plopped it into his eager mouth. "You are beautiful, do you know that?"

"No, no one has ever called me that. My older brother is most handsome. His hair lies flat. You'd swoon at the sight of him."

"No, I wouldn't. He's not you."

She nuzzled into his neck, nibbling his ear.

Speaking of duty-bound Edward brought Evan back to his senses. "But what can I be to you?" He sat up on the bed. "See, the sun is going down and I must leave soon. My absence is surely already being noticed in the hospital. Milady, this is wrong, for both of us. If this angers you or causes you grief, I'm sorry. But surely you can see that we have no future."

Joanna sat back, wondering what she might have said that had jolted him out of the moment. Annoyed at herself for being so careless, she took the measure for the first time of the man she had just taken to her bed. Not some silly boy to distract her and pass the time, but a young man of intelligence, integrity, and undeniable talent. It was already known that he had likely saved her brother's life.

The first time she'd seen him, sitting alone, drawing, on the Limassol sea wall, she'd felt a powerful urge to meet him. She'd been immediately taken with his unusual eyes and open, guileless face. Maybe someday, she would confess to him how she'd subsequently dragged Agnes and Nicolette along the walls of Limassol and Acre, hoping to spot him again. And then, to find out that he and the gifted young medicus who'd saved her brother were one and the same? She didn't believe in coincidences like that.

She'd had Pummeroy make discreet inquiries. He'd learned that Evan's father was a respected English baron who shied away from court politics. Pummeroy had gone on to say that Evan had quickly cured several infected wounds by an unusual treatment: placing mouldy bread on top of them. Most of the other physicians were now imitating this practice, as well as placing a drug-soaked sponge over patients' noses before they underwent surgery, a technique he claimed he'd learned from the Infidels, no less. Pummeroy had sounded impressed when he described the latter. He'd had no such luxury when one of his little fingers had been amputated years earlier. People were starting to ask for Evan by name; failing that, his squat young Cornish friend. Roger de Crécy was having him draw pictures of wounded body parts for some vanity project of his own.

How easy it would be for any other ambitious, capable young man to seize this opportunity for advancement and favour. A comfortable bed, clean clothes, and a woman beside him. Her life had not always been easy with William, but, fortunately, it had not yet begun to show on her body or her face.

She took his hand. "I know that. Richard's impatient to be out of here." She turned to him. "But, no matter what, Berengaria and I are to remain here. Who knows if we can ever see each other again, once you all depart. Can we not take this pleasure, now?"

"But what about our reputations, Milady? Should this get out, and it will—"

"Please. Don't you think we're past the 'Milady' stage by now? Call me Joanna. Don't worry about me. I'm a young, rich widow—that's if Richard doesn't spend all my dowry. I'm apparently unable to conceive a child. That will handicap my chances some. But I am a king's sister, and I won't be allowed to remain widowed. However, until that marriage takes place, as long as I am not foolish or open about it, I'll be left alone. My brother understands this. Everyone does."

"But I *won't* be left alone."

"Yes, I understand, for you it is another matter." Scarcely believing that she was actually about to end it when they had only just begun, her voice caught, though she quickly regained her control. "You are young, with a fine career awaiting you. I want no part of ruining that."

He caressed her face. She looked for hesitation or regret in his eyes and saw neither, only sadness. "If it's your wish that we not see each other again, I will agree."

"It's not my wish. It's our duty. I swore an oath never to embarrass my house. Montmorencys always keep their oaths."

"Don't presume to talk to *me* about 'oaths' and 'duty'!" she snapped.

"You're right. I apologize."

She pulled him to her and kissed him heatedly. Don't ever change your hair, she thought. I'll wager every woman you know wants to run her fingers through it.

His lips responded, as she knew they would, but she pushed him back. "Now, go."

The compline bells rang. He got up and slipped on his clothes. In the outer room, he reassembled his equipment, slinging his bag over his shoulder. He turned to wave goodbye. His heart was breaking, and he hoped she couldn't see it. But no, she couldn't. She had already turned her back to him.

"Goodbye, Milady."

As he walked back down the hallway, he thought he heard something crash against a wall.

Two days later, he was surprised and touched to find an array of small pots of dyes of various colours, including a deep red, tucked under his pillow.

-X-
Ayyadieh

July had long since turned into August, and Richard was still waiting on Saladin. The sum of two hundred thousand dinars in ransom for the almost three thousand prisoners was not forthcoming. Nor was the True Cross or the return of Christian prisoners that had been promised in exchange, a good faith gesture that was now meaningless. Meanwhile, Richard had these prisoners on his hands, using up valuable time, food, supplies, and manpower in the guarding of them. The heat was appalling, and everyone was irritable. He had a sneaking suspicion that Saladin was playing him for a naïve fool.

Evan and Gurci and the others at the hospital and under the tents were starting to see fewer injuries and more of the familiar complaints of static army encampments: contagion from bad water, collected refuse, and mounting fecal matter. The only cure for that, other than treating the symptoms, was to move on, and that didn't seem to be happening. At night, Evan tried not to think of the beautiful woman cloistered only a few hundred yards away, wondering whether she ever spared him a thought, or if she'd found someone else to amuse her.

On August 19, someone started a rumour, probably false, that some of the Christian prisoners were being killed.

On August 20, Richard had had enough. He ordered his men to round up the prisoners and herd them out to a small hill called Ayyadieh, beyond Acre's walls. Saladin's army was camped just beyond. Everyone could see what was about to happen.

It was well known that Muslims preferred death by decapitation. It was considered a nobler, more merciful form of execution. But Richard knew that would take too long. So, he ordered Lord

Robert de Sablé to separate out those prisoners who seemed to be of noble birth. They were freed, to return to the Saracen camp. Then, the rest of them were ringed with lanced horsemen, and at Sablé's signal, in full view of the Muslim army, soldiers were ordered to move into the arena space created by the ring of horses and kill them all—by lance, truncheon, or sword, whatever it took. Richard sat astride his horse behind the lancers, watching the whole thing.

It took a while to kill twenty-seven hundred people—mostly men, though some women and children. Over an hour, to make sure that all of them were dead. More than a few of Richard's men made a show of sword plunging, but "missed"; that soon stopped, however, as they too succumbed to the killing fever. The prisoners all struggled, at least initially, and holding them down was time-consuming. Mothers threw themselves on their children, to no avail; all were simply run through. Everyone for miles could hear the unrelenting screams, the prayers, the pleas for mercy, the roars of outrage from the Saracen camp. Eventually, the remaining prisoners realized that struggle was futile; they knelt, submitting to the will of Allah. With that, it was easy to behead them.

Evan was one of the many who rushed up the walls to see what was happening. When he saw the horrific scene, he staggered back down the steps, gagging. He ran back to the hospital, back to his duty, but nothing could block out those cries. Everyone covered their ears in silent horror. Nothing else was possible. In the breeze wafted the stench of the blood, fear, and loosened bowels of twenty-seven hundred bodies.

Afterwards, Richard's blood-soaked men silently withdrew, leaving the pile of bodies for the Saracens to retrieve. There was no feasting that night. Inside Acre, it was eerily quiet. Richard reportedly took his supper alone, in his tent.

Muslim custom required that the bodies be buried within a day. Still, it took a while for the ditch to be dug and for the corpses to be interred in a mass grave. The rest of the day, and all night, in fact.

By morning, the task was done.

The massacre was a clear statement to Saladin. No more playing around.

The Massacre of Acre, or Ayyadieh, was the blackest stain on Richard's reign. Whatever he privately thought of it, he would always stand by his decision.

It hadn't been arbitrary; Richard had consulted with his war council, who'd approved it. His position had been impossible: With endless delays by Saladin, what was he to do? His options were few. He couldn't drag the prisoners along with him. He couldn't leave them in Acre to be expensively sheltered and fed. Sell them into slavery? That would take time and manpower, too.

Word got out that the Muslims had begun executing their Christian prisoners in retaliation, chopping the bodies in pieces.

Evan lay on his cot, wondering what kind of monster he had vowed to serve. How could anyone just look calmly on that slaughter? Worse, how could Richard's men do that to innocent women and children? Combatants, he could almost understand, although being hacked down, defenceless, was a dishonourable death for those who had so staunchly defended their city. Somehow, he would have to try to understand this blood lust. He knew that at least some of the attackers had been men he'd cured under the tent. Having been healed, with God's help, was this how they gave thanks?

Eventually, he must have drifted off. Sometime later, when the night was blackest and everyone in town seemed to have finally fallen asleep, he was poked awake. It was Nicolette, carrying a candle and holding a finger to her lips. She gestured to him to follow her.

Evan hurriedly dressed, and they quietly made their way up to the fortress. To his surprise, he was not taken to the gates, but led around the side towards a grove of olive trees and thorny bushes. She took his hand and made her way through, groping until she felt a door that she opened and promptly locked behind them. Evan had just enough time to make out that it was painted to look like stonework. Then, they descended a set of stairs, the musty dark mitigated only by Nicolette's candle. At the bottom were three tunnels, an extraordinary, forked construction. "This way, Medicus Evan."

"Where do the other tunnels go?" he asked.

"One goes straight upstairs to the west side of the fortress. This one will take us to the east side. That one there is the longest. It goes south, to the port."

Their tunnel was perhaps ninety yards long. Those Templars! Who *were* those people, anyway!

When they eventually climbed another flight of stairs and opened the door at the top, he saw that he was now inside the fortress, in an empty room on the ground floor. They had crossed under the courtyard, it looked like. Opening the door, he thought he knew where he was. At the end of this hallway should be the flight of stairs that would take him up to Joanna's quarters.

"Thank you, Nicolette. I know where to go from here."

"No, I've been ordered to take you all the way and to wait until you leave, so I can escort you safely out the door and lock it behind me."

She opened her mistress's door. "You are to go straight in," she said. "I will wait here."

He strode into Joanna's bedroom and closed the door. She was sitting on her bed, her hair loose, clothed in only a white linen nightshirt, her feet bare. Her eyes were puffy from crying.

They flew into each other's arms, both weeping, clinging to each other's live bodies in the face of so much death.

"What has he done?" she sobbed. "I knew he was capable of cruelty, but this!"

"I know. We're all in shock."

"I couldn't look. But who could not hear?"

He held her, stroking her back, murmuring, "It's all right, we're here together," but knowing neither of them would ever feel quite cleansed of this day.

"Why didn't anyone try to stop him?" she mumbled into his shoulder.

"Because we can't pick and choose what orders to follow, Joanna. They will have to make their peace with God somehow about what they've done."

One of the executioners evidently could not make his peace: he had walked out to sea and, weighed down by mail, drowned himself.

"There will be no peace from this. Those people's souls will never be at rest." She turned toward her bed. "Come lie with me, please?"

And so, they made love. They took their time, tenderly relearning each other's bodies, extending the moment as long as they could until their desire could no longer be denied. Two people trying to restore a bit of love to their worlds after a day of such wickedness, to heal each other, just a little.

Afterwards, they dabbed one another with a dampened, scented towel. Joanna had lived in heat like this for over a decade and was used to it. Evan couldn't see how he ever would be.

"How do you stand it, seeing this carnage day after day?" she asked.

He paused a moment. "Well, it isn't always carnage. Lately, my biggest challenge has been figuring out what to do about someone's ingrown toenail."

"But isn't it gratifying that you've fixed that toenail?"

"Oh yes. That's what keeps me going. And, thanks to our interventions, some people do recover from horrific injuries. Left untreated, they would surely have died in agony.

"But when it's bad, the only way I can cope is to separate my horror from the medical problem in front of me. It's like a mask I put on when I start work in the morning. These men need me to do my job and I mustn't disappoint them."

"But when you take off your mask, at night?"

"Yes, when the mask comes off, it's like those screams of agony pierce my brain. It's why I draw. I can't go to sleep with the day still present in my mind. It's meant a lot to me, having you in my thoughts."

He would not tell her about the stench of rotting and burning flesh that no one could ignore—amputated limbs, tossed on the rubbish heap beyond the east walls. Saladin's forces were directly downwind, of course. But if the wind changed direction … Always, he had to remind himself that the young men whose body parts were burning on that heap were alive, to live, love, and sire children. He needed that hope.

She touched her lips to his cheek and nestled closer.

"A few of us weep in our cots. It helps to know that we're all suffering in some way. Some work through it in the taverns, gambling dens, and whorehouses, but that would shame my house. We don't judge each other; we're all coping as best we can. The older men are tough. Perhaps one gets inured to it after a while."

Knowing she had to pull him out of this dark space, she asked, "What do you keep in that pouch on your neck?" She'd taken it off herself this time.

He reached over to open the bag. He showed her the letter of credit.

"Those Templars are clever and efficient!" she said admiringly. "They're an organization to watch."

"Yes, I know! I've been in that tunnel."

"And what's this?"

He showed her the tiny frog. "My mother pressed it into my hand just as I was leaving. It has brought me good fortune so far." He kissed her eyelids tenderly.

"How adorable! Why a frog?"

"It's on our crest. It symbolizes harmony."

"Such a gentle creature. Ours is nothing so inoffensive. *We* must have fierce, snarling lions, claws bared."

"Tell me about your family," he said, as she gently swabbed his leg.

She gave him a rueful smile. "From the little you have said to me about your own, I think you were fortunate indeed. You have known very little loneliness or unhappiness in your life, am I right? You have this innocence, still, about you."

"Not entirely innocent! I've seen a few things, been a few places."

"Not quite the same as surviving in a golden cage, day after day, one's whole life."

"Tell me, then."

She lay back. "All right. It's a bit of a long story, I'm afraid."

Evan smiled. "I have till the cock crows."

She smiled back. "It may take that long! Well," she began, "I am the seventh of eight, but, do you know, half of us have died? Out of five sons, only Richard and John are left. We all wonder who's next. Strange as it is to say this, my mother could well outlive us all."

Evan wondered how women bore this. He would have had an older sister, Elizabeth, but she'd died shortly after her birth. Mama still lay flowers on her grave on her birthdays.

Guessing his thoughts, "I don't know how Mother bore that. I was enough of a wreck when Bohemond died."

"You *have* given birth, then? That was your baby's name?"

She paused. "Yes."

Evan waited, realizing she would elaborate in her own time.

She continued, "Mother was under house arrest when Henry, Geoffrey, and Matilda died, but she's not one to wear her grief publicly, in any case. After she moved to Poitiers in 1170, we rarely saw our father. And then, after the Great Revolt in '73—remember? when she conspired with my brothers against him?—she was confined back in England. We lived in various castles, wherever Father took it in his head to imprison her next. We were treated well, but his spies were everywhere. Actually, I was glad enough to be married to escape those wretched castles and Mother's bitterness."

"Your father had a long memory, to punish her so."

"Sixteen years' worth of long memory. She was only released when Richard took the throne."

She paused to organize her thoughts. "If you ask me, it's my sister Eleanor—Ellie—who's the best of us. She's married to Alfonso in Castile. So far, nine children, four of whom have died. But she keeps pushing them out, and I understand she rules very ably beside her husband. The kind of marriage Mother could have had if she hadn't started interfering.

"John is Mother's favourite. He's spoiled and useless and untrustworthy, and now that Richard's married, he's unlikely to become king, thank God. Richard was never meant or trained to be a king. But he was given Aquitaine when he was thirteen, and he's had to fight off rebellions ever since. He's never governed. Subordinates do that. Instead, he fights. It's what he does. And I'll tell you right now that there's no one better. He's like Ares."

"You'll get no argument from me on that."

"And yet, my mother did teach him the arts. He has a beautiful singing voice, and he's a master lutist. He speaks more tongues than I do. He writes poetry, did you know that?"

"Yes, I'd heard. He has many talents."

"He would tease me, call me 'Jojo.' He taught me sword craft when Mother wasn't around. I was four! Even if it was a small wooden sword he made himself." She laughed at the memory. Admirably imitating Richard's bluff voice, "'You never know when you might have to defend a castle!' he'd say. Richard taught Ellie and me to stare fear in the eyes. He made us climb trees, hold worms. I'm good on a horse and on a hunt. He'd pick me up when I fell and hold me in his lap when I cried."

A shadow crossed her face as the memory of the day's events muscled its way to the front again. "He does have a kind, sensitive side, believe it or not. It must be in there somewhere, still."

"Had you ever met your husband before you married him?"

"No, I was introduced to him on our wedding day. I was twelve."

"Were you afraid?"

"Do you have sisters?"

"Yes, one, Marie."

"Well then, you must have an idea of what it's like for women like me. From the earliest time I can remember, my sisters and I were raised to accept that we'd be dutifully married to some prince or duke, and we would not complain. We were to bear these men as many children as is humanly possible to secure whatever succession. That's all princesses are good for. We are nothing but two-legged brood mares. I knew that going in, so, no, I wasn't too scared about my 'marital duties,' not that I knew anything about those."

"Marie couldn't wait. Personally, I think she knew all about her 'marital duties.'"

She laughed. "She's fortunate, then! 'It's easier if you just submit,' I was told. Mostly, I was frightened of being alone, in an alien land, away from everyone I knew."

"What was he like?"

"You mean, on our wedding night, or in general?"

"Both. Neither, if you don't want to talk about it."

"I don't mind. He was a kind man. His people call him William the Good. I eventually came to care for him deeply. But Bohemond only survived a month, and I couldn't conceive again. His physicians could not discover the reason."

He took her hand. "I hope you don't blame yourself. The quality of the man's seed is equally important."

She smiled playfully at him. "*Voyons, entre nous, on se tutoie, non?*"

Evan was startled. She was giving permission to use the intimate *tu* with each other, and it gladdened him. She was his social superior, by quite a lot. Even between equals, many couples took years to cross the barrier of intimacy from *vous* to *tu*. Marie had told him that her in-laws never did.

"As you wish, *Ton Altesse*," he murmured, his lips brushing her neck.

She giggled. "Well, if we're going to be talking about marital duties and men's seed, it only seems fitting, don't you think?"

After a moment, she took a breath and continued. "I think the more intelligent ones in my class know that—about the man's seed—even if the Church won't admit it. Look at my mother. Louis annulled their marriage because she couldn't produce a male heir fast enough for him. Then she turned right around, married my father, and produced five boys! What sweet revenge! But I do think something's wrong with *me*. All the other women in my family breed like rabbits."

She turned to him. "Evan, you can't imagine the pressure on us to produce an heir. Berengaria's already starting to worry. 'Why am I not with child by now?' she asked me the other day. It was all I could do not to tell her that she needs a husband who wants to try."

"Was he much older than you?" Evan imagined a lecherous old goat with rotting teeth and crooked fingers.

"He was twenty-three. Actually, I thought him handsome."

Evan's revulsion at the thought of the lecherous old goat *touching* her immediately switched to wild jealousy. He wondered briefly, which is worse?

"This is difficult for you, I can see," he said. "You don't need to talk about it."

"No, I want to. It gets worse, and I've had no one else to tell it to."

She took a deep breath and pushed on. "Anyway, eventually, William became desperate for an heir, and I was desperate to give him one. I prayed, I took potions, we tried every position we'd ever heard of, from the uncomfortable to the comical."

Her voice now a monotone, "He told me, 'Joanna, if you wish to take a lover, I will look the other way, as long as you don't make a fool out of me.' I tried that. It didn't work, either."

She looked for a reaction on Evan's face. "Maybe I *shouldn't* be telling you all this! Women's affairs, are you shocked? Do you think me wanton?"

"Not at all. You forget my trade. I'm listening, I'm interested. I want to know all about you."

She looked into his eyes and saw that he was sincere. Oh Evan, you are a gem. "Well, I thought surely he'd annul our marriage, and I would be sent back to Mother in disgrace. But, it seems, he had come to love me, too, and he never did. Perhaps he might have, with time, but he died of the wasting disease. Such pain. He was only thirty-five."

"I'm sorry."

"Yes, I still miss him deeply. The day of Richard's wedding? That was the first day I didn't wear mourning black. I'd decided it was time. One of us had to live. And then I met you. It was like a sign, don't you think?"

"Me, I happened to feel a need to go alone to the sea wall that evening. I thought you were just some local grandee's wife and promptly forgot about you." He winked at her.

She laughed again and poked him in the ribs. He loved her laugh. It was warm and spontaneous.

"But, please! Enough of my prattling! Tell me about your own family."

And so he did—as much as he was at liberty to tell. He described a life of immense privilege and learning and stability, if not immense *wealth*. He spoke of loving, supportive parents, and of their devoted servants.

"I don't know anyone like you," she said when he fell silent.

"I don't think I realized until this moment how very fortunate I've been."

"You've given me a memory of a different sort of life, one that I might yet have. It's possible. I can hope."

"But not with each other. There is no magic that can make that happen, is there?"

"No, I suppose not. So, *mi corazón*, let's make the best of this night, until it's time for you to go."

As he took her again into his arms, he asked, "What is that? Spanish?"

"Yes, just a phrase I picked up. I love the sound of Spanish, don't you?"

A little while later, she said, "Thank you, Evan, for coming tonight. For a time, you almost made me forget."

"Yes, it was almost like it didn't happen." The heaviness in his spirit was beginning to creep back, and he ruthlessly pushed it down. "Do you know, I was aboard the *Reine-de-Sicile* from Cyprus, and I never saw either of you."

"You were one of those cooped up below whenever we took it in our heads to get a breath of fresh air?"

"That's right. Bets were taken on whether you really existed. All we knew was that we were shouted at to get our worthless asses below *right away.*"

"I'm sorry for that. That was my brother's doing. For our 'safety,' he said. I wouldn't have minded looking at someone else other than Berengaria all day!

"Fate," she said, shaking her head. "Driving us together and pushing us apart at the same time. I dare not ask it to make up its mind."

When he finally slipped back into his hospital cot, the first cock crowed but a few minutes later.

That afternoon, Evan was on the way to the apothecary to get more thread for stitching when he collided with a Templar. "My apologies, Medicus, I wasn't attending to where I was going."

Evan bowed, accepting the man's apology, and carried on with his business. Hmm, he thought a little later, how did he know I'm only a medicus? Reaching into his pocket for a rag with which to wipe his hands, his fingers alit on something slender and hard and metal. He hid behind a pillar. It was a key.

-XI-
A Careless Nick of a Knife

The key gave them four more nights. Each night, they joyfully reconvened, grateful that they'd managed one more encounter, certain that this time must be the last because Richard was desperate to get out of this place. They always needed to talk, afterwards. By tacit agreement, Ayyadieh was never brought up.

She was genuinely curious about how he spent his days. Evan learned he needn't filter to accommodate her supposed tender, feminine sensibilities, though he still censored the worst of it. She critiqued his sketches. He told her about his successes, as well as his failures. He talked about the frustration of recognizing a condition but being powerless to do much about it.

"Like William's wasting disease?"

"Yes, like that."

That very day, he'd lost a patient, one Wilfred of Rye. He was a year younger than Evan. It had started with an innocent cut. Wilfred had been whittling, a pastime of his. He was fashioning a sailing ship when the knife slipped and he gashed his left index finger. He bound it and tried to forget about it. By the time he visited the hospital four days later, feeling embarrassed over such a minor thing, the finger was black, too late for maggots or even mouldy bread. Evan amputated the finger, cauterized the stump, and dressed it.

Wilfred said, "I'm going to die, aren't I?" His eyes were frightened.

Evan said, "Of course not! You are young and strong, and you'll recover."

"I think not," Wilfred said quietly.

The following day, Wilfred's pulse was fast, his breathing shallow and rapid, and he was feverish.

He whispered to Evan, "It won't be long now, will it?"

Evan looked into that trusting young man's eyes and disobeyed Joseph's firm instruction. "No, not long. I'm so sorry. You're in God's hands now."

Wilfred lost consciousness an hour later. Evan held his hand as a priest administered last rites.

Blood poisoning, from a simple, careless nick of a knife. Just as lethal as any arrow wound. Wilfred had planned to use what he made on the crusade to get married. He'd wanted to continue apprenticing as a carpenter upon his return.

Evan felt irrationally angered by Wilfred's death. He had seen death many times before, but this was the first time he felt especially useless, powerless, and ignorant.

"Joanna, do you know how difficult it is to see a condition that must surely be easily treatable in some future time, but there's nothing we can do now?" Please don't ask me to elaborate, he thought.

Joanna found Evan's remarks curious. What did he mean by that? What future time? Physic was physic. It hadn't changed in a thousand years.

Not for the first time, she sensed that Evan was holding back, like he knew something he couldn't share. Given time, she could worm secrets out of anyone. If only they had the time.

Meanwhile, she only said, "No, I can't imagine. But, still, you are fortunate. You're doing exactly what you want to do."

"I know I have no desire to be an army surgeon."

Then he turned to her and asked, "If you had a choice, what would *you* do?"

The question stunned her. She had never, once, thought of it. She lay back on the bed and stared at the bare wall opposite them. An immense brown spider had made its home there. The local servants urged her to leave it alone: they said such creatures stayed on the walls, generally. *Generally?* They were harmless and ate other insects, like mosquitos. *Stare fear in the eyes.* One small thing of many she'd had to get used to in this strange land.

He gave her time. Finally, she said, "You're going to laugh."

"I promise, I won't."

"Well, once I got a little older, I was pretty good as a helpmate to William. He learned to trust my advice. If I really had a choice,

I would want to be like Ellie, or my mother, or yours. Even if she can't wield power directly, from what you've said, she certainly has power and has great influence over your father. And she's in charge whenever he's away, right?"

He nodded.

"Has the demesne fallen apart during those times?"

"Absolutely not. She's very capable."

"See? There you have it. So is my mother. But I'd need a husband wise enough to seek my counsel and not care that I'm barren. Not very imaginative, is it?"

"On the contrary. You're of Henry's and Eleanor's blood. You are not their daughter for nothing. You could still get your wish, you know."

She eyed him cynically. "So, what we both want is to keep doing what we're good at, but in different circumstances."

On the fourth night, his bag packed for departure the following morning, he thoughtlessly asked, "Do you want your key back?"

"Why? Do you think I may want to give it to someone else?"

"Well, yes, in case—"

"In case what? Someone more 'suitable' comes along? You think me so faithless? You're not giving either of us much credit."

"No, I didn't mean that! Just that—"

"Yes, I know. We have no future. Keep it to remember me. In any case, it's a duplicate."

He didn't want his last moments with her to end in silly misunderstandings and cursed himself for his stupidity. He reached for the knife he always had on his person.

"What are you doing?"

"I need something more than a cold, hard key to remember you by." Lifting a strand of her hair, he said, "May I?"

"Of course."

She got out of bed to rummage in a drawer. "Wait, here's a bit of ribbon to tie it with. Oh, I almost forgot. Berengaria and I picked you some of these today." It was a small bag of rosehips. He kissed her.

He might have been wiser to say what he felt: "I love you."

-XII-
Arsuf

On August 25, Richard and his army pulled up stakes and started their march down the coast. Only washerwomen were allowed to trail behind the army. All others, including Evan, found themselves back on the ship, slowly keeping pace with the army ashore. This strategy was something different from past crusades, and every man in the medical corps was grateful they were not being put in harm's way, trailing at the back as was the custom, slogging their way in the ferocious heat. All of the *Saint-Luc*'s passengers were together again, on *Misericordia*. This was a captured, rechristened Muslim ship, spacious enough to serve as a makeshift hospital.

Richard arranged the army in a layered formation: supply train closest to the beach, protected by his knights, who were in turn protected by the infantry. For the time being, these men would absorb most of the injuries inflicted by Muslim arrows. At both ends rode the Templars and Hospitallers; their positions were switched daily.

Mindful that this would be a long, difficult march, Richard had his men walk only four miles per day. Still, the weight of their armour, combined with sunstroke, took a toll. Adding to this were the tarantulas that came out in droves at night. Evan had known of the soothing properties of aloe vera since Messina, but aboard ship all he could do was apply cool compresses to the welts. Nasty little yellow scorpions killed a few marchers foolish enough not to shake out their boots in the morning, prompting a life-long habit for Evan. The marchers were harassed by Saracen arrows every step of the way, and it took constant exhortation and encouragement from Richard to keep his men in line, not to give in to the temptation to break ranks and counterattack.

The crusaders didn't take heavy casualties; most of the time, the arrows lodged harmlessly in their armour, making them resemble pin cushions more than anything else. The injured were rowed out, treated, and rowed back when they were sufficiently well to resume the march. Pressed by Evan and Gurci, Crécy persuaded the other physicians to move the injured up on deck, shaded under linen canvas; everyone noticed the improved morale, not to mention their more rapid recovery.

On September 7, the army emerged from the forest at Arsuf, relieved that the forest hadn't been set ablaze while they traversed it. Immediately, they found themselves surrounded by Saladin's forces in an open field. Saladin had apparently decided that harassing Richard's forces was a wasted effort; at last ready for battle, his forces easily outnumbered the crusaders. Seeing this, Richard tightened the formation and ordered his archers to launch their arrows; all others waited for the clear signal of six clarion calls before launching a counterattack.

Meanwhile, Saladin's forces made the most fearsome noises possible to disorient their foes: clashing cymbals, blowing horns, and high-pitched screaming rocked the field, but Richard kept waiting for the correct moment, urging his troops not to be agitated by the noise. Under attack at the rear, order started to break down. The Hospitallers pleaded to begin the counterattack but were told to wait for the signal. As well, the ranks of archers were showing the strain of being forced to fire and reload walking backwards. At some point, perhaps due to some miscommunication, the Hospitallers charged.

Richard realized he must act. With the enemy surging in much too close, too crowded to retreat—an unbelievable turn of fortune—he ordered the attack. Superior English crossbows obliterated the front rows. Then he ordered his cavalry to charge. There is not much an opposing army on foot can do against a concentrated charge of knights, leaning in on their lances with all their weight behind them.

Back and forth Richard rode, calling orders here, encouraging others there. The Saracens regrouped and pushed back, only to be mowed down again, and again. Finally, they retreated to the Arsuf forest.

From what looked like certain slaughter, Richard and his troops had somehow emerged triumphant.

As they patched up the wounded that evening, everyone agreed that they'd seen a magnificent victory. Seven hundred had died—the most notable of whom was Lord Robert de Sablé—but they had taken easily ten times that number with them. Emirs and other men of rank died that day; the plunder was rich. As Evan collapsed into his hammock that night, he had to admit that whatever else he felt about Richard the man, he was a splendid commander, whether by birth or by long training.

The march resumed. Saladin had no choice but to raze the villages in their path.

-XIII-
An Arrow to the Leg

Seventeen days after they left Acre, on September 10, the army reached Jaffa, whose port and walls Saladin had largely destroyed, and began immediate reconstruction. Richard was now faced with a dilemma: Head straight inland to Jerusalem and accomplish what he'd set out to do, or rest, recover, and repair in Jaffa? Richard himself was itching to head straight inland, but was called to listen to calmer souls who urged him to first refortify Jaffa; if he didn't, Saladin would have a base from which to attack from behind, and Jerusalem itself was well fortified. If he didn't, he'd be looking at another siege of Acre, but this time from the wrong side of it.

Something else: he'd lost men. The ranks of his forces had thinned through both attrition and death. He elected to remain in Jaffa and appealed to the Pope to see if more men could be summoned to the cause.

In the meantime, medical personnel rowed ashore to repair and get the hospital up and running again.

On September 29, a band of Muslims attacked a crusader foraging party. When word reached the crusader camp, Richard and some of his cavalry rode out in support. In the skirmish that followed, he took an arrow to his calf.

That evening, a Templar approached Evan as he was binding an injured man's leg. He said, "The King requires your immediate presence. He has a wound he would like you to inspect."

"Ah. If that's the case, may I also request Sir Roger de Crécy's attendance? He is our senior physician and is most experienced in these matters."

"What do you want, Montmorency?" Crécy muttered. "Can't you see I'm busy?"

When Evan explained who had summoned him, Crécy leapt to clean himself up.

In the royal tent, Richard was lying propped up on his litter. Even in pain, he dominated the room.

After Evan and Crécy bowed, Richard got right to the point. "I have an arrow wound in my leg. It isn't serious, but I've been told that you have some skill with repairing wounds."

Evan replied, "If you don't mind, Your Grace, may we see?"

Richard nodded to one of his attending physicians, who unbound the dressing. The arrowhead had been removed by pushing it through to the opposite side of his calf. The exit wound had been sealed with lard. The entry had been treated with wine, herbs and honey, the latter being a strong disinfectant.

He and Crécy exchanged glances and nodded. "This looks good, Your Grace, but it should be stitched."

"But, Your Grace, if we stitch it, the laudable pus will not form," protested one of the physicians. Evan presumed this was Sir Ralph Besace, Richard's chief physician.

Evan replied, "It has been our experience that the wound will heal more quickly if it is stitched, dressed, and kept clean."

Richard trained his eye on Crécy. "What's your opinion on this, Crécy?"

He replied, "Your Grace, in battlefield situations, we have found that there's no time to wait for the pus. Wounds do heal more rapidly if stitched and dressed right away. I would be happy to brief my esteemed colleagues here." This was an enormous concession for him. Crécy was contravening centuries of doctrine with this declaration, in favour of the undeniable evidence in front of his eyes. But he was also canny enough to attach himself to a young star on the rise.

Richard looked from one to the other and back at his physicians. "Do as this young man suggests."

Besace bowed his assent. Evan sensed the hostility, aware that he was challenging everything this very experienced physician had believed his whole professional life. Just as he'd finally got somewhere with Crécy, he was going to have to start all over again with this old buzzard. He'd need Crécy to grease the wheels.

Richard said, "All of you, leave us, except for Montmorency."

Startled, they all bowed and retreated. Being alone in the presence of the King was unnerving. Feeling vulnerable and unsure what to do, Evan opted for silence.

Richard made a show of inspecting his quill, then he turned his eyes on Evan, studying him. It took all Evan had to return his raking gaze, certain that every impious thought and deed he had ever committed was written all over his face. Eventually, Richard said, "You have made a most favourable impression on the Dowager Queen."

"Thank you, Your Grace. I have been honoured to sketch a couple of likenesses of her, at her request."

"Alone with her, in her chambers, is my information."

Absolutely guilty. No point denying it.

"Yes, Your Grace." He waited for the swinging sword to lop off his head.

The steel-grey eyes stared at him again. "It is not my concern what my widowed sister does until she marries again. Her sense of duty is too strong for her make a fool of herself. Can I expect the same of you? Can I assume proper discretion?"

Evan stood, silent for a moment. What should he say? Every time he was within one foot of Joanna he made a fool of himself.

Finally, he said, "My family's honour has been instilled in me since I was little. I would never knowingly dishonour our house."

"Good, we understand each other, then. God's feet, you will answer to me if you hurt her in any way. In the meantime, your skills are needed here, with me. My physicians are capable, but someone needs to bring them into the twelfth century before it ends, and I believe you're the one to do it."

"Thank you, Your Grace. May I bring two people with me? Sir Roger and a surgeon named Gurci Morgant? All three of us are in agreement about how best to treat battlefield injuries and illnesses. Sir Roger is also efficient at organizing people and procuring supplies. We work well as a team, and my task will be simpler."

"Safety in numbers, is what you're thinking."

"Exactly right, Your Grace."

"Very well. I will see that quarters are prepared for you."

"I am humbled by your generosity, Your Grace. Now, if you will allow me to see to your wound?"

-XIV-
The Wayward Stroke

Richard's leg wound indeed healed quickly, and within a couple of days he was up and restless to be at it again. While the troops rested up and repaired Jaffa, negotiations with Saladin continued over the next few weeks. Then, Richard caught wind of a possible attack on Acre. He sped up the coast to retrieve Berengaria and Joanna and shore up the moral fibre of the garrison there. The men were reputed to be enjoying the pleasures of Acre more than seeing to its stalwart defence and repair of the walls.

Prior to the siege and the massacre, Acre had been renowned for its nightlife and brothels. Once the situation stabilized, such venues and activities resurged. The Romani women were especially popular in the local taverns: although fully dressed, they danced in the most erotic and enticing manner, swaying and wiggling their hips. The men went wild; only burly Romani men prevented wholesale pandemonium, throwing overly enthusiastic audience members back into their seats.

Such lascivious behaviour was a persistent issue with crusaders in the Holy Land. Living here had its pleasures, no doubt: warm climate, abundance of food, elegant architecture, beautiful women, affable Arab hosts. Too long here and their fierce sense of purpose and righteous morality would trickle away like water in a leaky vase. Too long, and people might start to question what they were *doing* here.

Evan was starting to wonder just what he was doing here himself. The sorts of injuries he'd been treating lately were sunburn, bad backs, infected blisters, digestive complaints. Trickiest of his tasks was soothing the injured pride of Besace, whose nose was still out of joint that this *boy*, a mere *medicus*, had been admitted to Richard's inner ranks. Worse, he'd dragged another mere boy with him.

Evan took care to ask Besace's advice when in doubt. Some of the time, he followed it.

He saw the *Trenc-la-Mer* sail back into Jaffa harbour, and he watched as the royal threesome disembarked, willing her to look for him. She didn't. Joanna and Berengaria were hustled off to the best quarters in town—not a fortress, but the former abode of some Muslim grandee whose home had likely survived only by bribing Saladin. Richard strode off to his tent.

Evan stayed awake for seven nights, awaiting a summons that never came, feeling in turn bewildered, anxious, and angry.

On the eighth day after the ladies' arrival, a Templar—not Pummeroy—strode into the royal hospital tent and planted himself beside Evan. Evan looked up from washing his hands after attending to a *fluxus*-struck knight and asked, "Can I help you?"

The Templar replied, stiffly, "The Queen understands that you have a talent for portraits and wishes you to attempt one of her, at your earliest convenience."

The Queen *understands.* "I take it you mean Queen Berengaria?"

"Yes, Medicus Montmorency."

An inchoate rage stirred in him. "After supper today, then?" The Templar agreed to fetch him right after vespers.

Gurci grinned at him. "Quite a way with the ladies, does our Evan have. Had I known that scratching a few curves and lines on paper would bring me such success, I'd have considered another career."

"Be careful what you wish for," Evan muttered, echoing a favourite aphorism of his mother's. He was still angry at the sketch of a spurting penis that he'd found etched in the dirt beside his cot one day.

"Don't let those idiots bother you," Gurci urged. "They're just envious. But, my friend, be careful. Remember Iracus."

"I think you mean Icarus, and I'm less worried about being melted than I am about the sharp sword of the King's outrage."

Gurci himself had scuffed over a couple of such drawings before Evan had seen them.

He hadn't intended to betray his friend's secret. It had just come out, and he still felt bad about it. Some of the other physicians, doubtless envious of this aristocratic boy who suddenly seemed to be practically running things, and having noticed his absence from the brothels and taverns, were wondering if he was aware humans came in two sexes.

Gurci had scoffed, "You should be so fortunate, you dickless wonders. He's been fertilizing the royal garden for months. And this stays here, right?"

"*Riiight*," they all breathed, impressed, and even more envious.

The penis drawings had started right afterwards.

Roger de Crécy didn't miss much, and he had overheard the exchange. He'd heard the gossip—besides, it was hard to ignore those knights coming in and out of the hospital—and dearly wished to know how Evan had come to the Dowager Queen's attention.

He drew him aside and said, "Boy, be careful. You're running with *royalty* now. Don't you know how fickle they are? They can swing you from the gibbets as quickly as they elevate you."

"I know that, Milord. But what am I to do if I am summoned? I must go, mustn't I?"

There being no actual proof of anything untoward in their relationship—being caught in flagrante delicto would help—Crécy doubted that the boy was sarding the King's sister. He very much wanted to come right out and ask him; no matter what the answer, he'd be in a fine position to offer all sorts of fatherly or, at least, worldly advice. In his youth, he had cut quite a swath through the Parisian demoiselles, if he said so himself, before he married Lady Anne. But this was the closest Crécy had ever got to royalty; if things went wrong for Montmorency, he could take down both himself and the Morgant boy, merely by association.

Montmorency seemed not to grasp how quickly his star had ascended, and he seemed distinctly unawed by the company he was keeping. It was almost as if he considered himself one of them. How had he come to be that way? He'd doubtless been raised to be aware of his place in the tightly ordered scheme of things. It was the way the world worked. No good could possibly come of this association.

Crécy's heart wrenched at the great hurt that could very likely come this fine young man's way.

Finally, Crécy said, "Yes, you must obey a royal summons. But exercise the highest discretion. Keep your mouth laced shut. If anyone asks you anything about this at all, look him straight in the eye and say you refuse to dignify that with a reply."

The Templar came as promised and escorted him through the city walls, through its narrow, winding streets, and, finally, to a large, ordinary-looking door that interrupted a high, thick wall. The only thing special about it was the half-dozen guards at the entryway. Through the door was a courtyard and a substantial, though rather plain, one-storey residence.

From the unassuming exterior, he was not expecting the gorgeously tessellated hallway within, and he had to pause to stare in awe: tiled from floor to ceiling in jewel-like, star-shaped patterns of sea-blue and white. This hallway gave onto the central garden, the surrounding arched columns of which were also intricately tiled. Such elegance, such a feminine sensibility, compared to the stone abodes he'd grown up in! The concept of a living space as beautiful and tranquil, as opposed to functional and bustling, was a new pleasure for him.

Ah, roses, good. He wondered briefly if he could prevail on Joanna and Berengaria again for the hips. At the far end of the garden, by the pool, sat Queen Berengaria and three attendants.

He bowed deeply to her.

Gesturing to a stool placed in front of her, she said, "Medicus Montmorency, please do sit. Thank you for coming on such short notice. My sister-in-law speaks highly of you and I thought perhaps a small, portable likeness of me might please my husband."

"I'm honoured to try, Your Highness. I'm only just learning how to do human figures."

"I'm sure he'll be delighted with it."

As Evan set up his supplies, he thought about that. Something was off about Berengaria and Richard. People were talking about it, in hushed voices at night in their cots. Everyone knew aristocratic marriages were a stab in the dark as far as compatibility went, but for a newly married man, he seemed curiously unwilling to be long in his bride's company. Rumours even floated around about local prostitutes snuck into his tent from time to time. Well, he was charged with important matters, much was on his mind, or so went the consensus. Plenty of time to get started on an heir once this campaign was over.

Berengaria was modestly though elegantly clothed in an embroidered, pale pink dress, veiled and wimpled. She wore a large cross around her neck that seemed heavy for her small frame. She had a pretty face that just missed being beautiful. However, it held little of Joanna's strength, and, dare he say, intelligence.

Her best feature was her unusual eyes: one might say they were black, but there were gold lights in them. He'd never seen eyes like that.

She asked, "How would you like me to sit?"

"How you're sitting is suitable, Your Highness, but I believe the most favourable portrait of you would be of your face. Your eyes are remarkable, and I would like to capture them accurately."

She nodded, unsurprised. "However you feel is best." She settled herself into a placid pose and arranged her face into an equally placid smile.

He settled down to his task, chasing away the persistent, other thoughts that crowded into his mind as he worked. They remained silent, Berengaria similarly lost in her own thoughts.

After a while, as he stretched to work out a kink in his back, she asked him, "What is your opinion so far of the Holy Land, Medicus Montmorency?"

Seeing an opportunity for an actual sign of emotion in her face, he replied, "My acquaintance is scant, being confined as I am to the hospitals, but what I've seen of it is fascinating."

"Yes, Jaffa makes a pleasant change for us."

He said, "Your journey to Sicily and here were difficult ones."

"Oh yes, but every comfort was provided to us."

"Your husband is a brave man and an admirable commander."

She fingered her cross. "Yes, I pray every day for his safe return to me."

Evan thought, Return from what? The hazardous royal *tent* where he spends all his time?

He almost jumped out of his skin and his quill slipped when a gentle hand was laid on his shoulder, then quickly removed.

"Good evening, Medicus Montmorency. I'm sorry I startled you. The breeze is stronger here than in my chambers. I hope you don't mind if I sit here and watch you work?"

Willing his heart to stop pounding, he managed to croak, "Not at all, Your Highness. Unfortunately, I can't work much longer, as we are rapidly losing our light." He couldn't bring himself to look at her.

She took a seat on a bench beside Berengaria, right in his line of sight, Agnes and Nicolette behind her.

Addressing Berengaria, she said, "Your Highness, what the medicus has done so far is a good likeness. I believe you will be pleased. Pity, that wayward stroke there."

"No matter, I can make another picture," Evan mumbled.

He worked silently for a little while longer, drained dry of banal chitchat. Agnes and Nicolette exchanged puzzled glances. He wiped away a bead of sweat that was making its way down his cheek. Birds chirped. The fountain tinkled.

"I love Infidel courtyard gardens, don't you, Medicus?" said that so-familiar, honey-warm voice. "They're like cloister garths, only prettier. I will miss them when we must leave."

"Yes, most restful."

Berengaria joined in, "And the tiled columns are particularly elegant, are they not? Surprising, in a relatively modest home."

"Yes, indeed, Your Highness."

A peskily determined fly seemed hell-bent on trodding over his newly laid ink. A long, thick silence as he bore down on his task.

She said, "You are looking well, Medicus. Your beard becomes you."

"Thank you. And you as well, Your Highness." He swatted at the fly again. Indeed, she *was* looking well; in a vivid yellow, silk bliaut, trimmed in white, she stood out like tansy in a bouquet of daisies. He decided she looked best in strong colours.

The beard was recent. While he'd enjoyed the breeze on his clean-shaven face in this heat, since Arsuf, he and Gurci had been too busy to seek out a barber.

Another silence. Berengaria had finally given him something he could work with: interest and curiosity. Her eyes darted back and forth as she took in this drippingly stilted exchange.

Finally, the compline bell rang to end his wretchedness. He looked pleadingly up at Berengaria, who picked up on her cue. "Goodness! *Tempus fugit!* We must let Medicus Montmorency return before it gets too dark."

Evan stood to hurriedly gather his supplies. "Your Highness," he said to Berengaria, "I will make a copy of this picture. I'll see that you get it before this time tomorrow." He bowed deeply to her and Joanna.

Berengaria stood to leave and so did all the other women. "Thank you ever so much. This has been most enjoyable … and interesting for me. I bid you a good evening."

On the way back to his tent, Evan seethed. What was *that* about? What was she trying to do, torture him? May hell's dogs tear her throat out, then!

No, not that, he thought miserably as he lay on his cot, thinking of that lovely, slender throat.

Why was she doing this to him?

-XV-
"I am the toy."

Evan missed supper the following day so that he could redo Berengaria's portrait. He walked it to her residence himself, instructing the guards to see that she got it. He fumed as he downed a quick meal of fried chickpea balls from a nearby stand, thinking even villeins sat down to supper. Then he hurried straight to the safety of his cot. Trying vainly to get to sleep, he raged that those two ladies had reduced him to a simpering sycophant.

As if he didn't have better things to do!

This uncertainty—this *disharmony*—was new to Evan, and, being a true Montmorency, it crazed him like a pebble in his boot. He was short with Gurci, who barked back at him to take out his female problems on his cot. He was distracted at work, which deranged him even further. He reviewed their last conversation in Acre again and again. It had to be that asinine comment of his about the key, that was it.

He thought about Crécy's warning. Was this what people like Joanna did when they were bored or angry with someone? Drop them like a hot platter? And watch with pleasure as they shatter on the ground?

What if he got a note to her, begging her forgiveness? But whom could he trust with that note? He even started wondering if he could sneak into the compound, hidden in a wagon or something. But the thought of his embarrassment and dishonour if any of this went awry sent him back into agonies of frustration.

A fortnight after that sketching session, now into November, he was nudged awake. It was Nicolette. She raised her fingers to her lips and beckoned him to follow her. The full moon gave sufficient illumination that no candle was necessary.

"Is there a tunnel in these quarters, too?" he whispered as they made their way rapidly and stealthily through the empty streets.

She smiled. "No, merely six sleeping guards whose wine has been altered."

This angered him anew. Who did she think she was, summoning him at her merest whim? The spoiled, entitled arrogance of the woman!

True enough, all six were sitting propped against the wall, snoring loudly. They entered the residence. Past the garden, on the far side, through a series of rooms, they came to a door.

Nicolette said, "The drug is not a long-lasting one. You should try to leave before the matins bell rings."

Inside was a spacious, tiled sitting room with a high, domed ceiling. Low divans lay against the walls, and the same two chairs from Acre sat by the graceful, arched windows. Evan was not alone in finding Arab rooms cavernous.

"Through there," she said, pointing to a large door to one side. He stood for a moment or two, staring at the door, thinking, Get out of here, you fool, before you lose the last of your self-respect.

But he didn't.

"What the hell are you trying to do to me?" he demanded as he slammed the door behind him. "Summoning me from a sound sleep in the middle of the night? Do you think me a toy that you ignore and pick up whenever you feel like it? To torment at your whim?"

"*Toy?*" she shot back. "You think *you're* a toy? Believe me, toys are a lot easier to manage than you, second son of a middling baron!"

They glared at each other. "No one insults my family, not even you. I'm leaving. I came as you asked, but I'm leaving."

She stepped towards him and caught his arm. "*No!* Please don't! Please don't leave me … I'm sorry about that evening. That was stupid. I knew I had angered you, but I had to see you. I tried, I really tried, but, you see … I am the toy." Her voice faltered and caught in a sob.

He ripped open her night shirt and shoved her onto the bed.

Panting, they lay back from each other. Once they'd caught their breaths, she removed the rest of his clothes and pulled the fur up around them. In November, the nights cooled off here, quite a bit. She slipped into his arms, sighing in satisfaction. Both of them felt cleansed, renewed, at ease.

"Richard proposed my hand in marriage to Saladin's brother."

He sat up. "Come again? Is he mad?"

"That's what I said. I thought he was joking. Some desert chieftain's fourth wife? An *Infidel?* He was *serious!* He said he'd make me Queen of Jerusalem. This brother, Adil-something, said he'd give it serious thought!"

This was not as insulting as it sounded; the title "king" or "queen" of Jerusalem referred to not just the city, but all crusader-occupied lands surrounding it. In effect, this person would be the ruler of the captured Holy Land.

"Wait, you mean *Malik* al-Adil? Safadin? He's Saladin's emissary, the one the King has been dealing with all this time. He's an impressive man. You might like him."

Joanna shot him a withering, *"Et tu?"* look before she saw that he was teasing her. She continued, mollified, "I told Richard he could go eat shit, and I would throw myself in front of a chariot first. He asked, what if Safadin—that's what people call him?—converted to Christianity? He even floated it by al-Adil, who told him politely to eat shit."

"Is this a way for him to get Jerusalem without besieging it? I've heard he's thinking about invading Egypt, since that might help accomplish the same thing."

"Well, yes. He'd really prefer to avoid having to besiege Jerusalem at all. One thing about my brother is that he hates the needless waste of men. He figures that conquering Egypt would cut Saladin off at the knees, and he'll have no choice but to surrender Jerusalem."

"But the Egyptians aren't exactly going to lie down for a nap."

"Exactly. That's what his allies keep telling him. So now he's angry at me for spoiling everything, like this is my fault. Richard is terrible when he's in a sulk. I don't think this scheme of his would be allowed, anyway. I'm sure the Pope would excommunicate us both if he married me off to an Infidel."

Evan drew her to him. She contentedly ran her hand across his chest. "Perhaps the stress is starting to get to the King," he mused. "This is not a sensible proposal. There must be a calming tisane ....

I'll ask Besace. The King hasn't yet visited the local bath. That would also calm his temper—"

"Hush, stop your fretting, take off your medicus cloak, and come back to *us*."

But he couldn't. "Speaking of 'calming his temper,' what's going on between him and the Queen? He's rarely in her company."

"Berengaria is, well, confused. She's worshipped him since they first met, years ago, but with that betrothal to Alys, she assumed he was out of reach. Then, when he proposed marriage, she believed all her prayers had been miraculously answered. She's willing to be anything he asks of her, but to date, he has asked nothing, or almost nothing. She asked me when we were alone once if it was normal for a husband to get out of bed right afterward and not stay the night. I could only say that every man is different, and some men feel restless and need to leave the bed."

"I assume you added, 'from what I've heard.'"

"Naturally," she said, smiling.

Evan had already noted Joanna's utter lack of regret or shame for her dalliances. He knew he should feel jealous of those other men, but he didn't. There'd been no mistaking the detachment in her voice as she'd related what little pleasure she had taken, about as much as being leeched; performing her duty was how she saw it. None of those lovers had been allowed to see into her soul. He loved her candour and realized at that moment that however magnificent the pleasure he took in her body, the companionable talk afterwards was what he'd most treasured—and missed. Two friendly spirits sharing thoughts, memories, hopes, and fears.

No, if he were really honest with himself, it was William, the dead king, whom he was jealous of. Because he'd had the privilege of having her every night, as his wife and counsellor, something Evan could never have.

"Physically, they are an odd match," he commented. "Richard must be close to a foot and a half taller than his wife." In Evan's opinion, he and Joanna fit perfectly together.

She laughed and cuddled into him. "Well, this is true! And she is a bit meek for his taste. But his real problem is that he can only focus on one thing at a time. He might have thought he had room in his head for a bride, but he was wrong. We talk alone after supper, sometimes. This crusade is making him tired and distracted and short-tempered."

"I know. There's talk in the medical tent and among his staff."

"It's driving him mad that he's so close, and he's stuck sitting around in Jaffa. Richard has never taken inactivity well. It's all taking so much longer than he thought, his vast resources are depleted, and so are the ranks of his men. And the closer he gets to Jerusalem, the more evasive it seems. So, to answer your question, Berengaria is about the last thing on his mind at the moment."

"She may never be more than a ring on his finger."

"At least not a toy."

He held her close. "Joanna, I've missed you so much. Why didn't you call for me before now?"

"You kept saying we had no future. Richard certainly reminds me, often enough. I've had weeks with nothing to do except think about it. I started to agree with you. What's the point, I thought. Why do we keep fooling ourselves that we can have anything more than a few stolen nights? I told myself that you were just a passing diversion, we were finished, and I would get over you soon enough. I almost believed it."

"I angered you with that stupid comment about the key, didn't I. I'm sorry."

"Well, it didn't help, but please let that go. I knew you meant no offence. I thought I could handle it, just looking at you and Berengaria from my window. I was so wrong: I was frantic with jealousy! But, still, I tried. And then I woke up this morning with a need for you so great I curled up and cried. I don't care anymore if we have no future. We can have a present, can't we?"

He said, "Only if we play no more games with each other. I can't go through these past three weeks again."

"I agree. Neither can I."

"So, we're friends again?"

She lowered his lips to hers and gave him a long, leisurely kiss. "I was always your friend."

They lay quietly, savouring the transient sweetness of the moment. "Evan, Richard is sending us back to Acre. This is goodbye."

"What? Oh no, not *again!*"

"I know. I'm so sorry, I just found out today. It pains me, too. I meant it when I said that he can only focus on one thing. We women are too much of a distraction. And there's starting to be gossip about us."

"Yes. I don't know how."

Oh Evan, my love, you are still so innocent. In an anthill like this? Everyone knows, depend on it.

For all Joanna knew, it could have been one of her guards. Or even his physician friends, noticing that he wasn't in his cot some nights. But she wasn't about to destroy that innocence. Not tonight, in the little time they had.

There were already layers of protection for them that she was determined he never know about. Richard had thundered to his entourage that anyone overheard spreading gossip about either of them would shortly find himself missing a tongue. And, whereas other physicians were being siphoned off to remain in Acre and other captured places, he was keeping Evan and his two associates close at hand, where they could be more easily protected.

And away from *her*, she thought bitterly.

"But is Acre safe?" he asked.

"I think so. It's well garrisoned."

"But Berengaria—"

"I know. She isn't happy, of course. But it's not in her nature to complain. As for me, it seems that my main role in life for the near future is to rot in Acre and be companion and chaperone to her. No, wait, that sounds too harsh. As I've said, she has been a constant friend to me through this."

Evan chuckled. "And who chaperones the chaperone?"

She laughed in turn. "I don't believe you qualify. Anyway, as soon as he takes Jerusalem, we will be packed off, back to Sicily as a first stop, is my understanding."

He turned to her. "Joanna, we are always saying goodbye, yet we have always been granted one more time. I will not believe that this is all the Lord will allow us."

"We can only accept His will. But, yes, surely we will be allowed one more time."

He slipped back into his cot just before the matins bell rang, as usual tiptoeing past the sleeping Agnes and Nicolette on the divans. His pocket on the way back was a little heavier by a bag of rosehips.

-XVI-
Christmas in Latrun

On November 17, a week after Joanna and Berengaria's departure, the crusaders mounted an offensive on Jerusalem. It was a difficult march: Saladin had burned the orchards and destroyed every village along the way. These had to be repaired, and it was a slow job. Victuals had to be constantly transported from the coast, and Muslim bands harassed the food trains the whole time. If not Muslim bands, Muslim people, now reduced to begging for any bit of food or money to keep them from starving. The wet and miserable army was also dogged by persistent rain.

Evan, Crécy, and Gurci were among Richard's medical corps, not trailing at the back with the rest of the medical unit, the priests, and all the other camp personnel, but slightly farther up, surrounded by Hospitallers.

Horses and kit had been located for them without difficulty. Fine Arabian steeds, indeed; Evan didn't want to think how his own horse's previous master had met his demise. The horse was a *grisliard* gelding, grey dotted with white, with a long black mane and tail. Riding a gelding bothered Evan not at all, although they were rarely used in Northern European armies because they were thought too mild-tempered. The last thing he wanted was a high-strung, fire-breathing horse, so they would get along just fine, he told him. He decided to stick with his Arabic name: Wasim. It was the only name the horse knew.

"And just how do you know that?" Gurci wanted to know.

"He told me." Like Branwen, Evan had a sense of horses. Since young childhood, he had been able to communicate with them on simple levels. Branwen had always claimed that it was the Welsh in him. That was the only one of Evan's abilities he acknowledged as a gift; he still believed there was nothing in his medical or artistic skills that couldn't be learned, and he had a long way to go yet.

Gurci didn't scoff. There were people in his homeland, too, who had that ability. Usually women. "All right, smart ass, what's *my* horse's name?"

Evan approached the bay stallion, stroked his neck, and lay his head against it. After first of all complimenting the horse on what a brave, strong animal he was, Evan thought the question.

"His name is Muhtal."

"Mucktaal? Well, I don't much care for it. Too hard to pronounce. I think I'll call him Windy, for all his farting."

"Careful, Morgant. His name means 'trickster.'"

Evan had survived storms at sea, a shipwreck, and imprisonment, but this was the first time he felt he was a participant in a war. Any random arrow aimed somewhere in their midst could hit him and he would die without ever seeing the face of his killer. His skin crawled with the tension, his senses continually on alert, like a wild animal's.

The tension was palpable within the ranks—he even felt Wasim's—and Evan wondered how he and the other men could sustain this for weeks at a time. He thought again about that long, harrowing march from Acre to Jaffa, watching safely from the *Misericordia,* and felt awe for the simple bravery and discipline, day after day, of those foot soldiers. Some of them had begged not to be returned to the march after they were pronounced fit. Now in their shoes, it would not be so easy to callously thrust these men back into action.

The army did manage to make it as far as Latrun before Christmas. This hilltop village, about fifteen miles west of Jerusalem, boasted an old crusader fort; Richard decided to hunker down for the season, giving everyone a bit of a rest and a chance to get dry and warm. Well, maybe not warm, and certainly not everyone. There was a shortage of firewood, and what was available was damp. The infantrymen had to make do as best they could under their tents. Evan was not alone in preferring the radiant body heat of the stables, choosing to bunk down with Wasim.

With everyone chilled and under stress, coughs and respiratory ailments started to make the rounds, including Crécy, quite nastily. Alas, no chickens were running around to be cooked up into a soothing broth. Evan ignored his demands to be bled. Instead, from Jaffa, he'd brought along a small supply of camphor, commonly used in Islamic medicine for clearing the nasal passages, which he added to hot water so that Crécy could breathe in the steam. He kept him warm and hydrated with an improvised, bastardized variation of a brew of Mama's: cups of boiled, hot water infused with lemon juice, ginger, honey, olive oil, and an eye-watering, clear spirit, a cask of which had somehow found its way from Russia and been left in the fort—probably because no one liked it. The concoction didn't look like much, and it may not have cured the men's colds, but it cheered them up; in fact, they seemed to be growing rather too fond of it, in Evan's view.

Christmas dinner was a modest stew made from some sort of tough and chewy meat, of unknown origin, though Evan suspected camel. He thought of Christmases past. Mama would deck the outside doors with spruce branches and holly. Every Christmas Day, the castle invited the local villeins for dinner, with dancing afterward. The day was suffused with warm-hearted generosity and love. He would be comfortable and cozy, surrounded by family and friends, snug in his own bed. Following that miserable train of thought, he thought of being snug in Joanna's bed, her warm body curled around his. That plunged him further into his swamp of self-pity.

He was terribly homesick, and it took Gurci to snap him out of it, as usual. As they doggedly chewed at their stew, Gurci reminded him, "Remember, my friend, all of us here in this hall are on the right side of the ground, at least for today. You're not yet buried in some soon-to-be-forgotten mass grave that no one will ever visit. Give thanks for all that."

Gurci was nursing a tender behind, from where Windy had nipped him the previous day. The day before that, Windy had knocked him down with his nose. "Personally," he went on, "I believe I will die at the hands of my horse. The day after tomorrow. I'm resigned to it, actually. Think well of me after I'm gone."

Swallowing a chunk of the mysterious meat, Evan said, "As I say—"

"Ay, ay, I know … Mooktal, you say?"

"Sort of like that."

He wasn't sure when the tide of belief in the great cause of the crusade had gone out on him, but any idealism he once felt for this endeavour had mutated to a creeping belief that his countrymen were losing their lives for naught. But yes, Gurci was right. Every day that ended with him on the right side of the ground brought him one day closer to going home.

1192

Vintage etching of Jerusalem, showing the topography

The whole secret lies in confusing the enemy, so that he cannot fathom our real intent.
—Sun Tzu, *The Art of War*

-I-
Brothers Under the Skin

The day after Epiphany—January 7, 1192—the army set out again for Jerusalem. The way was clear: a Roman road led straight to it. Richard ordered the men to make camp at Beit Nuba, a village only twelve miles from Jerusalem. Unfortunately, the weather turned even worse: incessant rain and sleet, even hail at times. Though Richard pressed his allies to stay the course, he was reminded that everything and everyone, from the siege engines to the horses, would be mired in the mud. And there remained the ever-present threat of Saladin's army attacking from behind. Hugh of Burgundy said he would not join in any attack on Jerusalem. Wait till warmer weather, he said.

Hugh may have held the French standard in the Holy Land, but his conniving king still pulled the strings from Paris. Sensing Philip's long claws from afar, Richard furiously conceded and ordered a retreat back to Jaffa, but grumblings from within the ranks emerged. Had they come to conquer Jerusalem, or had they not? They'd marched in the cold and rain for nothing? To turn tail and march back, Saladin's forces laughing at them the whole way? While no one questioned Richard's personal courage, they did question that of his supposed allies. There were whispers of a noble cause being eroded from within by fear.

However, as they regained Jaffa, the men now out of their saddles or wet shoes, they began to see it was perhaps the wisest decision after all. They were still well-provisioned. They could afford to wait till things dried out.

Still, Evan knew that Saladin would always be capable of attacking from behind, no matter the season or the weather. And, sadly, this respite would work to Saladin's advantage, too. The crusader army had threatened Jerusalem as enemy morale was low from the loss of Acre and the catastrophe at Arsuf, and this delay would allow them to regroup. It seemed to him that the *idea* of capturing Jerusalem was becoming increasingly more appealing than the actual, highly dangerous execution of it. And who would stay to defend it if it were captured? The pilgrims straggling behind in the wake of the army, having attained their goal of visiting Jerusalem, would just go home. After all this time, really, all everyone else wanted was to leave once their mission was accomplished.

Evan was sure these very thoughts had also occurred to Richard.

Indeed they had, compounded by troublesome news from England: John was misbehaving. Richard had given him control of sizable duchies in France, in exchange for a promise that he'd stay out of England during Richard's absence. But Eleanor missed her favourite son and invited him back across the Channel. John had sacked Richard's senior officials, started setting himself up as an alternative ruler, and even, reportedly, sent out feelers on an alliance with Philip.

Richard was tired, frustrated, and cantankerous. Not the strongest position to bargain from, and Saladin must surely know this.

During the six months they had now been in Outremer, Richard had come to understand that doing business in the Arab world was a vastly different proposition from how things were done in Western Europe. He felt at a distinct disadvantage. At home, politics was conducted on a personal level; across a lavish dinner table, he could use his power and the force of his personality to bring people around, willingly or not. He was used to looking people in the eye. He was a master at reading body language, probing for signs of deceit or evasiveness.

Here, all transactions were done through intermediaries. The word he kept hearing was *wasta*: It had to do with a man entrusted with smoothing over the relations between two opposing parties, so that both retained their honour. If things went wrong, the *wasta* accepted responsibility. In this case, it was Saladin's brother Safadin who was the emissary—the same fellow that Richard had proposed should marry Joanna. Richard understood that, even saw the value in it. In fact, he liked the man. Brothers under the skin, he felt. While at first glance his offer of marrying Joanna to Safadin might have been construed as a joke, he still thought Safadin would have made a perfectly good brother-in-law.

He had long since accepted that he would likely never meet Saladin face to face, man to man, as he so fervently wished. He also worried that his messages were not being correctly transmitted, that subtle points of negotiations were being lost in translation. He could get no "read" on the man. And it all took so much more *time.*

These protracted negotiations had forced Richard to revise his opinion of Muslims as sub-human Infidels. He now grudgingly admired their courage, cunning, subtle reasoning, grit, and generosity. They were forever offering him gifts of expensive silks and jewels. He considered his own, mostly plundered offerings crude in comparison. They'd even given him a pair of camels. Atrocious-looking beasts and as stubborn as donkeys, though, true, they had their uses. They'd come in handy during the marches.

Able young Montmorency had requested an audience with him earlier that morning. He'd mentioned a bathhouse in Jaffa, saying, "Your Grace, I was in such a bathhouse in Limassol. It is a great gift from the Infidel world to ours. I promise you, you won't regret it." Apparently, it was highly recommended for stress, as well as aches and pains from wet weather.

Richard had learned about the ancient Roman fondness for baths and knew there were still some here and there in Europe in a pitifully ruined state. He'd always thought them vaguely sinful and degenerate, a symptom of the lassitude that had led to the Empire's downfall. Still, Montmorency had been in one and appeared to have suffered no ill effects. Quite a find, that young man.

Richard sent his chamberlain off to reconnoiter the place. Learning that it was not, as feared, a place of ill-repute (in fact, the chamberlain could not seem to wipe the smeary smile off his face when he returned), with a guard of two Templars, he marched into the local hammam the following afternoon. The startled attendants hurriedly cleared the place of disgruntled customers. He came out a changed man. God's feet, he had to get one of those! For, as he'd sat basking in the warmth of the bath, his active mind drifting aimlessly, an adage he'd heard somewhere popped into his head: *Confuse the enemy.* Two could play that game.

-II-
Melech-Ric

A week later, in late January, the word came that all were to pack up, save a garrison of a thousand men: they were heading down the coast to repair Ascalon, which Saladin had razed. It was a perfect jumping-off spot to invade Egypt. Richard was still fixated on this notion as an alternative to full-on assault on Jerusalem: conquer Egypt, with all its riches, and mortally wound Saladin's power base at the same time.

So, another trudge down the coast. Morale was low and people were disgruntled. They'd just reconstructed Jaffa, and now they had to start over again? Didn't they have better things to do? Like *capture Jerusalem?* An ironic toast started to make the rounds: "Next year in Jerusalem!"

When they arrived at Ascalon, Richard set everyone to work right away. They couldn't march on Jerusalem until Ascalon was rebuilt, so he stripped down to his chemise and hose, and carried stone alongside his troops.

With confusion of the enemy as his fresh credo, he started to find himself in no particular hurry to respond to Saladin's missives. He extensively employed loyal and able Hubert Walter, Bishop of Salisbury, as an intermediary. Although Joanna had furiously refused to marry al-Adil, Richard played for time by claiming envoys had been sent to Rome to seek a blessing on the marriage. He also delayed for weeks on the pretext of the return of the True Cross, a non-negotiable sticking point. Saladin replied that the True Cross was his to keep; it was a priceless relic for Islam, too. In fact, that dubious piece of wood was probably just some old rotten beam one of Saladin's minions had found, and Saladin had simply allowed the rumour to flourish. Richard knew it, he was sure that Saladin knew it, and he was also fairly sure that Saladin knew that he knew. But the game amused him and bought him time.

It gave him satisfaction that Saladin's hangers-on only wanted to deal with him. "Where is *Melech-Ric*?" they would ask. "Oh. So, when will he be back?"

"*Melech-Ric*" was "King Richard" in their tongue, and somehow that term had gained popular currency among Richard's men as well. "Look sharp," their overseer of construction would yell. "You don't want Melech-Ric to see you lounging about like grasshoppers!"

As the weather improved, and as Ascalon started to take shape, he and his Templars captured the town of Darum, on the outskirts of Egypt. The defenders put up a surprisingly good fight—five days' worth—and there were casualties. But Richard's mood was greatly improved. He'd needed a victory. For once, here was a town Saladin hadn't got to first, and it was one worth raiding for treasure and supplies.

But, morale booster or not, the ordinary men were quietly talking amongst themselves. A standing garrison at Acre. Another at Jaffa. Another at Ascalon. And, now, at Darum. King Philip had left, along with much of his army. So had the aggrieved Leopold of Austria, with all of his men. Many lives had been lost so far. So, would there really be enough to besiege Jerusalem?

Dissension was also emerging in the senior ranks. Hugh of Burgundy, representing the French, thought invading Egypt was a preposterous idea and was adamant that nothing should distract them from seizing Jerusalem. Richard reluctantly conceded and, in June, everyone was on the march again back to Jerusalem.

This time, instead of pelting rain, the marchers suffered the relentless heat of a Mediterranean summer. Again, Evan felt the prickle of constant danger. His mail was hot, sweat poured off him, his clothes clung wetly to him. The flagons of ale the men kept on them had to be carefully rationed; even so, by late afternoon dehydration was a problem. How did the men stand this, march after march? The obvious answer was that they weren't standing it. They were sick of it.

Since Ascalon, a common complaint from the King on down was gigantic, black bruises that appeared at the merest knock, Evan included. The problem had also arisen during the march to Jaffa, he heard, though the bruises themselves seemed harmless. He figured it must have to do with sweat excreting precious nutrients. He brewed up some rosehip tea, thinking it couldn't do any harm, then let it cool, so as not to sweat even more. He drank it constantly, all day. After a few days, his bruises were yellowing and any new ones were small and of normal colour.

He was granted an audience with the King. "Your Grace, may I offer you something cool to drink? It may help with the bruising."

Richard took a cautious sip of the ruby-red liquid, then another. "Well, if nothing else, it's refreshing." Guzzling the rest down, "Have you any more?" He told Richard to drink it, to the exclusion of anything else.

Richard's bruises, as well, yellowed in a few days and no new ones appeared.

Besace wanted to know if Evan had any more of those rosehips.

He could only say, "I'm sorry, I have enough for the King, that's all. But get as much fruit into the men as you can."

Richard bade Evan stay a moment as he brought him another cup of the tea one afternoon, along with some dates that he'd packed along from Ascalon.

Richard nibbled happily on a date. "Tell me, Montmorency, about this tea. How do you know about it?"

Evan had no idea if this was future knowledge or not; all he knew was that it was Stacey who'd had the row of rosebushes in the castle kitchen garden planted. He reached for Mama's tried-and-true explanation. "My mother is Welsh, Your Grace. The Welsh have knowledge about some things that we English don't."

"Is that right," intoned Richard.

Evan knew Richard was not an imbecile and that he should go easy on the "Welsh knowledge" angle. Pivoting quickly, he added, "But there is so much I still have to learn. As you know, I am not even a licensed physician yet. I'd like to continue my studies in Salerno."

"Ah. I've been in Salerno. On the way to Messina, in fact. Pleasant spot. Though one day while I was near there, I came as close as I ever have to meeting the Lord."

Evan started in surprise. In *Salerno?* "How did that happen, Your Grace?"

"It was stupid. I was touring around with just one Templar,

believing myself to be absolutely safe and capable of defending myself if some fool decided perchance to pounce on us. I heard the cry of a hawk from inside a house."

Richard paused significantly. "Of course, you know that only *nobility* may own hawks."

"Of course." Evan would have assumed that only nobility had the *time* to play with hawks.

"Well, I quite rightfully entered the house and seized the hawk. The local *rustici* must not have known who I was because they came as a mob at me. One man drew a knife and I struck it with the back of my sword, only to have the confounded thing *snap*. I'll tell you, I was in the fight of my life, with only sticks and stones as weapons. We only just managed to get away."

Evan considered for a moment that the whole fracas of the Third Crusade could have been avoided by an accurately aimed knife. On further thought, a silly, useless death. He worked frantically for something to say, but all that came out of his mouth was, "Shocking."

Richard cast a sharp look at him and then smiled. "Yes, I suppose it all sounds ridiculous in the retelling. But the lesson I learned that day is that we can't choose the manner of our passing. Despite our grand pretensions of a noble death, it may take us at any time, in the most undignified fashion."

He paused a moment and coolly gazed at him. "The Dowager Queen is most anxious about your safety. I've told her that I cannot afford you special protection. The effect on company morale would, in effect, make life more difficult for you, in the end."

Evan was now genuinely appalled. The last thing he ever wanted was to draw this sort of attention to himself. "I'm sorry, Your Grace. If I've had any part at all at causing discord between you and the Dowager Queen of Sicily, I beg forgiveness."

Richard waved his hand impatiently. "Yes, ordinarily, I would have your balls for breakfast. But, as it happens, I need you and your wizardly skills. I have said this before, and I'll repeat it: Be careful. Your honour is the one thing only you can take away from yourself."

Evan took a moment to consider his response. Richard must know that he and Joanna were far beyond the sketching stage. No use denying anything, then. "Yes, Your Grace. Both of us are only too aware of that."

"We're understood, then. That will be all."

Two days later, they reached Bethany, only two miles from Jerusalem. The men took in the landscape, rejoicing. They'd got here! And lo, wasn't that the Dome of the Rock that they were seeing? It shone as a gleaming jewel before them.

But Richard, staring at that glorious city and taking in its topography, felt his heart sink. It was worse than he'd feared. Jerusalem was built on a spur of flat land surrounded by valleys. They would have go around and try to take it from the north gates. This city was not sea-level Acre or Jaffa, which could be captured from the relative safety of ships at sea. Jerusalem's walls were solid, likely eight feet thick; the city's defenders, including Saladin himself according to spies, would throw everything they had on them. It would be a long siege, and even if they succeeded in effecting a breach and taking the city, he knew in his guts that it would be lost again within a year.

In addition, Saladin's forces would most certainly encircle them from behind, trapping them and making them battle on two fronts. Then there was the cold, stark fact that Richard no longer had the numbers. With garrisons at all the conquered ports, the mobile crusader army now totalled perhaps twelve thousand and would continue to shrink. Saladin, on the other hand, could always round up more men. How much longer could the crusaders get by, at a numerical disadvantage?

No, clearly, the only way Jerusalem could be taken was by surprise. There might be a shepherd boy in the faraway hills of Syria who didn't know the crusaders were coming, but he'd be the only one who didn't.

The crusader war council numbered twenty-five: five each of Templars, Hospitallers, the English, the French led by Hugh of Burgundy, and the Latin league that comprised Genoans and Pisans. All except Hugh now believed that besieging Jerusalem was folly, at least at this time. Similarly, all except Hugh supported the Egyptian initiative.

They argued for two days, each side laying out its reasoning. Capture Jerusalem or capture Egypt? In the end, Burgundy was intransigent: Jerusalem had been taken before, it could be taken again. Yes, came the reply, but that was because those crusaders didn't have *Saladin* to face. They could try to take Jerusalem, or they could try to capture Egypt, but, divided, they hadn't the numbers to do both.

Richard finally said, "If you want to besiege Jerusalem, go ahead. But I will participate as a simple soldier only. Any blame—or credit—will fall squarely on the Duke of Burgundy's shoulders."

Richard had called Burgundy's bluff. Faced with the challenge of actually having to take charge, he finally backed down. Richard had "won," but retreating back to Ascalon was a pyrrhic victory, indeed. In the larger scheme of things, he had failed at what he'd set out to do: raise the English flag over Jerusalem. Further, the once buoyant and united crusader coalition was now hopelessly divided. Worse still was the morale of the men who'd marched for so long and fought so bravely.

Always in the vanguard of the army, Richard now let his horse fall back to the rear. One of his Templars, seeking to cheer the King up, said, "My Lord King, if you ride up to the top of this hill, you can see all of Jerusalem clearly!"

Richard replied, bitterly, "Those not worthy to win the Holy City are not worthy to behold it." Word of this exchange ran swiftly through the ranks. Angry as they were, they admitted that their king could be noble in defeat.

-III-
"Shame on him who lags behind!"

While repairs continued at Ascalon, Richard used the time to replenish stores from Cyprus. The crusader leadership was disturbed, however, to hear that Saladin's naval forces were attacking supply ships sailing to and fro. Richard decided to stop that by attacking Saladin's base of operations in Beirut.

He advanced north, Evan and his colleagues back in the *Misericordia* with all the other medical personnel, who were amused at being rejoined by these "demoted" elites. Evan and Gurci settled into their accustomed hammocks in the hold, though there was some chest-thumping by Crécy and Besace over which of them got the choicer accommodations. Besace won.

The force stopped overnight in Acre, where Richard disembarked, presumably to check on the two women in his life. Most others remained aboard ship. Until the sun went down, Evan sat on deck, sketching the view of Acre from the sea. Mostly, he hoped to catch some sight of Joanna. And how would *that* be, you dalcop, he thought. Do you think she'll casually stroll along Acre's walls? Wave a handkerchief from a fortress window? He imagined rowing himself in to shore and skulking around town, sneaking into the premises. If it weren't so pathetic it would be comical.

Early the next morning, July 29, they were awakened by frantic activity. They were reversing course. Saladin had attacked Jaffa, had breached the walls, and those crusaders who hadn't been killed in the initial assault were barricaded in the citadel. No one knew anything more than that, but everyone did know—including Saladin, apparently— that those left behind in Jaffa were there because they were too weak or sick to accompany the rest of the army. For all they knew, the citadel had already fallen and the occupants slain.

Richard promptly assembled thirty-five galleys, comprising about two thousand men, with a land force of French, Templars, and Hospitallers meant to keep pace with them. Unfortunately, winds were not favourable, so only on the early morning of July 31 did they come within sight of Jaffa. The land force was nowhere to be seen.

Dawn rose. Muslim flags were waving all over the city. All that could be heard was the noise of looting and celebrating.

The crusader commanders did hold one vital piece of covert intelligence, however: in the wee morning hours, a priest in the citadel had jumped out unseen and uninjured onto the sand and begun swimming out to the ships. He was spotted by someone on the *Trenc-la-Mer*, who rowed out to retrieve him. He informed Richard that the citadel still held, though the situation was dire. They could hold out a few more hours, at most, but those still alive were combat-ready.

Richard had the galleys approach the shore, clearing the beach with crossbow fire as they got closer. Richard was among the first to wade ashore, still in his seafaring shoes, wearing no mail, and calling, "Shame on him who lags behind!" He ordered a beachhead established with timber, shields—anything that could be used for protection for the archers. Then, under covering crossbow fire, Richard and a company of others stormed the town.

Saladin had abandoned attempts to control the Muslim celebrants, now a leaderless mob thirsty for revenge for past humiliations, especially the massacre at Acre. Bent on plunder and celebration, they were disorganized and unprepared for the fierce crusader assault. They were also shocked to face the surprisingly alive and robust citadel defenders, who stormed out and attacked from behind.

In not much more than an hour, the crusaders regained Jaffa. Richard immediately sent envoys to discuss terms.

Saladin wasn't ready to give up, though. Richard's force was pitifully small, outnumbered as usual, and Jaffa's battered walls were in no shape to withstand an onslaught. The night of August 4, Saladin's army crept forward, hoping to catch the crusaders by surprise.

Evan and his company were wakened before dawn by repeated clarion blares. They heard later that a Genoese sentry had spotted the gleam of rows of Muslim helmets in the moonlight and sent word to Richard. Richard had just enough time to organize his men in a semblance of battle formation. Some of them were only half-dressed. The front rank knelt tight behind their shields in a "hedgehog" formation, their spears planted in the ground, points upward. Behind them were the crossbowmen, working in pairs: one firing, his partner loading another crossbow. But they were pitifully few against many thousands, with only about a dozen mounted knights held at the rear. When he wasn't slashing at the enemy himself, Richard continually strode back and forth at the front of the ranks, encouraging and exhorting his men not to lose heart.

After some time, it became clear to the Muslims that this formation would not break and run, and their casualty count was ruinous. As soon as Richard saw that the attack was flagging, he and his knights charged, again catching the enemy by surprise. The sight of the dreaded Melech-Ric bearing down on them like a demon possessed, roaring in rage, slashing his sword, hair flying, caused Saladin's men to scatter and flee. One man did bring down the King's horse before Richard sliced his head off. Being dismounted dismayed Richard not in the least, and he continued the pursuit on foot.

Even then, the attack wasn't over. Some of Saladin's forces had circumvented the battle, entered Jaffa, and engaged with Genoese soldiers who put up very little fight. Hearing this, Richard grabbed a horse and galloped into the town, rallying all the remaining men. By afternoon, Saladin sounded the horn of retreat, knowing the battle was lost.

Evan and company watched all this from the *Misericordia.* What they couldn't see, they heard from the rowed-out injured. "Incredible" was the word of the day. Was this a miracle? Everyone thought so: While Saladin directed the action from a safe distance, it was as if Richard encased himself in an invisible shield. Had the man no fear at all? How had he survived, with not a scratch on him? Two of his mounted knights and two hundred infantrymen had died. Their opponents had lost seven hundred men out of a force of seven thousand, along with twice that many horses.

Saladin, ever the gracious loser, gifted Richard with two stallions to replace the one he'd lost. The land force, delayed at Caesarea by a false report—likely planted by Saladin's men—of a Muslim army ahead of them, arrived the following day.

Evan knew that the Battle of Jaffa and the Battle of Arsuf would go down into English lore. No matter what Richard did before or after, these two battles would form the core of his legend. He was already known as Richard the Lion. Now, he was being called Richard Lionheart.

-IV-
The Threefold Cord

But Richard was just a man, like everyone else. All those punishing marches, withdrawals, and battles had taken their toll on him. He was worn out, and he'd contracted malaria. Moreover, he was out of time. Successive envoys from England informed him that John was now openly allied with Philip. It was time to make a deal and go home.

The conflict had also exhausted Saladin. The previously invincible sultan had thrown everything he had at the crusader force, but the most that could be said was that he'd fought Richard to a draw. He retained Jerusalem, but the coast belonged to the English and their allies.

The two leaders settled into serious negotiations, Richard from his sick bed.

The King summoned Evan to his tent outside the Jaffa walls in mid-August. Weak and feverish, he whispered hoarsely, "Cure me of this."

Malaria was commonly thought to be caused, literally, by "bad air" or "miasma." Knowing from Mama that it was actually caused by a mosquito, he was quietly experimenting with basic netting. But for Richard, right now, the most he could do was no harm. That included stopping the bloodletting and purging that Besace was inducing.

He could only proceed by following how Nasir and the other physicians had treated it. "Your Grace, there's no immediate cure for swamp fever. But you are strong and in otherwise good health. You will recover, but until that time, the most I can do is prescribe a very simple treatment: rest, a plain diet, lots of boiled liquids and fruit juices to replenish your fluids. I can help reduce the fever, headache, and chills. But most of all, you must have rest. The air is better out at sea, and the breeze is cooling. I suggest you recuperate aboard ship."

In fact, Richard's survival was no guaranteed thing. Malaria took people of all ages and physical conditions. But he needed Richard to believe he would recover.

Besace glared at him. "What, no magic potions or incantations? Just 'a plain diet and lots of liquids'? My mother could prescribe that."

"I know, Milord, but to my knowledge this is the best we can offer him."

Besace shrugged, as if to say, "All right, you handle it; your funeral."

Richard nodded. He said, "Everyone pack up, including you, Montmorency. We're going back to the *Trenc-la-Mer.*"

Evan was in a tiny, windowless cabin below deck, but at least it was his. Access to Richard's cabin was gained through the top deck and down a short flight of stairs.

For the cabin of a king, it was surprisingly Spartan. Evan had expected rich drapes, bejewelled whatnots, a grand bed. Certainly, chests of plunder. It was spacious and had windows; however, other than a fine oriental rug, it contained only a narrow bed, a washstand, and a large table around which were several chairs. An operational, functional room. His crown was on the washstand. Joanna had told him that however avaricious her brother was about helping himself to other people's money to fund his enterprises, she had never known him to spend much on himself.

He and Besace split Richard's care into equal shifts: being the senior officer, Besace took the day, Evan took the night. During the day and on warm nights, Richard lay outside, on deck, under his red awning. He slept as long as he wished, but during the few hours of the day that he was lucid, he attended to negotiations with Saladin.

Saladin, ever solicitous, sent him peaches and plums, which Richard devoured—but only after Evan and his comrades had thoroughly washed and tasted them first.

The Treaty of Jaffa was finally signed on September 2, 1192. It was a compromise in the best sense of the word. From the following Pasch, the truce was to last three years, three months, three weeks, three days, and three hours; this was inspired by the Biblical threefold cord that is not quickly broken.

The crusaders would retain control of those cities they'd captured, with the exception of Ascalon, which was viewed by the Muslims as too close to Egypt for their comfort. It was to be demolished again and returned to them. This had been a major sticking point with them and was the last of the terms that Richard agreed to; in fact, rumour had it that Saladin was so sure Richard wouldn't give up Ascalon that he'd been planning to suspend the talks and attack Jaffa yet again.

Jerusalem, of course, would remain under Muslim control, but pilgrims to the Holy Land would be allowed safe passage through to it.

By the time the treaty was signed, Richard was up and about, though still weak.

Besace drew Evan aside one day. He was a slim man in his late forties, bald on top, with penetrating blue eyes and yellow teeth. Once the King's health showed sure signs of improvement, he'd been quite civil to Evan. Besace had had little faith in this young upstart's abilities, but little by little had come to be impressed by the boy's polite, calm assurance that his way was the correct way. Though he would have eagerly thrown Evan to the wolves had the King died, he was now more than happy to take much of the credit.

Clearing his throat, he said, "It looks like, with the Lord's mercy, our king will yet see his homeland again."

Evan agreed. "Yes, it was a near thing for a while, wasn't it? I couldn't have done it without you, Milord."

Besace wasn't fooled by the obvious show of flattery, but he was impressed that it sounded sincere. It was a skill he'd never mastered.

He replied, "Indeed. But the reason I wanted to talk to you is that I've been trying to remember where I've heard your name before. I remembered just yesterday. Surprised I'd forgotten, really, because of the talk at the time. When I was much younger, before I heard the call to be a physician, I was a knight in our late king's household. Guy de Montmorency must have been your uncle, I take it?"

"Yes, he was!" replied Evan. "I have only the vaguest memory of him. He's been missing and presumed dead for going on twenty years now."

"Yes, curious affair it was at the time. I heard he rode out of your castle one night and was never seen again."

"That's right. I was only three. My parents still keep his room ready, in case he rides up to the castle gates again."

"Is that a fact," said Besace, thoughtfully. He studied Evan's face. "It's been a long time, and one forgets a lot, but I see the family resemblance."

"Yes, I resemble my father, and I'd heard that they looked much alike, except for Uncle Guy's dark hair."

"May I say quite frankly how pleased I am that you resemble him only facially."

Evan blinked.

"Why? Why would you say that?"

"I don't mean to speak ill of the dead, but there are some people in whose souls God's love does not reside, I've learned. He was a fearless warrior, no doubt about that, but among his company, there were bets on who would get to Guy first: an enemy sword, a betrayed 'friend,' or an outraged father. To our knowledge, the only living thing Guy cared about, other than himself, was his horse. That his disappearance was never solved frustrated the bettors not a little."

Evan was now intrigued. He loved puzzles, and this was an interesting one. What had happened to Guy? In the meantime, what to say to Besace, who was clearly hoping for some insider information?

"Hmm! Maybe it's why no one ever talked about him. When I get home, it'll be amusing to delve into it a little bit. But as you say, it's been a long time."

"Just so. Well, my boy, the only other thing I wanted to say, other than goodbye, is that the King will be taking only me on his passage home. I hope you aren't disappointed."

Evan was elated but tried to look a little deflated. "No, Milord. I thought as much. In any case, I wish to pursue my studies before I return home."

"So I've heard. For the best, then. I have served the King for some time, and I'm used to being on the move. Well, may fair winds be with you, and Godspeed, young man. I see a great future for you as a healer."

It may have been the last he would see of Ralph Besace, but Evan was resolved that it wouldn't be the last of that extraordinary conversation.

Richard summoned Evan to his quarters a few days later. He was still pale and he'd lost a fair amount of weight, but he was absolutely out of danger—enough so that he was turning away the bland soups and porridges he'd been having for the last month and requesting "manly" food.

After Evan checked his urine, felt his forehead, took his pulse, and studied his tongue, Richard got straight to the point. He said, "By my reckoning, I owe you my life three times over now."

"I was only doing my job, Your Grace, to the best of my knowledge."

"But with considerable tact and skill, and you've even got Besace espousing your ideas. That is no small achievement. I see a future in government for you if you ever tire of physic."

Evan bowed, "Thank you, Your Grace. I still have much to learn."

"I would like to offer you something as a token of my gratitude. Just ask, and I will see that you get it. Plunder? Books? I know you value those."

They both knew the only thing Evan really wanted out of all this would remain off the table, and he would not insult his king by bringing it up. So, what else? He had no desire for trinkets. He still had plenty of money. Books, yes, Mama and Papa would love some of those. But he was sure he could pick them up just as easily closer to home.

"Just one thing comes to mind, Your Grace. I would like brief leave to retrieve my horse. He's back in Ascalon."

"Your *horse*? Why *that* one? I can give you another."

"Wasim and I have developed a bond of sorts. I will need a horse anyway to make my way home."

Richard stroked his beard. "I understand that, the bond a man can have with his horse. Fanuel broke his leg on the retreat from Jerusalem. That, along with everything else, was a bitter blow. Saladin sent me a replacement right away. He seems particularly concerned that I never be without a horse."

He studied the exceptional young man in front of him. His blue-and-white crusader surcoat was clean but faded and showing signs of wear and tear. His hair could use a trim—or *something.* He had not a drop of royal blood in him. Yet for someone so young, he carried himself with surprising dignity and authority.

The small portrait of Berengaria that he had painted was an excellent likeness, especially of her eyes, which were fine. He had also, perhaps unintentionally, captured her essential vacuity. But Richard really had nowhere to put it.

While there was no doubt that Jojo was deeply attached to the boy, in his view, their differences in station and life paths made them fundamentally incompatible. Besides, much as Richard now trusted and even liked him, the stark fact was that for people like Joanna and Richard, when it came to marriage, it didn't matter what they wanted. Personally, he would just as soon not be married at all.

He was grateful that Montmorency hadn't asked for the impossible, for Richard had been through all this with Joanna. All the lad was asking for was a favour. Since Richard was dispatching ships anyway, to pick up the troops at Ascalon and Darum for the voyage home, it would be easy enough to put Evan aboard one of them to retrieve his confounded horse.

"Very well. I'll send you down the coast to get him. From there, the fleet will make its way back to Acre."

At the mention of "Acre," Montmorency's face lit up. In a poor attempt to sound conversational, he said, "Will the queens be accompanying the fleet on the way home, then?"

"No, I plan to send them off ahead of us, but I'm going to allow a day to get reacquainted."

Richard could offer nothing better than this.

"Be at the harbour first thing tomorrow morning, right after prime. Dismissed."

-V-
"Don't forget your key."

Arriving at Ascalon a day later, Evan was taken aback. He knew of the treaty condition that the city be torn down again (and what of the poor inhabitants, he wondered); he just hadn't expected it to happen so fast.

The mood in the city was odd. On the one hand, the crusaders were elated to be going home at last. The taverns and brothels were doing fantastic business—they'd be the last buildings to be demolished. On the other, a still palpable bitterness that they'd not done their job permeated the atmosphere. This frustration was manifest in the general surliness of the garrison as it took apart a city it hadn't even finished reconstructing.

Evan was relieved to lay eyes on Wasim and Muhtal, stabled in the citadel. Horses were valuable and it was unlikely they would've been just left there. Anyone could easily claim or steal them. The situation in Ascalon was hardly organized.

"Hello, my friend," Evan said, as Wasim nickered and nudged him in greeting. "You didn't think I'd just leave you here, did you? I may leave you for a time, but don't worry, I'll always come and get you. You too, Muhtal. Gurci misses you *so* much." Even now, Muhtal had a gleam in his eye.

It took another ten days for the troops to finish the demolition and load the ships with stores for the trip up to Acre and home. Time was starting to press.

The fleet gathered ships, men, and momentum as it made its way up the coast. They arrived in Acre on September 24. The mood here was much more upbeat—mainly excited anticipation to finally be going home, tempered by awareness that the loose living was shortly to stop dead. Troops were being allowed ashore on a rotating basis. The medical corps was permitted to disembark to assist at the hospital; there was an uptick in minor injuries from drunken scuffles, as well as a vexing spread of *fluxus*.

That afternoon, standing after examining a patient, Evan again collided with a Templar, who covered himself with apologies. As soon as he safely could, Evan ducked into the apothecary, closed the door, reached into his pocket, and pulled out a small, rolled piece of parchment that read: *Don't forget your key.*

That night, he waited till everyone was safely snoring on their cots before he got up and tiptoed out, carrying a lit candle with him. The streets were still full of carousing crusaders, so no one paid him any attention. Trying his best to look like any carefree soldier on the prowl for a good time, he slipped past the bored and distracted guards and snuck into the grove of trees. Groping around the wall, he found the door and the keyhole. The key slipped surely in. Through the tunnel and through the opposite door, he then blew out the candle. He made his way down the hall, up the stairs, to the left and down the hall again. He opened the last door to the woman pacing the room, waiting for him.

They lay quietly together, content as always in one another's company. No giddy catch-up on their lives tonight, no lively exchanges of opinion. This was it, and they wanted to wring every last, precious second out of it.

A year had passed since they'd last seen each other. For Joanna, planted like an oak in Acre fortress, endless days of shrieking boredom with nothing to do but embroider, simmering with resentment that she'd been confined, one way or another, "for her own protection" since William's death. She'd napped a lot in the afternoons; nothing to feel too guilty about there, since this was what people here did, she'd learned. She'd even picked rosehips to get herself off her chair and moving around. She walked the walls.

Finally, desperate, she'd reached out to some of the area's Greek, Arab, and even Jewish citizens and invited them to the fortress. She'd been surprised and pleased at how grateful and interesting they were. They wakened her slumbering curiosity and opened her eyes to their reality.

It appeared they were just as starved as she was for civilized company in this barbaric garrison town. She and Berengaria often invited the wives over for tea in the mornings; the ladies insisted on contributing their own homemade delicacies, opening her taste buds to glorious baklava and halwa. Admiring their exquisite, silk brocade dresses, she found out where they bought the fabric; the ladies also referred them to superior dressmakers in the area. She wondered how she had lived thirteen years in a cosmopolitan city like Palermo and never once thought to do this.

Still, she went to bed every night aching with loneliness, wondering if it would have been better had she never met Evan.

During the rare times she and Richard talked in private, he'd enthused about Evan's curative tisanes and innovative wound treatment, which he was also generous about sharing.

"That boy has a rare gift, I must say!"

She'd been telling him as much for over a year now and raged at his obstinacy.

"Jojo," Richard said, "I'm sorry but, remarkable as he is, he's but a landless medicus, and you're worth a lot more to me than that."

"Then raise him to a baron!" she pleaded.

"No. Do not press me on this again." His hard stare told her he meant it.

She thought, if I don't ask now, I never will.

"Evan, why do you know things no one else does?" Hearing his breath catch, "Don't waste our time denying it. We have little enough as it is."

Evan had been awaiting this question from someone for some time. Though unsurprised that it came from her, still, he had to pause to consider his words.

"I occasionally have vivid dreams. If I'm fortunate, they offer me a clue to solving a problem."

She sat up, interested. "Do you ever see yourself in some future time?"

After a pause, "Yes."

"How long have you had these dreams?"

"Most of my life, every two or three years. Not often enough! The reason for the King's illness came to me in just such a dream."

Please, let this be enough for her.

"Aha! So, you have the sight! Are you a sorcerer?"

Evan laughed, relieved to be given a way through, glad that she wasn't pursuing the implications of this "future time."

"No, only the second son of a middling baron who loves a princess beyond all reason."

She smiled and snuggled back against him. Having noticed how adroitly he'd changed the subject, she knew he'd told her some of the truth, but not the whole truth. How far in the future could Evan see? Perhaps it was better for them both that she not know the what or how of it.

"Do you still carry my lock of hair?" she asked.

"Always. Right here, in my pouch."

"May I have a bit of yours?"

"Certainly." He took out his knife and sat still as she selected a discreet strand. She put it in her cupboard, for the moment. As soon as he left, she'd need to find a permanent, hidden location for it in her bags.

They got back under the covers and slipped happily into each other's arms.

In the comfortable silence that followed, Evan's thoughts wandered to a persistent fantasy he couldn't seem to excise. In it, she had given up her royal position and inheritance and settled into a normal life, as a physician's wife. She would have to retain a couple of servants, of course; how could he expect her to scrub a floor or eviscerate a chicken? As proof of the Lord's blessing on this marriage, they would have at least two children. She would be a devoted mother and would even, occasionally, assist him in his practice. In leisure moments, they would sit together and read, just as his parents did. Lively discussions would then ensue.

They'd live in an educated circle of friends and family, ideally close to Shaftesbury Castle because that was the only place where learning was valued, to his knowledge. Not in the castle per se—Joanna would never consent to submitting to the will of Mama or even that of timid Jeanne—but perhaps Papa could provide him a manor close by. There were no rainy days in this fantasy, only sun-filled idylls of joy and family. Even if it were God's will that she could not bear children, that would be fine, he'd decided. He wasn't fussed about reproducing himself, and there was little dynastic imperative for it.

It was a lovely fantasy. But it always came crashing to earth when he realized that "giving up" her royal position, short of eloping together and vanishing, was nigh impossible. He'd thought a lot about that. Could she just vanish into anonymity? Unless they moved to the hinterlands of Scotland or Wales or even Ireland, there was no chance at all. Anyway, in no fantasy could he imagine Joanna happy in the hinterlands of Scotland, Wales, or Ireland. It did nothing but rain there, everyone knew that. He'd spent many a night on his cot thinking through how to bring this fantasy to life, and he always ran right into the wall of Reality. It was simply not feasible. He wondered if it ever would be. Mama would know.

Meanwhile, Joanna had allowed herself to drift into her own delectable little fantasy, which she'd often spun as she lay awake at night. Since she'd never be allowed to marry him, she imagined a world in which she *could* keep him: literally, kept as a courtier, perhaps as a court physician, discreetly warming her bed at night while her old fart of a husband was snoring away in his own. She could command it; it was in her power.

But, always, the little fantasy vanished like smoke when she thought even slightly ahead. She knew in her heart that no matter how much he loved her, his work was the mistress that would never go away. And, tending to the complaints of the powerful and privileged, Evan's considerable gifts would go to waste. That, in itself, would surely be a sin against God. He would become ordinary, no matter how skilled he was in bed, and, under her tutelage, he was becoming skilled, indeed. It would strip him of that which meant the most to him: his honour.

By continually summoning him to her bed, she had already done that a little, she knew. He was worthy to be shown off—"Look who *I* have!"—not made to slink up to her chambers in the dead of night.

Soon enough, she would tire of him, he would resent her. How long would it take? In her most dismal moments, she thought a fortnight, at most.

One of her mother's more bizarrely enduring legacies was the concept of *fin' amor*. It had started as a sort of game on chilly winter afternoons, a way to amuse Eleanor's predominantly female court at Poitiers. It was Joanna's most enduring memory of her mother and half-sister, Marie de Champagne, as they all sat by the fire. Little Joanna had tittered along with the grown-up ladies, wanting to be grown-up like them. Her young mind had not yet internalized how within just a few years, her breasts having only started to bud, she would be forced to be grown-up, just like them.

The basic premise of *fin' amor* was devotion of a knight to his chosen noble—and usually unattainable—lady, and the extents to which he must go to prove his declared love. There were elaborate rules and circumstances to be weighed. It was all silly, harmless fun, which troubadours quickly adopted as their own. It was still standard troubadour entertainment over dinner and supper, and Joanna was sick to death of it by now, although she did admit that it had smartened up the comportment of the knights at court.

But make no mistake: it was all talk. Such a love could never be consummated. The knight would likely be castrated if caught, the lady tossed in a convent if she were fortunate. The possibility of a lady's child being anything other than her lord and husband's was too horrible to imagine. The fact that her own William had not only looked the other way but had *encouraged* her desperate, joyless affairs was profoundly open-minded; nonetheless, it was grounded on the pragmatic need for an heir and the tacit understanding that she not come to *feel* anything for those seed-donors. The chances of being assigned another husband who would countenance her taking a lover were precisely zero.

What had begun as an amusing flirtation had rapidly evolved to the certainty that Evan was the love of her life. But the sand running through her fingers of their liaison had almost run out. A rapidly diminishing present, never any future, only the pile of sand that was their past.

He asked, "How am I supposed to manage, getting up every day, for the rest of my life, knowing you are out there somewhere where I can't have you?"

"Don't say that. You're still so young. I am your first, but I surely won't be your last. You will make a home with a suitable girl who will bear you lots of beautiful children."

"Stop talking to me like I'm a babe at the breast. I don't want some 'suitable' girl. I only want the entirely unsuitable woman beside me right now. I *love* you! I will *always* love you. Can you believe that I will *always* be out there, missing you, praying for your happiness?"

She nodded. "And I love you, too. For as long as I live, you will be first in my heart." She had never put any of those words together in a sentence, not even to William.

"Please tell me this isn't really goodbye. Tell me that you'll let me know where you are, so I can come to you."

No emptier words had she ever spoken than her wish that he would find a suitable girl who would bear him many children. The grubby truth was that she'd rather gouge out the eyes of that cow than bless their marriage. But one of them deserved a chance at happiness. She herself would just have to keep snatching at whatever small moments happened to come her way. She had never known anything different.

She made her decision and resolved that she wouldn't regret it, even if it took the rest of her life. But not wanting to rob Evan of all hope, she lied to him, for the first and only time. "I will try, *mi corazón*."

Joanna and Berengaria left aboard the *Reine-de-Sicile*, the following day, September 25, 1192.

Everyone else left a fortnight later, on the feast of Saint Denis, October 9. The Third Crusade was over.

-VI-
Sir Evan de Montmorency

From Limassol, the original plan had been to rendezvous at Messina, but the ships hit bad weather yet again. They had to put in at Corfu, an island off the far northwest corner of Greece. It was a pleasant place, and ordinarily Richard might have chosen to winter there till he could select a desirable route home. But John's antics were getting more worrisome with every informant. Although there was no particular rush for his army to get home, there was a rush for *him*. Since his army's interests no longer converged with his own, it was time to turn them loose to look out for themselves.

All his advisors informed him that returning via the Atlantic was not an option: it was too late in the year, and the weather was too unpredictable. Thus, he must proceed by land across Europe. However, he would be at particular risk on most overland routes, according to his spies, because he'd made three implacable enemies during this crusade: Philip of France; Leopold of Austria, who had never forgiven that slap; and Henry VI, son of Frederick Barbarossa, still annoyed that Richard had denied his wife Constance—and by extension, him—the crown of Sicily in favour of ugly little Tancred.

Constance had been an aunt of William's, and he'd even named her in his will as his heir. Joanna had warned Richard that allowing Tancred to stay on the throne would be a mistake, and he now saw that she'd been right; however, at the time Richard just couldn't see how some aunt, some *woman,* could be a superior leader to Tancred, who'd put up a good fight against him.

Henry had, furthermore, drawn up alliances with the kings of Aragon and Castile, as well as with the doges of Genoa and Pisa, making those points of entry hazardous, as well.

To even sail the Mediterranean, Richard had been obliged to leave the great, recognizable *Trenc-la-Mer* in Acre, in favour of the much more modest *Franke-nef* [Free Ship].

As far as he could see, there was only one option. His older sister Matilda had been married to Henry of Saxony until her death, and Richard was on good terms with him. If he could just get to Saxony, he could be afforded decent shelter and protection, and then make his way home from there via the North Sea. He thus planned to make the long trip up the Adriatic Sea, docking in Venice, to proceed overland from there. This trip would not be in the grand style of his passage through France on the way to his crusade. This time, he would need to travel incognito.

In early November, Richard summoned the shipmasters of his fleet, as well as those in charge of every other branch of the operation, including Roger de Crécy. He released them that day from his service, conveying his thanks for their fealty and care. After a visit to his treasurer for final compensation, they could make their way home however they judged most fit.

This news caused a stir among the shipmasters. After two years under military orders, they were on their own. What were they to do? Where should they go? After the meeting, they congregated into worried groups, asking others about their plans: Where are you going? Who with? With winter coming, many of them opted to just stay put in Corfu.

Crécy soon shared the news with the rest of the medical personnel, who expressed similar sentiments of abandonment: What were they to do now? Hitch a ride on any available ship?

Crécy drew Evan aside. "He wants to see you," he said. "But first, run a comb through that hair of yours."

Richard was quartered in the donjon of the citadel. When Evan found him in the great chamber, he was overseeing the counting of the chests of coin and treasure, which were shortly to be distributed to the men.

He looked over at Evan, who bowed. "Ah, Montmorency. Glad you could come. Sit."

Evan sat on a stool in front of Richard's desk. Richard said, "So, I assume you have heard the news."

Evan replied, "Yes, Your Grace."

"Tell me, what are your plans?"

"Well, I would like to make my way to Salerno, to resume my studies there."

"Yes, you've mentioned this before." He paused. "You have served me most excellently. You have saved my life and many of my men's. I would prefer for you to remain in my service, but on this trip home I'm taking only Besace with me, as you may know. He is an able physician and has served me well through the years."

What Richard was not saying was that Joanna, fearful of Evan's safety on this hazardous trip across Europe, had begged him to release Evan from his service. She'd been practically hysterical on that point.

"You know how badly he wants to pursue his studies! He can't learn his craft shackled to you. Let him go, to learn and grow on his own—for a time, at least. It can only benefit you in the end. Please, I'll marry whatever poxy old fool you want. Just do this one thing for him, for us."

Richard had finally acceded.

For a time, at least, then.

"Yes, Your Grace, Sir Ralph explained this to me," Evan replied.

"This will also free you to continue your studies. I will only caution you not to get too comfortable wherever you decide to put down roots because I will require your services again. But, as a final gesture of gratitude, I command that you kneel before me now. Walter! Fors! Get over here to witness this."

Surprised, Evan got out of the chair and did as Richard had asked. Richard withdrew his sword from his baldric, and for a horrified moment Evan thought Richard really would lop off his head.

But Richard whacked him, hard, once on each shoulder and said, "For outstanding service to your God, your king and your country, I dub you Sir Evan de Montmorency."

Evan had always taken whatever he hadn't spent at the end of each month to the local Templar commandery, wherever he was at the time. His letter of credit had got increasingly cluttered with deposits of odd sums of pence. This day, he took his severance straight into the Acre office, a little disappointed that his elevated status had not translated into a "raise." Giving Richard the best possible benefit of doubt, he wondered if the King figured the bragging rights of tending him personally were reward enough.

The Templar, pinching with distaste a corner of Evan's tattered and spattered letter of credit, burned it and issued him a new one. Evan now had a total of forty-four marks in his account. Pleased that he had a surplus, he knew that Salerno would take a big chunk of it. He would have to be frugal.

Richard left with only four attendants on a small galley, three days later.

-VII-
"I intend to die in a tavern."

By December, Evan, Gurci, and Crécy were rounding the boot of the Italian peninsula. Those of the medical personnel who'd opted not to winter in Corfu had found passage on the *Misericordia.* It was simply easier, in the end. Most of the army migrated to whatever ship had carried them to and around the Holy Land and accepted the itinerary and sailing schedule of that ship. Shipmaster John Harewood informed those aboard that the eventual destination was Montpellier, take it or leave it; it was his home. That suited his passengers just fine. The first thing Evan asked was if the ship could leave him off at Salerno. Harewood said, sure, he was taking on supplies there, anyway.

Crécy and Chapelle would remain on board to Montpellier, from where they'd make their way home to Crécy, a village near Paris.

Gurci had always been less conflicted about the crusade than Evan. Even in the worst moments of the treks to Jerusalem and back, it was all a grand adventure to him. "You don't come from St. Ives," Gurci kept telling him. Fighting for his place in the family hierarchy in damp, cold Cornwall held little appeal to him and he was not yet ready to settle down.

Evan had come to see that some men were natural soldiers, and Gurci was one, even if he'd never held a weapon. While most of the men Evan had treated at the end were exhausted and battle-weary, often mentally damaged, others still had a gleam in their eyes, even when they were in pain. They loved it all, every minute of it, and Gurci was among them. Like Richard, in fact.

Evan leaned on him to join him in Salerno.

"So, you want me to spend the money I made on the crusade on room, board, and tuition in some woebegone backwater town with nothing to do except hump fish? I come from a place like that."

"But I have money! I actually have more than I started with!" Gurci, in contrast, had spent almost all he earned on women and gambling. "Look, don't even think about the money. We'll figure it out. And Salerno has two things Cornwall doesn't have: Sun. Heat."

"Maybe you haven't noticed, but my Sicilian isn't too great."

"Neither is mine. Anyway, the classes will be in Latin, most likely."

"Latin? Are you *serious?"*

"Sure. It's the only language everyone will know. Don't worry about it. Look how quickly you figured out that Avicenna. I'll help you."

Misericordia stopped in Messina for two days to take on supplies. During that stop, Evan and Gurci dropped in at the hospital to help out and happily reconnect with Sayid Abdullah and Joseph ben Solomon. Crécy merely wanted a short holiday in an agreeable location before the long trip back to French shores, and home from there.

The night before the ship's departure, Crécy insisted on taking them out to supper. That evening, sitting in a portside tavern, over impeccably fresh, grilled tuna dressed with lemon and olives, along with a dry Sicilian white, Evan presented his book of drawings to a delighted Crécy. Evan fervently hoped that he would never again be expected to draw a sawed-off limb, an ulcerated toe, a stitched abdomen.

Although Crécy had only studied in Paris, whose *studium* was still fairly new, he knew all about Salerno's renowned medical school. Founded in the ninth century, the school was both a facility for advanced education and a teaching hospital that synthesized Greek, Roman, Jewish, and Muslim physic.

A licence from Salerno was strictly regulated. This was because the area's salubrious climate had always attracted the rich and ailing, looking for a cure and a seaside sojourn in the bargain. This, in turn, drew the usual assortment of quacks and crooks selling dubious cures, relics, and "magic" crystals. The school relentlessly turned them out of the city.

To get in to the Salerno school, one needed, first of all, a preliminary degree in the arts from a recognized *studium* such as Oxford or Bologna, or even Paris.

Crécy said, "Montmorency, my boy, there's no guarantee you'll get in, even with the comprehensive education you have. How good is your knowledge of the trivium and the quadrivium?"

"Well, I'm pretty sure my tutors taught me most of it."

Gurci said, "Say *what?*"

Crécy went on, "You'll have to take some sort of entry examination. And you're looking at four years of study even if you do get in."

"Couldn't I get credit for my two years' worth of experience in the crusade?" Gurci asked.

"I don't think you can get past that entry examination. Sorry, my boy."

Crécy sipped his wine. "Imagine this, *women* are admitted as both students and teachers! When I was your age, my father was shocked to hear that and, for that reason alone, told me I must study in Paris, under Hugo. I must say I agree with my father on that score. It's dangerous to give women too many ideas and ambitions. It's not *decent* for a woman to see an unclothed man other than her husband," he harrumphed.

"Those were the days. My first time away from home. I was a cleric, so the authorities couldn't touch us. What we got away with!" He paused, and a sly smile crossed his face as he recalled his misspent youth. "The most fun I've ever had." Perhaps he expected the others to ask him to elaborate on his exploits, but they sipped their wine pensively. Gurci would not be going to Salerno, and both were dealing with that let-down.

Looking out on the setting sun, Crécy said, "Some wise ancient said, 'I intend to die in a tavern.'"

Evan had never heard that quotation, but it did bring back a memory. One night, in post-coital bliss, his head had rested on Joanna's belly as she languidly ran her fingers through his hair—something that, for some reason, she liked to do.

He said, "I intend to die right here."

She'd let forth a great belly laugh, disturbing his bliss. She playfully scolded him, "Don't even think it! What am I supposed to do *then*, with your naked corpse in my bed? Now, put your head back there."

Evan pushed that memory back, to be savoured another time. He forced himself back to the moment.

He remarked, "The life here is good, you know, Morgant."

Gurci replied, "Ay, but without you to borrow money from, where's the fun?"

"Well, I won't be *that* far away! So, what do you think you'll do now?"

In typical Gurci fashion, he shrugged off his disappointment. "Who knows? I may sign on as a medicus on a merchant ship. Eventually, I may go home. Wherever the wind blows me." Both Evan and Crécy knew that Gurci would never have any money; he would always be a medicus/surgeon, but he would always find work because he was among the very best there was.

"What about Muhtal?" Evan asked. "You could get a good price on him."

"You mean Glue-Soon? Nah. He's my buddy. I think he's decided I'm the best human he's going to get. Besides, I need some kind of transportation."

Crécy suggested, "Why don't you come with me? I'm sure the King will need my services again, and I could get you on."

Gurci seemed flattered and said he'd sleep on it.

As the three men embraced for the final time when the ship docked at Salerno, Crécy said to Evan, "It has been a pleasure to serve with you, and I'll be proud to do so again."

"And so would I," Evan replied. He meant it.

He turned to Louis Chapelle. "Goodbye, Chapelle, and thank *you* for serving Sir Roger so faithfully." Evan and Gurci had found out pretty quickly who the magician was behind the appearance of all those medicinal herbs. Chapelle bowed solemnly, but when he stood up, he had a never-before-seen smile on his face.

To Gurci, Evan said, "You've been a true friend. You know where my family lives. It's not that far from St. Ives, really. Come and stay, any time. I, too, would be proud to work with you again."

-VIII-
"Many think the earth is round."

Salerno was a hilly seaside town reminiscent of Messina: large port, narrow streets, stairways opening onto unexpected, small squares. Most of the city was squeezed between the Tyrrhenian Sea and the steep hills behind it. A small river flowed through the city centre into the sea. The city held two dozen churches and nine monasteries and was blessed with bountiful sun and water, thanks to a still-functioning Roman aqueduct. This allowed almost anything planted to grow. Wisely, the streets were laid out so the welcoming sea breeze could blow through unimpeded. Roman-style villas of the wealthy perched on the steep hills surrounding the city.

Having started modestly, the Schola Medica Salernitana had gradually taken over various locations around town: a couple of old palaces, an old magistrates' court, the Church of Santa Maria della Porta, and rooms in the Salerno Cathedral. Students were housed in the Monastery of San Benedetto. Large, carefully tended beds of herbs were cultivated outside each building.

Looking around this prosperous town, soaked with learning, with its blessed location, warm for a December day, Evan said to Wasim, "This is beautiful. I think we'll like it here." It had never occurred to Evan for a moment that he wouldn't be admitted.

Prior Lorenzo da Bari was the one to see about admission, according to a student who pointed him to a building on his left. He was told to look for a bald man with a hunchback and a cane. He was also warned not to make the mistake of underestimating him because of that handicap. He found Bari inside, conversing with a group of other people, similarly authoritative in appearance. These were likely *maestri*, including one middle-aged woman.

Evan waited until the group had dispersed before he approached him. "Prior Lorenzo? My name is Evan de Montmorency and I come seeking admission to your school."

Bari may have been painfully handicapped, but Evan saw that his eyes were keen. He stopped and cast a shrewd glance over him, clearly assessing him. He said, "Aha. So, you're the Montmorency who saw to King Richard during the recent crusade?"

Evan started. He replied, "Yes, I was honoured to treat the King on a few occasions. Do you mind if I ask you how you know about me?"

"Come into my office. We have matters to discuss." He led him down to the end of the hall, made of solid, whitewashed stone.

"Here, take a seat." His shelves were crammed with codices, scrolls, and medical curiosities, including a bleached human skull and a heart in a glass jar full of pickling fluid, Evan assumed. Other than that, a beautifully woven oriental rug covered the tile floor, and two large, mullioned windows looked out on the monastery next door. His table was cluttered with rolled parchment.

Bari began, eyeing him curiously, "So, young man, your reputation precedes you. You have a patroness: the Dowager Queen of Sicily. We were honoured that she stopped by here on her own way home from the crusade and informed us that you'd be coming. She urged us to give you every consideration. A most lovely and gracious woman. May I say you come highly recommended."

Evan's breath caught as he took this in. Oh Joanna, I will love you forever, but I don't need your help.

Bari observed the play of emotions on the young man's face, confirming what he'd suspected. He switched from French to Latin. "Of course, we take our responsibilities here most seriously. We told the Dowager Queen that you would have to be assessed first and placed wherever your knowledge level was most appropriate. Can you tell me how much formal education you've had? You're too young to have attended a *studium generale*."

"That's correct, Prior," Evan replied, carrying on in Latin.

Very good, thought Bari. The boy had correctly understood that this formed part of his assessment.

"I knew of Jacob. Pity about his death. I assume you have been instructed in at least some of the trivium and quadrivium. How much have you had of them?"

"A fair amount."

"Let me ask you a few questions, then." He steepled the tips of his fingers and sat back in thought. "What proportion is the volume of a cone to its corresponding cylinder?"

"One-third."

"How does one calculate the volume of a cone?

"One-third of the sum of pi R squared times the height."

"What is the value of pi?"

"3.1415926."

"What else?"

"I know no other number after that, though I understand no one has calculated the limit."

"What is the farthest planet from the Earth?"

"Saturn."

"Of what sort of law was Cicero a proponent?"

"Natural law."

"What is the first thing one swears in the Hippocratic Oath?"

"To hold my teacher in this art equal to my own parents."

"Very good. Remember that while you are here."

And on it went, for some time. These questions were just the warm-up. Bari was enjoying himself, trying to test the limits of the young man's knowledge. Montmorency's memory seemed to him to be of near-total recall. He'd had a few other students with this gift, but this young man was indeed a pleasant surprise. He'd been expecting someone a little older, more worldly-looking, perhaps a bit louche, even dim. In short, someone easy to condescend to, not this fresh-faced but very clever youngster.

The lad had so far got only one wrong: a perfectly elementary question, surprisingly, that Bari had thrown in there for fun, expecting him to ask, "Is this a trick?" Asked what the shape of the earth was, he'd replied, "Well, many think the earth is round."

Hilarious! Everyone would fall off! He'd had to laugh at the very notion. But it proved that this young fellow still had things to learn.

Finally, as the bells rang for dinner, Bari sat forward. "Well, young man, there's no doubt about your qualifications. You are, of course, admitted to the school. You realize that this is a four-year program?"

"Yes, Prior. I was hoping to obtain some credit for my experience in Messina and Outremer."

"Well, we will have to see about that on the wards, but I'm sure we can settle on something. Now, about your tuition. It's not cheap. Including room and board, it is forty marks a year."

Evan gulped. He had it, barely. For a year. Could he graduate in as little as a year, even with advance credit? His heart sank.

"Fortunately for you, the Dowager Queen has already paid for your tuition in the form of a sizable donation to the school."

Evan gaped at him. He'd never anticipated this. He felt tears well in his eyes and determinedly blinked them away.

"She made it clear that there were no strings attached to this donation, of course, though she would prefer that it be used for a needy student such as yourself."

Evan did a quick calculation and cleared his throat. "Prior, may I ask a favour? That I cover my own room and board, as well as that of my horse? And that this sum be used to help a truly needy student? For my bed, I'm not particular. I've slept on all surfaces, in all conditions. I'll sleep anywhere."

Bari studied him again, a surprised smile on his face. "Very well. I'm sure we can make suitable arrangements in the San Benedetto next door." Looking out the window to see Wasim chomping on the parsley in one of the herb beds, "That's your horse? The grey Arabian? Spoils of war, I presume?"

"Yes, he's all I have."

"Fine steed. We will take good care of him. Now, if you'll follow me, I'll take you to our main office, where we can formally register you and show you to your quarters. I suggest you take the rest of the day to orient yourself to your surroundings. We will expect you in Maestro Alessandro Scalia's anatomy class promptly after prime tomorrow morning."

Evan was shown to a dormitory at the monastery, housing twenty students, and Wasim to his own quarters in the stables. Meals were taken in a communal dining hall.

First thing the following morning, Evan found himself in the company of fifteen other students, including three women, all listening to a lecture on the musculature of the human arm.

1193

A Medieval Infirmary

An ignorant physician is the aide-de-camp of death.
—Avicenna

-I-
Salerno

The morning of January 5, 1193, about a month after Evan's arrival, the hospital was abuzz with shocked whispering.

"What's wrong?" Evan asked no one in particular in a huddled group.

"Your king. He's been kidnapped."

"*Whaaat? Richard?!*"

"Yes, four days before Christmas, we heard. Somewhere in Austria. They say he was trying to cross Europe incognito and was recognized. I heard Dürnstein Castle is where he's being held, wherever that is. Any of you heard of it?"

They all shook their heads.

This would be Leopold's doing, Evan thought.

"I heard he was wearing too fancy a ring," someone added.

"*I* heard he was throwing too much money around for a modestly-dressed 'merchant,'" someone else had to say.

Evan couldn't resist putting in, "Have any of you *seen* the King?" No one had. "Well, he's a head taller than any one of us."

He now had everyone's attention. Placing his hand at about a 6'5" height, "How many people are this tall?"

Their mouths flew open. One of them said, "No one's that tall."

"It's true. I served with him. He made a lot of enemies on the crusade. His own brother has no wish to see him alive again. Anyone would have guessed that he was going to be making his way home by land at this time of year. All they'd have had to do is give a general description and stress that he is *tall.* Well-built. Arrogant. Carries himself like he owns the world. He'd be hard to miss. So, have any of you heard what they want for ransom?"

"A hundred thousand marks."

"I heard pounds."

"God in Heaven, how will they ever raise that? Will they even try?" Evan wondered aloud. His next thought was of his family. They're going to come after Papa again.

Although he was still new to the routine at the school, he already knew much of what was being explained. Even so, he'd found his "tribe": every one of his classmates, having been through the most gruelling elimination processes to qualify for entry to this place, knew exactly what they wanted to do with their lives. He also knew that, for once, his status would not mark him as a dilettante in the eyes of his classmates; one had to be rich to afford the education they'd received. He was no one special and he loved that.

There were five women of varying ages, and he was struck by how focused they were. There was none of the self-important strutting around that he saw in some of the men; it was like they felt they had something to prove. Since women were barred from studying at most *studia* that he was aware of, he wondered how'd they'd gained admission to this place. He asked one of them, Demetria Laskaris, how she'd managed it.

She looked offended. Evan hastened to clarify. "I'm not questioning your ability; I just wondered how you managed to get in without going to a *studium*."

"From what I've heard, I got in as you did. I had to take a test. My family is old and wealthy, and I am a third daughter. They fortunately believed that I should have an equal chance at instruction."

"You are fortunate, indeed. My parents felt the same way."

They soon became friends and study partners. They would grill each other on what they'd learned each day. Though the other students teased him about it, it wasn't *like* that, Evan insisted. He was pining for Joanna and confided that to Demetria, though he did not name her; as for Demetria—well, Evan sensed that she wasn't really interested in men, anyway. But even though they conversed in a tongue native to neither of them, in a way they spoke the same language: two privileged aristocrats, neither of them first born, raised in enlightened households with a lot and nothing expected of them at the same time.

The organization of the hospital was similar to the one in Messina, only larger. Here, a whole floor was devoted to surgical treatments.

Digestive complaints were treated in their own building. Their days began right after prime, every day except Sunday, following a quick breakfast of bread and a piece of fruit. Their patients were their instructors at this time of day. The students were taken from bed to bed, where they were briefed on each patient's malady and were taught to carefully palpate the afflicted areas, feeling for swelling and pain. The patient was involved in this process: How was he feeling that day? Better? Where exactly did it hurt?

Students were constantly examined and assessed based on their knowledge of diagnostics, as well as their manner around patients, as they touched them and adjusted their position in the bed. Lectures were based on Hippocrates, Galen, Avicenna's *Canon,* and al-Majusi's *Liber Regalis,* among others. Classrooms were mainly tiered rooms with benches, where their *maestri* would recite the contents of these books. Students were expected to remember, although the material was constantly reviewed. As visual aids, on the walls, someone had painted star charts, urine tables, and illustrations of human and animal anatomy.

While female students were integrated with the male students in the treatment of men, the reverse was not the case. It was still felt that women's diseases should be treated by women only. What struck Evan was how women's ailments were considered a worthy, separate field of study. Women were not disparaged in any way; in fact, Evan was taught that probably the greatest physician who ever worked at the school was an eleventh-century woman, Maestra Trota de Ruggiero. Every other day, Demetria and the other female trainees took off to learn about female conditions.

One of the best ways of remembering facts was to incorporate them into a poem. For this, the *Regimen Sanitatis Salernitanum* was an essential resource. It had been composed in the previous century, some thought by the great Trota herself. A lengthy poem written in hexameter, it offered advice on diet, herbs, humors, and bloodletting. It synthesized the essence of what was known in Mediterranean physic.

Some commonsensical advice on diet was presented like this:

"Eggs newly laid, are nutritive to eat,
And roasted Raw are easy to digest.

Fresh Gascoigne wine is good to drink with meat,
Broth strengthens nature above all the rest."

Practical advice on when and how to let blood was described in these terms:

"Three special Months (September, April, May)
There are, in which 'tis good to open a vein;
In these three Months the Moon bears greatest sway,
Then old or young that store of blood contain ..."

Despite this, Evan was determined never to phlebotomize in his own practice. While only about a cup of blood was taken and the procedure itself was probably harmless, an open wound always carried an unacceptable risk of infection, in his view.

In fact, there was much that he quietly disagreed with, beginning with the school's acceptance of both Hippocrates' and then, later, Roman physician Galen's theory of the four humors (blood, phlegm, yellow bile, and black bile), their corresponding temperaments (sanguine, phlegmatic, choleric, and melancholic respectively), and the necessity of keeping them in balance. The seasons, as well as the earth's alignment with the moon, sun, and planets all had to be factored in.

It was all fantastically complicated, and Evan knew that at some point, this would be debunked. However, he did appreciate how physicians made every effort to prevent disease by prescribing a careful diet, which included moderate intake of foods thought to throw the humors off balance, such as wine and dairy products. They were trying to treat the whole person, not just the patient's symptoms. Central to their belief system was balance, and the maintenance of it. He had no quarrel with any of that.

One of Trota's great contributions concerned pain and wound management, strategies now thoroughly standardized at the school, with a large catalogue of opiates and herbs for prevention of excessive bleeding and infection. Her experience with women was invaluable in developing this knowledge: treating the pain of menstruation and childbirth, with its frequent perineal tearing helped her to identify concerns and their appropriate management. She also observed that women were more prone to a particular "hemicranial" headache, a severe headache on one side of the head. Midwives and wise women had treated these for millennia, but it was not until Trota that "women's" conditions started to become thought of as human conditions.

While anatomy was important, to Evan's disappointment, no human cadavers were available to study—only those of pigs, considered the closest to human anatomy. The Church officially forbade examination of human remains; the main reason, however, was the understandable aversion of Salernitans to the idea of someone they knew being potentially carved up on an examining table. Pigs had the advantage, as well, of being easy to obtain. Each student in his class was assigned his or her own pig. Even so, dissections had to be carried out expeditiously, before the animal began to rot. Other than that, they did have Galen's anatomical drawings of monkeys at their disposal. And it was more than Evan had seen till then.

As the days lengthened and the weather warmed, he would ride up into the hills after supper. While Wasim grazed, he would sit under an ancient olive tree and contentedly look out on the vastness of what everyone called *Le Grand Bleu.* So peaceful to gaze upon from here, but he was now quite familiar with its capriciousness. He would think about Joanna, wondering where she was and whether she would drop by Salerno again. He fantasized about trysts in inns, or maybe that splendid villa yonder. Sadly, as the months went by, those fantasies crumbled away as he saw anew that stolen trysts now and then were all they would ever be permitted. And it wasn't enough, not anymore.

Updates on Richard's status came to Evan through many mouths and in many languages. From what he gathered, a serious attempt was being made to raise the ransom, which was indeed one hundred thousand pounds—or, one hundred fifty thousand marks. The Dowager Queen Eleanor had put herself in charge of this task and mandated that every free household, including churches, contribute one-quarter of their annual income to the cause. It was a staggering amount. In the meantime, Leopold had sold Richard to Henry VI, who'd moved him more than four hundred miles west to Trifels

Castle. Richard's location was not a secret; on the contrary, Henry bragged about it, taunting Eleanor, betting that she'd never come up with the money. The months dragged on. Both Leopold and Henry were excommunicated, but it seemed not to faze them at all. They'd worry about penitence, indulgences, or hellfire later. For now, there was serious coin to be gained.

To everyone's additional surprise, word reached the school in March that Saladin had died of a fever in Damascus, earlier that month. Rumours suggested that he'd died essentially penniless, having given away his vast fortune to the poor. Evan pondered the vagaries of Fortune and wondered what Richard and Saladin might have done differently, had they known that seven months after they signed their treaty, one of them would be imprisoned for ransom and the other would be dead.

Meanwhile, it became obvious to Evan's maestri that his training in Messina and on the crusade had more than qualified him to be a physician. He'd learned from the best, shared improved treatments with his fellow students and teachers, and even devised some of his own. The fact of the matter was that there wasn't a lot they could teach him.

As a result, one morning in August of 1193, about eight months after his arrival, Prior Lorenzo summoned Evan back to his office. Much to Evan's surprise and delight, after repeating the Hippocratic Oath, and further swearing to treat the poor and to avoid collusion with apothecaries, Bari presented him with a parchment licence to practise physic. He said, "Congratulations, Maestro Sir Evan de Montmorency."

The title caught Evan by surprise because he was sure he'd never mentioned being knighted.

Bari said, "All of us here believe that, with a little more training, you would do well as a maestro here. Would you consider that?"

While Evan was thrilled by the compliment, he replied, "Perhaps sometime I can return here, but, for now, I must return to my family."

Bari nodded in understanding. "Then, go forth and bring honour to this school," he said. "You have done your family proud."

As he awkwardly and painfully took Evan in his arms to embrace him, Evan felt his eyes sting with tears.

That afternoon, having said goodbye to Demetria and his other classmates, he and Wasim were on the road. Where to? He didn't know. In the general direction of Shaftesbury Castle, to be sure. Paris sounded good. He rode down to the harbour and booked passage on a cog heading for Marseille.

-II-
Arthur and Guenievre

Outside of Marseille, Evan fell in with a company of about twenty returning pilgrims and crusaders who had wintered in Corfu and then lingered for a while in the benign Provençal climate. From Aics, they picked up a Roman road to Lyon, as ever thankful that, although Rome's great civilization lay in ruins, its infrastructure still functioned. From Lyon, tracking along the Saône river would take them as far as Dijon, then cross country till they picked up the Seine to Paris. From there, still following the Seine, Evan would eventually reach the Channel. The travellers welcomed him into their midst; a physician was always an asset, and Evan was an armed knight, although he was at pains to clarify that he'd never used his sword on anyone.

Until they reached Paris, the travelling party would expand and shrink as people hived off to take their separate routes home. All were accustomed to sleeping in the open air, though they aimed for monasteries along the route where they could be guaranteed indoor accommodations and a modest, hot meal. There were wayside inns, of course, but few had money to pay for a room.

The pilgrims had spent the entire crusade and after begging for their keep. Like dogs around a campfire, they pleaded to those in the company to spare them what food they could. Some even stole from others in the group. Evan spared what he could from the change in his pocket, both annoyed at their utter lack of self-reliance and pitying their abjectness. Nonetheless, although he could well have afforded to bunk down in the odd inn, he found he was glad for their company.

As he rode past the sloping vineyards of ripening grapes in the Beaujolais and Burgundy regions, stopping here and there to find simple, though well-prepared, food, Evan sensed the *savoir-vivre* that seemed to permeate the very air. There was something about this place that all those who'd invaded it deeply admired and strove to emulate, he thought.

Take his own loutish Norse ancestors, for example. Barely a century after they'd been granted what would come to be called Normandy, they were so integrated that they spoke French and considered England an uncivilized backwater. They had long since dropped the Norse patronyms of Sigurdsson, Ericsson, and so on in favour of their Norman birthplace. They equally disdained the descendants of the Norsemen who'd lived in England for centuries. More than a century after the Conquest, Evan's people still tenaciously held on to that French.

Outside of Dijon, in open country, the travellers picked up a troupe of entertainers and a *trouvère* by the name of Crestien de Troies. Now in his fifties, and, by his own admission, getting a little old for cross-country journeys, Crestien was an established poet whose more recent works embroidered the Arthurian legend. He'd written several *romans*, and, at the moment, he was working on another, *Perceval.*

Evan gathered that Crestien was well regarded in court circles and financially successful, considering the precarious living most of his colleagues eked out. His problem was not income, although his *librarius*—the man in charge of parchmenter, scribe, illuminator, binder, and book broker—took the lion's share of the money. His problem was spending. He gambled excessively. He was on his way to Paris to sell a few love poems to keep the moneylenders at bay.

One evening, everyone's bellies pleasantly full from roasted rabbit, Evan asked Crestien if he'd sing one of his works for the company. The band members pulled out their instruments: a flute, pipe, tabor, frame drum, and lute. All instrumental groups kept a repertoire of melodies that worked well with octosyllabic rhymes. Crestien took a few moments to orient himself to their choice of melody and its rhythm; then, in a clear tenor, he sang the tale of Yvain: that of a hapless knight returning from a quest a little later than promised to suit his wife, Laudine. He is therefore banished and must perform several tasks before eventually winning her love back. One of these is rescuing a lion, who becomes his devoted companion.

The company loved it and wanted more. Crestien demurred; at over sixty-eight hundred lines, it was long, and he'd only got a quarter of the way through it. But he promised more another night.

After the performance, Evan took a seat beside Crestien and asked him about himself. He'd grown up in Marie de Champagne's court, the second son of one of her courtiers. Marie was one of Eleanor's daughters from her first marriage to King Louis, and was every bit as formidable as her mother. She was also Joanna's half-sister, Evan realized. It was all he could do to stop himself from eagerly asking him if he'd ever met Joanna.

Like Evan, he'd had to find his own way but had always known that he had an ear for music and a talent for transcribing stories into poetry. From there, it was not a long reach to composing his own works. In the last while, he'd turned to the Arthurian legend, a motherlode of potential material.

"What did you think of my *Yvain?*" he asked.

"Very entertaining!" Evan replied. "But, just a thought, isn't Laudine a bit of a ..." He searched for a word.

"Shrew? Bitch?" Crestien suggested, smirking.

"Well, yes, I guess. Just because he comes home a few days late? Come on!"

Crestien smiled and shrugged. "*Yvain's* been received well. It's what sells these days. At Poitiers, it's all you hear."

Evan replied, "Yes, I know. The reverend mother of the abbey next to my home often writes such tales, though hers are what she calls *lais*, very short."

Crestien looked more closely at Evan. "Are you speaking of the Reverend Mother Marie Martel?"

"The very one."

Crestien leaned towards him, grinning. "Did you say your name was Montmorency? Are you related to the Earl of Shaftesbury?"

Evan cocked his head. "Why yes. I'm his younger son, making my way in the world, just like you are."

Crestien laughed. "Well, I'll be foxed! I've had the honour of visiting Shaftesbury Castle. I've sung for your parents. Thrice."

Evan laughed in turn. "Not really! When?"

"Oh, let's see." He stared off into space for moment. "Always in autumn. 1170, I think, 1174, and again five years ago. In fact, I tried out my *Lancelot* on them in '74."

"Oh, too bad. For the first, I was barely a gleam in my parents' eyes. I was too young to remember you for the second. For the third, I was away squiring then."

The fall of 1170? Crestien would have sung for Stacey, Evan realized.

"Yes, now that I think of it, I do remember a little boy that night in '74. I remember being surprised that children were allowed at their high table." He smiled at him, winking. "You know they're Camaalot, don't you?"

Evan had heard of Camaalot as being the seat of the legendary Arthur and Guenievre but that was all he knew. "What do you mean?" he asked, puzzled.

"As far as we *trouvères* are concerned, your parents are Arthur and Guenievre. Do you not know how widely known they are in educated circles? How people beat a path to their door, knowing that, in addition to exemplary food and ale, they'll hear conversation second to none? Everyone knows that the Earl likes to maintain a modest profile. Out of respect, and because we don't want to ruin it for everyone, we don't post signs. Still, it's the worst-kept secret in Christendom. They are our muses, and when we say 'See you next fall in Camaalot?' everyone knows exactly what it means."

Evan beamed with pride. It was nothing he hadn't known, his whole life. But to hear it from someone like Crestien, well, that was something. "I've always known that I've been hugely fortunate. But for me, all those guests at dinner, it was my life. I knew nothing else until I left the castle to page." He winked at Crestien. "My mother called you freeloaders."

"There was only one thing your parents expected of us, an unwritten rule of sorts," Crestien went on. "We were to mind our manners. No drunk and disorderly behaviour. Hands off the servants. If anyone lapsed even a little, he was quietly escorted to the gates and never allowed inside again. The best of us try to bring something for them, to show our gratitude. The last time I was there, I brought a copy of *Erec et Enide*. I know how much they value books."

Evan nodded. He'd seen it in the great chamber cupboard, one of fifteen, the last time he looked.

Crestien eyed him shrewdly. "It's perhaps fortunate as well that you're a younger son. It would be difficult to live up to that father of yours."

"Yes, my older brother reminds me of that every chance he gets. You probably met him when you were there."

"Yes. Handsome lad. Quiet wife."

Evan chortled. "That's about right! Edward is intelligent, all right. I think he's just afraid to speak his mind. And Jeanne has a stutter that she's very embarrassed about. Troies, I'm glad we've had this talk. You're like a link to home. I don't feel so far away now."

Despite the age difference—Crestien could have almost been his grandfather—both men went to sleep that night pondering the happy serendipity that brought strangers together.

As their northerly passage progressed, they gradually felt the temperature drop and saw the leaves fall. They'd lost the warm lands of temperate fruits and olive oil, and were now in butter and apple and pear country. The aroma of fermentation and pressed cider filled the air.

-III-
"What was the crusade but a quest?"

King Philip may not have been much of a crusader, but at home he knew what he was about. A few years before the crusade, looking out his palace window and disgusted at his city, he'd ordered the roads paved. That work was still going on. Among the first things he did upon returning from crusade was capture much of Normandy east of the Seine away from Angevin control. Now, he was walling Paris's Right Bank against the danger of invasion from Richard if he was ever sprung free. This now seemed like a real possibility: sources informed him that Eleanor was raising the money. As for the Left Bank, it could wait. It was populated by ruffians of the working class—therefore expendable, in his opinion. As an additional defence, he'd also started work on a castle, Le Castel du Louvre.

Philip was still only twenty-eight. Within his lifetime, thanks to his massive building schemes and expansion of his kingdom, he would become known as Philip Augustus.

Nevertheless, Paris remained a crowded, rank city of a hundred thousand, dwarfing London. Like the Thames, everything wound up in the Seine, from animal and human excrement, to offal from slaughtered animals, to run-off from the tanneries, and even the odd corpse.

Evan followed rue Saint-Martin outside the walls to the Temple commandery, to redeem a few more French *sols*. This meant passing through the tannery district. The stench about took his breath away. How could people do this all day? Still, leatherworking was a profitable trade that likely paid for the handsome houses he went by on the outskirts of the city. This was where the moneyed townspeople lived. Between the tannery district and the expensive outer houses lay the textile shops. These were filled with the latest in exquisitely worked Italian brocades and silks and then transported everywhere through Northern Europe and across the Channel. The wall was a good distance beyond the last of the housing, thus incorporating some farmland. Clearly, Philip had assumed the city would expand considerably.

Crestien insisted that Evan stay with him and his wife, Aubine. They lived in a modest, two-story wattle-and-daub house on the Left Bank, on the rue des Escrivains. Out back was the well, her kitchen garden, mostly hibernating now for the coming winter, along with their cow and chickens, now joined by Wasim. No children graced the marriage, but one never asked why; the story would likely be a painful one. Evan knew that life hadn't always been easy for them, and, certainly, Crestien would never have been faithful to her during those years on the road. Still, they remained a devoted pair, or as much as was possible after thirty-five years of marriage. Evan bunked down on the tiled floor of their *salle.*

Despite the squalor, Paris had its charms, or at least the Left Bank did. Those in search of amusement of any kind hung around the scruffy taverns frequented by students, clerics, and travelling merchants. The nightlife was varied, the gambling was good, and so was Crestien's company.

Evan was glad for Crestien's insider familiarity with his neighbourhood. A lot of those taverns were frequented by low life characters, and brawls were common. Amongst the hard-working citizens lurked faux monks shaking down people for money, as well as petty thieves, whores, and swindlers outside the churches selling fake relics.

Crestien had told him, "I'm known around here. Mostly, people leave me alone. Don't wander around without me. Walk tall and don't look like a victim."

Crestien introduced him to some of his associates, including his friend, Robert de Boron, who was also embellishing the pagan Arthurian legend. His big idea was to interweave it with a Christian element: the chalice in which Joseph of Arimathea was said to have gathered drops of Jesus's blood. He waxed enthusiastic about the good story lines that would emerge from quests Arthur's knights could pursue in search of this chalice.

Refilling Boron's wine, Aubine griped, "But this has nothing to do with how things really are! What self-respecting man sets off on some fool quest to impress a silly lady? Who has time for that? If he wants to prove his manhood, he should stay at home and put food on the table."

Crestien replied, "But in a way, it *is* how things are, *chiere*. What was the crusade but a quest? Why do you think all those pilgrims are on the road? We're just dressing it up in a more pleasing form, with a dash of allegory to get people thinking. No one would ever want to read about a bunch of ordinary pilgrims slogging their way to some shrine."

Evan enjoyed these evenings, watching fertile minds inspire each other. However, it was now into October, the Parisian skies were a perennial dull grey, and he knew he had to be on the road soon if he didn't want to winter there. The last night of his stay, over cheese-and-chive-laced omelettes and a rough red wine, they discussed their long- and short-term plans. Evan basked in the cozy comfort of his friends' home, knowing it would be weeks before he enjoyed the like again.

Crestien's back was stiff and sore, and he was thinking about retiring to concentrate on his writing. He acknowledged that Paris was the centre of Europe now—everyone who mattered in his work lived there—but he missed his birthplace, Troies. He was trying to talk Aubine into moving back there. The air was healthier, he told her; there was less chance of being robbed and stabbed, too.

Evan had so enjoyed their company he wanted to help them out in some way, and an idea had occurred to him. He'd seen a few copies of Crestien's works sitting on his shelves.

"Troies," he said, "May I buy one of your books off you? I can't think of a better gift for my parents." Earlier that day, he'd made another, larger, withdrawal at the commandery. As a precaution, he'd been escorted back to Troies's house.

Crestien was delighted, and Evan could see the wheels turning in Aubine's head. "Which one are you thinking of?" she wanted to know.

Evan replied, "The *Lancelot.* It's the one they'll have heard. I know it'll mean a lot to them."

Aubine replied, "Well, what do you think, *mon amor?* You

only have the one copy. I don't think we can let it go for less than three *livres*."

That was too much, of course, but Evan knew it would certainly be at least one *livre*. A number of paid hands would have touched the book before it ever got into Crestien's. As the author, he'd have got a discounted price, but he would never have received a free copy. Eventually, with some dickering, they settled on one *livre*, ten *sols*. The life of a roaming *trouvère,* even such as Crestien, was not an easy one, and he knew this would help them out for a while.

Crestien said, "Why don't I introduce you to my *librarius*, Henri Dupont. He has a fair stash of books. If you'd like another one to keep the *Lancelot* company, I can take you there tomorrow before you leave."

The next day, Crestien took him to a house a few streets west on rue Pierre-Sarasin, where they found Dupont. It was there, in the back room, that Evan spotted *La Chanson de Roland*. He'd heard of this classic French tale and knew his parents would love it. For another *livre*, he now owned another book. And, into the bargain, something else: an Avicenna, in Greek. Few here read Greek, and it was Infidel physic, anyway. Evan knew just the right recipient for it.

I'm getting to be quite the fancy man, he thought, very pleased with himself. He tucked them down at the bottom of his bag, wrapped in cloth that Aubine gave him. He would guard them with his life.

He had once asked Mama what she missed the most about the twenty-first century. After a short pause, she replied, "Learning. And books. They are unbelievably plentiful and cheap, and everyone can read them. They are so cheap, they are often given away as soon as they're read."

To Evan's gasp of disbelief, she'd said, "I know. I couldn't believe it, either."

On the market, those three books could fetch a labourer more than a year's wage.

Before he set out, they crossed Le Petit-Pont, no more than a footbridge, to see the construction on the new cathedral, to be called Nostre-Dame. Construction had begun thirty years ago, and, to date, only the nave walls were complete. There was no roof yet. "It'll be beautiful when it's finished!" Crestien beamed proudly. "Look at how it's supported with the buttresses! So unusual and elegant! You wait. Someday, Paris will be grand!

"*Adieu, mon ami,* just follow the Seine," he said, as the pair embraced for the final time.

Evan sadly realized he'd never see him again in Shaftesbury. Crestien was a true ambassador for his country. As long as people like him kept crossing the Channel, hope remained that the two countries could find a way to get along.

-IV-
The Company We Keep

On the road leading north out of Paris, Evan picked up another company of travellers. Some were pilgrims intent on visiting Saint Thomas's shrine at Canterbury; others were like Diego, an itinerant Spanish rug merchant. He had supplied all the rugs in the bedrooms at Shaftesbury Castle, Evan was delighted to discover. Indeed, the Countess of Shaftesbury was his best customer. Evan told Diego how happy he'd always been to return home and have his feet alight on a clean, soft, beautiful rug first thing in the morning. Diego visited the castle every other year. Next year, he said. This year, only as far as London and then back to Spain.

Thankfully, they were also joined by a returning crusader, Sir Roderick d'Amiens, a Templar who'd supply needed protection en route. Like all Templars, Amiens rode with two squires, Gaston Blanchet and Erman Demirci, a Turkish mercenary he'd brought on in Cyprus.

Amiens said to Evan, "You may not remember me, but I remember you. You treated me for heatstroke on the march to Jaffa. You have my thanks, and I'm happy to see you again in different circumstances." While Amiens had the usual tonsured head and full beard of a Templar, by his roguish grin, Evan was fairly sure that in all other ways, he was not a monk.

Indeed, Evan didn't remember Amiens—he'd treated just too many—but he was glad to meet another veteran. With the crusade a year behind them, both men were able to put the experience into perspective. Not all of it was bad, they now agreed. He told Amiens that it had made a physician out of him.

For Amiens's part, although the failure to capture Jerusalem still weighed heavily on him, he'd had the privilege of serving under the greatest commander ever, in his opinion. "The battle at Jaffa?" he said with a rapturous grin, "I was one of his knights that day.

Only a dozen of us, part of a splendid force that beat an army three times our size. Best day of my life, and my men here would agree."

They both nodded, smiling. Demirci said, "Not every Turkish son of a blacksmith has such an honour." Once Richard was released, all three intended to join his service again.

Evan asked Demirci one day how he'd found himself in Amiens's employ.

He replied, "My family has always lived in Cyprus, though we're Turks. I was one of the guards in Komnenos's prison."

"Really? I was one of those imprisoned when our ships were wrecked on your shores."

It was Demirci's turn to be surprised. "Well, I never would have recognized you! I must say you clean up well."

"Sorry, I was too woebegone to take much notice of any of you."

"And 'woebegone' as you were, you all looked alike to *us*. Anyway, when King Richard took over, I saw a chance to see the world and serve under the Melech-Ric! Sir Roderick had lost one of his squires during the conquest of the island, and I offered my services. Sir Roderick's a good man. I'm always paid on time."

"But you're Muslim."

"Actually, no. I'm as Christian as you are, but I see nothing but hard times for us in Outremer in the years ahead. Islam is a strong religion."

Evan couldn't disagree with that.

Mildred Brewster, a London brewer, was also one of their party. Evan quickly developed an affection for this matronly widow who'd gone to Paris to purchase hops, a flavouring and stabilizer for ale. It had been used for some time in Germany, but it was a gamble in terms of her English customers' tastes, she told him. The bitterness it imparted to ale was an acquired taste; if it didn't sell, she'd swerve back to the old way of flavouring ale with herbs and spices. Mildred was everyone's adopted mother in this troupe, fussing over her fellow travellers, listening sympathetically to their various tales of woe. She was also happy to cook if others did the hunting and foraging.

Persistent threats were a fact of life for travellers. They were easy prey for gangs of thieves because their routes were so predictable: they followed the rivers and Roman roads, headed for the monasteries. They also had to watch out for the wolves, human-habituated and aggressive.

Finally, they couldn't always choose their fellow travellers for their own virtue.

One man in particular, Cedric, caused a kind of reflexive disgust among Evan's company. He claimed to have been on pilgrimage to Rome and was now heading back to England.

Amiens said to Evan, under his breath, "If he's been to Rome, I'm King Solomon. It is neither 'beautiful' nor 'grand.' It's a miserable place. There's nothing and no one to see there now except some old ruins, a cat, and two dogs."

If ape could become man, Cedric would be one. Dark hair and eyes. Husky, hirsute, slanted forehead. A dull expression that, at the same time, projected animal cunning, enhanced by prominent teeth that resembled a leer when he smiled. He drank too much and he stank. Three nights out of Paris, he tried to make off with Wasim, under cover of darkness, and was bucked off.

"Just trying to see what it's like to be on him," Cedric claimed with his smirky grin, his eyes evasive, when Evan caught him. "What're you so upset about?"

Evan had to constantly remind himself of his immense privilege, that a little Christian compassion would help, for a man who'd been cursed since birth with such a loathsome appearance.

Two days later, the company spent the night at the monastery in Aizier. The following morning, they set out again, always using the Seine as their guide. That night they had to sleep outside. The October night was warm, fortunately. Evan always slept lightly when he slept rough. Later that night, he woke to the sound of Wasim snorting and Cedric whispering angrily, "Shut up you, or I'll slit your throat!" He was rifling through Evan's bag.

Mustering what he thought was reasonable calm, Evan told him, "Get out of there, Cedric."

Cedric stared at him. Clearly, the ale had not only impaired his judgment but had made him careless and bold. "Try and stop me, you Norman toff." Brandishing his knife in one hand, he thumbed through the *Lancelot* in the other.

"Put that down. *Now!*"

"What for? You can always get another. This one'll keep my belly full for months."

"Last time. Put. It. *Down!*"

"And I say, try and stop me." His knife glistened in the firelight. By this time, the others were awake.

Amiens said calmly, drawing his sword, "Cedric, I will count to three." Demirci and Blanchet were also alert and had swords drawn.

Cedric ignored him and got up to leave.

Evan would always have trouble articulating what happened next. Perhaps it was the shame of Amiens coming to his rescue. Or perhaps it was the man's filthy, stinking fingers pawing through a precious book that so many others had carefully put together, soiling and defiling it. A book that had belonged to its very author. The lout didn't know what he was looking at, would never appreciate the beautiful words within.

Consumed with a primitive rage, he whipped out his own knife, sprang up, and before Cedric could react, jabbed it into Cedric's belly, thrusting it up to his sternum as easily as he had done to one of his dissected pigs. His teeth gritted, his voice low, "I am Sir Evan de Montmorency, and when I tell someone to stop what they're doing, they'd better *do it*."

Cedric dropped the book and fell like a stone, gasping, his eyes wide, not so much in fear or pain, but in surprise. Evan crouched over him, silent, waiting for him to die. The only sound was Cedric's gasping and gurgling of blood. A few moments later, his eyes turned sightless and his head lolled to one side. Only then did Evan withdraw the knife.

The others stood there, agape. Some had never seen a man murdered before. Some had killed, as Amiens had. But no one had expected a gentle soul like Sir Evan to be so ruthlessly capable, least of all Cedric.

Evan said, his voice flat, "He was going to take my parents' book."

Amiens said, "Don't feel bad. He'd have gladly killed you for it."

Evan was still crouched beside the body, staring at it.

"Is this the first time you've killed someone?" Amiens asked gently.

After a moment, Evan roused himself and replied, "Yes."

The others, now fully awake, started to organize. Mildred asked, "What do we do with the body?"

Amiens replied, "Throw him in the river. By the time anyone finds him, there'll be nothing to connect him with us. He'll just be one more nameless pilgrim who ran afoul of someone."

The others agreed. Together, they picked the body up, bore it down the bank, waded out about five feet, and lay him face down. The rapid current quickly took the body away, farther, farther, until he was out of sight. They all prayed that eventually he would simply wash out into the Channel.

"Good riddance," said Amiens. "You won't be missed."

When they came back up the bank, Evan said, still clearly in shock, "I killed a man. Because of a book."

Amiens crouched to shake him. "Pull yourself together, Montmorency." Evan looked up at him, now confused, like he'd just remembered where he was. "Men have been killed for much less. You will have to treat with God on this, but, for now, we're rejoicing that *he's* gone and not you. *Your* loss would have been mourned. For now, be grateful you're still alive."

"But I am a healer, not a murderer."

"That may be true, but first of all, you are human."

Amiens turned to the others. "Are we all agreed that none of us know anything about Cedric? That we parted ways at Aizier and haven't seen him since?"

Everyone nodded.

"Now, let's try to get back to sleep and put this night behind us." To Evan, he said, admiration in his voice, "'When I tell someone to stop what they're doing, they'd better do it'? By the gods, Montmorency, that took some balls."

"I said that?"

"Would I lie? I must try to use that sometime. Now, give it no more thought. He was a cur."

"Why would he *do* that, with four armed men in the company?"

"He probably never counted on your horse arousing us."

"How could he have thought we'd just let him leave with it?"

"Have you ever tracked game in a forest on a moonless night, without dogs? If you hadn't leapt on him like that, he could well have got clear of us."

Evan, still in shock, said vaguely, "My knife. I should rinse the blood off. My hands. I must clean them before I touch the book."

Amiens patted him on the back. "Wise idea."

Mildred said, hugging him, "You go get washed, and I'll put the book back, dear. See? It's undamaged."

Diego took him aside to reassure him, "Your parents will never hear about this from me."

Although only the shy night creatures could hear them, the rest of the group whispered about Cedric's family or lack of, chances of being discovered, and deserved end. Gradually, conversation petered out, and they fell back into snoring. But Evan remained awake. The realization of what he was—in the end, no better than any of the others, only human, possessed of no moral superiority whatsoever—rocked him to the smallest corner of his soul. What especially troubled him was that he didn't regret what he'd done.

-V-
Four Pairs of Gloves

Two days later, they reached Honfleur, on the Norman coast. After a rough Channel passage, during which Evan was again sick—but at least not into a barrel—he was finally back on English soil.

In Dover, he reconvened with many of the company, all eager to be back on the road again. For those journeying to Canterbury, it was the last leg and the going was easy, a good day's walk. They would follow the Roman road commonly known as Watling Street the entire way. Like all the Roman roads that still criss-crossed England, it was heavily trafficked and therefore relatively safe. Of course, he had to visit Saint Thomas's shrine.

Other than the stupendous cathedral, the largest Evan had seen, Canterbury was much like every other cramped, dismal English town.

He paid a couple of urchins to mind Wasim, then he and his companions went inside the cathedral. Evan was unprepared for the general bustle and noise in the nave, a true assault on the senses: incense, the stink of unwashed bodies, brightly painted walls of Biblical scenes. Above all this chaos, the soaring vaulted ceiling above and the diffused light of the jewel-like stained-glass windows. The Shaftesbury Abbey church could, at times, be crowded and noisy, but nothing like *this.*

It was difficult, making their way through the crowd to the mob of people waiting to see the shrine. Amiens pulled him through: "Follow me. You're not a knight for nothing."

Along the walls, people were sleeping, eating, and chatting; having come so far, many just camped out here. Lined up against one wall were hawkers of souvenir pewter flasks filled with "holy water," mixed with the "real blood" of Saint Thomas. Also for sale were pewter brooches with the image of Saint Thomas and other saints whose relics were also housed in the cathedral. Hopeful dogs lingered about, snatching dropped food; everyone had to watch for the turds. All this was screened off from the choir, the private part of the cathedral reserved for the monks and archbishop.

Becket's tomb was located beneath the floor of the crypt, under the cathedral. The tomb was covered with stone, with two holes, each large enough that one could stick one's head down to kiss it. Evan couldn't bring himself to touch his lips to it, and he felt a need to wash his hands afterwards.

What's the matter with me, he thought. Surely that's the point of visiting this sacred place? To be cured, not to get sick? Would God not protect pilgrims who had walked so far to honour Him and His saints? He tried out a few syllogisms: Holy relics have curative powers. Saint Thomas's tomb is a holy relic. Therefore ... But he always stalled at the conclusion because he knew his basic proposition was faulty. The fact was, he just didn't know if relics were curative. He slammed the door on the unsettling, dangerous, heretical direction his thoughts were taking him.

He purchased one of the Saint Thomas badges after a lengthy bargaining session. Jeanne would probably like it, he thought. He asked the seller if business was good and if it was always this busy.

The hawker replied, "Yes, to both. But this is nothing compared to Pasch and Christmas, and especially Saint Thomas's day. Then, you can barely move in here." The Feast of Saint Thomas was on December 29, the anniversary of his 1170 assassination.

Evan then asked if there were inns in town he'd recommend.

"Oh yes, lots," he replied. "Along the Stour," gesturing westward. "Look for the sign with the red lion, and tell them Alfred sent you."

When he exited the cathedral, the two urchins seemed relieved to see him. The older one, his eyes wide and tone impressed, said, "You've a loyal horse! Some snake just tried to steal him. He was bigger than us, but he got himself bitten and kicked in the *coilons* for his troubles."

"That's my boy!" Evan replied, giving Wasim a pat. "Wasim doesn't go with anyone unless I say so." He gave the boys another penny each and thanked them again. Evan was beginning to think he could leave Wasim alone in a crowded square.

Of course, there would be an arrangement between the innkeeper and Alfred, which would account for the inflated price of the room. Mildred, Amiens, and his men would have been similarly extorted. But, after weeks on the road, sleeping rough, and sleeping in dormitories when he was under a roof, he rejoiced to finally have some space to himself.

Three days later, still following Watling Street, Evan parted ways with his new friends as they approached London's outskirts. Before he did, he said, "If you're looking for a good physician here, seek out William Wolstone on the south side, Saint Olave Street. You won't get better. In fact, I'm heading his way right now."

Mildred and Amiens thanked him for the recommendation, both promising to stop by Shaftesbury Castle if they were ever in the neighbourhood. Demirci promised that his parents would take Evan in if ever he decided to visit Cyprus again. They all knew the chances of any of this happening were remote.

Having visited Paris, he realized that London had much the same demographic distribution: the established, powerful moneyed class resided on the north side of the city, with the scrubby, aspiring classes on the other side, south of the Thames. Like Paris, houses were adjoined and built of wood, wattle, and daub, making fires a continual threat. Unlike Paris, however, there was only one bridge, which was currently being rebuilt in more solid stone. The bridge was only a couple of streets away from William's house.

William looked up in happy surprise when Evan came in the door. "Montmorency!" he exclaimed. "I was wondering when you'd show your face inside these doors again! You're just in time to help me put this shoulder back in. Put your bag down and make yourself useful!"

Evan smiled. He noted the tile floor, so much more durable than wood. Also, the steel surface of the examining table. What an excellent idea! There was even a bench now, for people to sit, and long enough for Evan to sleep on. William must be prospering.

"Let me first put my horse out back." The patient laughed as Evan led Wasim through the house to the back yard. For company, Wasim had the same goat Evan had met before, a young pig, and four chickens.

"Where's Cat?"

"Oh, he's still around, earning his keep. So, let's see if that crusade taught you anything. You set it."

"Of course. If you steady him." Evan deftly massaged the shoulder back into place and then asked for some cloth for a sling. William probed the man's shoulder and nodded. Evan asked him, "Do you have willow bark?"

"Do pigs oink?" William fished in a cabinet for both. "Godwin, have Berta make a sweetened tea of this bark to control the pain for a couple of days. Try to drink milk along with it because it may upset your stomach. Wear that sling for five days. Come back here in a week, and we'll work on strengthening the arm."

Godwin nodded at all these instructions.

Evan asked Godwin, "Do you have tiles or flat stone in your house?"

"No, but I know where I can get a few, why?"

"Just put them outside to get cold and lie on them. It'll relieve your pain."

"Thank you, Physicians. I have no coin to give you, but Berta will bring you some fine sheepskin mittens she's making now."

"Thank you, Godwin," William replied. "Good day to you. Be gentle with that arm and do come back sooner if you have any more trouble with it. You should feel better quickly."

Briskly smacking his hands together as the door closed behind Godwin, Evan remarked, "So, that turned out well!"

"Yes. Good idea, about the tiles. I like it when I get a straightforward case of something I can treat easily. It helps with the word of mouth. Speaking of mouth, however, I can't eat gloves. I'll give them to my mother. I've already given her four pairs. She turns right around and sells them, so it helps her out. Edward bought a pair, she told me. But I don't mind. Mostly these people are poor, honest folk who pay me what they can spare."

The two men happily embraced, finally. "Let me buy you supper," Evan said. "It's good to see a familiar face again, old friend."

William locked his doors, and they set out for a tavern two streets away. "The owner is a patient of mine. He pays me in ale that's much better than the cat piss you had the last time you were here."

They came to a sign with a knight and castle drawn on it and went inside. As Evan expected, the small space had a dirt floor with several rough-hewn tables.

"That's quite a horse you have there, Montmorency," William said, when Harold, the taverner's son, brought over their ale. A hearty mutton potage followed. "In this neighbourhood, he's probably being stolen as I speak."

Evan replied, "I'd like to see them try. Wasim knows his own mind." Memories of Cedric jabbed his mind uncomfortably.

William did not scoff at this. He remembered Evan's way with horses from his years in the castle.

During this satisfying supper, he probed Evan about his experiences: where he'd been, what he'd learned. He listened, rapt, as Evan casually described treating the King.

That night, and in the days and evenings that followed, Evan happily recounted his days in Messina, Salerno, and even Paris. His memories of the crusade were more nuanced, and he edited those experiences as he recounted them. William, ever shrewd, continued to dig and eventually got the truth of the massacre, which had only been rumoured, as well as the truth of both retreats from Jerusalem. He was also treated to an eye-witness account of the splendid victories at Arsuf and Jaffa. But Evan did manage to get away with omitting all reference to Joanna—and to Cedric.

-VI-
When Darkness was Longest

Three nights after Evan's arrival, he was shaken from a deep slumber.

"Wake up. Be sharp. We have a body." It was pouring rain outside, as it had been all day.

Evan knew what that meant. They were going to dissect a corpse, likely a prisoner hanged that day and buried. There was an unconsecrated graveyard not far away, where prostitutes were interred, as well as prisoners and other people who couldn't afford a proper burial. The graves were unmarked, and not much trouble was taken with them. Still, knowledge of the recent arrival and of the body's exact location were obtained through underhanded means via a sympathetic, compensated jailer.

A dissection was always carried out in late fall and winter, when darkness was longest and temperatures coldest. Heavy rain was optimal because it camouflaged the sound of wheels and hooves and discouraged the locals from peering or moving about outside. Everything they wanted to accomplish, including the body's reburial, had to be completed before the matins bells rang at about two in the morning. People would be up and about then, and not all of them went back to bed.

William opened the door, and two other men came in carrying a shrouded body on their shoulders. Both men looked to be in their late twenties, William's age, one blond, one with brown hair. The body was placed on the examining table and unwrapped.

William said to Evan, "For safety's sake, I won't introduce you to each other, but rest assured that we are all physicians, all dedicated to our calling." He'd lit several candles, but not the brazier. "We are sharing the risk, as much as we can. They see to the transport of the body back and forth, but it is my house we use. Tonight.

We change houses each time. We must be finished by the time this candle burns to here." William indicated two notches down from where the flame was now.

Evan recognized this type of candle. Father Benedict used them so he would know when to ring the bells for the various services each day. They had two hours. William handed him an old smock and put one on himself.

The body was a middle-aged male who had obviously been hanged, to judge by the rope burn on his neck and by his open, gagging mouth. He was dirty, and he'd been underfed for an indeterminate amount of time. A scar on his right cheek indicated he'd known violence. His left shin looked to have been broken and poorly set, meaning he would have walked with a limp and, likely, in pain. Did anyone care about him? Did he have a sorrowing wife and children, perhaps even mother and father still alive? Unlikely. Death claimed the poor early.

"Do you know how we can estimate how long he's been dead?" William asked Evan.

"No, how?" Everywhere he had practised, no one gave it a thought; bodies had to be buried quickly because of the heat.

"Two ways, though a lot of factors can throw us off. First, the blood tends to eventually settle towards whichever side of the body is closest to the ground." Turning the body on its side, "See the bruising on his back? He has not been beaten. Secondly, it stiffens by degrees." Gesturing to his blond colleague, "How long would *you* say?"

The blond took the man's clawed hands and tried to move the fingers. He could not. He said, "I would say he died about eight this morning." The others nodded. He turned to Evan. "This stiffening starts about three hours after death and spreads throughout the body. The hands and feet are last. The entire process takes about twelve hours, although it can vary according to the seasons. It took us more than a few dissections to learn this; it's not in any book that we know of."

"All right," William said. "We must get started. First, we observe certain rituals here. Even though he doesn't have a name, this person—this body—deserves respect. Whatever he did, we must assume he had his reasons and that he probably died frightened and alone. In his death, he is a great teacher. We always begin by saying a prayer of thanks to him, with the hope that he died in a state of grace."

All four joined hands and bowed their heads as the brown-haired man uttered a prayer of thanks in a low voice.

"For our protection, we must wash him." William brought a basin of water and some soap, and all four swabbed the man down. He then said to Evan, "We next cover his face and whatever part of the body we are not working on tonight. This helps our concentration."

They re-draped his lower body and his face with the shroud. Tonight, for Evan's sake, they were working on the upper torso: they were going to expose the heart and lungs. All three of these men had worked on these organs on their first dissection, but they were glad enough for another look. Evan watched as William expertly made the first cuts lengthwise, down the sternum, and crosswise, under the clavicle, with knife in one hand, clamp in the other. He then peeled back the skin and very thin layer of fat, at last revealing the musculature. They all helped to pull back the rib cage to expose the heart. Superficially, the arrangement of the organs resembled that of the pigs he'd worked on.

William turned to Evan. "What do you notice about the human heart?"

Evan said, "It's shaped differently, like a trapezoid. Not like the pig's, which narrows."

William replied, "Exactly. *Now* you can really understand how important this work is."

Evan nodded. "I could study this body for a month, and I still wouldn't know its secrets. There's a whole art to this, isn't there?"

Brown-haired man said, "We've been doing this for six years now. We're only beginning."

The men determinedly went back to work. Working only by candlelight, they strained to see the delicate tissues and blood vessels. Evan remembered the brightly-lit room in his Steven dream and thought how fortunate twenty-first-century people were to possess such light.

Eventually, he commented, "Look," pointing to a clot of blood in one of the lung's arteries. "Do you think this might have caused a problem for him at some point?"

William replied, "Hmm … possibly."

They quietly worked on, watching that candle clock. Three lobes in the right lung, two in the left, unlike a pig's four and two. How many other differences were there? Still, Evan again marvelled at the thought of all this crammed into such a small space, each part vital to the entirety. If even one of these parts was missing, the body wouldn't survive. How was it that one could cut into a precise area of any creature and, having studied others of its kind, almost certainly know what organ lay underneath? This arrangement must have been determined from conception. And how was that?

Such was their concentration that the next time they looked up, the candle clock had almost burned down to the second notch.

"Now we put everything back and close him up." Following that, they washed their hands and once again held hands and gave thanks to the gift that had been offered them tonight. They re-shrouded the body and hoisted him into the cart outside, covering him with hay.

Evan embraced Blond and Brown. "Thank you, gentlemen. It has been an honour to work with you."

"And us with you," said Blond. They quickly got on the wagon and made their way down the street in the continuing rain.

"This is incredibly dangerous!" Evan exclaimed when they were alone, exhilarated both by the risk they had taken and the fact that they looked to have gotten away with it. "God help them if they get caught!"

"I know. More danger from the Church if they hear of it than from the authorities because, from their standpoint, what do they care after the man's been buried? Graves have been robbed for centuries. We have all vowed that, if any of us are caught, we will not give up the others. We don't make a pattern of it. No more than twice in six months and, as I said, never twice in a row in the same house. We take every precaution we can."

"Times are changing, Wolstone. Already, in Salerno, I heard noises that it should be legalized. Not in our lifetimes, but perhaps in our children's. Wouldn't it be wonderful to do this in broad daylight, without stealth?"

They repeatedly scrubbed the table down with soap, water,

and soured wine till the room reeked of it.

"Now, let's open the shutters, to let some air in," William said. "Give me that smock. We'll put them to soak overnight."

Evan said, "Thank you for tonight. It's really opened my eyes. But be cautious. I shudder to think what would happen if you were caught."

"I know. And we *are.* Now, let's try to get a bit of sleep. Good night."

The matins bell rang about half an hour later and, shortly after, the street began to stir. Though he heard William snoring in the next room, Evan knew he wouldn't sleep that night. More than anything, he wanted to talk to someone else about this experience—someone who would be interested, not disgusted. He missed Joanna so much his gut ached.

-VII-
"We aren't gods."

During the fortnight Evan spent with William, he barely strayed beyond William's neighbourhood. He was too busy: days, he helped William out in the treatment room; evenings, over supper at The Knight and Castle, William quizzed him on what he'd learned. Primarily the lesson Evan wanted to leave with William was this: "You say this herb works? How do you *know* it works? Have you seen it for yourself, or is it just that you think it *should?*"

They made daily house calls. This, too, was an education. He was shown into dark, rat-infested one-room dwellings that housed a whole family on a lice-ridden bed, with the cow stalled in the back. He pitied the wives who tried to keep a clean house and failed because the only water supply was two streets away. He saw the dirt floors, packed down to a hard surface that could never, of course, be washed. The women who were almost constantly pregnant, with children that were, almost as constantly, dying. They were always invited to break bread with the families afterwards, and they always accepted. One never asked if they were freemen or escaped villeins.

Nevertheless, Evan went to bed each night satisfied that he'd spent the day productively, believing he had helped. Most conditions they saw were run-of-the-mill: boils, infections, seasonal afflictions. For a few, however, little could be done: *phthisis*, apoplexy, *oncos*—all so poorly understood, all centuries from being curable or treatable, and completely oblivious to wealth or social class. He and William would look across the table at each other and shake their heads, ever so slightly. All they could do was relieve the symptoms.

In cases like that, William was honest. He informed the patient, "I've done all *I* can do, but you're welcome to take your chances with another physician if you wish." This was not necessarily a death sentence. Some did look elsewhere and were sold a quack cure. Once in a while, William admitted, these baseless "cures" worked—likely to the great surprise of the quack, as well. Some staggered off on a pilgrimage. Sometimes that worked, too. Evan had told him about the strings of crutches hanging like ugly necklaces in Canterbury Cathedral. Had their owners truly been cured of their lameness by kissing Saint Thomas's tomb, or were the crutches just cynical decoration? Who knew? There was so much that neither of them understood.

"Are you ever frustrated that you do everything right, and some people still die?" Evan asked one evening. He talked then about Wilfred, whose death still haunted him.

"Of course," William replied. "It's happened to me. But I always remember that we aren't gods. There's only so much we ever *can* do. In the end, if God wills it that our patient die, the best we physicians can do is try to provide him a good and peaceful death."

That made sense to Evan; he was coming to think that himself. He wondered if, even in the twenty-first century, physicians still agonized over the loss of their patients.

However, despite their limited options in some cases, William told him one night, "What a difference it makes to the people here to have a physician! No longer do they just suffer, pray, and beg for a miracle cure. Now they actively seek treatment before all that. This has to be a good thing, don't you think?"

He cut off a slice of trencher and chewed into it. "You know, you could stay here. We could work together. Between your looks and my brains, who knows what we could do." He looked up at Evan and smiled.

Evan chuckled. He had, in fact, been thinking along those lines. They did work well together. But William had been making a life for himself, and it was his own. Everything he had, he had toiled to achieve. He didn't need Evan coming in with a fancy education, taking over. And Evan most certainly would. It couldn't be helped. It was what Evan did, something he had realized about himself in the last few years. He was fairly sure William had only asked him out of politeness.

"Yes, don't think I haven't considered it. I'm flattered you asked. I'm a country boy at heart, I guess. But, Wolstone, one last time. Your mother isn't getting any younger. At some point, she's going to need your assistance."

William shook his head resignedly. "Yes, I know. The last time I was home, one of her neighbours took me aside to mention that she's forgetting things lately."

Evan was alarmed to hear this. This incapacity occurred sometimes in the very old, but not many people got to be very old. Joanne was young to be afflicted.

"Can she manage, on her own?"

"So far, she can. She has good neighbours who look in on her. But I agree with you. I will have to move back there *at some point*. You'll understand, however, if I don't pack my bags right away."

Neither man brought up the subject of a partnership again.

William had a lady friend, Margaret, to whom he was introduced one day. A daughter of a neighbourhood baker, she was blonde, blue-eyed, and had cheeks that dimpled attractively when she smiled. Though younger than he was by about ten years, an understanding was in place between William and her parents that the two would marry; as to when, William was a little vague. He wanted to be able to bring Margaret home to a house a bit larger than his cozy, two-room abode. Evan figured that would not be long.

It was mid-November, and the weather had turned chilly when it wasn't pissing rain. It was time to be on the road.

"Wolstone, before I go, I want to give you something. I got it in Paris, and I hope you can use it." He dug into his bag and produced the Avicenna, glad to no longer have that tome weighing down his sack.

William gaped when he saw the precious tome. "Do you know we were forbidden to try to get a copy of this? Do you know how long I've waited for a book merchant to tell me he'd somehow obtained a copy?" He stood to embrace Evan, his eyes watery.

"Are you still able to read Greek? I wasn't sure." Both men had learned it from Rabbi Jacob.

"It's rusty, but I'll manage. Thank you, Montmorency. But, why aren't you keeping it for yourself?"

"I don't need it. I have it memorized."

William believed him.

-VIII-
Saffron and Cider

On the Sunday of the third week of November, 1193, in gusting snow, Evan and Wasim finally entered the castle bailey. Recognizing Evan as the lone hooded horseman plodding up the hill, the guards alerted the rest of the castle. The comforting aromas of stew and baking bread were first to greet him, followed right after by the ecstatic embraces of his family and the entire castle staff.

Branwen took him in her arms, running her hands through his messy hair, as she'd always done. "My boy! Look at you! You're brown! You're alive!" she wept, laughing through her tears.

Robert exclaimed, "Welcome home, son! It's been a long three years without you." His hair was entirely grey now; otherwise, they both looked well.

"And who's this?" Branwen smiled, patting Wasim. "Aren't you a handsome lad! Wasim, you say? Fine name!" No one was surprised that she "knew" his name. Wasim preened under her admiring gaze. "Ah, I see you have been altered. Never mind. You are welcome here."

To Tom, she said, quietly, "For the first week or so, stable him away from Merlin."

Edward was starting to turn grey; Jeanne looked much the same. Isabelle was now a young woman, pretty like her mother was, if more sturdily built. Evan took in her rebellious and defiant look and knew she would never be some lord's demure and obedient wife, even if she was likely be married off soon. Pierre would still be away but would be home at Christmastide, as was castle custom. He must be fourteen by now. A young man!

A towheaded boy of about nine lingered shyly along the sides.

"Hello, I'm Sir Evan, and who are you?"

Branwen wrapped her arm around the boy's shoulders. "This is Gilbert de Clare, the Earl of Clare's younger son. He's been paging with us for the last two years." She looked at the boy expectantly.

"Delighted to meet you, Sir Evan," Gilbert said politely, bowing to Evan, prompting a smile from the latter. He remembered all this.

Branwen said, "Come, my dear, let's get us all out of this cold! Should I have a bath drawn for you?"

"Yes, I'd love that. I haven't had a bath in over two years!"

Two maids dashed off without having to be told.

Tom said, "Gilbert, as soon as you take up Sir Evan's bag, we have work to do."

He led Wasim off to the stables, where Evan knew he'd be immediately groomed and pampered.

"And as soon as you're out of your bath and in clean clothes, come join us in the great chamber. Cider wassail will be waiting for you. We have so much to catch up on!" Branwen paused for a moment to happily take him in again. "You're home! I can hardly believe it still! Why didn't you let us know? We would have slaughtered the fatted calf!"

"We would have sent you an escort!" Robert chimed in.

"I did write, from London. I've been with William the last couple of weeks."

"Oh, very good. You must tell us how he is. No, we only got one letter, from Salerno, to say you'd been admitted and that the King had knighted you."

"Hmm, I wrote from Messina, Jaffa, Salerno, and London. I guess one out of four isn't bad."

As he, Gilbert, and Branwen made their way up to his first-floor room, he asked Gilbert, "Who's tutoring you?"

"Lady Montmorency is, Sir Evan," the boy replied.

"Until I can find an acceptable tutor, that is," cut in Branwen.

Evan said, "Good, you're getting the best, young man."

"You take as long as you need. We'll be waiting for you." She hugged him close again, kissed him on the cheek, and said, "God has answered all my prayers."

She closed the door.

His room was unchanged from when he'd last slept in it. He collapsed on his bed. A real bed. His bed. He was home. In Camaalot.

He luxuriated in the ground-floor bath for some time, thinking back to that hammam, feeling nested and secure in the cocoon of familiarity. Eventually, he climbed the stairs to the great chamber, where everyone, including Gilbert and Father Benedict, was waiting for him by the fire, having got a head start with the wassail. Gilbert was passing around small, round, light-as-air cheese pastries of Jack's invention that Branwen was trying out on the family first. From December till about the end of February was a quiet time in the castle for mealtime guests, who preferred sticking close to home in winter weather. It allowed those in the castle a welcome, private time for repairs, improvements, and, for Branwen and Jack, trying out new recipes.

Once she'd poured him a cup and the warm, spicy liquid trickled down his gullet, the first thing Evan wanted to know was how the castle had coped with Eleanor's levy. It was all he'd heard about in the inns and taverns he'd dropped in on, on the way home.

His father sighed heavily, and they all exchanged glances. "We paid it, of course. At least it was just a quarter of our *income,* not a quarter of all we *have.* But it was a huge sacrifice, especially when we were taxed just four years ago for the crusade. For most, it's been horrible: How many people have that amount of money just sitting around? Thankfully, the harvests were good this year. Prices for wool are good, too. All that helped. But Villiers had to go to the moneylenders. He was far from the only one. The Jews aren't made of money, either, and many had to call in existing loans. You can imagine how that's gone down here with people."

Evan could well imagine.

Edward added, "But you know what? We think Eleanor's going to come up with the money. God only knows how she's going to get it all to Germany."

Robert nodded and went on, "It doesn't help that that goblin Prince John is up to his usual tricks. Have you heard what he's doing to undermine the whole thing?"

Evan replied, "Well, I heard that he's offered Henry and Leopold fifty thousand marks to keep Richard imprisoned."

Robert smiled. "We heard eighty. In any event, obviously John is not motivated to see his brother home. He has a lot to answer for. The only bright side in all this is that his great father's efficient clerical service has become entrenched, since it's been so neglected. There are laws, customs, and procedures now that'll be difficult to overturn."

Branwen said, "But enough about all that. We have so many questions, Physician Montmorency! At least, we *assume* 'Physician'!"

Evan replied, "Oh yes. I finished in August. Let me show you what I brought back." He reached into his bag. "I didn't want to draw a target on my back, so I couldn't bring you much, unfortunately."

He pulled out a few bags of spices that were expensive in England but ubiquitous in Salerno: black pepper, dried hot chilies, cinnamon, even a little saffron. A small bottle of a sweet, lemon-infused spirit that monks there made and sold. As well, seeds from Dijon to make a condiment that was the latest rage in Paris; Branwen beamed, knowing all about mustard. And the precious two Paris books. He had often heard his mother bemoan the lack of reading material in the vernacular, something more contemporary than the "old masters." The *Lancelot* was practically brand new.

Branwen, so controlled and dignified, squealed in delight at these gifts and leapt up to embrace him. "Another of Troies's! I *love* his work!"

"Mama, you should see what's going on in France now. So much writing! Scribes are working full time, copying and translating it all." Once again, he saw the frustration in her eyes. Paris was nothing compared to what she'd known in the future, but it was a start.

He dug out the brooch and handed it to Jeanne.

"F-for me?" she exclaimed. "Thank you! I'll wear it often!"

He pulled out and unrolled his parchment Salerno certificate. "And this here proves that I actually attended the Schola!"

They all exclaimed as they examined the elegant Latin script, with "Maestro" attached to Evan's name. An illuminator had drawn, in gold, the symbol of medicine—a rod with a single snake twisted around it—at the top of the parchment. Circled around it was printed "Schola Medica Salernitana."

"And this is for all of you. I don't need it anymore. The images are all fixed in my head." He brought out his small book of drawings. It was all there. Jabal Tariq, Marseille, Messina, Limassol, Acre, Salerno, Paris, London. People he'd met: Richard, Morgant, Crécy,

Besace, Troies, and Amiens—with two notable exceptions. Those sketches had been given to the subjects.

Everyone oohed and aahed as the book was passed around. No one seemed particularly surprised that he'd drawn these images himself, and Evan wondered why. "I'll explain all about them if any arouse your curiosity. Almost all of them are good memories that I'll be happy to relive."

"Yes, I can see many an enjoyable winter afternoon in front of the fire as you tell us all about them. But what did you buy for yourself?" Branwen asked.

"Just Wasim—and he was plunder."

Over supper, he was peppered with questions. Robert's were mainly on the logistics—how many, how, when. Everybody else's were more along the lines of, what was it *like?* Just as curious to hear his tales as the family, the servers lingered over their tasks, hovering in the shadows a little longer than necessary.

Branwen eventually said, "Harry, Wil, you might as well have a seat so you can hear the story correctly! Gilbert, you, too." One of Gilbert's duties was refilling the water cups at meals. Father Benedict forgot about compline that night.

Evan went to bed warm and comfortable, so much so that he slept through the matins bells.

-IX-
The Fawn in the Forest

The following morning, as he was dressing, he heard a knock at his door. He opened the door to find his parents.

"May we come in?" Branwen asked.

Robert barred the door behind him. As far as Evan could remember, that door had never been barred.

Branwen glanced around the room in approval: Evan had already made his bed and put away all his belongings. But this was Shaftesbury Castle, he was Sir Evan de Montmorency, and this was what maids were for. He would have to get used to having things done for him again, just as she'd had to when she'd returned to this time. She noticed a key lying on his bedside table. It aroused her curiosity, but she decided he would tell them about it if and when he chose.

"Sit with us, dear. We have something to give you." They all sat side by side on the bed. "We wanted to wait until we could be alone to give you this."

Out of her pocket, she handed him a folded piece of parchment, sealed with red wax, imprinted with a crowned woman holding a fleur-de-lys. Joanna's. On the front, she'd written *Sir Evan de Montmorency, Shaftesbury Castle, Dorsetshire.*

Evan's heart lurched as he stared at it.

"When did it arrive?"

Robert replied, "Towards the end of September, would you say, love? Yes, just before Michaelmas. Two Templars delivered it. We had them stay the night. They were most informative about the political situation in France, although, obviously, they could say nothing about the letter's contents, or even the whereabouts of the Dowager Queen of Sicily."

Branwen asked, "Would you like to read it alone? We'll leave, if you'd like."

"No, Mama. In fact, I'd appreciate it if you both stayed."

He stood to lean against the wall in front of them. He broke the seal and unfolded the parchment. There, in a clear, elegant hand he read:

Saint Giles's Day, 1193

Dearest Evan,

First of all, I send you assurances that I am well, although there is a large hole in my heart that only you can fill. I was delighted to hear that you graduated early from the Schola, as I knew you would. I am so proud of you! I hope that by the time this letter arrives, you will be safely at home with your family.

Evan, mi corazón, *you have a daughter, Jane. Yes, I was as shocked as you must be now when I realized I was with child. I immediately journeyed to Fontevraud Abbey, where the nuns took me in and where we waited out the pregnancy. She was born on the Feast of Saint John the Baptist of this year. I wanted to wait until it was clear she would thrive to tell you. I have learned that both our names derive from "John." I don't believe "Jane" is a common variation of our names, but I wanted to give her a name that was in some way similar to her parents'.*

She is beautiful and healthy, although it is too soon to tell which one of us she favours. It is peaceful there, and she will be safe. I will ensure that she receives the education and instruction she deserves.

Other than Agnes and Nicolette, who are absolutely trustworthy, only the nuns at the abbey know of her. I will leave it up to you to decide whether you wish to inform your family. I'm sure whatever decision you make will be the right one.

I know you love me, and you know I love you. That thought will warm me in the chill of the years to come. I wish only good things for you, but I believe that my wishes are but a feather on a stream. You are meant for great things. I feel it.

Please don't try to find me. We were not destined to be together in this life. But, God willing, we will meet in heaven.

Yours, always,

Joanna

Breath heaving, he refolded it. His first thought was, At least she's all right. His second was, Why in Heaven did she not call for me?

"What's the matter, dear? Can you tell us?"

"We—I mean Joanna and I—have a daughter. Jane. She's being raised at an abbey in France. Why didn't she tell me? I would have gone to her!"

Branwen said, "Sit back down and tell us about this. As much as you feel comfortable saying."

And so he did. How they'd met, the frustrations they'd both felt as circumstances pulled them apart, their mutual sorrow that they had no future, along with their certainty that they could never love again as they'd loved each other. He revealed that it was Joanna who had partially funded his time in Salerno and advocated for his admission. He finally said, "She must have known she was with child then."

Branwen took his hand. Robert wrapped his arm around their son.

"Mama, Papa, what do I do? She's my daughter. She deserves more than being raised as a foundling by well-meaning nuns. We have to bring her here."

His parents glanced across at each other and shook their heads slightly in unison.

Branwen said, "Believe me, I would love to have another little girl in the castle to hug and fuss over! But Joanna placed her child there so that her secret would not get out. Bringing her here would only endanger that."

Robert asked, "May I see her letter?" Evan handed it over to him. He skimmed the contents, the "mm's" becoming increasingly loud, and then passed it on to Branwen, who did the same.

"Fontevraud. I know of it," he said, finally. "I'll confirm with the Reverend Mother, but I'm sure she'll say it is large and well-endowed. I agree with your mother. Joanna has weighed what she believes will be the best interests of her child. She explicitly states that Jane will be safe at Fontevraud. This is her wish. Son, as a princess and then queen, she has been given very little control over her life. She has done you the courtesy of letting you know, but we urge you to respect her wishes in this matter."

Branwen added, "Joanna left her there, certain that her identity would remain protected. That anonymity could not be guaranteed should the child be brought under this roof. This is, after all, not such a large country. We gentlefolk all know each other. You know how people gossip. Are you very sure there was no gossip about you during your, shall we say, time together?"

Evan looked down. "We were hardly ever actually together. But, yes, there was talk. We tried hard to keep it secret, but it got out, somehow."

"With that in mind, more than anything, she will want to protect that child from the designs of her brother or whoever succeeds him," Branwen pointed out. "She went to some lengths to hide her pregnancy and the child's birth, and it wasn't only because of the stigma. It hasn't stopped marriages before."

Evan had to take that point. While he'd been in France, he'd heard that King Philip was shopping around Richard's discarded Alys to various dukes.

She continued, "If you'll permit me an analogy? Think of a doe that leaves her fawn in the forest while she goes to feed. One might think, how could a mother abandon her offspring like that? But the fawn is well-camouflaged, and the doe is always close by and alert to danger. To continue the analogy, if anyone came by thinking he could 'rescue' the fawn, he would cause the most enormous distress to both creatures, not to mention endanger the life of the fawn.

"This is a child conceived with love, and she's all Joanna has of you. Joanna will ensure that she is properly and lovingly raised. When Jane's of age, she may be fortunate enough to marry a man of her choice, or perhaps no man at all. She already has a freedom her mother has never had."

Though Evan understood the logic of his parents' argument, he was still unwilling to give up. "So, I'm just the stag that plants his seed and then leaps off? Can't I at least visit my daughter?"

Again, his parents shared a glance. "Joanna hasn't expressly forbidden it," Branwen said after a moment. "There is probably no legal reason why you couldn't be allowed to see her, but we would advise against it. It would be too tempting to override Joanna's wishes."

"What about Edward and Jeanne? Can I tell them?"

His parents shook their heads, eyeing that barred door. Branwen said, "A wise man will say one day, 'Three can keep a secret if two of them are dead.'" Evan nodded. "Well, your secret is safe with us, but there are too many ears in this castle. Tell no one else about this child."

She took his hand. "And may I say one more thing. It is my opinion only. From what she says in her letter, almost more than anything, I believe that she doesn't want to hold you back."

"Me?"

"She has enormous respect for you and your capabilities, that much is obvious. Look at what she has already done to advance your career. Do you not realize that protecting this secret protects you, as well? Nothing—or nobody—should hold you back in the fulfilment of your destiny. You are only twenty-two."

"Everybody keeps telling me that. But even if what you say is true, can't I have both—my daughter and my work?" But even as he spoke the words, he knew the answer. To take her out of that abbey, he would have to argue that he could offer her more, and he couldn't. He'd have to be a father for her. Not just at the end of the day, or when it suited him, but when it did not. Although he was fully licensed now and able to practise physic anywhere he wanted, he had no clientele yet, no steady source of income. And there remained the issue of protecting Jane's identity.

Crushed, frustrated, and powerless, Evan finally said, "So that's it, then? Why did she write this letter? Why not just let me remain happy in my ignorance and false hope that someday, maybe we could see each other again?"

Branwen replied, "I agree. It's a decision I might not have made myself. Perhaps, fearing that the child's identity would get out, she wanted you to hear it from her, not from malicious gossip. And it's always hard to say that definitive Adieu. Perhaps this was just her way of reaching out to you one last time before she's married off to whomever."

"Yes, 'one last time.' It was our motto. Somehow we were always given one last time."

Branwen's heart broke for her son's misery. But really, what did he have of Joanna but a few nights of what was, presumably, excellent coupling? She stifled an odd discomfiture at the thought of her little boy doing *that*. He hadn't known Joanna when, tired or stressed, she just didn't feel up to doing it; when she was irritable on the days before or during her courses, or in the last months of a pregnancy. He hadn't known the terror and exhilaration of a childbirth; he hadn't smelled her sour morning breath or heard her pass wind; he hadn't watched as taut body parts started to sag, as the first white hairs became the many. Could what he felt for her be, in any sense, called love?

She took a fresh look at her beloved younger son, not as a mother, but as a woman. She and Robert knew that Evan had a gift, one grounded not so much in radical discovery as in being open to the vast array of knowledge, then synthesizing and adapting it to serve his needs. And, despite all he'd lived through, he remained a kind-hearted, generous soul. All these sterling qualities notwithstanding, however, he'd never have attracted a woman like Joanna if he had a face like a frog. Among family and friends, Edward had always been informally known as the handsome one, Evan the clever one, Marie the naughty one. But looking at Evan now, she saw that, while he had his father's fine bone structure and his own remarkable eyes, the key to Evan's appeal was the utter lack of guile that could never hide his intelligence and decency. Yes. Any woman would find that compelling.

Evan, my dear, she thought, you will not be alone except by choice.

An unsettling thought leapt into her mind. Evan had always possessed an innate self-confidence, but what might those well-meant epithets have done to *Edward's* confidence? She pushed it back, for now, but she must take it up with Robert. Soon.

She wrapped her arm around her son. He laid his head on her shoulder, and for just that moment, she had her little boy again. Oh, how she missed this simple gesture from her grown children!

"Evan, my dear," Branwen said, "poets and trouvères are fond of saying that we are allowed only one great love. I personally believe that this notion is naïve, and your father would agree with me, as you know." Robert nodded. "You have so many years left, and we beg you, don't barricade your heart because of her."

"I will never love anyone like I loved Joanna."

"Perhaps not. But there are other, wonderful ways to love. We understand how great your pain is now. But, trust us, that pain will gradually diminish to a sadness, and finally a poignant memory. Maybe even a happy one."

"Mama, in the future, can someone like me marry someone like Joanna?"

She sat back, trying to remember. She finally said, "Yes, you could, but it will have been only recently accepted. Until the twentieth century, royalty mostly still marry royalty. Even when I was there, it was still noted that a royal member was marrying a 'commoner.'"

They came together in a group hug. While the rational parts of Evan's brain understood all this, his instincts told him that there'd never be another Joanna. In the "so many years" he had left, it would be up to him to find a way to live with that knowledge.

1194 – 1199

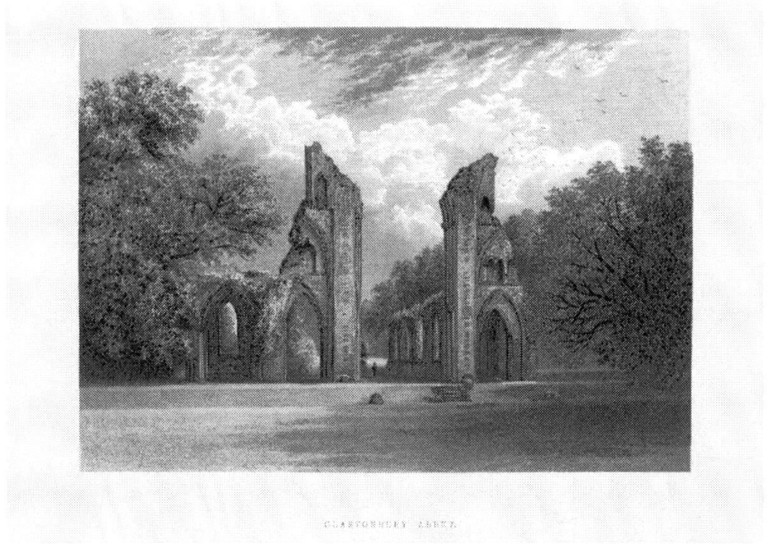

Vintage engraving of Glastonbury Abbey ruins

The first degree of humility is prompt obedience.
—St. Benedict of Nursia

-I-
The Locked Room

That winter, Evan rattled unhappily around the castle. For three years, he'd dreamed of coming home; now here, he felt frustrated and at loose ends. Having been away for so long, he looked at his home with new eyes and saw what an efficient operation it was. They didn't need his help. Edward had had fifteen years to absorb the lessons his father had taught him, and the demesne would be in good hands when the time came. Jeanne was slowly growing into her role as the future Countess of Shaftesbury, though Branwen quietly worried to him that she was still too tentative and anxious to please.

Isabelle, it turned out, was to be married that summer, as planned, to Simon d'Argentan, Lord Hubert d'Argentan's older son. The Argentans were hosting the wedding. As Robert and Branwen had done with Edward, they'd arranged for the betrothed couple to meet once or twice a year for supervised visits throughout their childhoods; however, since she'd "become a woman," Isabelle had shown herself reluctant to become a wife. It taxed Jeanne and annoyed Branwen. While she totally understood Isabelle's truculence, upper-class women had infuriatingly few options. If Isabelle didn't take the veil—and many did, to avoid precisely this—an unmarried lady's life could be confined and bleak. She could serve as some royal woman's lady-in-waiting, that was about it.

Branwen knew this from experience: if Lord Ralph, Robert's father, hadn't become aware of her through court circles, she would have remained back in Wales, tending her parents, hidden away because of her epilepsy. Those afflicted were met with fear and revulsion. If it had become known, she would certainly not have been married to the heir to a barony.

For ten years, terrified Robert would find out about her malady and annul their marriage, she'd camouflaged her fear with a cool, competent, castle-chatelaine façade. She'd persuaded herself that she didn't love him, though she'd always respected him. But, during her time in the twenty-first century, she was startled to realize that she missed Robert and wished he could be there to share that adventure with her. She realized that respect was the basis of love.

When she'd awakened in Robert's arms from the "return" seizure, her first thoughts had been of terror. She was sure he'd cast her out right then; even if he didn't, she knew she could never match what he'd had with Stacey. But he tended her with gentleness and discretion, and they had the talk they should have had right at the start. To her surprise and joy, he told her that he'd known about her affliction since almost the beginning and had always loved her in spite of it. She was now free to be herself, to love him in return, beginning the most remarkable journey for both of them. In the deepest, most private part of her being, she knew they were still not what was called, in that other century, soulmates. Stacey was that for Robert, she felt sure. But what they did have was stronger and more intimate than any romantic fantasy. She could not imagine life without him.

Since her return from the twentieth-first century, she'd thought a lot about that century's obsession with finding The One, and how often that led to The Wrong One. In her experience, very few couples enjoyed the combination of physical desire and easy compatibility that Jean and Marie seemed to have. She fully granted that arranged marriages could be disastrous. However, Branwen believed that, assuming both parties wanted to make it work and neither of them was a dastardly, abusive character, a successful marriage could potentially be made with many partners. Edward and Jeanne, for example. They might not be a match made in heaven, but they were a perfectly good match on earth. Yes, her stutter was tiresome, but Branwen had assured Edward at the time of the wedding that it would probably make Jeanne a better wife, and she'd been proven right. They were full partners, working to the same goal, which was how it should be. Again, mutual respect was the key.

Evan was still young. Marriage to his "one true love" was impossible, but, surely, he'd find another girl who would bring him joy. She was sure Isabelle would come around, too. Simon, at least, seemed like a well-brought-up young man. The stickler would be how someone as strong-minded as Isabelle would get along with Lady Blanche, her mother-in-law. Meanwhile, Branwen presumed wedding preparations were going as planned. Neither she nor Jeanne had any say in it and she couldn't care less.

Evan treated bumps, bruises, aches, pains, sprains, breaks, and other minor ailments in and around the castle. He consulted with Sister Marguerite and, sitting by her brazier, confided a curated number of his anxieties to her. Robert's health was starting to be a bit of a concern; he was complaining of shortness of breath and fatigue. Taking Branwen aside, Evan told her that these weaknesses were often symptoms of an ailing heart.

Robert had always been fit, and she saw to it that the castle denizens ate healthfully. He had never drunk in excessive amounts. All this worked in his favour. Evan prescribed a tincture of hawthorn berries, and, while not discouraging him from vigorous physical activity, he did counsel avoiding stress. Perhaps he should offload more of his responsibilities on Edward.

Other than that, Evan read the books his parents borrowed from the abbey after they were finished with them. He tutored Gilbert. He flew kites with Isabelle and nephew Pierre, when he came home for Christmastide. He brushed up on his gentlemanly hunting, chess, and *jeux de tables* skills.

He dropped in on Marie, Jean, and their three boys at Amesford Castle. There, he was pleasantly surprised by his sister, who'd once said that all she wanted was to be married to Jean and have his babies. Having efficiently produced an heir and two spares, Marie had asked Jean to give her a bit of a rest. She wanted to start a school for the children in Amesford. She was already quietly tutoring the servants in their letters, and their children.

She enthused, "Egbert—he's our groom's son—is such a clever boy! When he gets older, I don't see why I can't send him to Oxford! Well, why not? William went, didn't he?"

Evan could think of a dozen reasons why not and one big reason why: because it would give a deserving boy a chance.

"What do Lord Rupert and Lady Christine have to say about that?"

"What do you think?" she smiled. When Marie smiled, she dimpled prettily. She usually got what she wanted, in the end.

She looked around furtively and lowered her voice. "Of course, they're all shocked and scandalized. But they won't be around forever, will they? And Jean agrees with me." Evan would have been surprised if he didn't; he'd had the same instruction as his wife.

He toured the countryside, looking for a village lacking a qualified physician or needing a second one, but he found that the so-called physicians at the villages he did stop at were suspicious and territorial.

One afternoon in January of 1194, coming home from his daily ride on Wasim, he took a moment to watch Marshal Oliver Longstreet in daily sword practice with the guards. Longstreet's father, Geoffrey Longstreet, had died the previous year. Thinking about knightly activities, Evan now recalled that puzzling conversation with Besace. Yes, whatever had happened to Uncle Guy? This could be a useful little project, something to fill his spare time.

Tom Atwood had worked in the castle since he was a boy. He'd started out as stable hand, worked his way up to groom, and then head groom. "Genial" seemed to be the word that stuck to Tom. His face, though now middle-aged, remained open and cheerful. His and Ellan's two boys were now working as an apprentice baker and shoemaker in the village. She was pregnant with their third child. Branwen had instructed the boys in their letters when they were younger, and they had pretty much grown up in the castle alongside the other children. The castle commune without Tom and his family was unthinkable. If anyone knew anything about Guy's disappearance, it would be Tom.

As he and Evan stripped Wasim of his tack, Evan decided to broach the topic. "Atwood, can I ask you something in all confidentiality?"

Tom stopped, intrigued. "Why yes, Sir Evan, ask away."

"What do you think happened to my uncle?"

Tom momentarily froze. "You mean Sir Guy, of course."

"Yes, who else?"

Stalling for time, he filled a bucket of oats for Wasim.

Why's Gilbert never here when I need him, he thought irritably.

By the time he turned to face Evan, he had found his usual cordial expression.

"Hmm, whyever would you ask that after, what, almost twenty years?"

"Well, it seems the world is a small place, right? King Richard's senior physician was once a knight in Henry's household. He served with Uncle Guy." And Evan went on to relate what he'd learned about Guy's unsavoury reputation and the frustrated bettors who could never collect on the manner of his passing.

Tom listened to all of this, his face frozen in cordiality as he brought back to mind the prepared answer he'd given all the authorities at the time.

When Evan finished, Tom said, "I'm sorry, Sir Evan, I can't help you. I last saw him alive that afternoon. I think you know that he left the castle late that night, with Marshal Longstreet."

"Yes, pity that the elder Longstreet has passed on, otherwise I'd ask him." An awkward silence ensued. "That's all right, Atwood, don't worry. I just thought I'd ask."

This was starting to gnaw at Evan. Atwood knew more than he was saying, that much was obvious. If Atwood knew something, someone else must, too.

Enith. Enith noticed things. There was nothing she didn't know about this castle because there was essentially nothing else in her brain, and she'd never minded gossiping before.

He found Enith where she typically was at this time of day: in the great hall, mending hose. Enith had had a withered left arm from birth. Evan had always admired how dextrously she compensated for that handicap. Her mending was better than anyone's. As usual, she was with her friends, Ellan and Winnifred, the dairy maid. Perfect. Surely one of them could help.

He cordially greeted them and apologized for the intrusion, pulling up a chair by the fire. He said, "I'm just trying to solve a little mystery in my spare time. I'm trying to figure out what happened to Uncle Guy. I know it's been a long time, but perhaps there is some small detail one of you might remember, some clue, however small. Who knows, it might lead to solving the mystery of his disappearance."

All three women started in surprise and glanced at each other. The silence in the room was thick. Winnifred, who'd always been the most forthright of the three, eventually said, "Sir Evan, you know we hold your family in the highest regard. So please forgive me for saying this, but Sir Guy was a terrible man. None of us were safe when he was around."

She paused to let him absorb that and, seeing Evan's shock, continued, "No one's sorry that he's gone. But we last saw him alive that afternoon."

He tried to imagine their terror whenever Guy would ride up to the castle gates, their powerlessness in the face of a man who could, and would, ruin them in any number of ways. Winnifred had had an illegitimate son whose father she had always refused to identify. The child had been raised with his grandparents. The full horror of it started to sink in.

"Was Aldred—"

The three women stared at him, mouths clenched.

"I see. I'm so sorry. Do my parents know this?"

Winnifred said, "Ultimately, it came out. They wanted to bring him here to live with me, but my parents were the only ones he'd ever known. Aldred still believes I'm his sister. Sir Evan, it's all a long time ago and he's gone." The look on her face said the rest: Please don't go stirring things up again.

Evan shook his head and said, "I'm sorry I troubled you. Please carry on."

The secret to Guy's disappearance was in this castle, he was sure, and his death was most likely suspicious.

The following day, after dinner, Branwen casually said, "Evan, my dear, before you take Wasim out, would you join Papa and me in the great chamber? There's a matter we'd like to discuss with you."

When they were assembled, Robert closed the door and sat down, fussing with his sleeve. After clearing his throat, he said, "It's come to our attention that you've been making inquiries into my brother's disappearance."

Evan was taken aback. He felt like he'd been caught thieving. "Enith told you? Am I in trouble?"

Robert replied, "No, no *trouble*. We just want to know why you're asking about it after all this time."

"Well, yes, I have," he replied defensively. "My attention was drawn to it while I was away." And he related Besace's story again. "Surely, Papa, even if he was a bad character, isn't it best to know what happened to him? So he can have a proper, Christian burial?"

His parents stared at each other, their faces troubled. "Should we tell him?" she whispered. Robert nodded.

He said, "Son, I could tell you to drop this inquiry of yours in its tracks. But it's been my experience that telling people to stop trying to solve a puzzle is like the priests telling people to stop fornicating. We cannot have you disturbing the servants any more than you already have. Our only choice is to trust you with the truth. You've shown yourself capable of keeping secrets before. If we tell you what happened, will you promise to drop this?"

At that moment, Evan would have promised one of his kidneys. "I promise."

Branwen said, "I suppose I'll go first." Robert took her hand. "Whatever your uncle was, he was not a Christian, and he deserved no 'Christian burial.' He will never be found alive because I killed him."

Evan gasped.

"I came upon him in the act of interfering with your sister."

Evan gasped again. "Did he—"

"No, it hadn't got that far. Believe me, I've watched Marie for signs of nightmares, memories surfacing, but to my knowledge she has no memory of it—she was only two at the time. So, don't you start introducing notions into her head! I have prayed on this so much, but to this day I cannot beg the Lord for forgiveness. I'd do it again. In fact, I'm glad I stopped Guy in time."

Mama had a small scar on the mound of her right thumb. She absently rubbed her middle finger against it. She had injured herself that day, Evan now understood. He thought back to his young childhood with his sister. No, he couldn't remember any behavioural problems, night terrors, or other signs of distress.

He racked his brains: Had Marie mentioned anything about it at the time? Again, no. Evan had only been three, after all. If she had, all memory of that day was lost.

If Mama hadn't come upon them when she did … Evan felt a chill run up his spine.

"Mama, Papa, I think I'd know if anything she experienced that day lodged unpleasantly in her mind."

"Yes," Branwen replied. "You knew her better than anyone."

Robert said, "One of us would have had to kill him, eventually, to save the family honour. Your mother and I and Tom Atwood are the only ones still alive who know what happened after that. The rest of the staff have collectively decided that what they don't know can never be brought back to hurt them. Guy's body was transported out of the castle and buried. Even I am not sure where, and I've never thought to look. Do not try to get it out of Atwood. He'll never tell you and he has served this castle too well to be put in such a position."

"But Guy was seen that night leaving—"

"Well, you can't always trust what your eyes see."

"But …" Evan's mind worked feverishly. How had the body been snuck out? And who did leave the castle that night, if it wasn't Guy? How did they get rid of the horse?

"Evan, it's done. Exactly how we disposed of the body is not important. What is important is that when your mother took his life, the balance between good and evil in this world was restored a little bit. But I must command you, as your father, to drop this now."

"So that's why no one goes in Guy's room."

Branwen shuddered. "Evil lived in that room. Murder was committed in that room. Who knows, maybe his ghost still lives there. I don't want to find out. That room will remain locked."

The secrets they had kept all these years. Surely that went a long way to explaining their solidarity as a couple. He was sure he could trust them with his own guilty secret.

"Mama, do you remember killing Guy? Do you remember what you felt when it was happening?"

After a moment, she said, "Yes, every bit of it, to this day. When I saw him exposed like that, with my innocent, tiny daughter, I was consumed by a white-hot rage. I had never felt that before and never have again. If I'd had the strength, I would have torn him apart. In hindsight, I suppose what helped was that he'd always made my skin crawl." Robert wrapped his arm around her shoulders.

"I don't know what would have happened if your father and Geoffrey Longstreet, with cooler heads than mine, hadn't taken charge. I was not myself for some hours after that." She studied him curiously. "Why do you ask?"

Now was the time. He took a breath and said, "I, too, have killed a man—and not during the crusade."

Seeing his troubled face, she took his hand. "Oh, my poor dear. How? Why?"

"It happened the night after we left Auzier. He was trying to steal the Lancelot. I wouldn't have it. But, unlike you, Mama, when I put my knife in his belly, I swear, I barely remember doing it. It was like someone else took me over."

There was a silence as his parents absorbed this.

Robert asked, "Was he unarmed?"

"No, he had a knife drawn."

"So he might have killed you."

"Yes, I try to remember that."

"Have you told anyone else about this?"

"No one. The other travellers know, of course, including Diego." He'd told his parents about that happy coincidence. "He, like the others, promised never to tell anyone."

"How do you feel about this now?" she asked.

Evan replied, "I still can't believe I got all the way through the Third Crusade without ever drawing my sword, only to kill a man fifty miles from the Channel. Like you, Mama, I have yet to feel remorse. Well, I am remorseful for having killed, but not for having killed him. What bothers me is that I ought to be."

"What do you mean by that?" asked his mother.

Evan paused, conjuring the memory of the man. "Cedric was ugly, brutish looking, like a gargoyle. I was repulsed by him. Would I have killed him so readily if he'd been handsome? He couldn't help how he looked! Who knows how I would have turned out if I had to go through life looking like that. Besides, it was just a book! I could have got you another!"

Branwen said, "It's not surprising that someone like Cedric would become what everyone assumed he was from his appearance. On the other hand, people like Guy walk freely among us because they are handsome. It is tragic and unfair."

Evan nodded and added, "And now what bothers me is that, perhaps, I am really no better than Uncle Guy. Maybe his spirit even possessed me in that moment."

She gasped and crossed herself. "Do not ever think that! You are a good man who broke a commandment. So you're not perfect! Are you only just now realizing this? In an ideal world, no one would ever take another life. But ours is a violent world. You killed a man who would surely have killed you. You've returned from a war in which your comrades in arms killed ordinary men who had mothers, likely wives and children, too, at home. That is glorified, but it's still murder, isn't it? Sufficiently provoked, all of us are capable of it."

After a moment, Evan said, "Have you heard of the massacre at Acre?"

They nodded. Robert said, "Yes, we did. We heard three thousand victims."

"No, not quite that many. More like twenty-seven hundred."

"Does that make it better?" she asked. "In the twenty-first century, the King would be tried for war crimes. Your father and I disagree on whether he was even vaguely justified."

Evan replied, "I still don't know myself. Richard was in a difficult position. But at the time, I was more upset about the men who carried it out. It's one thing to issue an order, it's entirely another to be the ones to actually do it, isn't it? The prisoners were unarmed, and some were women and children. They were penned, like animals. How do you draw your sword and run them through? How do you bludgeon a child to death? I never understood how—until that night outside Auzier. Like me, I think the executioners were in a sort of blind fog. I think we all persuaded ourselves that we were killing something not quite human. I suppose like the mob that killed Rabbi Jacob."

Loyalty to a friend who had confided the most shameful moment of his life stopped him from saying any more.

Robert said, "Do you know what the real difference is between you and Guy? Weeks later, you're still preoccupied by it. If he thought he could get away with it, Guy would have knifed that man because he was bored, or out of curiosity for how someone suffers before dying. And then would have carried on with his dinner. Never put you and him in the same breath."

He said, finally, "I think all you can do is repent before God and try to atone. Resolve that you will carry on doing good, doing the best you can. And what has been said in this room today stays here. Do you swear?"

"I swear."

-II-
Here Lies King Arthur

One day in February of 1194, Evan rode into Glastonbury, Somersetshire, a little over a day's ride northwest from Shaftesbury. He was curious about the village's growing fame as a pilgrim destination. Glastonbury's distinguishing geographical feature, visible for miles around, was Glastonbury Tor, a conical pimple of land rising from the otherwise mostly flat landscape, on top of which was a modest wooden church. However, the church was of secondary interest to the tor's growing renown as a vortex of Arthuriana.

Glastonbury was similar to Shaftesbury, known also for its walled Benedictine abbey, a short walk from the tor. Its abbot, Robert of Winchester, had officiated at Edward and Jeanne's wedding. Now, it was Savaric of Bath. In 1184, a fire had burned almost the entire complex to the ground, although reconstruction had begun almost immediately. The Lady Chapel, the dormitories, the kitchen, and the refectory had already been rebuilt. The largest and most expensive project, now underway, was the great church.

It was an impressive complex, built to be as self-sufficient as possible. The abbey grounds occupied some thirty-six acres and contained fish ponds, dairy cows, large gardens, and an apple orchard that served to make cider, as well. It was rich in income from the surrounding lands, but more cash than that was needed to fund the rebuild, to create an impressive and longer-lasting church. Like everyone else, the abbey had been required to come up with its share of the ransom. Fortunately, the abbey was more creative than most in attracting paying pilgrims.

First of all, was the legend of the Holy Thorn. Local lore held that in biblical times much of Somersetshire was under water, making the tor an island. The apparently well-travelled Joseph of Arimathea was said to have arrived by boat. Disembarking on dry land, he climbed Wearyall Hill and plunged his staff in the ground as he rested. The following morning, miraculously, a hawthorn tree had started to grow. Anyone could see that the tree was ancient. It flowered in spring *and* around Christmastide, surely testament to its divinity. Miraculous healing powers had been attributed to this tree and access to it was strictly controlled. A fee was charged to anyone wanting a leaf or a sprig; nonetheless, a cutting from it had been planted on the abbey grounds.

Furthermore, rumour had it that Joseph had come to the area with a cup of Jesus's blood and buried it somewhere in the vicinity. Troubadours were now calling this cup the *Saint-Graal*. There was a spring right at the base of the tor that spewed a sort of reddish-coloured water that was obviously symbolic of the rusty nails on the cross: this must be where the *Graal* was buried! To drink of this water must be a cure for whatever ailed.

Evan remembered Robert de Boron's nascent work back in Paris and thought, Well, that didn't take long.

By far the most exciting story was the collective "vision" that the monks had three years before, which led them to discover in the abbey graveyard a casket of two skeletons, one male and one female. The casket was neatly labelled, *"Hic jacet sepultus inclitus rex Arthurus in insula Avalonia."* For centuries, this Celtic legend, as written by Welsh and Breton bards, had been popular after-dinner fare in the West and Southwest. But now, aided by trouvères such as Troies and Boron, the Arthurian Legend was particularly abloom and pilgrim activity picked up accordingly.

In addition, the abbey already housed a massive collection of holy relics: a part of Moses's rod, a fragment of Jesus's cradle, some bits of the five loaves with which Jesus fed the masses, a few threads from one of the Blessed Virgin's gowns, a bone from Saint John the Baptist's forefinger, and one of Saint Paul's teeth, among many others.

By now, Evan had a physician's doubt of the healing powers of supposed relics. A lot of it was pure chicanery, if not downright dangerous. Still, he did know that the mind—call it faith—could play a huge part in effecting a cure. He had witnessed it himself. Even so, he understood that the abbey's ambitions had more to do with the commercial than with the miraculous.

He was impressed with the energy this place exuded, and it seemed to Evan that someone like him might be useful at this critical time in the abbey's history. The abbey needed every good man it could get; there were only seventy-four monks—not that many, considering the size of the abbey. It would mean he'd have to take holy orders, but the chance to do something meaningful, to set up a real hospital in a place where there was probably only a single medical room was positively thrilling. The more he thought about it, the more this seemed like the right thing to do. He just knew he could be of great help here; in the process, he could expiate some of the guilt he still felt at Cedric's death. Besides—and he would admit this to nobody—on the remotest of chances that someone did come looking for him, he'd have sanctuary here.

And there was something else, perhaps the most important factor of all. Eleanor had come up with the money. Even now, it was being transported to Germany. No one had any idea how a sum that great could be safely shipped; even getting it all to London had been a logistical and security nightmare. One of the conditions Henry and Leopold had set down was this: if any of the sum got lost on the way for any reason, well, she would just have to find a way to replace it. It was reportedly being transported in instalments, shipped from and arriving at various ports, with no particular guard; it was less likely to attract attention this way. Eleanor was shortly going to travel to some agreed-upon place in Germany to ensure her son's release.

Assuming his captors were men of their word, Richard would be released, perhaps any day now. Knowing the King as he did, Evan believed he would spend very little time tending to his kingdom. Richard was a warrior. Idle for thirteen months, he'd roar out of the gate to get back at Philip and retrieve his lands. To accomplish this, he would want a physician or two, or three. He would come looking for Evan.

Evan never again wanted to see hacked-up bodies and the sacrifice of young men in their prime. He could not look anymore at full wards of suffering men, crying for their wives or mothers. This could not be his destiny, surely. He wanted to heal as a normal physician would. He wanted to be somewhere where Richard could not get at him. And that was in holy orders.

This particular morning, the abbey grounds were busy. Soil was being turned and stone hauled. Evan asked one of the monks if he could have a moment of the Father Abbot's time. The monk looked appraisingly at Evan with his upper-class French and his well-made, though hardly luxurious clothes, and took in his beautiful, proud, exotic horse. Clearly, a horse like that could only have been obtained as booty on crusade.

The monk did not reply to him, merely nodded his head in the direction of a man at the church construction site, conferring with one of the masons.

Savaric was an energetic Saxon in his thirties, exactly the sort necessary to supervise this project. He looked up from a parchment plan of the new church to cast an assessing eye on this young visitor.

Evan kneeled to Savaric. He said, "Father Abbot, I am Sir Evan de Montmorency, just returned from crusade. I'm a qualified physician, and I've come to offer my services here, as well as take holy vows."

Savaric took another look at the young man. He was not the first returned crusader who felt a desire to leave the world of sin and vice. He was a knight; ergo, he came from money. His entry fee would come in handy. Montmorency, did he say? He must be the Earl of Shaftesbury's younger boy. That would explain the escorts. Add another thirty or so marks to the fee.

He said, "While the abbey will always welcome novices to the fold, we do have a physician. You would be welcome to assist him, of course."

Of course. How could I have been so stupid as to think I could just walk in here and start running the place, Evan thought resignedly. Here I go again. But if I could do it with Crécy and Besace, I can do it here. Lord, give me patience.

"Father Abbot, I have studied in Messina and in Salerno. I was King Richard's personal physician towards the end of the crusade. While I'm anxious to put my skills to peaceful use, I will serve however you bid me."

Both men knew that Evan's qualifications and skills far surpassed those of whatever physician was currently on the grounds.

Savaric said, "I'm sure your skills will be of use." He switched to English. "We speak English in this abbey, by the way."

Evan replied, in that language, "That's not a problem."

"May I ask why you are not still in the King's service?"

"He released me at Corfu, Father Abbott. He knew I wished to continue my training. In any case, it was his intention to travel in the company of only a few other people."

Savaric commented drily, "Just as well that you were not included in that select company. Otherwise, you'd be keeping the King company in some German castle at this very moment."

"Yes, I consider myself most fortunate."

.

Savaric sensed that Fortune often tilted this young man's way. He'd survived the Third Crusade, for starters. Savaric's nephew hadn't. Back in '89, when the call to arms came, Savaric did his part in rounding up young men for this endeavour. Two hundred men from Glastonbury and the surrounding area joined up. Why shouldn't they: all-expenses paid, see the world, rescue the Holy Land in the bargain. Forty of them did not return, and those that did were generally not the same men they'd been before. The ultimate sacrifice for the glory of God, a secure place in heaven. These platitudes were thin gruel indeed to the mothers who would never see their sons again, would never even have a grave to visit. In his darkest moments, which he clamped down on with increasing fervour, his guilt ate at him like an ulcer.

In Savaric's experience, good fortune often led to the sin of pride. This young man would have to be managed carefully.

"You realize, of course, that this is a Benedictine abbey. There are demands and sacrifices required of you to be part of this brotherhood. In addition to chastity and obedience, you must forgo all trappings of wealth, all personal belongings." He eyed Wasim. "These are difficult demands for any man, never mind someone of your background."

"I understand, Father Abbot." What Evan understood was that Wasim would henceforth reside permanently at Shaftesbury Castle.

He returned to the castle, excited that he had a plan for his life and that he could answer his calling by peaceful means. Over dinner the following day, he told everyone what he'd decided.

The reaction was unexpectedly muted. Second sons (or even daughters) often took holy orders. "One to the Church" was a common phrase in England at that time. It was easy and straightforward and got this extra child off people's hands. Many noble families told these children that they were destined for the Church as soon as they were old enough to understand. That had not been the case in Shaftesbury Castle, however.

Branwen chewed her lip worriedly. It was commendable that Evan was exercising his right to choose his life's path. But why did his every choice have to involve leaving Dorsetshire? The thought of losing her son in this way tore her heart open.

She said, "You've only just got home, and now you're leaving us *again*, probably forever? Are you sure this is what you want, dear?"

Robert added, "You realize you can't jump in and out of the abbey whenever you want. From the moment you pass through those gates, we will have to come to you, rather than the reverse. You know that we waited long years for your return. We had hoped that you'd spend a little time here before you disappear on us again."

Evan hadn't considered that; in fact, he really thought that he'd be doing his parents a favour. Yes, it was true: he might never see his beloved home again. But, still, there was a principle involved here. This time, he had made an oath to himself.

Robert said again, "Are you sure this is what you really want? You've spent the last four years on the move. You will now be rooted in one spot, for the rest of your life."

"Papa, I must. It's the only way I can keep out of Richard's reach. None of you have seen what I have seen. Or, done what I have done. I can't be a party to any more violence."

"Ah," his parents said in unison.

Edward voiced what everyone else was thinking, but not saying. "But, you'll be celibate."

"Yes, I've thought this over carefully. I know what it's like to 'know' a woman. I have known the only woman I care to know. I'll be fine. I'll have my work."

The others weren't so sure. Branwen, in particular, couldn't hide her consternation. Oh, my dear boy, she thought. I so wanted you to know the joy Robert and I have had. I so wanted to hug your children, my grandchildren …

Robert eventually said, “Well, we’ve always said that your life is yours to do with as you wish. You’re a grown man. I think we speak for everyone when I say to think it over carefully. Give it a month.”

Evan agreed, though he knew he wouldn’t change his mind. He glanced over at Edward and caught an unguarded look of envy before it was wiped off to a studied neutrality.

-III-
Each Day Provides Its Own Gifts

Richard was released on February 4, 1194, but not without some last-minute skullduggery on Philip's and John's parts: both connived to get Henry to renege on the deal and keep Richard in custody. When Philip did hear of Richard's release, he sent a message to John: "Look to yourself. The devil is loose."

On Richard's arrival back in London, John threw himself at his feet and begged forgiveness for his transgressions. With an uncharacteristic lack of foresight and judgment, Richard gave in to pressure from Eleanor and magnanimously forgave his brother, a fact that caused some alarm in court circles loyal to Richard. As long as John was pardoned and unfettered, he would continue to undermine his brother at every opportunity. Richard did, however, have himself quickly re-crowned, so no doubt would persist about who was in charge. Then, he set off for Normandy to regain the territory Philip had captured. Although the very capable and implicitly trusted Hubert Walter was left to run things in his absence, Richard himself never again set foot on English soil.

Across the land, general celebration ensued at the news of the release of the Hero of the Holy Land. But in Shaftesbury Castle, this announcement was met with a mix of relief, weariness, and cynicism. Neither Robert nor Branwen had any illusions that their coffers would be left alone. There would always be more causes to fund.

In March, Evan began his three-year-long postulancy and noviciate in Glastonbury Abbey. Everyone promised they'd visit him, though the abbey was hardly around the corner, practically speaking. It was a more than a day's ride away. A long way to go for what would amount to only a brief chat.

He missed Isabelle's wedding on June 26 and was almost glad he did; the thought of beautiful young people holding hands at a church door hit too close to home, and he pushed it out of his mind. He had no idea if the wedding was a success or not, or if, in fact, the wedding had taken place at all. From then on, the only news he and his fellow monks would hear of the world was what the Abbot felt fit to share with them.

Evan was immersed in the culture of prayer, humility, and obedience; he was stripped of all his possessions and provided with a change of robes and a pair of sandals only. He lived in a dormitory sleeping ten monks. The Abbot himself lived in fine style, however: his residence was a grand, three-storey affair, richly decorated from gifts to the abbey. He even had his own kitchen.

Days were strictly regimented: five hours of prayer, including the seven daily prayer services; five hours of work, during which Evan was regularly cycled from the kitchen to the stables, to the garden, to the scriptorium; four hours of spiritual readings. Since talking distracted from communication with the Lord, silence was the general rule, except for exchanges with the Abbot—and physicians with patients.

At meals, there was enough to eat, but only just. All meat from four-footed animals was forbidden, unless one was very ill or weak. There was never any breakfast, and, except for Easter season, as Pasch was called in English, only one meal was standard: dinner or supper, taken at varying times of the afternoon or evening, according to the season. During Lent, they had to wait until supper to eat.

Evan was lonely, though he was rarely alone. The Rule of Silence inhibited forming friendships with the other monks, though they'd all become adept at a common sign language and a rich range of facial expressions. In fact, there was so much "chattering" going on that he wondered why they bothered with silence. Accustomed to being praised for his accomplishments, he was regularly castigated for his pride and impatience, his "lack of humility before God."

He had never felt before that his confidence and eagerness were character flaws. But that was then and this was now, and he knew there was no room for pride here. It was all about humility.

He still half expected a band of authorities to ride up to the abbey gates inquiring about a Montmorency, wanted for questioning about the murder of a certain Cedric. But no one did, and while Evan could never entirely forget, he gradually forgave himself and tucked it away in the drawer of his brain marked "Reasons for Humility."

He missed his tiny frog. Although it would have been confiscated anyway, he wondered whether leaving it at home was a bad omen. As well, it had been some time since he'd had a Steven dream, and he wondered why. What was Steven doing with his life? Did he have children yet with Gaby? Cut off from everyone he'd ever known—and cut off from Steven, it seemed—Evan felt adrift.

Late at night, his thoughts turned to Joanna, wondering where she was and whether she still thought of him. "Please don't try to find me": those six little words were as hurtful now as when he'd first read them. He understood now that she'd never intended they have "one more time." Sometimes he wondered whether he'd eventually forget what she looked like; indeed, it was becoming increasingly difficult to conjure the lines and contours of her face, her light, flowery perfume. The lock of her hair was safe, of course, back in his room at home. He knew she could not be happy. How could she be, waiting for her brother to decide her future for her? Was the knowledge that he loved her even faintly enough to comfort her anymore? Was she, too, lying awake at this moment, trying to remember his face?

These thoughts inevitably led him to Jane. How was she growing? She would be over a year old—probably walking. What had been her first word? Which of them did she resemble? Was she being treated well? Sometimes he even wondered about Gurci. Had he found his place in life? Met a pleasing girl? Fantasizing about all of them, living their lives, got him to sleep at night. And he continually reminded himself of the greater good he would accomplish, once he was allowed to start the hospital. Surely, his family must think of him and be proud. Finally, concluding this train of thought, he thanked God again for blessing him with the strong family and friends who'd supported and loved him.

On the positive side of his life here, he had strengthened his faith. One afternoon during the past winter, alone with his parents, he'd asked them, "How do you reconcile what the Church preaches with what science tells us?"

Branwen had paused for a while, to gather her thoughts.

"How do you reconcile what happened to Stacey and me with science and reason?" she finally said.

"It makes no sense, and yet it happened. You know that phrase, '*certum est quia impossibile est*'?" It is certain because it is impossible? The thing about faith is that it is just that: faith. It doesn't have to be proven; if it did, it wouldn't be faith, would it? Even while I was in that future time, I went to church every day. I needed to in a way that had nothing to do with fear of damnation if I didn't. It gave me comfort, and what's wrong with that?"

Robert had added, "A lot of blather, shall we say, comes from the Church. It is immensely powerful and rich, and it needs to control us with fear; otherwise, it'd no longer be powerful and rich, would it? What we have learned to do is shut that out and listen to the basic message of the Faith, which is love, forgiveness, and an intimate relationship with our Lord."

"Do you shut out Father Benedict's sermons, too?"

They laughed. "Especially those," Branwen said. "I plan the daily menus during prime."

"This would be blasphemy, would it not?"

"Of course," they'd both said.

She said, "Someday, centuries from now, one will be able to talk freely about such matters, but until then, keep your beliefs to yourself."

He remembered what they'd said every day. The prayers, the chants, the meditations: he felt his soul enveloped by love and peace during those times. He was able to shut out the Abbot's blather and soothe his loneliness.

He knew that no work on his hospital could be considered while he was still a novice; the Abbot reasonably counselled patience on that. Every month, Evan put in a few days' work in what passed for a hospital at the abbey. It was just a room with a couple of beds, with an apothecary attached, erected in a hurry after the fire destroyed the previous space. According to Brother John, that hadn't been much more. Evan's obedience was expected and absolute. He bled the patients as he was ordered to do, then quietly gave them a restorative tea. He watched as John gave them skullcap to treat headaches, then just as quietly pressed willow bark on them.

At the same time, he was learning that everyone had something to teach him, if only he would listen. He saw that John's treatments occasionally worked, mainly because John impressed on the patients that they would. Evan learned that he shouldn't be ashamed of availing himself of this trick of the trade if he suspected the patient's symptoms were related at all to their state of mind. A surprising number of monks, for example, came in claiming they had trouble sleeping. Lacking valerian, Evan gave them jars of a "special" honey that he swore would have them practically fall asleep on their feet.

"Be careful of this, now!" he'd urge them. "You don't want to fall asleep during compline! Take only one spoonful just before bedtime!"

Asked later how they were sleeping, they claimed that it had worked like a charm.

Time passed. The days turned into the months and, before he knew it, the years. He marked the passage of time not by events, anniversaries, and birthdays, but by the cycles of the monthly duty roster, the seasons, and the religious calendar. He looked forward to the first snowdrops, the first calf, the first frog song in spring, the first apple blossoms, the first Perseid meteor shower, the first cider. He loved the soul-cleansing, majestic power and beauty of seventy-eight male voices chanting in harmony. He took as his maxim Marcus Aurelius's "Each day provides its own gifts."

In March of 1197, he took his vows. He was now a full monk. Shortly after that, Savaric announced at dinner that, thanks to the Lord's will and the generosity of the abbey's donors, building the new hospital could be commenced. Evan launched himself full throttle into the project.

He never did get a Steven dream.

-IV-
As Oil and Water

In January of 1198, along with Edgar—his personal servant—Gilbert, and two guards, Edward rode to the abbey in the pouring rain. He looked for and eventually found his brother, as expected, in the still-unfinished though serviceable hospital beside the chapter house and dormitories, close to the east wall. His plans were close to fruition, Edward saw, and he was amazed at how his brother could organize all this in such a short time. Mama and Papa had been kept apprised of Evan's progress at the abbey and had been as proud of the building of this hospital as they'd been of his growing fame as a healer.

It had been almost four years since he'd seen his brother. He took in the drab fustian monk's robe, the cross dangling from his neck, the sandals on bare feet. Edward, bundled in layers under a fur-lined cloak, felt chilled just looking at him. A cowl covered his tonsured head. He was clean-shaven, and he was clean. Edward hadn't been sure what to expect. Mama had told him to take careful note of his appearance: "Does he seem healthy? Any sign that he's being mistreated?"

He looked for signs of birching but saw none. How could he unless Evan bared his back? He was definitely thinner. On the ride to the abbey, Edward had pondered whether he'd have some sort of saintly aura about him, some air of piety. But no, he saw none of that. While his eyes still shone with intensity, no trace remained of the old innocence.

The brothers warmly embraced. "Come," Evan said, bending his mind from English back into Anglo-Norman. "Let's get in out of the wet."

As they warmed their hands in front of the brazier, Edward said, "Brother, I come with bad news. It's Papa. He suddenly passed away the day before yesterday."

Evan groaned in despair. It was not unexpected, but it hit him like a body blow. "How? Tell me he wasn't alone."

"It was quick, mercifully. He was getting on Merlin for his morning ride when he collapsed, clutching his chest. Mama had just enough time to take him in her arms. The last words anyone heard him say were, 'I love you.' And she said, 'And I love you, too.' And he died."

"We should all die like that, in the arms of our beloved spouse," said Evan, wiping away a tear.

"Yes … but, something strange: Atwood could have sworn she then said, 'Now find her.' Find who? Do you know what she meant?"

Evan said nothing to that. "How is she taking it?"

Edward said, "You know Mama, dignified as always. Everyone else is crying rivers … Evan, you know I've never wanted this."

Evan looked up at his splendid brother, who looked every inch the part. Jeanne, in her quiet way, had always seen that Edward turned himself out well. Evan saw not the rightful new Earl of Shaftesbury, but a scared man. He felt a distinct twinge of annoyance. Edward was now in his thirty-seventh year! By Heaven, if he wasn't ready now, when would he be? Didn't he realize that, in some ways, Evan was as much a prisoner of his "destiny" as Edward was? On low days, when Brother John and the Abbot got under his skin like bed bugs, when he had to wheedle, beg, and pray for every little innovation, he was tired of this "great-healer" destiny and wished he could be just Brother Evan, a regular monk.

"Edward, you'll be a worthy successor to Papa, have no doubt. He trained you too well, and you're too fine a man to fail. Listen, every powerful man I've been around who's been confronted with a frightening situation has one thing in common: no matter how sweaty his feet may be, he acts like he's the one in charge. Go ahead and ask advice, take it if you think it's warranted, but remember, this role is *yours*. It's your birthright. No one will think to question you."

"Thank you. You're coming to the funeral mass, I assume?"

"I would assume so. I must ask Father Abbot, but he'll surely grant me permission." He took Edward's arm. "Here, let me show you around." Already completed were the treatment room and the general recovery ward, with the apothecary beside it. Beyond was a room for intestinal complaints. And beyond that, unfinished, a room for overflow.

"See?" Evan enthused. "We have a garden out back here, both medicinal and aesthetic, with benches for people to sit and contemplate. Do you see how the wall is low? I want people to have a clear view of the tor and beyond, so they feel at once protected and free. Granted, not many will want to sit out on a day like today, but it's a start! I've always believed that a little fresh air does wonders for one's spirits and health."

Edward expressed surprise that so much had been done.

Evan merely shrugged. "Well, it's nothing fancy. On the contrary. Four stone walls with a roof. Simple and restful is the key. The biggest fight and expense was getting the glass windows in." Waving his arm around, "See the tile floor? So much cleaner than dirt. See how solid it all is? It's not coming down in any fire, I'll tell you."

Aware he was bragging, he paused. There was more to the world than him and his precious hospital. "So, what news from home? Is everyone well, apart from this? Is Isabelle adjusting to being married?"

"Well, Grandmama Generys died last year." While Evan was sorry to hear that, like Edward, he'd hardly known her. The last time either of them had seen her was at Marie's wedding.

Edward continued, "Everyone else is well. Isabelle miscarried her first, but she's expecting again and seems to be doing well. She's driving her mother-in-law crazy, as she tries to clean up that castle! Do you recognize Gilbert over there? His voice has broken, and he's as tall as you are, now."

Evan peered, and spotted him. He waved; Gilbert smiled and waved back.

"We're bringing Pierre home in a couple of years. You'll be pleased to hear that Marie's school in Amesford is prospering. Isabelle wants to try that herself. Oh, and William married his sweetheart four years ago, and they have a son now."

Evan was pleased to hear all this. "What are your plans now? Why don't you stay? The abbey has room for guests and Father Abbot will want to see you."

"No, thanks for the offer, but I must get back. Arrangements are being made as we speak. I'm going to get dry and warm at Sir

Godfrey's manor." Godfrey Carreu was one of the knights in his barony. Both men knew that Robert had not been shy about dropping in on these knights; it kept them on their toes and provided useful, unfiltered information about the goings on in the demesne.

Edward mounted his horse but made no sign of leaving. "Evan, it occurred to me just now that you'll be out of touch with what's going on in the broader world out there. On the home front, Richard's squeezing us once again to build some giant castle in Normandy. But lots else has happened in Europe. You remember Duke Leopold, one of Richard's captors? Well, you'll be pleased to know he died of gangrene after a botched foot amputation. But more important, not long after you came here, King Henry—the other of Richard's captors?—used his share of the ransom money to conquer Sicily. Richard's shown no interest in trying to regain it, so that's the end of the Normans there, I suppose."

This abbey has changed me, Evan thought. Ask me if I care.

Edward went on after a pause, "The bad news for you is that Henry's men sacked Messina and Salerno. I'm sorry, I don't know if the school was destroyed in the process. Anyway, he's dead now, too. They say he was poisoned."

"They *sacked* Messina and Salerno?!" My God, he thought, Prior Lorenzo, Demetria, and all his other friends? What would have happened to them? And Joanna? Where was she at the time? What about Messina, and Sayid Abdullah and Joseph?

Reading his thoughts, "Sadly, that's all I know. I know a lot of your friends live in the area. We all pray none of them got caught up in it."

While Evan was still trying to process this horror, Edward added, "And, speaking of Sicily, your friend, the Princess Joanna? She was wed a while back, to Count Raymond of Toulouse. She's his fourth wife. I can't imagine that this is an ideal marriage, though it does secure Aquitaine's southern border."

Evan felt his heart twist. Of course, it had to happen. Oh Joanna, when it gets bad, think of me and know that I love you.

There was much to mourn and pray on, but not right now.

"When?"

"Over a year ago. October, I think. I'm sorry to be the one to tell you this news. Take care of yourself, Brother. You're thin."

At least she was safely out of Sicily. "Well by now, I'm used to being a little hungry all the time. I'll admit there are times I'd give my left thumb for a thick slab of roast lamb. Suppressing urges and cravings is good for the soul, we're told."

"Aren't you cold in just that?"

"It's all in the mind, they keep telling me. I find excuses to go into the kitchen. Please give my love to everyone, and tell them I hope to see them very soon."

As his brother and escorts rode off, it struck Evan that this was the most number of original sentences he had strung together in almost four years.

Savaric had been informed of the gist of the conversation, if not the specifics. There was no such thing as privacy in this place. He watched out the window as the elegant earl left the grounds with his entourage, their horses splashing up mud and sod in their wake, Brother Evan staring after them for some time.

It wasn't so much the fact of the ever-present, damned *Normans* that bothered Savaric. It was the accident of birth that entitled both of them to wealth and privileges he'd had to scheme for his entire life. They had no idea how fortunate they were. He was still a little vexed that the cunning steward of the late earl had bargained Evan's entry fee down to twenty marks, rightly claiming that his services at any other abbey would be eagerly sought after for free.

Both brothers had broken Chapter Fifty-Three of The Rule, which addressed the appropriate protocol for the arrival of guests. While the new earl might be forgiven because of ignorance, there was no excuse for Brother Evan. Visitors were to be taken straight to the Abbot. Monks were not allowed to speak to guests, never mind commit the sin of pride by showing off their accomplishments. In any case, Savaric would have been pleased to welcome the Earl to his table: start things off on the right foot, so to speak. So, he was more than a little disappointed as well as irritated that Lord Montmorency had simply ridden off. He was fairly certain the late earl wouldn't have made that mistake.

He reflected on the perplexing case of Brother Evan once again, while he waited for the knock at the door.

In just four years, Brother Evan had gained the respect and, dare Savaric say, the affection of the other monks. He was highly literate, energetic, and intelligent—in short, an outstanding new asset to the abbey. His reputation as a healer was known outside of Somersetshire boundaries, and those he'd treated had swelled the abbey coffers.

Relations between the growing medical community and religious institutions could not be called cordial. The Church had always resented encroachments on its turf; giving patients the notion that human skill and knowledge could cure them (with some help from prayer) was dangerous and threatening to the established order. Ordinarily, Savaric might have put Brother Evan in his place by accusing him of heresy, but it would have been patently absurd in Evan's case. His treatments were simple and intuitive. He had no secret potions, jealously guarded. No spider webs or frogs' tongues boiled up. No complicated star charts. No bloodletting. No incantations. Just various combinations of plants and herbs, mostly, combined with rest, good diet, air, light, and an odd obsession with cleanliness and boiled water. Everything he did, he openly shared—in fact, urged on the others.

Although Brother Jocelyn, the abbey prior, had relentlessly advocated for Evan's hospital as a way of bringing in extra income (all for the glory of God, of course), Savaric had delayed turning the sod as long as he could before any more delays would be unconscionable. He believed it was necessary for Brother Evan's spiritual growth. Evan himself had cleverly parlayed the delay into further profit for the abbey by exclaiming to his bejewelled and grateful patients, "Think how much more we can accomplish with an actual hospital instead of this modest room!" Turned loose on the project, Evan had immediately produced a plan he'd been carrying in his head, along with a cost estimate, assuming they could quarry the limestone at nearby Doulting.

He even had an acolyte—a sort of disciple, one might say: Brother Thomas, who had come to the abbey the previous year wanting to soak up whatever Brother Evan could teach him.

At this time, he was only in his twenty-seventh year, if memory served. Savaric was certain that, were he to die tomorrow, his brother monks would elect Evan to succeed him, despite Evan's youth and Jocelyn's seniority. This was because, in his own unobtrusive way, as surely as oil will sit on water, Evan was doing what Savaric knew he had done before: rise to the top. Savaric had no problem with this in principle; while the Church promoted the best, as long as Savaric lived, he could never be removed from his position. Still, he saw Evan as a younger, less devious version of himself. He knew Evan chafed at the rules of this community and the dim-wittedness of Brother John. So, assuming Evan would eventually become abbot, the trick was to manage and train this racehorse to lead the pack of mules. But to do that, he first had to thoroughly break the horse in to being ridden.

What, really, was Evan doing here, Savaric often wondered. Some men came because it was expected of them. Others because they genuinely felt a call to God. Savaric himself had had a dream of himself as a shepherd and had awoken convinced that it was a calling to serve. Others came because they were running from something or trying to atone for some malfeasance, the knowledge of which was torturing them. Ceaseless probing during confession and other times had failed to get anything out of him except the usual banalities of desire to serve God by doing good within a brotherhood of like-minded men. Savaric would have accepted that in any other man but Brother Evan.

There was a knock at the door. Kneeling when he was admitted, clearly reeling from mental turbulence, Evan said, "Father Abbot, I have just received word that my father has suddenly passed away. I request leave to attend his funeral mass and assist my family."

"I am so very sorry to hear that. The late earl was a much-admired man. But tell me, why did you not bring your brother straight to me, as required?"

Brother Evan looked mortified. Savaric watched as he mentally scrolled through the chapters of The Rule, realizing his mistake. Good.

"I'm so sorry, Father Abbot. I forgot. I beg your forgiveness."

Monks were frequently granted permission to leave the abbey, accompanied by another monk, on short journeys, either on personal or abbey business. On the outside, they were, of course, subject to all the usual earthly temptations. If they decided to leave the abbey permanently, they usually came back to guiltily retrieve whatever possessions they'd surrendered when they entered. During those returns, they had to explain their decision to the Abbot, and more often than not, he could persuade them to stay.

But Brother Evan was different. He'd brought with him a nag of a horse and the clothes on his back, easily replaced. If he went off the grounds at this juncture, before his spirit was entirely broken to obedience, Savaric was fairly sure he would not come back. But that would mean giving up his precious, unfinished work here. If he ignored an order to stay and then returned, he'd be subject to the usual harsh punishments, perhaps even more, given his growing stature among the other monks. An example would have to be set of him. This request, Savaric clearly saw, was a means of testing the young man's priorities.

"You are forgiven; you were understandably carried away by the moment. However, as you know, my son, one of the founding tenets of this abbey is commitment to the monastic way of life. We take this quite seriously."

"Yes, Father Abbot."

"You took the vow of stability. This means staying put, not wandering about whenever it suits your purpose."

He noted Brother Evan's quickly suppressed start of shock and annoyance.

"I hardly think—"

"Request denied."

Savaric observed the descending scale of emotions on Evan's face. Disbelief. Anger. Frustration. Sorrow. Finally, acceptance. His face couldn't hide his thoughts. Sufficient training usually rectified that weakness.

"Yes, Father Abbot. As you will it." He bowed and took his leave.

Evan strode furiously into the chapel. He needed to think.

He was mainly upset with himself: How could he have been so *stupid!* In his pride in his new hospital, in his need to show Edward that his decision to come here had not been an impulsive whim, he'd forgotten that in this place, he was only a monk, subservient to The Rule. The Abbot may have forgiven him, but forgiveness was always followed by atonement in this place. He should have known.

All his filial instincts told him he must go home, if for no other reason than to help out Mama. But he couldn't forsake his vows, not yet; he'd no longer be safe from Richard. *Could* he disobey the Abbot? What if he left and came back to suffer whatever punishments Savaric had in mind?

The previous year, Brother Gareth, a talented Welsh copyist, had done just that. He'd left for a silly reason: he'd heard somehow that his former lady friend was marrying. In fact, Gareth himself had broken off their engagement because he'd felt called to God. The Abbot correctly told him to forget about this girl, but like the proverbial dog in the manger, Gareth left anyway in the dead of night.

A week later, he sheepishly returned, having come to his senses. What happened next wasn't pretty. He was first stripped naked and birched by the Abbot himself, in front of all the other monks. For men required to dress and undress under the covers, that in itself was a shock to his brother monks. The sight of Gareth's scrawny, naked body shivering in the rain had jarred Evan because he suspected that he looked just like that, now. Ten lashes, and Gareth had to wear a hair shirt over his wounds for a week. Evan had begged to be able to salve the man's back, and after two days was permitted a daily inspection of Gareth's wounds.

Further, Gareth was excommunicated for six months. In effect, he was shunned. No one could even give him a hand signal. He ate at the back of the refectory, alone, all backs turned to him. He slept alone in a cell. He shovelled manure into the gardens, all day every day. At the end of six months, he was absolved and welcomed back into "the arms of Jesus," but it took longer than that for the other monks to come near him because of the lingering stench of manure that seemed to have seeped into his pores.

Life in an abbey was difficult. What held the men together was their sense of community. Being a social outcast in such a place was a lethal blow to a person's spirit, worse than any physical punishment.

Several weeks after he'd been reinstated, Gareth tapped Evan on the shoulder when he was alone, culling the mint, to signal that he needed a sleeping draught. When Evan produced his "special honey," Gareth said, in Welsh, in a low voice, "No, please, the real thing, as much as you can spare."

Evan immediately understood what Gareth was contemplating. In his sanctimony, Evan spouted all the usual bromides that Gareth's family would be shamed, that he'd been welcomed back into the fold, that it was a mortal sin, that endurance would make him stronger, and so on.

A fortnight after that, Gareth's body was found floating in an abbey fishpond. A plausible explanation was concocted for his drowning, both to spare his family and to spare the abbey a minor scandal. It was said he'd tripped, fallen in, and couldn't swim. Everyone smoothly accepted the lie, though he was "accidentally" buried just outside the perimeter of the abbey graveyard.

Like he had with Wilfred of Rye, Evan felt a profound sense of having failed a man in need. He continued to pray for Gareth's soul and for the wisdom to know how to treat such men in the future.

On a practical level, everyone learned the eleventh commandment: Thou shalt not defy Father Abbot. If he could do that to an ordinary monk like Gareth, what would he do to him? He'd get all that Gareth had endured and more: he wouldn't be able to practise his craft, the only thing that really mattered to him. For how long? More than six months, for sure.

No, he was the second son of the Earl of Shaftesbury. The proud blood that ran in his veins from as far back as the Norsemen would not stand for it.

He prostrated himself in front of the altar. "I'm sorry, Mama, forgive me, I'm not strong enough. I can't do it!" he wept. "You know I love you and only want to make you proud. Papa, do you really care if I attend your funeral mass? *Do you?* Please watch over me and know that I will always love and miss you."

Savaric was informed of what Evan had said and that he was still there when the sext bell rang. He had read Evan correctly.

-V-
A Country Within a Country

Branwen—so capable, so clear-headed—seemed at first to handle Robert's loss with admirable stoicism. She oversaw his burial and Edward's investiture as the fifth Earl of Shaftesbury. But once the urgency of these matters was over, the now-Dowager Countess of Shaftesbury withdrew into herself. She became listless, withdrawn, and uninterested in castle matters. She had to be urged to eat, and in fact often missed meals. She was overheard crying alone, either in the solar or the great chamber. She would take Wasim out, unaccompanied except for two guards, to sit at Robert's grave or at her "thinking place" by the river. She couldn't even be bothered to read.

Visitors to the castle, concerned about her absence at the table, were told that she was in deep mourning for the Earl.

People let her be, fairly sure she wanted neither comfort nor companionship; Lady Branwen had always been unusual about wanting to be alone.

One late April morning, by the fire in the great chamber, she gazed out the window and said listlessly to Edward, "Your father loved and understood me like no one else could. Without him, I find myself tired of this world. I'm ready for the next, if the Lord wills it."

He was profoundly shocked but could only take her hand and utter the usual comforting platitudes.

On the morning of the summer solstice, 1198, Enith came into her lady's room to discover she had passed away that night. It appeared she had simply died in her sleep. Everyone agreed that Lady Branwen must have died of grief.

The Earl of Shaftesbury of six months rode out again to convey this news to his brother. This time, a monk met him at the gates and led him straight to the Abbot.

Evan was summoned from his hospital. He knew it had to be bad news.

Savaric looked from one brother to the other. Although they resembled each other, Lord Montmorency had been blessed with his mother's reputedly beautiful colouring, and he was about two inches taller. They shared the straight-backed Norman bearing. The older brother was the handsomer of the two, but his face lacked Evan's focused conviction and self-confidence. The Earl apologized for not having paid his compliments to the Abbot on the previous occasion. Savaric nodded and invited him to stay to dinner.

He replied, "Again, I apologize, Father Abbot, but duties at the castle mean I must be right back on the road." Turning to Evan, "Brother, I come again with bad news. It's Mama: she passed away two nights ago."

Evan stared at him in shock, then collapsed, pounding the floor, moaning, "*Nooo* … Not her, *too!*"

"I know, we're all reeling from it."

Savaric, genuinely upset at the staggering blow Brother Evan had taken, said, "I am most sorry to hear this. And so soon after the Earl! She was a great lady, learned and beautiful, at the same time."

"Mama, how could you leave us like this?" Evan cried to the heavens. To his brother, "Wasn't she healthy? If only I'd been there, I might have noticed something."

Savaric thought, he is indeed grieving, otherwise he wouldn't have said that in my presence.

The Earl said, "I don't think there's anything you could have done, Brother, except cheer her up by your *presence.* She took Papa's death very hard." He related that odd statement of hers.

Savaric, listening to this exchange, had noted Lord Montmorency's mild reproach. The Earl had to know that it was Savaric himself who'd prevented Brother Evan from "cheering her up." He was starting to feel like the villain in the piece, and he didn't like that thought.

Evan replied, "Are you sure? That's exactly what she said?"

Lord Montmorency was surprised. "I think so, yes. Why does it matter?"

He muttered, "No particular reason."

But Savaric could see that it did matter, for Brother Evan seemed oddly consoled.

"Go forward bravely, Mama," Evan mumbled.

"Are you sure you wouldn't like to stay to dinner and service at nones, Lord Montmorency?" Savaric cut in gently. "It may calm your soul."

The Earl's face was bleak and full of regret. He would like nothing better, Savaric knew. "Once again, I apologize," he said, "but I am expected at Sir Edwin's manor. May I request permission to speak to my brother privately for a moment before I go?"

"Of course."

The two brothers bowed deeply to the Abbot and took their leave, arm in arm. Obviously, they were a close family. Savaric had had no contact with his own family since he'd taken vows two decades ago. He sat back and waited for the imminent knock at his door.

On the way back to the horse and escort, all waiting patiently in front of the stables, Evan took a breath, wiped his eyes, and said, "Edward, both of them have gone to a better place. It's up to us now. But, please, Shaftesbury Castle is special. You know that. Whatever you do, don't let what they started die."

"You remember the dinner conversations we'd have with our guests? How either Papa or Mama always knew the probing question, the witty riposte, the appropriate quote from some wise ancient? How can we match that? And what about Jeanne now?"

Evan replied, "You can't. But you can listen. You can guide the conversation without having to offer an opinion. The best minds in the country have eaten in our great hall, so think of them as teachers. For Jeanne, Mama was a strong presence at the table. But on her own now, Jeanne may start to speak up, you never know. Why not practise standard phrases and replies with her in private? Mama once said, 'It's better to keep quiet and be thought a fool than to open your mouth and remove all doubt.'" He knew it was actually someone clever from the future who'd said it first.

Edward smiled. "I'll tell her."

Glancing at Papa's signet ring, which Edward now wore, Evan said, "I know you'll do him proud."

"Thank you. I'll remember that. Will we be favoured with your presence this time?" he asked starchily. "We all missed you for Papa's."

That was twice today. He resisted the urge to snap at his grieving brother.

"No offence," Edward went on, "but you can hardly pontificate that it's 'up to us' when you've entrenched yourself here, disinclined to leave even briefly. We could really use your help now."

Evan snapped anyway. "*Excuse* me? You think I said to myself, 'Ho-hum, I'm *disinclined* to attend my father's funeral'? Edward, I took a vow. All I can do is ask. The Abbot's word is always final."

He didn't say how much time he spent castigating himself for the choice he'd made. For he *had* made a choice. Another reason for humility.

"I'm sorry. Poor choice of words. But what kind of man wouldn't permit you to attend your own father's funeral? It's not right. Mama said something about 'power corrupts,' and I think she had a point. She was pretty upset when you didn't come home."

Evan winced. "I am so sorry. I hope she forgave me."

He looked around to see if anyone was in earshot. Of course, there were four, at least, all looking purposefully busy and unconcerned. The Abbot made it his business to know everything that went on here; it's what capable leaders did.

His voice barely above a whisper, he said, in Welsh, "This place is a country within a country, and while I'm here I obey its ruler or face the consequences."

Edward nodded and switched back to French, his tone conversational. "I see your hospital's finished."

"Yes, we're all proud of it. It's getting busy."

He asked Edward how things were, otherwise.

"Well, every day has its challenges," he replied wryly. "Jeanne is fussing about Enith. What should we do with her?"

Evan considered this. Enith had tended to Mama since both were girls. A relationship at once intimate and distanced. "What about Reginald Poole? What's he done?" Poole had been their father's manservant as long as anyone could remember.

"He decided to go back to Poole."

"Hmm, why don't you ask her? She may wish to return to her people in Wales—although everyone she cares about is in that castle. I expect she'll want to stay. You certainly can't turn her out. My thought? If she wishes to stay, put her in charge of housekeeping. I'm sure Jeanne will think of other things she can do."

The dinner bell was ringing. He had to be back on the road. He embraced his brother again, saying, "Please come home."

As he and his escorts rode off, Edward thought, not for the first time, that the wrong man was wearing Papa's ring. Evan would know the question, the riposte, the quote. He would have made a perfect earl, though Edward had never heard him wish even slightly that the birth order had been different. Why should he? His life was made up of choices, acted on as he wished. Or had been, until he joined the abbey. He didn't have a high-strung, stuttering wife to worry about, either. Jeanne was a sweet, caring woman whom he was devoted to and protective of, but the strain of always having to compensate for her at mealtimes was wearisome, especially since Papa's passing.

He could never tell Evan of the hurt he felt as Mama fussed over Evan's absence in the months following Papa's death—how she'd look out the window every time someone rode through the castle gates, asking hopefully, "Is it Evan?"

There'd been something secretive and special about Evan's relationship with his parents. He hadn't been the only one who'd noticed the closed or barred doors, the conversations quickly terminated if someone else came in. He still wondered about those two Templars of the Dowager Queen of Sicily's, wanting to speak alone with Mama and Papa. It had to be something to do with Evan. What could be that much of a secret? That he had never been privy to any of this was another source of hurt.

"If only he'd been here!" she kept saying, irrationally.

The little boy in Edward wanted to say, "What about me? *I'm* here. I'm the one who stayed and has done his duty."

Jeanne scolded him, "Your mother isn't herself. She would be horrified if she knew you were thinking this. You know how much she loves you and depends on you, especially now." For no reason they understood, Jeanne's stutter vanished during the rare times she was cross.

Sometimes, he just felt like talking freely to someone as a friend. When his loneliness was strong, he visited Joanne Wolstone.

When he was younger, he'd occasionally visited her as a "client," but by now, that was the farthest thing from his mind; she was like another mother to him. She sat him down at her table, listened carefully, and occasionally counselled him. In return, he helped her out where he could; he now owned two pairs of sheepskin gloves and two scarves. Jeanne had one of her shawls. He really didn't care what the villagers thought about his horse tied up out front of her house; let them think what they wanted. However, for the last while, her memory had been failing. The last time he'd visited her, she'd tried to clean the table with her broom. He was seriously considering bringing her to the castle, where his folk could keep an eye on her. Hmm, maybe *that* was what Enith could do.

"Stop with your pathetic *whingeing!*" he could almost hear Papa say. "At least you're not a villein scything wheat all day!"

True enough, counting his blessings had never been one of his strengths. Somehow, he must stop being envious of his brother and learn to embrace this role. He must find a way to see it not as a burdensome task, but as an opportunity to expand and improve on what his parents had started. That was the key—building on their legacy. They never said he had to follow the same path as they did. He must find his own path, and he must now bring Jeanne along on this journey too.

Savaric again expressed sorrow and regret for the loss of the Countess of Shaftesbury. "Such a tragedy, so soon after the Earl's passing!" However, he reminded Evan of the vows of stability and, particularly, *obedience.* This time, Evan's eyes betrayed nothing before he bowed in submission.

I have broken him to obedience, Savaric thought, and I don't think I'll have to do this again, thank the Lord.

Still, he was intrigued. The truth was that Brother Evan's reputation was such that he could build his own hospital, closer to home, and he wouldn't have to submit himself to a soul. There was nothing to stop him. Or was there?

Weeping, kneeling in front of the altar, knowing he was failing his family again, Evan silently reminded himself of the resolution he'd made after the last time. He would stay here until it was safe to leave, and not one day longer. He'd done enough soul searching to know that his greatest flaw was not his pride, as Father Abbot kept telling him, but its near cousin: hatred of submission.

His whole life, with one significant exception, Evan had always got what he wanted. Leading by strong example and reasoned persuasion, he brought people around to his way of thinking. Why, he'd even made a physician of the pea-brained Brother John.

Evan had not been surprised that his request was denied. Still, the Abbot's decision was hard to fathom. It was like he was being punished or, at the very least, played with, to test the boundaries of his oath of obedience. But why him? What had he done to deserve this?

God, give me strength, he pleaded. Until that sometime-future day, everything he did would be in honour and memory of Mama and Papa.

-VI-
Without a Glance Back

A month after that, Savaric was fairly sure he'd solved the riddle of Brother Evan. A well-dressed knight rode into the abbey grounds, requesting to see the Abbot. He was an emissary from King Richard, still in Aquitaine, still draining the state treasury to get God-knew-what bit of acreage back and erect that monument of a castle of his. The knight, a snooty Norman by the name *Sire* Gregory Beauchamp, wanted to know if a physician named Sire Evan de Montmorency was indeed on the premises, as was his information.

Savaric confirmed in English that *Brother* Evan was here, and what did this concern?

A duel in opposing languages commenced, both men determined to assert their superiority.

Sire Gregory replied that *Sire* Evan had served the King well on crusade—in fact, the King himself had knighted him—and his services were required again.

"Why is the King only now asking for him?" Savaric wanted to know.

"Because his primary physician died."

Savaric countered that, unfortunate as that was, *Brother* Evan was absolutely committed to honouring his sacred vows.

Beauchamp responded haughtily, "I demand to see him to confirm this for myself."

Savaric retorted, "You may not. You are in my jurisdiction here. He is under my protection, and you have no authority on this property. Now, I regret the time and trouble it took you to get here, but I must bid you good day."

Beauchamp bowed. Before he left, he intoned, "The King will not be pleased."

Fine, Savaric thought. Let him be displeased. There is nothing he can do.

He never told Evan of the visit. He later heard through channels that the King had pursued the matter with the Archbishop of Canterbury—Hubert Walter, wearing two hats as Richard's trusted justiciar—but the Archbishop had said no. It was a question of inviolable sanctuary. Not wanting to recreate a Becket situation, Richard had backed off in a fury, Savaric was told.

However, Savaric now knew what kept Evan here when he knew in his heart that the man was unhappy. He agreed with Evan's reasons. It came to him that he and Evan had misunderstood each other, right from the beginning. Such a pity.

"You're welcome," Savaric said to himself.

In the latter part of Lent, 1199, Savaric received word that King Richard had suddenly died in Aquitaine of a wound suffered in battle. Three days of mourning, fasting, and prayer for this glorious Christian warrior were immediately decreed at the abbey. The day after Palm Sunday, to Savaric's great disappointment, Evan left Glastonbury Abbey on a horse that was due to be put down anyway, without a glance back.

-VII-
Just Another Princess

When Evan rode up to the castle gates, he knew without a doubt that never again would he stray far or long from his home. Modest as this castle might appear to be, there was nothing else like it, even without Mama and Papa.

"The prodigal son returns, just in time for Pasch!" Edward exclaimed. "Batten down the cakes and ale!" Everyone laughed, looking at the scraggy, tonsured man with the pitiful horse. The tailored clothes he'd left the castle in five years before were hanging on him.

Tom commented, "This four-legged creature that sort of resembles a horse looks like he has hours to live."

Evan replied, "No, Bramble has time yet. Just give him a bit of care and attention. Believe it or not, he's much better than when he was given to me."

And it was true. Everything in this castle seemed to thrive, including his old friend Wasim, who trumpeted a greeting from the stables.

Edward said quietly to him, "The timing of your departure is interesting, may I say. Can I assume you are here because you now consider it safe to be here?"

Evan nodded.

Evan saw with satisfaction how confidently Edward was growing into his role. He'd only needed the absence of his father's shadow to prove it. If he felt nervous or hesitant, he didn't show it. He smoothly settled local disputes and carefully protected the castle's finances, as Papa had done. Sitting quietly behind him and Michael Halliwell during these meetings was Pierre, a strapping young man of eighteen, the image of his father, now home for good and being groomed in turn. With the help of the experienced and capable castle staff, the place remained the well-oiled machine it had always been. Edward seemed proud when he mentioned that, after a lull following Mama's passing, dinner and suppertime "freeloader" traffic was picking up again. While Jeanne remained quiet at the table, she was starting to venture an opinion or two, based on those offered by previous visitors to the castle. Like Evan, Jeanne listened and remembered.

He was surprised to see Joanne Wolstone occupying one of the rooms on the south side. Although she had a disarming tendency on occasion to flirt with any young man who crossed her path, mostly she kept harmlessly to herself, weaving decorative, much-appreciated wool blankets for the castle staff. Enith saw that she ate and dressed herself properly.

Evan was pleased with this brave decision, for Joanne's arrival would have raised some eyebrows.

Like Enith's. What would she have felt when she was informed she would be seeing to Lord Robert's former mistress and the village *puterelle?* But looking after a woman was what Enith had always done, and it gave her new purpose. And Father Benedict? He'd actually taken it rather well, apparently, seeing Joanne as a soul that could still be saved. Indeed, Joanne was now no threat to anyone. The castle denizens protected her as they might a wounded pet. And William could relax, knowing his mother was safe and well-looked-after.

All happiness aside, however, Evan had gained enough experience, self-awareness, and, yes, humility from his years at the abbey to know he must set boundaries between his responsibilities and Edward's.

One night at matins in Edward's solar, he said, "Brother, I want to make clear that what goes on here is totally under your domain. I haven't the slightest ability or desire to poke my nose into castle affairs. Of course, if you seek my advice, I'll offer the best I know. But all I want is to be left alone to heal people."

Relieved, Edward smiled and embraced him. Castle visitors during Evan's years away had confirmed what he had only modestly hinted at: that no matter where he wound up, as great leaders inevitably did, he rose to the top.

He said, "Thank you. I must confess Jeanne and I were a bit worried. You do have a somewhat fearsome reputation for usurping power, you know."

Evan laughed. "Hmm … Let me cast one of my evil glares at you."

Edward laughed in turn.

Over the next several weeks, with Edward's permission, he took over the room where he'd treated his father's leg and set up a basic clinic, open on Edward's "town hall" Mondays. He scoured the meadows and streams for marigold, elderflower, feverfew, dandelion, chickweed, willow bark. He got the guards to be on the lookout for them, too. Those Mondays quickly became busy, and he was delighted that he seemed to have acquired an apprentice in the form of young Gilbert de Clare, still squiring at the castle.

Though he enjoyed doing what he loved in the bosom of his home, of course, everyone knew he was biding his time. He needed room: room to treat the more seriously ill, room to plant his own herbs. Sooner or later, he would have to fly on his own.

On Ascension Day (May 27) of that year, John I was crowned King of England in Westminster Abbey, as had been his brother ten years before. Again, the redoubtable Dowager Queen Eleanor was by his side; John was estranged from his wife, Isabella. The Montmorency and Villiers males were in attendance. The occasion was not nearly as lavish as Richard's had been, but at least it was not marred by bats flying about, nor by the murder of innocent Jews, nor by ominous lights in the night sky.

All through that day Evan looked first in hope, then in anguished disappointment for Joanna. Why wasn't she at her brother's coronation? Was she well? Something or someone must have prevented her attendance. Perhaps her husband? Evan needed to believe that Count Raymond was a decent man and that Joanna had made a good life with him. He was now beset by a niggling worry that he couldn't quite dispel.

On September 4, Evan awoke, heart pounding in alarm. He'd seen Joanna on a bed, moaning in pain. "Evan! Where are you? *Help* me!" she was sobbing. She was surrounded by nuns.

"I *can't!* I can't … *move!*" he cried uselessly in the dream. "Be strong! I love you!"

Perhaps it was because of the guilt he still felt for not being here to help Mama and Papa in their final days and months, he rationalized. But a persistent blackness was settling in him. He slept fitfully.

Michaelmas, at the end of September, signalled the time of year when the crops were in and rents collected. On September 29, a crisp fall day, Evan rode out with Edward, Bailiff Scrivens, and Steward Halliwell, offering medical assistance to tenants in need of relief from whatever ailed them. It was a particularly satisfying day all around, a day in which he forgot his worries. He and Edward worked well together, he thought. Edward had brought along Pierre and Gilbert, ostensibly to help out, but mainly so they could learn how a properly run demesne functioned. As was the custom, they supped on goose at a tenant's house. Evan was looking forward to doing it all again the next day, and the next. It usually took at least three.

By the time the group returned, the family was just getting up from the supper table and the dinnerware was being cleared; the castle staff knew Lord Montmorency and the others would have supped elsewhere. A band of French minstrels had entertained the family at supper. Edward invited them to join them all around the table and to sup. Jeanne summoned meals for them. More wine was brought. Everyone was relaxed and content, looking forward to an amusing evening of good gossip.

What news from France, Evan asked.

The minstrels were proud to talk of the building going on: King Philip's new castle, the continued work on the Nostre-Dame cathedral with its recently installed bell, the astoundingly rapid construction of another magnificent cathedral at Chartres. They dared not bring up the jubilation at the news of Richard's death, instantly removing the thorn in practically every European monarch's side. However, they did feel comfortable reporting that, unfortunately, his younger sister had died earlier in the month, in childbirth.

This news was greeted by shocked silence at the high table. The younger Montmorency blanched, visibly distraught.

Lady Montmorency gently took his hand. "I'm s-so sorry, Evan."

"Where?" he managed to ask.

The minstrels glanced at each other. They had expected this to be greeted by a mild show of dismay, nothing more. Just another princess, no one of consequence, really, although the ranks of Henry II's children were thinning alarmingly. They were down to two, only one of them male: that weasel, John. He'd just had his marriage annulled and, if he didn't start reproducing soon, the direct line would die out. Everyone knew this usually resulted in backroom manoeuvring, double-dealing, and, sometimes, civil war.

One of them said, "We don't know for sure, but we heard it was at an abbey. Maybe Fontevraud? I'm sorry, Sir Evan. We didn't realize you were acquainted with her."

"She was a good friend." Turning to Lord and Lady Montmorency, "Milord and Milady, may I be excused? I suddenly feel a bit unwell."

1200

The cloister garth in Fontevraud Abbey

The first beginnings of something cannot be
distinguished by the eye.
—Lucretius, *De Rarum Natura*

-I-
A New Century

The now twenty-nine-year-old man rode up to the gates of Fontevraud Abbey on his beloved Arabian. Apart from his mail and a sword, he was simply dressed. It had been a long journey, much of it in the company of a band of pilgrims to the Holy Land, but his mission was almost complete.

When asked his business here, he replied, "I am Sir Evan de Montmorency. I come in peace, seeking an audience with the Abbess."

"Very well," replied the guard, "but your sword remains with us."

Evan agreed. He handed over his sword and got off Wasim.

"Come this way."

He followed the guard to an outer building adjacent to the church and the abbey proper. It was a simple room with bookshelves, a desk and chair, and a crucifix on the wall behind.

"Wait here," he was told.

It was the year 1200. A new century, a new king, albeit an incompetent one. Now was a good, safe time to take a step forward in his life. Sister Marguerite was old and failing, and the fact was that he was a physician of some repute now. The abbey needed a hospital, and he was the one to build it.

The Reverend Mother Mathilde de Bohême rose from her morning prayers to see a guard waiting patiently for her at the back of the chapel. He said, "A knight begs an audience with you, Reverend Mother. He's waiting in your office."

The knight knelt to her as she entered. Startled, she stared down at him. Not classically handsome in the Roman-statue sense, but a pleasing face, brown from exposure to the sun. Perceptibly intelligent, with intense, earnest grey-green eyes. Dishevelled light-brown hair. There was no doubt who he was. She knew this day might come eventually; she had prayed not quite so soon, for the child was exceptional. He had every right to ask what he was about to ask.

"Good morning, you may rise. What can I do to help you?"

He stood and replied, in educated French, "I am Sir Evan de Montmorency, veteran of the Third Crusade under King Richard and a licensed physician. With your permission, I would like, first, to pay my respects at the Countess of Toulouse's tomb. And, second, I would like to take our daughter, Jane, home."

-II-
Mi corazón

Steve is standing in front of several dozen seated people, all lightly dressed. He is wearing black breeches and a black jacket, too many clothes for this warm weather. He is surrounded by several people in front of this gathering.

Right before him, Gaby is smiling up at him, exquisite in a long, white silk dress, her dark hair bound up with lilies of the valley threaded throughout. She is carrying a small bouquet of the same flowers. Behind her is a pretty girl dressed in dark blue, carrying a similar spray, who looks to be her sister. Behind Steve stands another young man. Evan intuits that this is Steve's now-grown younger brother.

In front of them all is an older man in grey breeches and jacket.

In the front row are his parents, older now, beaming at him. Right across the aisle from Steve's parents is a proud-looking, deeply tanned woman, alone. She has direct brown eyes, and, curiously, she is smiling, not at her daughter, as one might expect, but directly at him, as if she could see him … God in Heaven—Mama?! It is, he knows it is!

The place where they are gathered is not Calgary, with its rolling hills, distant mountains, and ice-blue, cloudless sky. This place reminds him of Outremer. They are overlooking an ocean; palm fronds are swaying gently in the late-afternoon breeze. A less formally dressed man and woman are hovering close by, alternately crouching and standing up, holding small black boxes with thick black tubes to their eyes, clicking. Who are these people?

The grey-clothed man, who seems to be some kind of priest, turns to Gaby and asks, in accented English, "Do you, Gabriela Renata Rivera Silverman, take this man, Steven Robert Rickert McAllister, to be your lawfully wedded husband, to have and to hold from this day forward, for better, for worse, for richer, for poorer, in sickness and in health, to love and cherish, till death do you part?"

"I do," she replies, smiling.

After Steve has slipped the slim gold band on her finger, she squeezes his hand, and they both look back at the priest.

"I now pronounce you husband and wife. You may kiss the bride."

Not in the habit of kissing her in front of a lot of people, he shyly takes her in his arms. She leans into his kiss and when he releases her a delicious moment later, everyone in attendance claps and cheers. She lays her head on his shoulder, looks up at him, and murmurs, eyes sparkling, "We've finally done it, mi corazón!*"*

Evan awoke, elated.

That evening, he knocked at the bedroom door beside his own. Jane called, "Come in, Papa!" It was time for their nightly bedtime story. Her attendant, Alice, a French orphan who had looked after her since Fontevraud, slept on a pallet along the side of the room. She would normally listen in on these stories. However, tonight, Evan said, "Alice, please excuse us." The girl bowed and left the room, Jane's eyes wide in curiosity.

He often read Crestien de Troies to them. Sometimes, he regaled them with stories about his adventures abroad. Other times, about people he'd known, especially her mother. If he was in the mood, he'd occasionally embroider his stories with tales of great sea monsters, goblins, and wizards.

Tonight, he sat down on the bed and wrapped his arm around her little shoulders. She nestled into him. Of all the unexpected joys of being a father, story time was surely the best. Her grey-green eyes looking up at him in eager anticipation, her smile endearingly gap-toothed, he said, "Jane, my sweet, tonight I want to tell you the true, secret story of your Grandmama and Grandpapa de Montmorency."

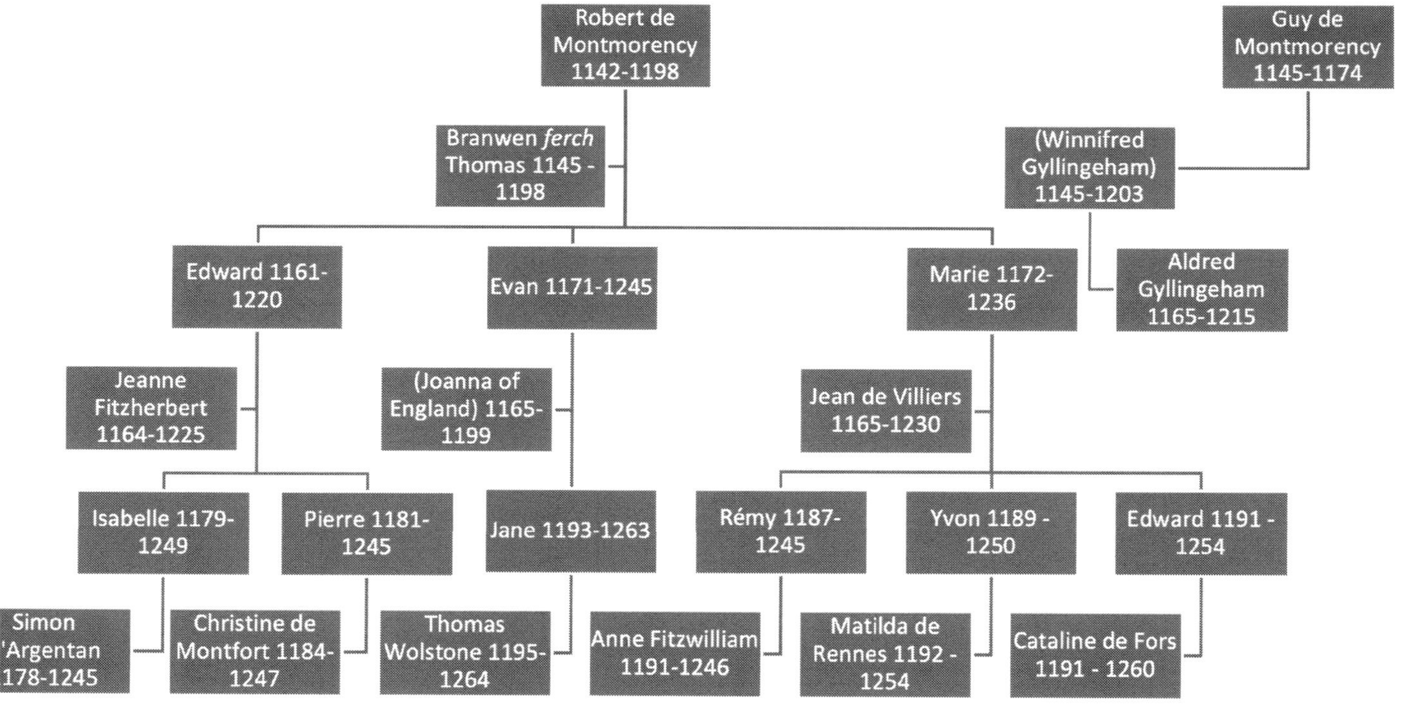

Unofficial family tree, to the third generation of surviving Montmorencys

ACKNOWLEDGEMENTS

Effigy of Richard I, at Fontevraud Abbey, France

One of the frustrating aspects of researching the twelfth century is the often-contradictory nature of one's sources. Events, places, dates, motives, numbers are all flexible, I found. Sometimes, I chose which of them worked best for my story; if an alert reader spots information contrary to his or her understanding, believe me, I read it somewhere! In the main, I stuck to John Gillingham's authoritative biography of Richard or to the historian Ambroise's contemporary account, *L'Estoire de la guerre sainte*, excerpted in Hallam's *The Plantagenet Chronicles*. Readers looking for an engaging and comprehensible rendering of the early Angevin kings should seek out Thomas B. Costain's *The Conquering Family*; however, his accounts do differ from the majority of scholarship in some instances. In the absence of any information at all, there was nothing for it but to make an educated guess.

And, what would any modern writer do without Messrs. Google, Wikipedia, and YouTube?

I gleefully picked the brains of some of my knowledgeable friends, and I'm so grateful for their assistance.

Since all trace of the Salerno Medical School has vanished, my deep thanks to Giovanna Naylor for researching Italian documents that, finally, got me on the right track to locating where in Salerno it might have been located. She also was my beta reader for the relevant pages.

I had an enjoyable conversation one afternoon with Dr. Sheldon Roth, who took me through how a primitive form of penicillin could be produced. He and his wife, Karen, kindly helped me rephrase Evan and Gurci's Hanukkah dinner paragraph.

Drs. Bryan and Evelyn Donnelly and Dr. Ronald Sandler helped me sort out in my own mind how the four medieval medical colleagues would have performed a dissection, as well as their feelings as they approached the task. The Donnellys also vetted my dissection sequence. Thank you, Bryan, for referring me to Sue Black's excellent book, accredited after this. And thank you, Evelyn, for the lovely turn of phrase: "on the right side of the ground." I liked it so much I used it twice.

Any remaining technical errors on these subjects are entirely my own.

Florin Safner from upwork.com generated the custom maps. It really is a new world when this can all be accomplished online, in a correspondence between a writer in Calgary and a mapmaker in Venezuela.

Donna-Lee Wybert of Textual Matters was my most capable and patient editor again, and Regina McCreary of Human Powered Design did her usual great job with the formatting.

Finally, regardless of its reception, may I dare express my gratitude to this project for carrying me through what was surely the lowest time of my life: the misery and isolation of chemo during a Canadian winter and a pandemic.

Partial Bibliography

Black, Sue. *All that Remains: A Renowned Forensic Scientist on Death, Mortality, and Solving Crimes.* Arcade Publishing, 2018.

Costain, Thomas B. *A History of the Plantagenets: The Conquering Family.* Doubleday & Company, 1962.

Della Monica M, Mauri R, Scarano F, Lonardo F, Scarano G. 2013. The Salernitan School of Medicine: Women, Men, and Children. A Syndromological Review of the Oldest Medical School in the Western World. *American Journal of Medical Genetics Part A* 161A:809–816. Accessed February 8, 2021.

Ferraris, Zoë Alaina, BA and Ferraris, Victor A., MD, Phd. *The Women of Salerno: Contributionto the Origins of Surgery from Medieval Italy.* Annals of Thoracic Surgery, 1997; 64:1855–7. Accessed February 1, 2021.

Flori, Jean. *Richard Coeur de lion: Le roi-chevalier.* Paris, Editions Payot & Rivages, 1999.

Gillingham, John. *Richard I.* New Haven: Yale University Press, 1999.

Hallam, Elizabeth, editor. *The Plantagenet Chronicles.* Weidenfeld & Nicholson, 1986.

The Holy Rule of Saint Benedict: Introduction to Study. Annotated by Fr. Philip Lawrence, OSB, Abbot of Christ in the Desert. www.christdesert.org [Accessed February 5, 2021].

Mitchell, Piers D. *Medicine in the Crusades: Warfare, Wounds and the Medieval Surgeon.* Cambridge University Press, 2007.

Regimen Sanitatis Salernitanum. www.medicinetraditions.com [Accessed February 5, 2021].

Rose, Susan. *England's Medieval Navy* 1066 – 1509*: Ships, Men & Warfare.* London: Seaforth Publishing, 2013. *Kindle edition.*

Walsh, James J. *Old-Time Makers of Medicine: The Story of the Students and Teachers of the Sciences Related to Medicine During the Middle Ages.* Fordham University Press, 1911. Accessed as a Project Gutenberg EBook, January 25, 2021.

AUTHOR'S NOTES

Entrance to the Templar Tunnel in Akko, Israel

So darn much *happened* before, during, and after the Third Crusade that readers may be forgiven for thinking I took the most absurd and fanciful licence with actual events, for the sake of a better story. May I assure you that I invented nothing; all I did was insert Evan into the panorama as a sort of undocumented Zelig who rubbed shoulders with the outstanding personalities of the age. In fact, my challenge was boiling it all down into something that didn't drown my readers in needless detail. Those familiar with the Third Crusade will have noticed the absence of a few key, though peripheral, characters—a tough decision based on the need to keep the story lean. Apart from that, I adhered to the generally accepted, albeit ruthlessly pared down, chronology of events.

Joanna's name has been variously spelled "Joanne" and "Joan." I called her Joanna mainly because I already had a Joanne, and I'm personally not fond of the name "Joan"—with apologies to Joans out there who are reading this.

I wish I could say that all ended happily for Joanna. Her dowry squandered by Richard, she spent the next four years after the crusade living at Eleanor's and John's courts. Although opinion is divided as to whether her marriage to Count Raymond of Toulouse was a happy one, in three years she birthed three children, two of whom survived to adulthood. Their son Raymond would become Count Raymond VII. What *is* known is that, in the last months of her life, pregnant with her third child, she single-mindedly tried to be inducted into holy orders—difficult for a pregnant, twice-married woman, though she did succeed in her final days. She died in childbirth at Fontevraud Abbey, almost five months to the day after Richard, who had been entombed there. Her baby, also named Richard, only lived a few weeks. Her effigy was, unfortunately, destroyed during the French Revolution. Otherwise, present-day visitors to the abbey would see hers, beside those of three extraordinary monarchs who had coincidentally all died nearby: Richard; his father, Henry II; and that grand matriarch, Eleanor of Aquitaine.

Berengaria would remain a neglected wife. Chastised by both the pope and his mother, Richard did try to spend a little time with her, but no children were forthcoming. After his death, she struggled financially for years, unsuccessfully petitioning John for Richard's dower to support herself. Eventually, John's successor, Henry III, settled four thousand pounds and properties in Le Mans on her. There she remained and took the veil. She spent the rest of her life devoted to charitable works, dying in 1230. For a woman of so little consequence in the scheme of things, it is interesting that she ranks as one of the best known of English queen consorts. A luxury liner was even named after her. I think it's because her euphonious *name* carries much more gravitas than the woman herself.

As for Richard, opinions as to his character, capabilities, and even sexuality have varied widely through the ages. Trying to capture his essence was like trying to grasp at smoke. While the coronation was beset by much-remarked-on ill omens—including the northern lights and the bat!—in fact, Richard was far from the worst of English sovereigns.

Although glorified as an English king, in fact, he was thoroughly French. He didn't even speak English. Spending only six months of his ten-year reign in England, he likely thought of it merely as an uncivilized, rainy outpost and cash cow to fund his various projects. His priorities always lay in the defence of his lands on the Continent.

In the twelfth century, actual pitched battle was relatively rare. It was costly in terms of knights and horses, and dangerous for kings, who in those days took personal charge of their armies. Generally, they preferred destroying the land, laying siege, starving their opponents out. We moderns are accustomed to images of chateau generals directing the course of action from the safety of some war room elsewhere, so it's hard—at least for me—to imagine the commander of an army, never mind the King of England, fearlessly *leading* the charge. Richard was a great general and a cunning tactician, able to think quickly on his feet, reckless of his own safety but cautious with his men's. He was also a disloyal son and a terrible husband who should never have become a king. He inherited a wealthy country and bled it dry. He could be astoundingly cruel and generous in equal measure. He ran with scissors and did not play well with others.

While not rejecting the theory that he might have been bisexual, I chose to accept the current thinking that he was not strictly gay. In my opinion, quite simply, he had too many enemies for such a secret not to come out and be capitalized on. I took the line that his seeming indifference towards his wife was not so much that he was incapable of fulfilling his marital duties (he did have at least one acknowledged bastard child and had been accused of "ravishing" village women), but rather that his attention was clearly elsewhere. He was addicted to the adrenalin of warfare, having waged war since he was sixteen. He seemed to me to be one of those men who are at their relaxed best around other men, like modern-day career generals, gone from their wives and families for years. I think he and Patton would have had much to say to each other.

Although estimates of what Richard's ransom would amount to in today's currency vary, the most conservative is two hundred million pounds. Using that as a guide, a bit of arithmetic told me that Robert's "contribution" to the crusade would have cost him the equivalent of over two and a half million pounds.

The Third Crusade marked the apex of Richard's achievements. He spent almost all of his remaining years on the Continent, regaining territory captured by Philip and putting out fires here and there. The outrageously expensive castle he built in Normandy, the Château Gaillard—alluded to twice in this work—was considered for its time to be an advanced piece of engineering and design. Richard himself is thought to be the architect.

In late March of 1199, he was besieging the unremarkable castle of Châlus-Chabrol, in the belief that treasure could be found there that he felt was owed to him, when he took an arrow to the shoulder. While it shouldn't normally have been a fatal wound, a botched job was made of removing the arrow and gangrene set in. He died on April 6 of that year.

The *léonardie* that afflicted Richard within five days of his arrival at Acre, and Philip about the same time, has puzzled doctors and historians for eight hundred years. It was certainly too early to be scurvy, and it doesn't square with malaria's or trench fever's symptoms. Since no one else is sure what it was, I took that as my cue to finally plunge Evan into the heart of the action.

The late twelfth century marked the apex of what is called the High Middle Ages, a sort of mini-Renaissance. It was a time of general prosperity, good crops, increased urbanization, a flowering of the arts, and a rediscovery of learning. Because people were eating well, they tended to be a good height; Richard really was 6'5". Were it not for the calamitous, plague- and war-ridden fourteenth century, the general European Renaissance might have started much earlier.

Twelfth-century spelling was highly unregulated, even personal. For the spelling of well-known words such as "Notre-Dame," "Camelot," and "Guinevere," if I found a version I was confident was the medieval spelling, I went with that. I used the same rationale for the few French names and expressions in this work. Otherwise, I used the modern spelling.

I did lengthen Chrétien de Troyes's life by a few years, with apologies to his scholars.

While Roderick d'Amiens may have been exaggerating about only "a cat and two dogs" living in Rome at the time, repeated invasions and political instability had caused the population to plummet from over a million at the Empire's height in the second century CE to a mere thirty to forty thousand at the time of this novel. Some estimates have it as low as twenty thousand.

Jacob d'Orléans, a renowned Jewish scholar, was indeed murdered the day of Richard's coronation on the footsteps of Westminster Palace. I highly doubt he tutored upper-class Anglo-Norman children, but it was fun to imagine he might have.

For Evan's struggles with what we understand as perspective: the trick of drawing in perspective was understood in Greek and Roman times but lost after the fall of the Roman Empire. Like many other medieval artists, Evan was reinventing the wheel. The science of perspective was only regained during the Italian Renaissance.

I allowed myself free rein with the layout of the real Acre fortress, which lies destroyed beneath an Ottoman-era fortress in modern Akko, Israel. However, the secret tunnels remain intact.

Being a near-complete scientific and medical ignoramus, one of my unexpected pleasures in researching this work was learning about the state of European and Arab medicine of the time. The twelfth century coincided with the Muslim golden age of cultural and scientific advancement, in some fields two hundred years ahead of their Frankish and English counterparts.

I'm fairly sure I rushed the term "physician" by a few years; at that time, Evan would have been called a *physicus*. But I found the word distracting and clumsy to work with and therefore exercised a bit of writer's licence. "Doctor" to describe a medical professional was centuries away.

It would have thrilled Evan that, within his lifetime, secretive, back-alley dissections were no longer forbidden. In 1231, the Holy Roman Emperor Frederick II issued a decree mandating that a human body should be dissected at least once in every five years for anatomical studies, and attendance was compulsory for everyone intending to practise medicine or surgery. By the last half of the thirteenth and early fourteenth centuries, human dissection was legalized in several European countries.

Parallels can be drawn between the crusades and the present day: a well-intentioned, well-financed, and well-equipped invading army that—after years of horrifying loss of life on both sides, including that of innocent civilians—must withdraw, if not concede defeat. Were the crusades an utter waste of time, in the end? A gigantic historical catastrophe? In my opinion, not entirely; given the flood of new ideas and trade that flowed into Europe as a result, the crusades cannot be called a complete failure. It is entirely within reason that a gifted young man such as Evan could return from his adventures and help open the door to progressive medical practices. There must have been many like him.

November 30, 2021
Mesa, Arizona

Manufactured by Amazon.ca
Bolton, ON

23909986R00203